The McCarron's Daughter
Fancy's Story

Sharon K. Middleton

Black Rose Writing | Texas

ISBN: 978-1-68433-248-9
PUBLISHED BY BLACK ROSE WRITING
www.blackrosewriting.com

Printed in the United States of America
Suggested Retail Price (SRP) $19.95

The McCarron's Daughter is printed in Adboe Caslon Pro

Acknowledgements

I would like to thank my husband, Gary, for putting up with me writing and neglecting the house when my head is full of stories, and for inspiring scenes from time to time.

I would also like to thank my dear friends, Dawn Anderson and Judy Steckman Broussard, who helped me with proof reading and listening to countless hours of plotting stories.

Special thanks to Angela Wollam, the Brazoria County Law Librarian, for her endless hours of putting up with me in the library as I write and pitch story lines to her.

And last but not least, to the many abused and neglected children I worked with when I was a social worker with Texas Children's Protective Services: your voices have rung in my heart and in my mind for years. I hope Fancy managed to tell your stories well. This is your chance to be heard. I dedicate this story to you.

The McCarron's Daughter
Fancy's Story

Chapter One
Fancy, January 1780

"I need my Daddy." I sobbed against my brother Will's shoulder. He wrapped the quilt tight around me, as he murmured words of comfort to me.

"It's okay, Fancy. No one will hurt you now. Le Grande is dead. He won't hurt you or anyone ever again. But honey, Daddy is dead. You're gonna have to make do with your big brother now."

I shook my head. "No, not Daddy Jo. My real daddy. I need Marc. Can you write him? I need to tell him I'm sorry. I … I should have gone with them to McCarron's Corner in December."

Will's wife, Sassy, gasped at my words, her eyes wide with shock. "Marc? Marcus McCarron is your real daddy? Will, what is this all about?"

Will looked grim and rattled, his eyes clouded with confusion. "I don't know, but I'm damned sure gonna find out."

My name is Fancy Selk. My real name is Francesca Marie Selk. My Daddy Jo used to call me Francie, and I pronounced it Fancy. Everybody thought that was amusing so the nickname stuck. I've been called Fancy most of my life.

My real mama was Tamsin Selk. She was the natural child of Josiah Selk. When I was born, Daddy Jo and Miss Belle adopted me and raised me as their own daughter. I was a spoiled, entitled little girl, wearing extravagant silk gowns, and I had my own French maid. I had tutors teaching me reading, writing, grammar, math, history, geography, music, dancing, and of course, French. I was learning to play the pianoforte and the harp, like Miss Belle. Daddy Jo called me his Wee Duchess, and I was treated like royalty.

"Why do you call me that, Daddy?" I recall asking him once.

He laughed. "Because, my love, you are little but you are fierce, and someday you shall be the Duchess of Ranscome."

I laughed and skipped away.

I was still small when Tamsin ran off and married an Irish lord. It was a big scandal. Miss Belle got sick and died not long after that. They said she died from a broken heart because her real daughter, Ginny Lee, died in childbirth the year before. Things were little different at first after Miss Belle died. But over time, Daddy Jo drank more and more and I got less and less attention. My brother, Will, took his three daughters back to Puerto Rico to their plantation because things at Belle Rose were too chaotic to keep the girls there any longer. He asked Daddy Jo to let me go, too, but Daddy said he had already lost too much and refused.

Four years later, when I was 10, my Daddy Jo died. My big brother, Tom, was the new owner of the plantation. Within the week, my tutors were all dismissed. Most of my pretty dresses were taken away. My maid was assigned new work and I no longer had a maid. I went from being my Daddy's Wee Duchess to being little more than one of the servants.

And then, Tom broke my heart the day he informed me that because my mother was a person of color, I would never be a white girl, no matter how white I looked. Daddy Jo used to tell me it didn't matter. Except Tom didn't call me black, he called me that "N" word that Sassy won't allow folks to say here at Belle Rose any more.

Tom's wife, Charlotte, tried to keep him under control. Charlotte was a sweet soul who always saw the good in people. She tried to dissuade him from his determination I should be taught to be a worker, not one of the privileged elite class to which I had been raised before my Daddy Jo died. With Charlotte's help, I was even allowed to keep a few pretty dresses, to wear when special company like Sir Calvin came, and a locket with a picture of my real mama in it.

But, when I was 12, Charlotte caught typhus. In less than two weeks, both Charlotte and their son, Charlie, were dead. I was scared. No, terrified. What would my world become now that my one defender was gone?

Tom soon complained it should have been me, not Charlotte or Charlie, but the no-account little colored gal who should have died. I felt numb. How could my own brother hate me so much? Why did he hate me so much?

Well, things went from bad to worse then. Tom became Mistah Tom. I was never to mention our 'relationship' to visitors. After all, he was the Master at Belle Rose Plantation now. I was little more than a maid. I was nothing more. I was damned sure no longer the Wee Duchess of Belle Rose. "Not now, never will be, little girl. It doesn't matter that Daddy talked some about his foolish pipe dream of making you into a Duchess now and then. So, you turn your pretty little ass around, go wash those drawers and shut your damned mouth."

He didn't want me to talk like I had ever been educated. He liked it the more I talked down, using colloquial, broken English like the slaves speak. And while Daddy Jo had been freeing slaves each year for about 30 years or so by then, ever since he bought Marcus in Puerto Rico that fateful day in 1743, no slaves were freed while Tom was in charge. In fact, he shocked the fire out of us all when he bought a few more. He was much freer with the whip than Daddy Jo, too. In fact, I don't ever remember Daddy Jo whipping anyone at Belle Rose.

I hoped it might be better when Tom went to fight at Saratoga. Tom hired an overseer, a man named Simon Le Grande, to run the plantation in his absence. Le Grande came highly recommended from Mama Belle's relatives in Louisiana. But I learned pretty quick that Le Grande didn't take 'no' for an answer. He beat me the first time I told him no.

Tom always told me not to ever tell a white man 'no'. He warned me a white man could beat me for saying 'no' and might even kill me. After all, Tom insisted, all white men knew you were a "N" if you had one drop of black blood. And if you were even one drop black, you were just a N-slut, and everyone knew you wanted it. If you told a white man 'no', he could beat you. Heck fire, he could beat you to death.

I was seventeen when Simon came. Hattie warned me to keep out of his way. "Chile, that man' ain't no good. You're a mighty pretty little gal with your light skin, those big blue eyes and all that pretty red hair. You stay plumb dab away from him. That man is evil. He will hurt you."

It was a few days after Tom left when Le Grande made his demand.

I remember Le Grande called me into the study. Simon leaned back in the big leather chair that had been Daddy Jo's and Tom's and put his boots on top of the desk like he owned it. He was tall enough to be a Selk, but he had dirty, mud brown hair and tended to sunburn somethin' awful. I recall he was sitting in Tom's big chair, picking at his teeth, with his boots propped up there on the desk. Chills went down my spine when he smiled at me. I felt like some kind of slime slid over me as his eyes lingered on my bosom way too long. "You come to my room tonight, little girl."

I was shaking so hard I could hardly stand up. I managed to raise my eyes to his and whispered, "Mistah Simon, you know what my brother said…"

His hands hit down on the desk so hard I jumped. "Your brother's gone, little girl. Ain't no one gonna say a word now. You come to my room tonight. You hear?"

I nodded, my mouth drier than dried out cornmeal. "Yes, sir, Mistah Simon, I hear you, but…"

His pale blue eyes narrowed as they darkened with rage. "Ain't no 'but' about it, Fancy. You'd best come to my room tonight."

I didn't go. He came to my room, madder than a colicky mule that needs to be puked. "You running a little bit late tonight, little girl?"

I slid back along the wall. "No, sir, Mistah Simon."

"Then why the hell ain't you in my bed pleasuring me right now? You coming with me?"

"No, sir." I whispered.

"What did you say?" he growled, his voice full of menace, as he stepped towards me.

I swear I didn't know a person could shake so hard and live to tell it. I lifted my head, swallowed hard, and answered again. "No, sir, Mistah Simon. I … I ain't coming. I'm a good girl."

He snorted. "A good girl, huh? That what you call it when you don't obey your Massa?"

My mouth went dry as chaff. He had never called himself Massa before. I was pretty sure it was a real bad sign.

It was.

He caught hold of my arm and then grabbed me by my long hair. He dragged me down stairs by my hair. He was so rough with me I thought he might pull it out. I was crying as he yelled at my Uncle Tobias to get everyone together. He dragged me outside right there in front of God and everyone. He ripped my dress right down the back, cut my stays loose, and ripped my shift before he tied my hands to the post. I was shaking like a leaf, my clothes pooled at my feet except for my stockings and shoes.

He had this look on his face that scared me, a look like I hadn't ever seen on anyone before. He snapped, "Little girl, you gonna learn some things right here and now. First of all, I am right. You are wrong. Second, you are nothing but a worthless little colored girl and you are gonna learn to obey me right here and now. Third, you will do as I say. I am the center of your universe now. You don't even need to bother to think about yourself anymore. You just think about me, and how you can best make me happy. Because, you best remember you are a worthless little girl who ain't ever gonna amount to nothing."

With that, he unfurled the horsewhip and commenced to lay it on me. He only had to beat me with that whip one time. Oh, he hit me with his belt and a hair brush after that, and with his fists lots of times, but that was the one time he ever tied me up and beat me with a horse whip. He told everyone that he was beating me for being disobedient to him. Hattie Mae cried as he lashed me.

I was lucky. He stopped at 15 lashes of the whip.

Afterwards, he let Hattie Mae clean me up and help me change my clothes. She put some unguent on my skin to help it heal. I remember it stung something fierce when she rubbed it into my skin. She reassured me my skin was bruised but he hadn't broken the skin very bad. After she got me cleaned up, I went to his room as he told me to do. He made me take my shift off and crawl to him, naked, like I was a dog. I did what he told me to do. I didn't fight him. I damned sure didn't tell him 'no' again. I did what he wanted me to do, no matter how dirty it made me feel. Over time, I learned I could do whatever he told me to do, but I could put my mind somewhere else, back in happier days when I was little. With my Daddy Jo and Miss Belle, or with Will and the girls. Sometimes, I remembered when Uncle Marc and Aunt Lily used to come to see us, and how sweet they always were to me. About playing with their son, Michael.

Anything to keep from thinking about what Simon Le Grande was doing to me.

The letter came in November 1777. Simon summoned me to the study again. I had learned to dread his summons, and my heart was beating fast and erratic that morning when I went to the study. My heart does that when I get scared. Simon was holding the letter in his hand when I came to the study. "You know what this is, little girl?"

I shook my head, trembling so bad I wasn't sure I could stand up. "N… no, sir, Mistah Simon. I sure do not."

He smiled, and then held it out for me to take it. I hesitated for a minute, and then with a heart filled with dread, I took the letter from General Arnold.

Tom was dead. My damned fool brother went and got himself killed at Saratoga. It wasn't even a bad wound, just some little ol' bitty scratch that went bad, the letter said. Lily told me later he 'went septic'. I don't have any idea what it means except 'septic' will kill you.

"You see, little girl? I told you your brother wasn't goin' to save you. You are mine. Body and soul."

Not long after that, Hattie Mae had the midwife check me. She advised Simon that I was biggin'. All I knew was I was numb. Simon was pleased as punch he had me biggin', but he got meaner and meaner towards me as I got bigger and bigger. Lord knows it seemed nothing I ever did was good enough to please that man.

In April, Sir Calvin Hobbs came to talk to Simon about buying the tobacco crop. I have known Mr. Hobbs most of my life. He was a fine gentleman, always very attentive, polite and kind. He was tall, with a smattering of grey making his dark hair aristocratic. He must have been Tom's age but he still had all his teeth. He had kind brown eyes that always sparkled when he saw me. That day, they were not sparkling. He looked plumb dab shocked, near senseless, when he saw my condition.

"Fancy, my dear, are you breeding?" he gasped. I thought his eyes might pop out of his head.

I was so ashamed. I hung my head as tears welled in my eyes. I blinked fast to keep the hot tears from spilling over. I managed to whisper, "Yes, sir, Mr. Hobbs."

And then, Simon Le Grande came waltzing into the hall. He popped me right on my butt right there in front of God and everyone, and to my horror, he began to grope my breasts right there in front of Mr. Hobbs.

"Mr. Le Grande, I am shocked," protested Mr. Hobbs. "Have you been taking liberties with this girl?"

Simon shrugged as he continued to fondle me. "Aw, hell, Hobbs, she ain't nothing but a little ol' mixed breed gal. She likes it. Don't you, Fancy?"

I could feel my cheeks burning red with shame, but I knew Simon would hurt me bad if I denied it. I hung my head as I answered. "Yes, sir," I whispered.

Simon frowned. "What say, girl? Speak up. Mr. Hobbs wants to hear you."

I was shaking by then. He was getting angry and that always meant he would be hitting on me later. Shaking, I gulped, and then answered again, a little louder that time. "Yes, sir, Massa."

Mr. Hobbs' eyes narrowed. "Why in the name of all that is holy is Fancy Selk calling you Massa, Le Grande? She isn't a slave. She is the daughter of this house."

Simon laughed and grabbed my arm to pull me close to kiss me. "She's my little sex slave. She does whatever I tell her to do. Don't you, Fancy?"

I was shaking so bad I wasn't sure my legs would hold me up much longer. I was eight months pregnant, big as the side of a barn, and I knew he was gonna beat the snot out of me when Mr. Hobbs left. I looked at Mr. Hobbs, imploring him with my eyes. "Mr. Hobbs, please, I'm fine. Please, sir…"

"Bull!" Hobbs bellowed, as his face turned red with fury. "This girl is shaking like a leaf. Fancy, you do not have to stay here and be abused by this … this animal."

My eyes must have been big as sand dollars then. Hattie and Tobias both came to the door of the office, worry written across both their faces.

Simon forced himself to laugh. "Aw, Hobbs, if you want the girl, you should have said so. Take her on upstairs. You can do whatever you want with little Fancy. She loves it all."

Mr. Hobbs looked like he might choke from a fit of the apoplexy. After a minute or two of coughing, he caught his breath and narrowed his eyes. He looked from Simon to me, and then back to Simon. He nodded, and grabbed my hand, dragging me upstairs to my room. Simon laughed like a fool as I struggled against Mr. Hobbs all the way upstairs.

"Hush, Fancy, you don't honestly think I intend to violate you, do you? My God, don't you know by now how I feel about you? I've wanted to marry you for years, and by damn, Tom should have let us marry last summer when

I visited," he muttered when we got to my room. "Now, grab some things quick, put them in a pillow case, and let's get you out of here."

Hattie Mae had followed us up the stairs, and kind of sobbed when she heard him. "Oh, praise the Lawd, my prayers have done been answered!"

"Shush! Help her get some things together, Hattie. We need to high tail it out of here before that blasted maniac realizes what we are doing."

We threw a few of my things into a pillow case. Mr. Hobbs and I tiptoed down the back stairs to the kitchen. I wrote a note for Tobias to send by the carrier pigeons over to Mount Vernon. Mr. Hobbs was going to take me there because it was close and he knew Mrs. Washington would protect me. Hattie sent Mina out to the pigeons to send the message, and then she checked to make sure Le Grande wasn't on to us yet. Once she gave us the all clear, Mr. Hobbs and I scurried out the back door. Within minutes, we were in his carriage headed away from my nightmare. Within two hours, Mrs. Washington was fussing over me, shocked at my delicate condition.

As she started to take me up the stairs, I stopped. "Mrs. Washington, ma'am, I am so sorry, but I think I wet myself."

She looked down, her eyes widening in shock as she paled. "Callie, go fetch the midwife right now. I think Fancy's waters broke."

Mr. Hobbs swung me up into his arms and carried me on upstairs, even though my skirts were soaked. I was impressed an older gentleman like he could carry me like I was a little old sack of flour. I didn't know what 'breaking your waters' was or what it meant, but by midnight, my baby girl was born. She was tiny, I reckoned a month premature, but she was perfect, with curling, dark hair and blue eyes like my mama and just about all the Selks have. She was beautiful, even if she was Le Grande's get. I named her Bella after Miss Belle.

Mrs. Washington was real good to me. She would not let Simon Le Grande anywhere around Bella or me. She told me every day I didn't have no reason to be ashamed of what he did to me. The shame was on Simon Le Grande's head, not mine. It might be true, but it was mighty hard to believe it. I was the one who bore the baby. I was the one people looked at like I was a fallen woman.

And to make matters worse, little Bella had dark hair and blue eyes, like a Selk baby. Simon took full advantage of that, too. The sorry excuse for a man claimed Tom must be the father of my baby instead of him. While I protested it with vehemence, some people must have believed him, because they looked at me like I was Satan come to earth in female form.

In August 1778, William came back to Belle Rose. He was horrified to learn that the no-good overseer had violated me. He damned near beat Simon to death when he learned I gave birth to Simon's baby and Simon dared say Tom was her daddy, not Simon. Will tarred and feathered Simon Le Grande, and dumped him over in Delaware, the other side of the Chesapeake Bay. Will must have told me a thousand times he was sorry he left me when he took his girls back home to Puerto Rico, but he would make sure I was safe now. He offered to take Bella and me to Puerto Rico, but it was hurricane season and I was sure enough afraid to move there.

Besides, like I told Will, I didn't speak a lick of Spanish. I could say 'gracias' and 'tortilla,' but that was about it. Will tried to convince me I wanted to go to Ireland, to live at Ranscome Manor. It turned out Daddy Jo always wanted me to become the Duchess of Ranscome, which was why Tom was more than a little bit mean to me for all those years.

I told Will, "I got no interest in going to Ireland. Tamsin went there when I was 4. Went off and left me to chase after an Irish lord. Left me here to be abused by a white overseer who thought I was less than him because of the damned blood I got from her. I got no interest in going anywhere near her."

If I keep telling myself that, maybe someday I'll believe it.

In September, Will and I agreed he would take my baby and me out west to Indian Territory, where Bella and I would live with the Widow Sassy Winslow at a place called McCarron's Corner. Uncle Marc and Aunt Lily live there, too. In fact, Uncle Marc founded that little town back in Indian Territory around the time I was born. Will advised me the Widow Winslow was a fine woman, and she was a seamstress and quilter. Will was getting orders all up and down the east coast for her quilts, and he figured I could live with her and help her with her orders. I do love to sew. So, Bella and I moved out west to Indian Territory and lived with Sassy, until she moved to Belle Rose in '79 when Will and she married.

I came back then, too, with my little Bella, to be the housekeeper here. I didn't want to come back to Belle Rose, and yet I did. Like Sassy would say, it was complicated. How could I love and hate the same place, at the same time?

I wasn't at all sure I wanted to go back to Belle Rose, but I would conquer my demons and go back to the home of my youth.

Things went fine at first. Will and Sassy had a big, fancy wedding. Sassy gave birth to twin boys in November. Christmas in 1779 was the very best I remembered in my whole life. But then, Will and Sassy had to go to Philadelphia for some big party given by General Benedict Arnold there, the same general who wrote the nice letter when Tom died at Saratoga in '77. It was some hoity toity political thing, and General Washington wanted them to attend. I would have liked to have gone to meet the man who was with Tom when he died, but I stayed home to keep the plantation on an even keel and to watch over their twin boys and little Bella. And like I said, things were going pretty good until the day Will and Sassy were due back, when Simon Le Grande showed up.

It was a bad day, like three years before when Simon was abusing me every single day. I thought I would about die when Sassy marched straight into my room, and saw what Simon was doing to me there. I was afraid she would think I was just a mixed blood, no account, little gal with loose morals, like Simon always said. But, I should have known better. Sassy is way better than that. She pulled a gun on Le Grande and shot him dead that night when she caught him abusing me. And, then Will fed his sorry carcass to the pigs. Like Sassy always says, hungry pigs can devour a human body in 10 minutes.

That was when I said I needed my daddy and Will and Sassy learned who my real daddy was. I remember Sassy marveled, "My land, it never did make sense."

But then, for Sassy, lots of what happens here doesn't make sense.

You see, Sassy came here from another time. Things are very different where she came from than they are here. There ain't no slavery there. Why, she says in the future, they will even have black leaders in Congress and a black President! Sassy says black women where she came from got no idea what being a slave is all about. She claims one woman felt like a slave because she earned a 'mere 12 million dollars a year'! I cannot imagine how much 12 million dollars is. Others say they are slaves if they have to do what their employers ask, even when they are getting paid big wages for their work. They got no idea what slavery, racism, or discrimination are all about, at least from my perspective. Their perspective must be a heap different from mine.

I am considered to be a person of color, but I look white. I have fair skin, blue-green eyes, and what they call ginger hair I inherited from Marc's mama. But believe me, I know what it is to be treated like you are inferior. I'm one-eighth black and as such, I am what they call a free woman of color. I have more than that single drop that most folks around here think taints a person's blood. I can never marry a white man in the Southern Colonies, where Belle Rose Plantation is located. That was why Marcus didn't marry my real mama, Tamsin. The foolish woman wouldn't go with him to Indian Territory, where they could marry. So, when I was born, Miss Belle and Daddy Jo adopted me, with the plan that someday, I could take Daddy's Irish title. Don't ask me how he thought he could pull that off. And then when the English King made Daddy Jo a Duke, Daddy Jo thought it would be amusing to name me to follow him. After all, he figured, if I were a Duchess, I could make a good marriage no matter what was in my blood. Daddy always told me Queen Charlotte was mixed like me and good King George loved her anyway. Her mixed blood made the King no never-you-mind at all. Daddy never made me feel bad about being a mixed girl. And the plan might have worked if Daddy Jo hadn't up and died before he put it into his will.

I may be of mixed race, but I am a human being. I have a soul. I have feelings, hopes, dreams. I refuse to ever be a victim again. Sassy insists I am a survivor, and I need to write down my story. She says survivors need to journal. This is my story.

Sir Calvin Hobbs of Spring Haven is a good man. I know he loves me. He has been asking me to marry him for years now, even before he saved me from Simon. He begged me to marry him the day Bella was born. I couldn't burden him with the responsibility of raising my child as his own then. If he married me before she was born, she would be his legal child. I reckon I should have done that, but it didn't seem fair to him that day, and things were happening pretty fast. He told me he asked Tom for my hand in marriage when I was sixteen, and again before Tom went to Saratoga. Both times, Tom insisted I was too young. That's kinda funny, don't you think? Funny and sad. I was too young to get married but not too young to be violated by scum like Le Grand.

I may not be able to marry Calvin here in Virginia, but Will and Calvin both assure me Calvin and I could marry in Bermuda, where his estate is. I believe I will tell him 'yes' the next time he asks, providing he proposes again. After four rejections, he might not ever bother to suggest marriage to me again.

At first, I couldn't even think about marrying anyone. Then, about the time I was thinking about accepting him and settling down, Simon struck again. Calvin hasn't been coming as much of late with the war and all, but he writes me pretty regular. I can tell from his letters he is still very interested.

Heck fire, I know he loves me. He would be a good husband. I just don't know how good a wife I could be for him. Calvin deserves a wife who could come to him with open arms and a loving, open heart.

That was when Sassy suggested I write this journal. She isn't keen on Calvin. She thinks the Good Lord has someone else in store for me. I know Calvin is in his 50's, the same age Tom would be now. Will's gonna be 50 this year himself. Calvin's dark hair is going silver, but he is still fit and trim. He is handsome and rich. More important, he is a good man, and he loves me. He has loved me for years. I remember when I was little he used to tell me he was waiting for me to grow up to marry him. Can you imagine? And, he saved me from Le Grande in '78. That ought to count for something, shouldn't it?

"Sassy, tell me again why I need to write in this journal?" I felt frustrated with my attempts to write down everything that was happening at Belle Rose.

Sassy is my very best friend, and not just because she killed Le Grand for me. She grinned, with her lopsided dimples flashing at me. I say lopsided because one dimple is much more distinct than the other. "It will help you to remember and to learn from your memories."

I shrugged. I have tried to explain to her over and over again I do not want to remember. I want to forget all about that awful time and move on with my life. And at that, she wanted me to write down all the stuff that happened to me since I was a little girl. Heck fire, I don't remember half of it.

Little girl. Damn, I hate it when people call me that. Makes my skin crawl. Always seems like a put down, an insult. I wonder why? I mean, I know Simon called me that, but Tom did, too. Daddy Jo did, too, although he called me his Wee Duchess more often. It never bothered me too much before Simon. Of course, I was a little girl when my Daddy Jo called me that.

Calvin Hobbs don't ever call me little girl since I'm a grown woman now.

I shrugged. Fine. Make her happy. Write it all down. Maybe one day I would understand why 'little girl' bothers me so danged much.

And so, I wrote about the doll.

Like I said before, my real mama ran off with Lord Jay Fitz Simmons to Ireland when I was four. It seemed like almost everyone went after her to try to get her to come back. The interesting thing was Lord Fitz Simmons was Marc's older brother. Marc was captured by Barbary pirates in Europe when he was real young. The pirates sold him as a slave. Daddy Jo bought him and later freed him, but Daddy Jo never knew who Marc was until Jay Fitz Simmons showed up hunting for Marc. I remember Lord Fitz Simmons resembled Marc a lot. I always suspected Tamsin ran off with Lord Fitz Simmons because he looked so much like Marc.

But whatever her reason, she went off and left her own flesh and blood here.

Well, everyone went after her except Tom and Charlotte. Charlotte was biggin' with Charlie and didn't want to go, and someone had to stay and run the plantation while the others went gallivanting off to Ireland. Tom was the heir so it was logical he would stay home and run the plantation. They all got back a couple of weeks after Christmas. Will brought his daughters to Belle Rose because their mama died in childbirth right before Christmas. My land, Belle Rose was a noisy house with Will's three, Lily and Marc's baby, Michael, Baby Charlie, and me! Lily and Marc brought presents from Ireland for all of us, including dolls for all of us girls.

My doll was a little red-haired girl with blue eyes. She wore a blue dress and a blue bow in her hair. I always love a pretty blue dress. I thought she was the most beautiful doll in the whole wide world. Uncle Marc – well, I called him Uncle Marc until I learned he was my real daddy – told me that the doll looked like his sister, Dara, when she was a girl. I fell in love with the pretty porcelain doll and named her Dara. Marc looked very pleased and assured me his sister would have liked that.

Dara was my favorite toy and my best friend for years. After Will took the girls back to Puerto Rico, I didn't have any other little girls to play with. So, I made up stories and played with Dara.

At least, I did until Daddy Jo died.

When Daddy Jo died, Tom took away most of my pretty dresses. And he took away Dara. I cried and cried, begged and begged, but he insisted that I was a big girl, and I did not need to play with dolls anymore. He didn't throw her away though. Sometimes, if I was especially useful, compliant, obedient, and if I did exactly as he said, that silver-haired devil let me play with my doll for a little while.

Humph. It seemed like I never quite scrubbed that floor clean enough, mended his shirts neat enough, or did anything else quite as good as he wanted, because he sure never let me play with my doll very much, I tell you for sure.

But the doll was there, and I got to hold her and play with her sometimes. Of course, by the time Tom left for the war, I was a big girl. I didn't have no more time for playing with dolls. I was the housekeeper at Belle Rose by then, and my duties took pretty near all my time.

That still didn't justify what Simon did to the doll when he came. Breaking my doll was not necessary. It was mean spirited and done to hurt me. And, you would have thought he had hurt me enough that day by beating me, and then raping me.

But Simon was never satisfied.

Tom confided to Simon that the doll had been mine when I was young and that it was still special to me. So that night, after Simon had his way with me, he made me break the doll myself. When I had to drop the hammer on Dara's pretty head, I cried. No, I take it back. I sobbed like my heart was breaking in two. He sounded plumb dab evil when he laughed. He picked up a shard of her broken porcelain face and scraped it down the side of my naked breast. It was like I was looking at something but I wasn't there. I remember the blood drops welled up one by one from the broken skin. I thought, hot damn, it hurt more to break the doll than for him to cut me. He made me pick up the pieces to throw them away.

But, I didn't throw Dara away. I hid her. Someday, maybe I can get her repaired for my Bella.

Now, why on earth does Sassy think I need to write this down? How on earth can it help me to heal? That don't make no sense at all to me. No sense at all. I need to get on about my life, lickity split, and never look back. I have a great big house to manage and a child to raise. I don't have time for this nonsense.

I pushed the journal aside and commenced brushing my hair before I got ready for bed. Sassy swears that a hundred strokes a night gives our hair a luster and sheen women in the future would kill to have.

"You think this journal thing will help?" Will frowned.

Sassy nodded. "Oh, yes. They taught us to have women journal at the women's shelter in Williamsburg where I volunteered in my other lifetime. There is something there that is eating at her. I would swear whatever this is, it's about to kill her. This can help her remember what it is."

Will's frown deepened. "Worse than being raped for months and months by that sorry assed animal, Le Grande? My God, Sass, what in the blazes do you think happened to her?"

Sassy was silent at first. She had to think how to word this. She didn't want to upset the man she loved more than life itself. "I think there is more than she has told us, Will. There are too many blanks in Fancy's memory. She doesn't remember much at all from around the time Charlotte died until Tom went off to fight in the war. That isn't normal."

His brow furrowed as he frowned. "What do you mean?"

She shrugged as she chewed the inside of her mouth. "I don't know. But, it isn't normal."

If only Rick were here. Rick studied psychology. It was his undergraduate major before med school. He worked as a volunteer at the Women's Center, too, and counseled with a lot of survivors. It helped Rick heal, too. Sassy's first husband, Owen, locked his son up in a mental hospital when Rick was 15. That was a God-awful time for Rick. She may have forgiven Owen for it over time, but Sassy knew Rick never would. Sassy adopted Rick after his mama died. She considered him to be her son, even though she was a mere ten years older than Rick.

Sassy knew if her son were here, he would know what to do. But, Rick was more than 200 years in the future. Sassy sighed. She would keep writing him, by way of relatives back home, to keep until the future. Maybe someday Rick would manage to come. And then maybe he could figure out how to help poor, sweet Fancy to heal. Fancy deserved so much better than she had received so far in life.

Okay, let's face it, Sassy thought. Fancy deserved a man like Rick. Sassy prayed every day the Good Lord would send Rick, or if not Rick, the right man, for Fancy. Will thought the right man was Calvin Hobbs, the tobacco buyer from Bermuda who saved Fancy from Le Grande. Hobbs had been asking Fancy to marry him for years now. Thus far, Fancy always turned him down. There had to be a reason why. Sassy knew Calvin loved Fancy, but she also knew Fancy did not feel the same way about Calvin. Sassy worried that one day, Fancy would cave in and marry Calvin instead of waiting for the right man to come along. Calvin was a dear man, and he seemed to be a good man. But, Sassy believed he deserved more than to be married to Fancy just because she felt she wasn't worth a man to love, or that she felt like she needed to take whatever crumbs got thrown her way.

Sassy knew Fancy deserved to find her own twin flame like Sassy did with Will. Besides that, Calvin was 55, way too old for a woman as young as Fancy. My heaven, she thought, Calvin is old enough to be her father!

Dear Lord, Sassy thought, please send Rick soon!

Chapter 2
Fancy, 1780

Three weeks after Simon's assault on me, Calvin appeared at Belle Rose. He paced back and forth, livid the scurrilous dog had again managed to harm me. And that time, when he asked me to marry him, I accepted.

"Fancy, my darling, please marry me. Tom should have let us marry years ago and you would not have had to endure all this horror. Please, my darling…"

"Yes. I'll marry you, Calvin."

He stopped dead in his tracks and his mouth fell agape in surprise. I almost laughed at the shocked expression on his face. "You … you will? I … I mean I'm delighted, my darling, but … are you sure?"

I nodded. "I am quite sure. I already made up my mind if you came back and offered for me again, I would accept. If you still want me, after all the things that horrible man did to me, after all he shamed me, then I would be honored to become your wife."

He rushed to my side to pull me into his arms. "Oh, my darling, Fancy, I love you so much. I have waited so long to hear you say you would marry me. Oh, my dearest, I will be the best husband in the world, I swear!"

I struggled not to laugh. He had never married. He often claimed he waited for me to grow up and marry him. He always claimed he fell in love with me when he first saw me in the cradle. Bless his heart, I've heard him swear to that story as long as I can remember him coming to Belle Rose. But even as a first-time husband in his fifties, I was convinced he would be a kind, patient and loving man.

We agreed Sassy and Will would take me to Bermuda at the end of March for the wedding. Calvin was ebullient as he departed. "You go over to

Williamsburg, my darling, and buy anything your heart desires for our little Bella and yourself."

He kissed me before he boarded the ship for Bermuda to make ready for our wedding.

Sassy was subdued when I told her. "Are you sure about this, Fancy? You don't have to marry him. Marriage is not the time to make do with whatever man is available. Are you sure?"

I bristled at her words. "Make do? I am marrying a handsome, kind, wealthy man who loves me beyond compare. Why on earth do you think I could do better?"

Tears welled up in her eyes. "Oh, Fancy, just wish you said you love him."

I didn't reply. How could I explain I wasn't sure I could ever love a man? I wasn't even sure I could engage in marital relations, eager and ready to please. But I would try. I would do my marital duty. Somehow. Besides, Calvin loved me. He was willing to take me as I was. He knew my shameful history and still treated me like I was precious, a treasure beyond compare.

I sure hoped and prayed I would not disappoint Sir Calvin.

One reason we waited was so I could be sure I was not carrying Simon's get. I sighed with relief when my monthly came in February and again in March. And then, one day as I was packing, I laughed. I would be the first Selk bride in over 20 years to go to her wedding without a bun in the oven, as Sassy put it. Sassy, Lily, even Tamsin when she married Lord Fitz Simmons, were all pregnant Selk brides. If I had married Calvin back in '78, I would have been another pregnant Selk bride. Lord knew I was not going to him a virgin, but I did not go to Calvin with memories of ever loving another man.

So, on March 30th, in the year of Our Lord, 1780, a year to the day after Will and Sassy were hand fast at McCarron's Corner, I became Mrs. Calvin Hobbs, in a little Church of England chapel overlooking the Atlantic.

My gown was made of silk, of course, as befitted the wife of the third Earl of Spring Haven. I wore a pale celadon green quilted, silk petticoat, over panniers and several very full, starched cotton petticoats. The outer, silk petticoat was topped with a white robe a la polonaise covered with pink embroidered flowers. The dressmaker assured me the flowers were hibiscus, and she read in a book that hibiscus grew in Bermuda. The robe a la polonaise laced up the front over a matching stomacher with pink ribbon. The sleeves were edged with white Irish bobbin lace engageants I found in Mama Belle's things. Will said he thought Miss Belle bought the lace on a long-ago trip to Ireland. A sheer, pale pink, silk fichu filled in the neckline. I wore white stockings and shoes that matched the robe a la polonaise, white with pink embroidery, with jade green heels and diamond buckles. I wore jade earrings, matching jade bangle bracelets, and a jade necklace that all matched my pretty jade wedding band Calvin obtained from China. They also matched the celadon green of my silk petticoat. Set into the top of the jade wedding band was a large, rose cut diamond. I thought it was perfect.

Calvin informed me jade was considered the most precious stone in China, where it is called 'the essence of heaven and earth.' In fact, Calvin claimed it is not legal to export it out of China. The captain who brought the jade set for Calvin did so at great personal risk, which told me Calvin must have paid a lot for it. Jade symbolizes purity and moral integrity. I cried when he told me that.

"But, I am not coming to you pure," I wailed.

"Oh, my darling, nothing Le Grande did to you could in any way have affected your purity. You are the light at the end of the tunnel. You calm the storms within my mind. You are the purest soul I will ever know," he insisted as he slipped the ring onto my finger. "The Chinese say gold is valuable. Jade is invaluable. That was why I ordered the jade set when I determined to marry you, my darling. You are invaluable, like the most precious jade that could ever adorn the body of an Empress."

So of course, I cried even harder, determined to be the bride he wanted, the bride he deserved.

Our wedding was small. At the wedding, Sassy stood up for me, and Will stood up for Calvin. Calvin's sister, Caroline, was also there. Caroline was a widow. And we had my precious Bella, the prettiest little flower girl in the whole wide world.

Calvin proclaimed to everyone that she was his natural child, conceived when I was young and Tom refused to let us marry. He claimed our wedding was delayed when Tom was killed at Saratoga and with 'the little Rebellion,' as Calvin calls the war raging in the Colonies. Even Will appreciated the deception. Both men swore they did not ever want Bella to know Le Grand fathered her in violence. With her dark hair, I admit she looks more like she could be Calvin's child than Simon's. Calvin's sister, Caroline, believed him, and the minister allowed us to baptize Bella as his child after we married.

It was foggy the morning we entered the church for the wedding ceremony. When we came outside, the sun was shining bright, and the picture before me took my breath away with palm trees, pink sands, and the greenery from the native junipers that filled the rocky shore.

Calvin boasts the weather will be mild most of the year. I am still worried about hurricanes, but he claims none have hit here for the 30-odd years that he has lived in Bermuda.

While I brought lots of linen and cotton to make clothing, I indulged and brought silk gowns from Williamsburg as well. It had been a long time since I wore silk gowns. I didn't know whether to exult in the sensual feel of the fabric against my skin or to despair over the cost of the extravagant gowns Sassy urged me to buy. I also brought along a dozen of Mama Belle's beautiful, old gowns to remake into more fashionable styles, since they were all at least 15 years old now.

Calvin owns a typical Bermuda home, built of limestone. As we approached the house, I saw a wall encircling the property, covered with native junipers. We passed through what Calvin said was a moon gate to enter the magical gardens of the Spring Haven Estate. They call it a moon gate because it is shaped like the full moon. As he promised, our home was painted bright flamingo pink, with canary yellow shutters and door. The roof was also made of limestone, terraced to allow for easy collection of rainwater. All the drinking water on the island comes from fresh rainwater, so it is imperative the settlers collect rainwater.

The gardens themselves took my breath away. I had not expected a formal English garden. Roses, frangipani and hibiscus lent color and scents. The gardens were edged with more junipers and palms.

Bella ran through the walkways, enamored of the exquisite gardens. "Ooh, Daddy, this is pretty!"

I smiled. It thrilled me he was so accepting of Bella and he wanted her to call him Daddy. What a good man I thought. How kind and thoughtful of my child as well as me.

Calvin beamed as he bent down to hug my little cherub. "Yes, darling, it is. And I'm glad you like it, my little pumpkin."

Located on a bluff above the azure waters, we could look out at the sea beyond and at the pink sands. Will said the pink sand was formed from the waves crashing upon the coral reef. Tall coconut palms flanked the house, with a flared stairway up to the entrance. Calvin explained they call that style entrance the 'welcoming arms'. The house was decorated with beautiful furnishings Calvin brought from England over the years.

I was lucky. My husband was not just rich and handsome, he was patient with me. Under his tutelage, I realized I could engage in marital relations with my lusty old man without fear. I could enjoy our relations, something I never thought possible after Le Grande.

But, I soon learned that life is not perfect even in paradise.

We were both ecstatic when we realized I was *enceinte* in June. Calvin says a Countess says *enceinte* rather than biggin' when she is expecting a baby. However, it seemed almost as soon as we learned our good news, I suffered a miscarriage. I never dreamed the loss of a baby could be so painful. Not just the physical pain of my baby being torn from my body. Not just my emotions, my inordinate sadness, my downright grief over the death of a precious little soul who lived such a brief time inside my body. Grief over the loss of the little person I never got to hold, to kiss, to tell how much I loved him. And with the loss, I lost part of myself, part of my hopes and dreams. And I felt so guilty. What had I done to cause this?

The doctor insisted we wait at least six months to try again for a baby, but my Calvin was not a young man. We did not want to waste time waiting and by Christmas I was again with child. I lost the second baby as well by February. And again, I blamed myself. I wept. I grieved. My body ached. Even worse, my mind ached. What was I doing wrong? Why couldn't I carry his child?

And Calvin, ever supportive, began to look at me askance. As if he were also wondering, why? So, we both grieved for the loss of that wee child for whom we had such hopes and dreams. How could this be happening to us? Why was this happening to us?

That time, the doctor threw a veritable conniption fit, adamant we should have no marital relations for at least six months. But, Calvin's sister died not long after that, and sure enough, I found myself consoling my old man in my bed.

Not long after Caroline's death, I received a letter from Sassy. As I read it, I shook my head at the incredible story unfolding before my eyes. No one but

Sassy Selk dares pull shenanigans like this one!

"You won't believe what Sassy has done this time," I muttered as Calvin sat reading beside me.

He looked up from his book with a wry smile. "I would believe almost anything about Sassy Selk. The woman is incorrigible. What has she done now?"

"It seems in January, Patty Jefferson and the children fled Monticello with Gen. Arnold and Col. Tarleton nipping at their heels. They went to Belle Rose, and of course, Sassy gave Mrs. Jefferson and the children refuge."

Calvin blinked. "Oh, my merciful heavens, did the British catch them there? They have been after that prize for some time."

I shook my head. "I think not. When the Redcoats arrived at Belle Rose, Sassy pulled a Sassy."

Calvin frowned. "Meaning she lied to them?"

I nodded.

He shook his head and sighed. "Oh, dear. Then what happened?"

"Col. Tarleton and Gen. Arnold searched the house. Tarleton found a nanny and children in the nursery but did not realize the nanny was Mrs. Jefferson."

Calvin looked surprised. "But I would swear Gen. Arnold knows Mrs. Jefferson."

I nodded. "He does. In fact, after Tarleton left the house, Arnold hung back long enough to tell Mrs. Jefferson it was good to see her again and to stay safe." I chuckled. "Well, Sassy always says 1781 will not be kind to young Colonel Tarleton."

Calvin looked horrified. "Oh, dear lord, I would not toy with Col. Tarleton like that. He is a brash young man with a fiery temper. Do you know what Tarleton's Quarter is? He gives no quarter. More than once, he killed every man standing after the rebels surrendered. The man is merciless. I dread to think what he would do if he learns of Sassy's deception. He would take it as a personal affront for which he would need to obtain satisfaction. And if it becomes known that Gen. Arnold covered for Sassy and Patty? Well, it would be very bad for Gen. Arnold. The Crown is already skeptical about Arnold's motives and true alliances by changing sides during this little rebellion. This would in no way enhance his reputation with Gen. Cornwallis if the General learned Gen. Arnold knew Mrs. Jefferson was there and did nothing to arrest her."

My cheeks burned with embarrassment as I realized I had confided something to my Loyalist husband that could be used against Sassy and even Gen. Arnold by the English. I grabbed his arm in dismay. "You can't tell, Calvin. My God, it could have horrible ramifications for Sassy!"

He looked uncertain, as if he might argue with me, but at last, his shoulders slumped. "Oh, no, of course not, my dear."

But I wasn't at all sure he would keep my new-found information secret. And if he didn't, I shuddered to think what kind of quarter Tarleton would give Lady Sarah Selk. Tarleton had been trying to flush Will out for over a year now. His soldiers had gone to Belle Rose more than once trying to get either Will or Sassy. If he obtained this information via my husband, and harm came to my family, I would never be able to forgive him or myself for having leaked the information to Calvin, which was used against them.

By May, I knew I was again with child. Should I be any less thrilled I was breeding again? But I am terrified. Yesterday I began cramping. Calvin and I both know that to be a sign of an impending miscarriage. I had to tell Calvin. I did not expect his anger, much less his outburst yesterday when I told him of my pains.

"I do not understand why you would carry a child spawned on you by that … that … creature and yet you now refuse to carry my child to term."

"Refuse? You … you think I am somehow refusing to carry my own baby to term?" I was never so wounded in all my life. I struggled not to cry, but I could not hold the flood of tears back as he continued to berate me. It was when he inferred that I was somehow rejecting his babies and that I had wanted That Man's baby when I lost my temper. "My God, how dare you say that to me? You of all people should know how much I wanted my babies. Our babies. How much I want this baby. You know what I endured with that creature and you … you dare to say I am rejecting your baby and wanted his? That's a horrible thing to say to me! I want our baby. I am desperate to keep this baby."

"It does not appear to me you want my child," he snapped, lips thin with rage. "This will be the third you have rejected. What else am I to think?"

I could feel the blood drain from my face. I felt like he had punched me in the belly.

"I tell you what. You have such a poor opinion of me? Then you take me back to Belle Rose. I don't want to be here with a man who does not believe me."

So, now I am packing. I will return to Belle Rose. Maybe the midwife there can help me. I carried my Bella close to term there before despite horrible circumstances. Maybe it is the water here. But these things I know for certain.

First, I am not rejecting a baby of my body. I want to give my husband a baby. I want my baby.

And, second, I will not live with a man who does not trust me and does not believe in me. Calvin shook me to the core when he accused me of rejecting his babies. His words have meant nothing to me several times when his actions said something quite different. But when he attacks me with both, well, then it is time for a change. After all, when someone is not treating you right, no matter how much you love them, you have to love yourself more and walk away. I will never be in the position again, to be controlled by an angry, bitter man who is intent on hurting me and the world around me.

I never dreamed I would leave my husband. I came to this marriage with the intent to make this marriage last. It will look like I am going back for a visit. After all, Calvin promised I could go back every year to see my family. But if he does not realize I want this baby, even if I lose this baby, then I will stay at Belle Rose.

I was so pleased I could feel pleasure with him. I love him, even if not the same way he loves me. I know what I feel for him is much more gratitude than true love, the kind of love I have seen between Marc and Lily, and between Will and Sassy. I knew when I married him I did not feel that way about Calvin. But, even so, I will not remain here and be bullied by a man who claims to love me with all his heart and soul.

I was bullied and controlled for too long before.

    ·   ·   ·   ·   ·

I awoke in a cold sweat. I realized I had the dream again. This time, I am writing it down since I just awoke.

It was dark. It seemed like everything was topsy-turvy.

Someone carried me to the bed and removed my clothes. I couldn't resist. It was as if I were boneless. Then, they were touching me, kissing me, telling me they loved me.

Oh, to be loved like that!

My heart swelled in the dream, and I wrapped my arms around his neck. "I love you, too," I whispered.

I still don't know who it was. Why can't I remember?

Hmm. Maybe it hasn't happened yet.

Chapter 3
Commencing in 2018

Rick Winslow worked hard to learn everything he could about the Selk family after he learned where his mother was. He lost a girlfriend over his 'crazy' search a mere two months ago when he announced he was going to Ireland to see Ranscome Manor, the Selk's ancestral home. Now, Rick knew it had been the right decision to come. He learned a lot about Will Selk's family on this trip. And now, standing in the painting gallery at Ranscome Manor, he had seen paintings of his Mom, Step-Dad, and even his half-siblings. But he never expected what he discovered with the painting he stood before now. He stared in awe at the painting of the beautiful woman before him. Gorgeous red hair, with that fair, translucent complexion Irish redheads have, and the most beautiful aquamarine eyes he ever saw. By damn, he was sure that was what Sassy told him was the real name for Will's sister, Fancy. Sassy wrote Rick about her for years. Sassy was convinced Rick and Fancy should someday meet if Rick could manage access through the time portal. Now, he could see why she wanted to introduce them.

He smiled. It looked like they would indeed meet.

Beneath the portrait was a placard that stated the elegant woman was Lady Francesca Marie Selk, the First Duchess of Ranscome, beloved wife of none other than Dr. Richard Winslow.

He smiled. His plans were all in place. He resigned from his job with the hospital before this trip. He had made a couple of trips to Williamsburg for period correct clothing over the course of the past year. He did reenactments often enough in the past with his folks that he knew the clothing he selected was appropriate for a doctor in the 1780's in the young United States of

America. He was close to the same size as his dad and was able to claim Owen Winslow's period appropriate clothing as well. Dad passed away before Mom went back in time. Dad would have appreciated the frugality of recycling his old attire.

When he got back stateside, Rick would trek down the Beech Bottom Trail right before full moon, as he had figured out Mom did. It was a shorter, more accessible path, a mere 4 ½ miles to the falls from the trailhead as compared to 8 miles up from the Jacks River trailhead his mom had traveled. He hadn't been able to go through the time warp the other times he tried, but it wasn't right before full moon then. Gibbous moon and full moon hadn't worked. The next full moon would be May 15th. He planned to try to go through the time warp every day for the week before that. He hoped he would catch the right day this time, and he would be able to go back in time to find his future wife.

He could care less that Francesca was a Duchess, but he was more than ready to meet this beautiful woman. Sassy wrote she was strong, resourceful, and not just a pretty face. He thought the story about why they called her Fancy was hilarious. She must have a great sense of humor.

Sassy also mentioned Fancy was a survivor. Rick wasn't sure what she survived other than the Revolutionary War. He suspected the woman endured some trauma. Well, they would cope. His specialty might be emergency medicine, but he took a lot of classes in psychology as an undergrad, enough for a second major. He damned near did his medical specialization in psychiatry. Even so, he knew he was better qualified to help Fancy deal with whatever issues she might have than anyone else in the eighteenth century. At least, he hoped he was. Besides, if he was this drawn to her by a painting, how would he feel in person when he met her?

Sassy wrote him in letter after letter that the sole reason you can travel back in time is to meet your one true love. Rick was so ready for love. He was ready for the beautiful Lady Francesca Selk. He figured he knew more about her than any living man in her century or his. He squared his shoulders, blew a kiss at the woman in the painting, and sauntered out of the elegant 16th century manor house he would someday call home.

Three weeks later, Rick felt more than a little frustrated. It was May 12th. He had not been able to pass through this damned hole in time thus far, and full moon was the next night. He sighed. He checked the cinches on the two pack mules, loaded down with medical supplies and his own things, and then mounted his horse.

He had a pass to take the horses up the southern part of the Appalachian Trail for the next two weeks, starting at the trailhead to the Beech Bottom Trail. He knew from Sassy that both Lily and she fell back in time in a meadow near the Jacks River Falls. He was sure he knew right where the meadow was that they had both passed through. He could feel an electricity in the air there, wild, like where lay lines cross, even though there was no electricity for miles around. He would try one more time, and then he would have to wait until next month. Dammit.

Rick swung up onto the horse. He clucked to get the big roan and the two mules moving. The damned mules were a royal pain in the ass, but he didn't know any other way to get all the equipment he wanted back in time. He was taking loads of antibiotics, a portable, battery operated ultrasound machine, even 'morning after' pills for rape victims and shots for Rh negative women to help carry their babies to term. Rick was Rh negative, as was his biological mother. He knew the Rho GAM shot helped many Rhesus negative women carry their babies to term. He also had suture, needles, anesthesia, and state of the art bone saws. Those bone saws still made him cringe, but he figured they might come in pretty handy during the Revolutionary War. He wanted to make sure he had everything possible when he got there. God knew he didn't want to ever have to use a freaking bone saw, but he was betting that he would before it was all over. After all, he figured the War was still going on. If he was right, and his timing was accurate, Yorktown would be the next fall. It would be so exciting to be there when the English surrendered! He damned sure wanted to make it in time for that.

He kicked the horse and started down the trail again for the umpteenth time.

•   •   •   •   •

Lily McCarron started down the trail to the Cherokee Village. She had sick to tend there, and Gentry was getting close in time to when her baby would be born. Lily stopped and smiled. This would be her first grandchild, born to the Bright Star of Hope, also called Gentry, and to the Red Wolf, Michael, who was her and Marc's son. It was an exciting time to be living in Indian Territory!

A movement below on the trail from Little Froggy caught her attention. She frowned as she leaned forward to try to see better, shielding her sensitive eyes with her hand. Her eyes had never been the same since that fateful day at Belle Rose in 1764 when that blasted horse kicked her in the head. Her vision returned as the blood clot dissolved, although it was never as eagle crisp and clear as before.

With a start, she realized a man was riding down the trail, with two pack mules behind him. Her heart began to thump with excitement. By damn, that young man looked an awful lot like photos she had seen of Sassy's deceased first husband, Owen Winslow, even if this young man was better looking. She turned and started running down the trail.

"Oh, my God, I bet it's Rick Winslow! Marcus, come quick, we have company!"

Marcus McCarron came running to see what was going on, fearful at first that his beloved wife had been injured. When he spotted the young man approaching, he broke into a broad grin. "It looks like the lad has managed to come at last!"

It was almost like old homecoming week, except Rick had never met these people before. Once Lily returned from the Village, they talked until late that night about changes in medical science over the almost 20 years since she wound up in 1763. He also described the various medical and obstetric equipment he brought. Lily trembled with excitement because Rick brought a portable, battery operated ultrasound machine, in addition to the most modern anesthesia. Of course, he also brought antibiotics, suture, needles, syringes, and surgical equipment. Lily felt like a kid in a candy shop, not knowing what to examine first.

In contrast, Marc went straight to the tactical shotguns, AR's, and reloading equipment Rick brought. "Damn, with a dozen of these, the war could be over in a month," Marc marveled.

Rick laughed as he clapped Marc on the back. "I only brought these, but the war will be over at Yorktown, in October. I hoped I would arrive in time for Yorktown, but I wasn't sure I would get here in time. That's just a few months. And we'll be there!"

"You'll learn soon enough it is not the same here," Lily said. "I know you grew up doing reenactments at Williamsburg, and you think you're ready for this century. But I have to tell you, Rick, the reality of life in the eighteenth century is quite different than playing dress-up at reenactments."

Rick laughed. "Oh, I think I can handle it."

Lily shook her head. "Yes, but…"

Rick shook his head. "Don't worry, Lily. I may look like some weak-kneed city boy, and yeah, I love my silly, little, fidget spinner, but I can hang. Dad made sure of that. We did lots of camping, hiking, and horseback riding in addition to reenactments every summer, all summer long, at Williamsburg. I'm ready for this."

She frowned. "My step-dad took us camping all the time, and I visited his Cherokee relatives every summer, but this is different, Rick. At the end of the summer, you are still here. It's tough. I'm not saying it's impossible. I love my life here with Marc. But, it is an adjustment. And believe me, I would have dearly loved to have had a flushing toilet and a steaming, hot shower every single day I have been here!"

•　　•　　•　　•　　•

I had that topsy-turvy dream again. I don't know why I can never see the face of the man. He tells me he loves me and promises he will come back, and we will marry. I weep when I awaken and he is not here. Why can't I remember any more about a man who so adores me? Is he nothing more than a dream?

We arrived at Belle Rose less than a week after I told Calvin I wanted to go home. Calvin and I were terse, with few words to one another. He looked like a pup who had been kicked to the street. I felt pretty much like that myself. My anger and hurt over his accusations had grown by leaps and bounds to the point I could not focus on anything other than what I perceived to be my husband's rejection of me due to my apparent inability to carry another child to term. All I could think was, I thought you loved me, not my ability to reproduce. I remembered Miss Belle loved Daddy Jo so much she got him to take my Gramma to bed when the doctors said any more babies would have killed Belle back in '40. My own mama was born from his relationship with my Gramma. I could not imagine my husband abstaining from my bed even if threatened that future pregnancies would cause my death. You could have cut the tension between us with a fork when we arrived at Belle Rose. I never could have guessed how tense it was about to become.

The morning after we arrived, we were eating breakfast when we heard horses outside. Sassy rushed to the window, where she let out an excited squeal as she ran to the front door.

Calvin frowned in disapproval as he peered over his new spectacles after Sassy. "What on earth is the ruckus all about?"

I shrugged as I continued to nibble at my tea and toast. "I have no idea."

But no sooner were the words out but that I recognized the Irish brogue calling out to me. "Fancy girl? Where are ye, lass?"

I jumped up and darted into the hallway in thrilled surprise. "Marc, I never expected to see you this trip!"

He grabbed me up and spun me around like he has done every time he came since I was a child. One of my happiest childhood memories is of my 'Uncle Marc' spinning me around like a top. I was giddy and dizzy when he stopped. Still giggling like a schoolgirl, I struggled to catch my breath, and realized a man was with him. I held out my hand. "Hello. I'm …"

"Francesca Selk, I believe," finished the handsome young man as he bent over my hand to kiss it. "And I am Dr. Richard Winslow."

And just that quick, I knew why Sassy never wanted me to marry Calvin. Mouth dry, heart racing, I stammered as I pulled my hand back. "No… no … no one ever calls me that."

He smiled. "They should. It's a beautiful name for a beautiful woman. Although I must admit I find the story how you came to be called Fancy to be quite endearing."

Oh, merciful heavens, now what do I do?

Calvin strode to us, placing his arm around my shoulders as if to protect me. I figured he wanted to show his claim to me. "This is my wife, Lady Francesca Selk Hobbs. I am Sir Calvin Hobbs, Fancy's husband."

Dr. Winslow's face paled under his new sunburn. He began to stammer. "Mrs. Hobbs, I did not realize you were married. I apologize if I were overly forward."

I tried to smile. "No offense taken, Dr. Winslow."

Dr. Winslow paused, as a grin began to tug at his lips. "Sir, did you say your name is Calvin Hobbs?"

Calvin frowned. "Yes, I did, young man. Why?"

Dr. Winslow chuckled. "My father used to tell me stories of a lad named Calvin with an imaginary pet tiger named Hobbs. I never expected to meet anyone with that name."

He winked at me, and Calvin huffed up in annoyance. "Harrumph. It is an old and well-respected name." His eyes narrowed, and he pulled me close to kiss me before he smiled at Dr. Winslow. "Fancy and I have been married about fifteen months now. Fancy wanted to come home to visit her family before she gets too big to travel with ease. *Enceinte*, you know."

I swear, he was laying it on thick enough to puke a mule. "Yes, if I can carry it to term this time." I quavered, my voice higher pitched than usual. Nerves, I reckoned.

"No, no, my dear, you'll be fine now that we are back here. You'll see. After all, you carried our darling Bella with no problems." Calvin beamed with pride as he pulled me close and kissed me soundly again.

I noticed Dr. Winslow's eyes narrowed at that. I wondered if Sassy wrote him about Bella and me. I knew she sent letters to her relatives in Texas, to be given to her family in the future. I would have to find out what she told him about me. Knowing Sassy, I imagined quite a lot. I sure hoped some of it was true!

Breakfast was tense but we somehow all survived it. Later, Calvin prepared to leave. "I'll be back by mid-July, my dear. Rest as much as possible, but I trust you'll be fine now that you are back at your beloved Belle Rose."

I nodded as I chewed my lip. They say silence is golden. I figured this was what Sassy calls a 'less is more' moment.

"Is there any way I can reach you in case of emergency?" I didn't ask where he was headed. I suspected he was going to Middleton Place in the Carolinas, General Cornwallis's headquarters. We had an unspoken agreement that I did not question him about his Loyalist work and he didn't question me about Will's 'treacherous leanings.' Middleton Place was known as the Jewel of the Carolinas. It was a most desirable headquarters because the owner, Arthur Middleton, was one of the signers of the Declaration of Independence.

He shook his head. "No, my darling, I'm afraid not, but I'll be back by mid-July. Take good care of our child and drink lots of the famed Belle Rose water. I love you with all my heart. I am sorry I have been a tad short tempered with you of late. It will be better soon, I promise. I'll see you in a few weeks." He bent over to kiss my cheek, and then frowned. "And stay away from young Dr. Winslow. I don't like the way he looks at you, the presumptuous pup. He all but drooled on you this morning."

Wordless, I nodded. Ironic. Once again, Calvin thought our disagreement was all fixed with a few sweet words and a kiss on my cheek. I sighed. Would he never learn? I know he was older when we married, and they always say you can't teach an old dog new tricks. But he must realize he hurt me something awful with his insane accusations!

However, I already knew I would be well advised to avoid young and handsome Dr. Richard Winslow. Why on earth did his family call him Rick? Richard is such a masculine yet elegant name. It suits him so much better than Rick does. I did not need to be around any man that made my heart race like he did with his piercing, amber-tinged eyes. Odd. He was all golden, his eyes, his complexion, his disposition was golden as sunshine on new-mown hay. Even his hair was sun streaked gold from the long ride from McCarron's Corner.

And he was forbidden fruit for this married lady.

I forced a laugh and slid my arms around Calvin's neck. "Now, why would I want a pup when I have a man?"

Calvin growled as he pulled me into his arms and kissed me hard. "I quite agree, my dear."

•　　•　　•　　•　　•

"What's the problem with her pregnancy?" Rick inquired. He realized his mouth was bone dry, as he forced his voice to somehow sound much calmer than he felt.

Sassy shrugged. "I don't know. Of course, I didn't realize she was pregnant until he made his little announcement a few minutes ago. They arrived last night. She was very tired and went to bed straight away. She's been unusually quiet since they arrived."

Sassy did not add there seemed to be a definite and most worrisome chill between Fancy and Calvin.

Marcus frowned. "She is A negative, like I am. Lily says that causes problems carrying babes to term."

Rick jerked his head up. "She is? Yes, it can. In fact, I brought Rho GAM with me for Rh-negative mothers."

Sassy frowned. "I'm O positive. So is Will. It never occurred to me there could be a Rh incompatibility factor before. So, what is this Rho GAM?"

"Hemolytic disease of the newborn is caused when a mother's rhesus negative antibodies try to destroy her baby's red blood cells, which can be life-threatening to the unborn baby. The Rho GAM Inoculation is administered to Rh-negative moms. It is never injected into babies. While there can be mixing of blood between mom and baby, the dose of antibodies in Rho GAM given to Rh-negative moms has never been shown to harm the fetus. I brought enough for 10 pregnancies. I figured it might come in handy for someone here. I never considered it might be needed right away."

Marc looked surprised. "Ye mean there are things to help prevent miscarriages for a Rh-negative woman?"

"Yes, assuming the miscarriage is caused by Rh incompatibility," Rick replied.

Silent, Marc got up and walked over to the window. Sassy felt a tug to her heart as she saw him swipe at a tear. "We're both Rh-negative, but my Lee had several miscarriages," he mumbled.

"Miscarriages can occur for other reasons, Marc," Rick began, utilizing his most professional bedside manner, calm and reassuring. "It could be from endocrinological problems or auto-immune problems. Rh-negative women often have endocrinological problems which hurt their fertility. But she's a doctor. She could have been cross-contaminated by blood from a patient, since she often serves as doctor and midwife for the Cherokee."

Marc nodded. "Aye, Lee said the same. I had no idea that in the future ye could give an inoculation to prevent miscarriage from such…"

Sassy felt alarmed as Marc's voice broke. She knew Lily suffered repeated miscarriages in Indian Territory over the years after Michael's birth. She knew it was the one great regret of Lily's life, that she had never been able to have more children. Lily confided to her that Marc convinced Lily to perform a vasectomy on him after the last miscarriage almost took her life. Marc had never mentioned the miscarriages in her presence before. Sassy sure wasn't going to raise the subject of the vasectomy, even though she thought it was incredibly brave of Marc to undergo one in 1770. She didn't think he ever told Will about it either. Of course, Marc was not a big talker. He was the quietest man she ever met, in marked contrast to her talkative husband who never met a stranger and could weave the best stories you ever heard.

Marc took a deep breath and squared his shoulders. "Are there any adverse effects to this inoculation?"

Rick nodded. "Yes, but none are significant. It can cause a headache, nausea, perhaps a bit of diarrhea. She would be tender at the site of the injection for a day or so. In fact, patients often complain that it is a painful shot. Ibuprofen helps. It a mild anti-inflammatory I brought with me. She might get a mild rash. Benadryl can take care of that. I brought it, too. But the important thing is she would not lose her baby."

"Then, she needs to have this inoculation thing. Now." Marc's tone was determined and resolute.

"I'll talk to her," Sassy offered. "She had two miscarriages since they were married last year. Besides, she knows where we are from and she knows Rick is a doctor. Let's hope she will be receptive to this idea."

"Aye. Otherwise, can I hold the lass down while ye jab her, Rick?" Marc growled.

Rick grinned and nodded. Sassy laughed shaking her head and walked out of the dining room to the kitchen.

"You never mentioned she was married. But then, I didn't know she was your daughter either." Rick kept his voice low.

Marc blushed. "Aye, well, ye never mentioned ye were interested in her."

"Fair enough." Rick grinned as he pulled out his wallet and found the picture post card be bought at Ranscome Manor of the painting. He held it out to Marc.

Marc let out a low whistle. "Well, then, by 1789…"

Rick nodded. "By '89. If not sooner." He hesitated a second, and then laughed. "Dad."

Marc looked surprised, and then chuckled as he patted Rick on the back. "Indeed, son! And I will feel better calling you son than a man older than me. Hmm. I wonder what Calvin's fated end will be?"

Rick shrugged. "I don't have a clue. I didn't know she had married before me." He winced as he rubbed his tailbone. "Well, you warned me this would be tough. That ride was something else. I'm gonna ache for a month."

Marc laughed. "Aye, tis a long, hard ride to Belle Rose from McCarron's Corner. 'Tis every bit of six hundred miles, lad."

"Yep, I believe you. But, you know Marc? What I can't figure out is, how did I wind up here now?"

Marc's eyes narrowed. "What do ye mean, lad?"

"It's 1781. I remember one of Mom's letters was dated from 1782."

"Marc's eyes narrowed in speculation. "Ah, but did she write that one to you?"

Rick frowned as he scratched his head. "You know, come to think of it, I think she wrote that to Uncle Jim."

Marc grinned. "Well, there you have it. You know something about her future she doesn't know yet."

"Maybe. But she didn't mention I was here." Rick frowned. "I sure hope I didn't screw up the time – space consortium, or whatever the Hell it is that brings folks here from there. That I didn't come at the wrong time. I mean, could that screw things up? Could I adversely affect the future if I came at the wrong time?"

Marc looked shaken. "I know Lily came as a child and they sent her back. They said it was the wrong time. Lily calls it a time hole. She says it makes her think of something she calls a worm hole, whatever the blazes that may be. My God, Rick, what do you think could happen if you arrived too soon?"

Rick shook his head as he nibbled on a thumbnail. "I have no freaking idea."

Marc laughed and clapped his hand on Richard's shoulder. "Ah, don't worry, lad. You're doing fine. You've adjusted far better than I dared hope."

Rick grinned. "Now, if I can ever get used to chamber pots and outhouses."

Marc nodded. "Aye. And what did ye say on the way here? The lack of running water in the houses."

"And air conditioning, bathtubs, showers, refrigerators, electricity, the internet, gas stoves, cars, and air travel." He swatted at a mosquito. "Not to mention mosquito repellant. God, the damned mosquitoes are big enough to carry off my horse! Thank heaven I've been inoculated against malaria."

"Your mam never complained."

Sassy walked back into the room then and clasped Rick on the shoulder. "No, I never fussed about mosquitoes, but I always felt like I was finally in the place where I belonged. The time where I belonged. Tell you what, I can burn some coffee grounds. That will help repel the mosquitoes," Sassy suggested.

"Lily taught me the trick."

"Oh, really? I didn't know that would repel mosquitoes. Well, let's face it. Mom, you're a bit crazy over this era," Rick said.

"I'll go start burning some coffee grounds. Makes good use of coffee grounds and smells wonderful." Sassy laughed and kissed Rick on the cheek. With another grin, she turned to go fetch coffee grounds from the kitchen.

Marc laughed. "I think you have to be a bit daft to be a traveler."

Rick arched a brow at the older man. "Is that what you call those of us who come from Beyond?"

Marc nodded. "Tis what the Cherokee call them. Travelers."

"How did Lily adjust? Was all this hard for her?"

"She missed indoor plumbing and what she called central air and heat. And something she called Tampax. I'm not at all sure what that was. But she's an old soul. Old Selu Corn Tassel was the shaman when Lee came. Selu used to say Lily adjusted with ease because she was meant to be here. Perhaps that is why your mam adjusted so easily as well."

Rick felt a twinge of concern at Marc's words. Could he have come too soon? Was he supposed to be here at this time? He pulled out his little fidget spinner and gave it a good spin. Of course, I'm supposed to be here, he thought, as he looked at the picture of Fancy again. But, is this the right time? Am I supposed to be here now? Or later?

• • • • •

I sighed with regret as I watched Calvin ride away out the window of my rooms. I never imagined I would wind up in such a situation. I had no idea if being at Belle Rose would help me keep this baby or not. I was sure my marriage was over if I lost this baby. I wasn't at all sure my marriage would survive even if the baby survived. But in any event, my children and I were welcome here. I knew we could stay forever, if I so chose.

I was resting when Sassy knocked at my door. "Can I come in?"

I sat up and motioned for her to enter. "Of course, you can. What's up? I'm surprised you are up here when you have so much to talk about with Richard."

Sassy blushed. "Well, that's why I'm here…"

"Sassy, I don't think this is the time," I began.

She shook her head. "No, it's about your pregnancy. He's a doctor, for heaven's sake! He knows you are Rh-negative. He says the negative Rh factor can cause miscarriages."

I felt the blood drain right out of my face. "Are you serious?" I asked, as my voice quavered, hoarse with unexpected terror.

She nodded. "Yes, but he brought medication that can help keep you from losing your baby. I thought you would want to let him explain it. If you are willing, he can administer it to you to keep from losing your baby."

For the first time in weeks, I felt a ray of hope. "Oh, yes, of course, I want to talk to him about it!"

She stopped me as I started up. "If it's okay with you, I'll bring him up here."

Eager to hear what Dr. Winslow had to say, I nodded as I hurried to straighten my clothing and my hair.

A few minutes later, Sassy, Marc, and Dr. Winslow all poured into my room. Dr. Winslow explained the Rh-negative blood type I inherited from Marc is incompatible with Rh-positive blood type and can cause miscarriages.

"So, Calvin is right? My body is rejecting his baby?" I stammered, the stunned horror I felt clear in my voice.

He looked surprised by my question. "Well, if you want to be technical, yes. But, you are not doing it on purpose. Plus, there is medication to prevent such a miscarriage. Back home, doctors administer it to Rh-negative moms right after a miscarriage, so the next pregnancy will be successful. Otherwise, in Rh-negative mothers, we give the shot at 28 weeks and again after birth. In this case, since you have lost two babies by miscarriage, I recommend administering it now, again at 28 weeks and postpartum."

I frowned. "What is post partying?"

He chuckled. "I'm sorry. Medical jargon. Postpartum means after you give birth to this baby."

"And you're sure it won't hurt my baby?" I pressed. My heart was doing its crazy flip flops again. I wasn't sure if it was from nerves or excitement. Maybe both.

But maybe it was from being this close to Richard Winslow.

"It will not hurt your baby. It should keep you from miscarrying it, so you will have a healthy, live birth."

I nodded as I thought about this unexpected information. I could have the inoculation and might be able to carry my baby to term. Or, I could refuse the inoculation, and it was pretty much given I would miscarry in the near future. "Give it to me."

"I will warn you: it's a painful injection. It may give you a headache, or an upset stomach. It will make the injection site sore, and you might get a rash from it."

"If it keeps me from losing my baby, I could care less. Give it to me."

Sassy held my hand tight while her son gave me what he called 'the shot'. I laughed. "Does that mean you shot me? In my *derrière*?"

He grinned, his amber eyes glinting dark gold. "Whatever. But, I will say this is the prettiest little ass I ever shot."

"Oh, now, you sound like your mama!" I exclaimed, as I swatted at his hand. "Except when she says 'whatever'…"

"You know to watch out?" he interjected.

I giggled as I nodded. "I remember the first time I heard her say 'whatever' to Will. I backed out of the room."

"You're a smart woman. Yes, if she said 'whatever' to Dad or me, we both knew to duck."

"She threw a shoe at Will." I giggled at the memory of my big brother cowering as little Sassy pelted him with that shoe.

"He deserved it," Sassy retorted, prim as an old maid schoolmarm. "As well you know."

He's easy to talk to, I thought, with an odd mix of excitement and dismay, as my heart sang an odd, jumbled tune it had never played before.

"So, where is Will anyway?" Richard inquired.

Sassy and I both fell silent. After an awkward pause, I said, "We don't talk about where they are, Dr. Winslow. My husband is a Loyalist. Will is a Patriot. If we don't ask them about it, then we don't know where the other one is … although to be honest, I don't know where Calvin has gone. My guess is Sassy doesn't know where Will is either."

Sassy nodded. "I don't. That way, I can't be forced to give his whereabouts to the Redcoats, if and when they show up again."

Richard looked concerned. "If and when they show up again? You mean they have come here before?"

"Sassy nodded. "Oh, yes, several times. Why, this last winter, we were visited by Benedict Arnold and Banastre Tarleton." She chortled. "They were hunting for Patty Jefferson, who was in the nursery, disguised as the nanny. It was hilarious! I told Col. Tarleton that the Jefferson baby, Lucy, and my Rosie were twins. He believed me. And then as they were leaving, Gen. Arnold whispered, 'keep safe, Mrs. Jefferson,' to Patty. Tarleton never realized he had her right here under his thumb.""

I saw shock and concern flash across his face before he answered. "Mom, with the reputation Butcher Ban Tarleton has, you would risk pissing him off?"

She shrugged and tossed her hand. "Oh, he'll never find out. And what was I to do? Hand my friend and her children over to that animal? I don't think so! Besides, I haven't had to shoot anyone in over a year now."

Richard shook his head. "You haven't had to shoot anyone in over a year? OMG, Mom, how many people have you shot? I knew Dad shouldn't have given you that gun!"

"Well, be glad he did, because I would have been taken prisoner twice if I hadn't been able to defend myself."

"Not to mention you managed to defend us both against that awful man when he broke in last year," I added, my voice soft as a whisper.

Frowning, Richard studied my face. "What happened then?"

I didn't answer but shook my head as I stared out the window.

Sassy responded. "He, um, he hurt Fancy. So, I killed him. He was the third."

Richard blinked. "Mom, you do realize they classify you as a serial killer if you kill three or more people, don't you?"

"Oh, nonsense. I shot twice in self-defense, and once in defense of Fancy. Besides, there's a war going on."

I could not look at Richard as the hot tears of shame welled up in my eyes, so I walked across to the window. I could not bear to talk about Simon. How could I mar the beauty of this day by talking about that awful night? Or any day or night Simon had scoured into my memory, like a sore that never healed? I stared out at the sunshine glistening on the Potomac, weaving its sunlit magic, drawing in the beauty of the day before I answered. "It's a gorgeous day. Do I need to stay a'bed, or could I go outside on the veranda?"

I'll give the man credit. He isn't stupid. He stared at me, surprise written across his handsome features for a second, before he dropped the verboten subject. "Wait a few hours. If your cramping subsides and you aren't spotting, I think it would be okay to go outside. But no epic walks today, or the next week for that matter. Once we are sure you're not at risk, walking would be good for you."

I laughed and gave him a snappy salute. "Yes, sir, Dr. Winslow!"

He laughed. "You can call me Rick, you know. Everyone does."

I tilted my head as I grinned. "Everybody calls me Fancy, but you call me Francesca."

He blushed. "Well, it's a beautiful name."

I nodded. "So, I think I'll call you Richard. Rick sounds like a child. Richard sounds like a grown-up."

Marc and Richard stayed until July 1st, in part to make sure I was okay. I could see they were both loathe to leave. They had been at Belle Rose for two weeks. Marc confided to me as they were leaving that they would be joining Lafayette's troops, and would remain in Virginia.

My heart clinched when he told me where they were going. "Oh, Marc, you aren't supposed to tell me!" I wailed. "What if the Redcoats show up?"

"Ah, love, they'd be looking for Will, not Rick or me. They won't have any idea we are anywhere around. Heck, they don't even know who Rick is." He grinned and kissed my cheek, hugged me close, climbed onto his horse, and then wheeled the horse around to leave.

Richard held back a minute, yearning written all across his handsome features. "You take care of yourself, Mom, Mrs. Hobbs. I would hate for anything bad to happen to you two ladies. And, take care of those children, too. They are the future's promise for our country."

It was hot outside, but I shivered as if a possum had run across my grave. I pulled my silk shawl close around my shoulders.

Sassy nodded. "We'll be fine. You men will be in battles. You be careful. And remember to drop my pistol off with the gunsmith in Charlottesville when you drop the children off for their visit at Monticello."

Richard laughed. "Yes, ma'am, we sure will!"

Sassy laughed. "You can sleep well knowing I won't be killing any Redcoats while you are gone."

Richard laughed again and kissed her cheek. "That's a relief."

Tobias started the team of horses up after the men with the children sequestered safe and sound in the coach. I am sure Sassy's heart thudded as her babies left, the same way my heart ached to see my precious Bella leaving. Bella and I had never been apart before.

The children being gone a few days would give Sassy a chance for her milk to dry up. Now that Rosie was 7 months old, we all insisted that it was high time a proper lady like Sassy stop such foolishness as nursing her own baby. She turned Rosie over to the wet nurse just this week. So, the twins, Baby Rosie and her wet nurse, and my Bella all went to Monticello, while Sassy fussed that her aching breasts and she both hoped her husband would be able to come home soon.

Sassy updated me on the War once the men left. She confirmed General Arnold turned coat last summer, just as she foretold. He had been with the British ever since. It made me sad. I always dreamed of meeting General Arnold, and now one of the greatest American heroes had turned on his country. In December 1780, Arnold sailed from New York to Portsmouth, Virginia, with 1500 soldiers, defeating Richmond in route to Portsmouth. Washington then sent the Marquise de Lafayette and 1200 troops to Virginia. Once in Virginia, Lafayette joined ranks with Baron von Steuben, who had been sent to Virginia earlier to assist the Virginia militia. They were also supposed to hunt down Arnold, but Sassy swears they will never catch him. He has since been reassigned to New England.

In January, Arnold was at Belle Rose with Butcher Tarleton. In late March 1781, Arnold was joined by 2300 troops under the command of Major General William Phillips. They resumed raiding with successes at Blandford and Petersburg. The burning of Richmond was prevented by Lafayette's arrival. Little Lucy Jefferson died April 15[th.] Tarleton left the Carolinas right away to head north to join forces with Arnold. The British then withdrew to Petersburg in early May.

On May 28th, Jefferson wrote Washington, advising him the focus of the war appeared to now be in the state of Virginia. He begged Washington to join the action in Virginia.

On May 29th, General Charles Cornwallis arrived at Petersburg, Virginia, with 1500 men after suffering heavy losses at Guilford Courthouse. Calvin and Charles Cornwallis had been friends for years, since they were boys away at boarding school. Cornwallis assumed command when he arrived because General Phillips up and died of some fever. Cornwallis had not received permission to abandon the Carolinas from General Henry Clinton. He figured Virginia would be easier to capture than the Carolinas. He also figured Virginia would be more accepting of the invading British army. Let's face it: the Carolinas were not.

At that point, the British army numbered 7200 men. Lafayette's men numbered 3000. Cornwallis wanted to push Lafayette and set out for him on May 24th, but Lafayette withdrew from Richmond and Cornwallis did not pursue them. Instead, he sent raiders throughout Virginia to raid depots and supply convoys.

"That was a big mistake, too." Sassy smirked.

I could feel my brow furrow as I frowned. "How?"

"He could have defeated Lafayette then. Now? He's lost his window of opportunity. And Yorktown is a'coming, Fancy."

On June 2nd, British troops captured a missive from Lafayette to Jefferson. It revealed that Jefferson and legislature were hiding in Charlottesville. Cornwallis then ordered Banastre Tarleton to capture Jefferson. As Sassy put it, "Tarleton and his dragoons rode hard for Monticello. In fact, 1781 has not been successful for Tarleton. He failed to capture Patty Jefferson at Belle Rose in January. He failed to capture Francis Marion and Will in the Carolinas. They have stayed one step ahead of Tarleton at all times."

"It helps to be married to the historian?" I suggested as I arched an eyebrow at her.

She nodded with a grin. "Yep. Plus, Tarleton suffered his first major loss at Cowpens in January, and then he lost two fingers at the battle of Guilford Courthouse in March. However, the Brits still won that battle. Dammit."

She went on to tell me that on June 3rd, Tarleton and his men raced to Charlottesville to try to capture Jefferson. That evening, he let his men stop at a tavern for three hours to rest, eat and drink. A man named Jack Jouett slipped outside and rode fast to alert the Governor that Tarleton's Dragoons were again coming. He stood before Jefferson by 4:30 a.m., warning him the Redcoats were on their way. He then rode on to warn the rest of the Virginia legislators in Charlottesville. Because of Jouett's selfless bravery, Jefferson was able to send his wife, children, and slaves to be hidden in a nearby farm. Jefferson watched the advance of Tarleton's troops through a telescope. He didn't leave Monticello until a mere ten minutes before they arrived at his door. He then managed to evade Tarleton using mountain trails unknown to the British.

"That was a bit brazen," I marveled, awed by Jefferson's audacity.

"I know. Jefferson is young. He can be quite ballsy. Tarleton's men did not burn Monticello, although they did burn Elk Hill. Cornwallis has used Monticello as his headquarters since then. I know when he leaves, they will burn the tobacco and cotton crops, take all the livestock, but they won't burn the house."

I frowned. "Why not?"

"I suspect some British officer wants it, when they win 'this little rebellion'."

I felt my brow furrow with worry. "Aren't you nervous with Tarleton so close by? What if he comes back?"

She sniffed and tossed her long, braid over her shoulder. "We'll be fine. There is no historical record of Belle Rose Plantation being destroyed by Tarleton. General Arnold will warn Cornwallis to locate his permanent base away from the coast. But, Cornwallis does not have a good opinion of Arnold and pretty much ignores him. Cornwallis says an officer of the British Crown does not heed the advice of an American traitor. Plus, Cornwallis pretty much will get ordered by General Clinton to go to Yorktown."

She told me on June 20th, Cornwallis headed to Williamsburg, and Lafayette's troops, then numbering 4500, followed him. After a series of confusing orders, in August, Cornwallis would end up in the waterfront village of Yorktown, where he will be instructed to build a deep-water port.

"So, now what?" I asked.

She covered her mouth to stifle a yawn. "Now, we have lots of little stuff until Yorktown. The war will end at Yorktown. Cornwallis surrenders there. You can bank money on it."

I shook my head as I chuckled. 'Bank money', another one of Sassy's odd expressions from the future. I learned in '78 that Sassy knew what she was talking about regarding the future. Even General Washington heeds her word. I didn't ask for specifics to come. Calvin might manage to get the information out of me. It was better if I didn't know about things that were going to happen someday in the future. It was enough I knew Will was with Francis Marion in the Carolinas and Yorktown would be the deciding battle of the war. And I wasn't supposed to know either of those!

"So, what happens to General Arnold?"

"He will get sent back to New York. He won't be popular there, in large part due to his criticism of British commander-in-chief Henry Clinton. But, the transfer back to New York will save him from capture at Yorktown. From New York, he will be sent to England."

"Tell me again the story about General Cornwallis's dogs," I urged. I loved the story and never tired of hearing it.

She laughed, her green eyes flashing merry twinkles. "Oh, Fancy, Will must tell you that story when he gets back. You know he can weave a story so much better than I can! With me, it's called dry history. Will says the patriots overtook troops taking supplies and personal items being sent to General Cornwallis at Middleton Place. The dogs were among the personal items. General Cornwallis owned a pair of German mastiffs, given to him by King George. Marion's men wanted to eat the dogs, but Marion and Will refused. They knew those dogs could hunt and track, not to mention that mastiffs are fabulous guard dogs. They were far more valuable alive than dead as hunting and guard dogs. The dogs adore Will. They follow him everywhere."

"Daddy Jo always called Will the dog whisperer." I smiled at the memory of Will coaxing the Irish wolfhounds we used to have to do his bidding. "Remember how it would gall you when you first came, the way your Skyes would hang on his every word, like he was made of goose liver? Those wolfhounds Daddy used to raise lived for Will, I swear."

Sassy looked up at me in surprise. "The dog whisperer? Interesting. I didn't know that. I knew they used to have Irish wolfhounds. He misses big dogs, even though he is fabulous with my Skyes. Yes, I'll never forget the first time he called out, 'come on, dogs!' My own dogs trotted after him and left me standing in my tracks."

I laughed at the memories of her funny little dogs fawning over Will's every word, as they ignored their beloved mistress. I laughed even harder as I recalled the shocked look on Sassy's face as those dogs took off after Will, and the way the shock turned to indignation in short order.

Chapter 4
Fancy, 1781

We cleaned the house top to bottom after the men and the children left. I felt great, full of energy, excited and optimistic about my pregnancy. At last, the house was spic and span. It was the 4th of July 1781, Sassy and Will's second anniversary. It had been a hot, clear day, but as the sun sank, a cooling breeze came in through the windows off the Potomac. I could smell the coffee grounds burning to ward off mosquitoes like Lily taught us to do years ago. We didn't need the coffee grounds to burn that night, because the breeze was keeping the mosquitoes out of the house for the most part.

The Jeffersons sent word the children were doing fine. Poor Miss Patty had been feeling pretty low since little Lucy's death in April. Sassy and Mr. Jefferson came up with the idea for this visit. Mr. Jefferson hoped being around more kids would help her spirit. She had plenty of young ones around now!

Sassy was plumb dab feverish hoping Will would come home while the children were gone. He'd been gone for three months, we figured most likely with Francis Marion in the Carolinas. Sassy assured me the patriots had been kicking ass and taking names. Sassy hoped the wily old Swamp Fox would let Will come home for their anniversary. As the sun sank, I could see her heart sank, also. It looked like there would be no anniversary lovemaking at Belle Rose that night.

Sassy sighed. "Well, three years and this was the first time we haven't spent the 4th of July together. Not too bad during the Revolutionary War."

She looked so dejected. I hugged her and reminded her that it would all be over soon.

Sassy and I went back inside, where she grabbed a ripe apple in the kitchen, and went upstairs, where she changed into a cool night rail. I tagged along with her as we continued talking plans for sewing projects and other tasks to get done the following week.

Sassy smiled as she looked at her reflection in the looking glass. The night rail was low cut, sheer batiste. My land a'mercy, you could see right through it! Her figure was mighty fine for a woman thirty-seven-years old who gave birth to 3 children in less than 3 years. Her breasts, in serious need of a baby to nurse, were full of milk, turgid, round, plump, fecund and inviting. Her belly was flat, her waist narrow, and her hips broad, the way Will often announced he liked. He always laughed when I blushed at that comment. Yes, it was clear she was still hoping against hope that maybe somehow Will would come in tonight. Maybe.

She finished her apple, brushed her teeth in her wash basin, and then unbraided her hair. I brushed it out. One hundred strokes a night, to brush the dirt out and smooth the perfumed pomade down through the long hair resulted in hair with a luster and sheen that Sassy says future women would weep in dismay to know their frequent shampooing stripped from their hair. I couldn't imagine washing my hair every day. What a waste of time, energy and good, clean water! After I brushed her hair the hundred strokes, I braided it again in a long braid down her back.

Still hoping her man would come back tonight, she dabbed perfume behind her ears, between her breasts, and after a slight hesitation, and with a devilish grin to me, dabbed some between her legs, shivering as the stinging tingle warmed her delicate flesh. I felt my cheeks redden as she touched herself down there.

"You are so naughty," I muttered.

"Does it embarrass you if I do that, Fancy?" she teased. She tossed her head as I nodded. "Will loves the smell and the taste of the perfume. He loves it everywhere. He says he loves the way it tastes on my skin." She grinned at me again, with a saucy little smile she gets sometimes when she is being naughty.

I blushed and arose to leave, but before I left, I turned back to her. "So, do you like it when he diddles you?"

She tilted her head at me. "Diddles me? I don't think I ever heard that expression before. What does it mean?"

My face must have been burning scarlet then. "Oh, Sassy, don't tease. You know. When he touches you… there… until you quiver with desire, beggin' for more. You know. Diddles."

Green eyes sparkling, she chortled. "Oh, you're a naughty girl! You mean does he pleasure me? You betcha. But, I never heard the word 'diddle' before. I guess it's an 18th century expression."

Well, I was so embarrassed by then I could have died, so I grinned, and winked at my friend. "Good night, Sassy. I hope your man doesn't disappoint you."

She laughed, her pretty eyes sparkling with what Will calls 'Sassitude.' "Me, too. Sweet diddle dreams, Fancy!"

As I shut the door, I heard her sigh, and then she blew out her lamp. I figured she was going to sleep.

Sassy told me later it must have been a couple hours later when she awoke. She said she could feel his weight over her, balanced, as he began to fondle her aching breasts. She moaned, and reached up for him. She intended to pull his head to her breast, to suckle her. His hands grabbed hers and raised them over her head. Sassy said she moaned again, arching up towards him. Her eyes flew open when the chuckle she heard was not the voice she expected. She told me she started to writhe and struggle against the strong, well-muscled young man who was pinning her down. And then, her head began to spin, as he smashed his fist into her face.

"You will refrain from struggling against me, Mrs. Selk, or I shall be compelled to take less lenient action against you, as a traitor to the Crown."

Sassy began to shake as she told me this. I have no doubt she began to shake at his words. She said he held her hands together with one hand and resumed groping her breasts with his other hand. She tasted the hot tang of copper in her mouth, as the hot rush of blood flowed from her nose. "Yes, Colonel Tarleton."

He chuckled again, a laugh Sassy and I both presumed he thought was sexy and inviting to women. "No, no, my dear, you must always address me as 'my Lord'. After all, I am a Baronet. And you are … nothing."

Terrified, Sassy nodded, still trembling, and swiped her tongue across her teeth again. She told me she was pretty sure he wasn't made a Baronet until after the war, but it seemed he expected the title and wanted to rub her nose in the fact that after the war ended, Will and she would no longer have titles. Of course, truth be told, a baronet is the lowest title there is. The holder can be addressed as Sir, but they are still pretty dad-blamed common, if you ask me.

Sassy replied, "Yes, my Lord."

He smiled. "Very good. Then, remove your night rail, or I shall be obliged to remove it for you."

She hesitated a moment, and then she saw the gleam of metal in his hand. No, best not fight him. Not while he sported those brass knuckles. He snickered again as she pulled the thin rail over her head.

"I remember you claim you seduced 20,000 women in the Colonies," she began, with far more starch in her words than she should have even thought about using. "Is this your take on seduction?"

He snatched the rail from her hands, and after sniffing it, smiled, and then tossed it aside. "Quite right, my dear. Twenty thousand, you say? My, even I am rather impressed at that number. Now, shall we get started?"

And thus, began her nightmare.

Sassy later told me that by morning, she lost count how many times he took her that night. As the sun arose, I came knocking at the door. Sassy tried to rise, remembering too late he had tied her to the bed posts. "Who is it?" she called out, her voice hoarse.

I laughed as I started to open the door. "You silly thing, you know it's me..." I gasped in shock as a naked Banastre Tarleton swung the door open. Eyes wide and wild, I looked from him, to Sassy, spread eagled on the bed. I threw my hands up to my mouth and dropped the tray with the two coffee cups and the pot of hot coffee I was bringing to Sassy.

"Oh, my dear, that is dreadful. You'll have to clean that up. We would not want anyone to get hurt on the broken china," he commented, as he pulled me into the room.

I let out a little cry, for which I was slapped hard before he wheeled me around to look at Sassy. "Stop it, stupid girl, or you can take her place," he growled.

"No," Sassy begged. "Leave her alone. This is Lady Hobbs. She is married to Lord Calvin Hobbs. She is with child. This is between us. Please... my Lord..."

His cold eyes jerked back towards Sassy. "What are you saying, Sarah?"

I was shaking, and I struggled not to cry. Sassy looked like she was trying mighty hard not to cry, too. She gasped, "Please, you can do what you will with me, but this is between you and me. Lady Hobbs is *enceinte*. Her husband is a Loyalist. Please, my Lord, don't take it out on Fancy."

She didn't tell him I was also a Selk.

His eyes narrowed as he considered her words. "You are Lady Hobbs? Married to Sir Calvin Hobbs, the third Earl of Spring Haven?"

Surprised, I nodded. "Yes, sir, I mean, my lord."

Tarleton's eyes narrowed as he looked me over. "My, my, old Hobbs snagged a prize in you, didn't he? No wonder that old fool is always talking about his beautiful wife." He jerked his head in affirmation. "Fine. Get someone to clean up this mess and then get out, Lady Hobbs. And have a slave bring me a pot of hot tea and some breakfast. Tell the others not to disturb Miss Sarah and me."

With trembling hands, I picked up the broken china and then I high tailed it out of that room lickety split. I wasn't about to stay any longer than I had to around that naked assed man. But as soon as I got downstairs, I sent messages to Mount Vernon and Monticello that Tarleton was at Belle Rose and we needed help as soon as possible.

I was pretty sure I knew how she must be feeling. I've felt that way before. When you felt empty. Dirty. Foolish. No. Downright stupid. I remembered when I felt like the most stupid human being on the face of the earth. And how I felt hollow. I don't think anything feels as bad as to feel empty, to feel hollow, where just yesterday you felt alive. And more than anything, back then, I wished I were dead. Yes, I was mighty sure that was how Sassy felt right about then.

So, I waited outside Sassy's room, sunk onto the floor watching in case Tarleton came out. I wasn't sure what I would do if he came out, but I would be there for Sassy.

I could hear a lot from that room in my place outside the door. Through the long hours, he instructed Sassy on his rules. I reckon men like Le Grand and Tarleton always have rules like these. No talking, except to respond to him when questioned. To always call him 'my Lord'. Not to cry out, no matter how bad anything hurt. She was less than nothing. She had best satisfy him if she knew what was good for her. If she must cry, she had best keep it quiet. And not to fight back, no matter what. I know when I heard him say that, I shivered.

Those were the same rules imposed on me years before.

Tarleton made sure she understood he could do whatever he wanted to her, as long as he did not hurt her people. Later, she told me that by nightfall, the insides of her mouth were raw where she bit her cheeks over and over to keep from screaming. She bit through her lip as well. She told me later she prayed throughout it all that the horrible nightmare would end soon.

Her violation continued for hours, until darkness was creeping through the window again. Around 8, Tarleton strode to the door, and threw it open.

I jumped up, stiff and awkward, as he opened the door that evening. "Lord Tarleton, may we help you in any way, sir?"

He smiled and clucked me under the chin. "Yes, Countess, fetch me a glass of Mr. Selk's finest sherry, and then go assemble the house servants downstairs in the parlor. Miss Sarah and I want to see them."

I was pretty sure that Miss Sarah could have cared less right then. But I saw her eyes fly open at his words. Somehow, even through the horror of the past 20 hours, we both knew something was about to get much worse.

I ran for the sherry.

Tarleton cut Sassy loose from the bed and jerked her up by the loose rope still attached to one hand. Naked, bruised, battered, filthy from his repeated abuses, he dragged her horrified and sobbing downstairs.

At the base of the stairs, his men snickered as Tarleton hauled her down in front of them. With a few quiet words, a man brought him more ropes, and she was tied up to the stairway post. Tarleton tied her up so she had to stand on her tiptoes to avoid dangling from the post.

"I am sure you are all wondering what has brought me back to Belle Rose," he began, as women all around us began to sob, soft and low. "You are all aware that Mrs. Selk lied to me in January when she told me that Mrs. Jefferson was not here. I am here to punish Mrs. Selk for her traitorous behavior, and to make an example out of her such that other colonial wives will not make similar errors of judgment in the future."

The room went quiet as death at his words. I glanced around, and paled as I saw him take a horse whip from one of his men.

"Mrs. Selk is in serious need of immediate discipline. Since her husband is absent, and as agent and representative of King George here at the Belle Rose Plantation, I am the designated authority to administer said discipline.

Mrs. Selk."

Sassy swallowed hard. "Yes, my Lord?" she gasped.

He smiled, but it didn't reach his eyes. They looked cold and unfeeling. "Will you accept the punishment I allay to you?"

She nodded, unable to control the trembling of her body. "Yes, my Lord. As we discussed upstairs."

Holy sweet Jesus Christ. This is like what Simon did to me in '77. He said he beat me to discipline me, too. I began to shake as my own breathing came fast and shallow. I figured my heart was going to jump right out of my chest! I remembered the feel the bindings on my wrists, the chill air against my bare skin. The humiliation of being stripped bare before the people of Belle Rose. Shame and horror as his hands roaming free over my helpless body.

I felt sick with the knowledge of what she was about to undergo.

Col. Tarleton smiled, as he stroked first her face, and then ran his fingers down her naked breast. She cringed, struggling not to flinch from his touch. "Mr. Andrews."

A young man stepped forward with a sharp salute. "Yes, sir, Colonel Tarleton, sir!"

"How many lashes does a colonial receive for lying to an agent of the King?" Tarleton inquired.

"Forty, sir!" responded young Mr. Andrews.

Even though Sassy was tied up, she swooned. Forty lashes comprised a death sentence. I tried to swallow, but my mouth was dry as sand.

"Is that the prescribed number for a woman, also, Mr. Andrews?" pressed Colonel Tarleton.

"Yes, sir!" came the young Sargent's snappy reply.

Heck fire, I was scared shitless. I could not believe he was about to do this to the wife of a Duke of the Realm.

And then the lashes began. I cringed with the first, struggling not to cry out. I was not sure what he would do, but I knew it would be bad if any of us screamed. It was always worse for me if anyone protested while I was being disciplined.

Sassy made it to three before the tears began, and to 12 before she could hold the scream back no longer. Tarleton stopped, and dragged the rough edge of the whip down her ravaged back before forcing it between her trembling butt cheeks. "Now, Mrs. Selk, you must control yourself. If you are good, and do not scream any more, I will perhaps cut this short."

Trembling, she nodded. I sobbed against my uncle's shoulder, and Russell held Mina tight to keep her from running to Sassy. Hattie Mae sobbed in silence into Tobias's other shoulder. I knew I had to hold myself together for our people.

He resumed the lashes. At 20, Sassy fainted. He roused her by throwing a bucket of cold water on her before he finished the beating. He then had her cut down. He told us not to come into Sassy's room unless he gave permission or we would suffer the same fate. He sauntered over to me and dragged the whip down the side of my face. "Of course, my beauty, if you want to join us, you would be most welcome."

I trembled, but I managed somehow not to turn away from him. I knew it would merit a beating of my own if he sensed the revulsion I felt at that moment. I've been beaten before and I damned sure don't ever want another beating, especially when I'm biggin'. "Thank you for the kind invitation, my lord, but I believe my husband would prefer I abstain tonight. We are so excited about this baby, you know."

He laughed and dipped his head to force his tongue between my lips again. "Another time perhaps, Lady Hobbs. Or should I say… Duchess?"

I felt a pang of alarm. "Duchess? What on earth do you mean? Sarah is the Duchess, not me."

He laughed, his voice low and sultry. I reckoned he thought he sounded seductive, or as Sassy would say, sexy. "No longer, my pet. Hobbs said you will be most reluctant to accept the title. Well, my beauty, time shall tell. You shall know soon enough."

Oh, Calvin, what have you done? I felt a coward for not taking her place, but Calvin and I wanted this baby so much, and after two miscarriages, we had almost given up hope. Sassy was right. I couldn't stop this and by trying to help her, I might well lose this baby, too.

I crept up the stairs behind them, to resume my vigil outside her door.

Upstairs, I listened as he tied Sassy to her bed again, this time face down. Later, she told me she came to as he pushed himself between her butt cheeks much like he had pushed the whip minutes earlier. "It will only hurt for a little while, my dear. You might even come to like it."

Terrified, Sassy struggled to try to inch away from his huge erection. "No, no, no. *Por favor*, my lord, I beg you…"

"No, no, no, dear Sarah, do not try to evade this. It is inevitable. Why? Have you never had relations in this manner before?"

I cringed. I knew without a doubt what he was about to do to her. It was the worst thing anyone ever did to me, other than out and out beating me. Believe me, it has been done to me more than once. Oh, yes, I became accustomed to it, but it turned my stomach to think of him doing that with the intent to hurt, to punish, someone as sweet and kind as our Sassy.

She must have shaken her head. She said he then slid his spit-wettened fingers in to try to lubricate her so he could enter her rear entry easier. "Never. Please, Lord Tarleton, please…" I heard her beg, the panic creeping into her low voice. "Please, no…"

"Now, Sarah, I find it difficult to believe that a woman your age who has been married twice has never been disciplined like this before." I could hear him slap her. Later, Sassy explained he slapped her again, and again, sliding his fingers in and out, in and out, in and out, until at last, he slid his fingers out and shoved his member inside her.

Sassy told me that was when she screamed and fainted. It was when I heard her scream that I laid my face down on the polished pine floorboards and sobbed.

The next morning, Tarleton came out dressed like he was ready to resume his military duties. I scrambled up. "May I get you anything, my lord?" I inquired, as I struggled to make my stiff limbs work again.

He gave me a sweet smile and clucked me under the chin again. "No, no, my beauty. You might assist Miss Sarah. I suspect she would appreciate a bit of assistance this morning. I would venture to guess she is not quite her usual self. I must say this is a gorgeous plantation. Gen. Cornwallis plans to take Monticello after we resolve this nuisance of a rebellion. He promised Belle Rose to me once we win this insurrection against the crown. Perhaps with a bit of luck, I can convince him you should be part of the package. After all, someone will have to take the title since your brother is no longer the Duke. And as old man Hobbs says, who better than Selk's sister?"

He bent over and kissed me right on the mouth again as he had done before.

My heart lurched with fear. How did he learn I was Will's sister? "But, my lord, I am married…"

"Yes, but many good men die in battle, my love." He kissed me again, pushing his tongue deep into my mouth. "Until next time, Countess. Or should I go ahead and call you Duchess? A reluctant Duchess. The very idea of a woman taking the title. How amusing."

And with that, he bounded down the stairs shouting to his men that it was time to go. I turned and spat, and then I realized with a start he was swinging Sassy's braid to and fro as he walked along, like a prize he won at the county fair. The damned bastard cut off her beautiful hair to take with him like it was some kind of a trophy! As he left the house, I wiped my mouth with the back of my hand as I stared in shock as the Redcoats followed him, pouring out of the house to mount their horses and leave.

Duchess? What the blazes was that all about?

Tarleton and his men rode out with Belle Rose horses, cattle, and food supplies. I cringed as I saw Tarleton mount Calvin's favorite black stallion. Calvin left the stud at Belle Rose to be bred to one of Will's thoroughbred mares. Calvin won't like that, I thought, as Tarleton jerked Cole's reins to make him rear up on his hind legs. Tarleton doffed his hat at me, with what I figured he thought was a sexy, beguiling smile. He wheeled the horse around and pushed him into a fast gallop alongside his men, tipping his hat to me as he rode by. "Until the next time, Duchess."

I turned and ran into Sassy's room. He had cut her loose from the bed before he left. She was curled into a little ball, hugging herself, as she cried. I gathered her into my arms. "He's gone, Sassy. It will be okay. He's gone."

She shook her head. "It will never be okay again, Fancy. My God, how did you endure it for all that time? What will I do? What will William do?"

Girl, you don't know the half of it. And William Ranscome Selk will kill that sorry son of a bitch when he finds out.

She laid there curled into a little ball, sobbing, as I stroked her butchered hair. I picked up her hair brush and began to ease the tangled snarls out of it. "It'll grow again, Sassy. I promise, it will be all right."

"But why did he cut my hair? I don't understand. My hair hasn't been cut short since I was 10 years old. It has been trimmed, but never cut short since my parents died." Bless her soul, she was crying so hard she began to hiccup.

I shrugged. I don't understand menfolk. I wasn't about to tell her the son of a bitch was swinging it like it was a trophy of some sort.

I washed her back with witch hazel like Hattie Mae did for me years before. I cringed as she flinched from the sting of the astringent on her raw wounds. She was injured worse than Le Grande injured me. After I cleaned it, I smoothed a healing unguent onto the livid red stripes.

"It's not too bad, Sassy. The skin is just broken in a few places. It will hurt like the blazes and it will more than likely bruise solid black, but it should heal with little to no scarring. The sorry bastard knows how to wield a whip so he doesn't leave long-lasting damage to a lady's skin."

She clung to me and cried, terrified, heartbroken. I felt like my heart was breaking as each new sob racked through her body.

I didn't have the heart to tell her it could have been worse. It could have lasted for weeks, or months, or even years instead of days. Or that it could have been when she was a young, virginal girl, innocent, naïve, untouched and unschooled in the art of lovemaking between men and women. No, there were some things best left unsaid. After all, rape is never pretty, whether it lasts a few minutes or a lifetime.

By the same token, Will and Calvin never need to know how I was treated during those long, desperate years after Charlotte died. Nor did Marc. Marcus McCarron held enough guilt because Simon Le Grande raped me. I wasn't sure what it would do to him to learn how Tom treated me, too. Those were secrets I intended to take to my grave.

I swore, when I started this journal, I would not discuss some things, but now it seems I can't quit thinking about them. But I don't want anyone to go nosing around and see what I might write. I don't think I could bear for that to happen. My God in heaven! What if Calvin read it? Or Will? What would they think? And, even now, I don't remember it all. Sassy says I have suppressed memories, whatever that means. I am not sure I want to remember. But since Tarleton was here, I seem to be remembering things – no, it is more like I am reliving things - either in nightmares or what Sassy calls waking dreams. I seem to be right back there when bad things happened, but I'm remembering it.

Last night, I woke up, and I was sure that he was lowering himself on me again like he used to do, covering my mouth with his hand so no one could hear me cry. I cried as I struggled to breathe. It felt like he was smothering me.

Even after I woke up, I could still feel his grasping touch, and taste the whiskey on his tongue after he forced me to open my mouth for him. Better his tongue than the alternative. My face was wet with tears I had not shed in years. It took a long time to go back to sleep, and right before I did, the cock crowed. I shivered, because that was what used to happen, too. He'd leave my bed just before the cock crowed, and I couldn't sleep until the next night – unless he came again then as well.

Sassy tells me those are flashbacks, like when she wakes up screaming that Tarleton is back. She can't get past hers yet. She swears we have to remember to heal. I am afraid to remember. I want those bad memories to stay hidden far away from me. But, if I won't let myself remember, can I ever get past it either, or am I always going to be that scared little girl, afraid of every shadow?

I don't want to be a scared little girl. I want to be that bad ass survivor Sassy thinks I am.

So, what do I do?

I say enough of all this. I'm ready for my old man to come back. Maybe we should go home to Bermuda. Maybe that would help put my mind to rest.

Chapter 5
Fancy, 1781

The next morning, the workers were installing bars on the windows when Marc and Richard Winslow returned. They had just installed locks on all the doors, but the front door was still unlocked when they rode up as Uncle Tobias and I were outside checking the work on the windows.

The men frowned as they swung off their horses and hurried up the steps. Marc gathered me into a bear hug. "What's goin' on, lass? Have ye women had trouble whilst we were gone?"

I nodded as I struggled not to burst into tears. "Yes. Bad trouble. Tarleton came back."

Both men froze in their tracks. "What did he do?" Richard choked out the words.

"He called it discipline. I would call it…"

"Jesus Christ, the sorry rat bastard raped my mother," Richard growled as he rushed up the stairs in leaps and bounds. Half-way up, he stopped, and turned back to me. "When?"

"He left yesterday."

"Francesca, please fetch me a vial of pills from my medical kit. They are marked 'morning after.' It should prevent her from conceiving a baby." Richard turned back to bound up the stairs before the words were even out of his mouth.

I ran to where we had his medical supplies hidden to retrieve the vial of pills he requested. I would make sure the other women raped by Tarleton's men got the pills as well. After a moment's hesitation, I picked up the black leather bag he called his medical kit to take with me. Minutes later, I slipped into

Sassy's room.

She sat on the edge of her bed, clinging to Rick as she sobbed. Silent, I sidled up beside him and slipped the bottle into his pocket. "I'll be in the hall if you need me."

Sassy grabbed out for my hand. "Don't go, Fancy." She pulled me close to Rick and her as she continued to struggle to tell him all that happened when Tarleton showed her no quarter for those horrible two days.

Rick, white faced and tight lipped, listened without interrupting as she told her difficult story. He paled as she told him about being horsewhipped in front of everyone. "My God, Mom! He beat you? Let me see."

Sassy trembled at his words as she tried to push him away. "Oh, Rick, please, no…"

He shook his head. "No, I need to see. Hell, I need to do a full exam on you. Francesca, you will stay with us, won't you?"

Silent, I nodded as I helped Sassy slip her robe off her shoulders to reveal her battered back.

Rick gasped. "Jesus Christ, what kind of sadistic animal is he?"

"He's a dad-blamed crazy animal. He sure ain't human," I muttered.

Richard traced his long, slender fingers along the worst lines, cringing each time his mother winced in pain at even the lightest touch. "Francesca, look in my bag there and get me a jar of Lidocaine. It will numb the pain some. And, there are some pills labeled Vicodin. Get those out, too, please."

I hurried to fetch the items requested from his medical kit and handed the jars to him. Silent, he applied the pain-relieving unguent to her tattered back. I was impressed by the gentle manner in which he applied the unguent. "Someone has been tending to this. It looks like they cleaned it and put some sort of unguent on it."

Sassy nodded. "Fancy has been doctoring it for me."

"Well, she did a great job. There. That should help, Mom."

She nodded her head as I helped her pull her silk robe back up on her shoulders. "Thank you, Rick. Yes, thank God for Fancy. And thank God for you. You're a good son. But honey, you have to understand. It was all my fault."

Rick looked shocked. He placed his hands on her shoulders as he peered into her eyes. "No, Mom. It was his fault. There is nothing you or any other woman did to merit those sorts of sadistic repercussions. I don't care if you did lie to the asshole. You did nothing to merit being horse whipped, raped and sodomized. Not once, but over two days. It is inhuman behavior, in fact, it's the behavior of a sexual pervert, a predator. You've volunteered at Women's Shelters before. You must know you did not cause it."

Sassy could not look at Rick. My heart ached for her as she sat there on the edge of her bed, head bowed, eyes averted, weeping in silence.

I reached a tentative hand over to her shoulder. "How many times have you told me that same thing, Sassy? You know he's right."

She reached to her shoulder and patted my hand. "Oh, Fancy, you don't understand…"

I snorted. "You don't think I understand? You think I had it easier than you? Or that I deserved to be raped less than you? Get over yourself, girl. He's an asshole, like Simon Le Grand was an asshole. Same as … any man who takes advantage of a woman or a girl is an asshole. What did you call Le Grand? A narcist?"

"A narcissist," Richard interjected.

I shrugged. "Well, like your mama says, whatever. LeGrande was a crazy mean bastard who never showed a wit of compassion for any other human being. Tarleton's cut from the same corrupt cloth of evil. Will is gonna kill him when he learns what the demented little toad did to you."

Sassy looked up, grabbing both my hands, with alarm written all over her face. "But, Fancy, that's the problem!"

Rick frowned. "You don't want Tarleton dead?"

She shook her head. "You don't understand. Of course, I do. But, he came here, he did this, to call Will out. He wants the confrontation. He wants Will boiling over with rage and to come after him in a blaze of anger. If Will does, Tarleton plans to kill my Will."

I felt lightheaded as the blood drained from my face at her words. "He wants to kill Will?" I said, my voice hoarse with shock. "Why? Will never did anything to Tarleton. Will won't even be Duke when all this is over. Are you sure, Sassy?"

She nodded, as tears again filled her eyes. *"Si, de veras,"* she whispered, as tears began to trail down her cheeks. "It's true. He told me that the fact Will is still alive is a personal affront to him. *Ai, Dios mio*, what do I do? William will go after him over this, exactly like Tarleton planned."

"Well, don't worry. I may kill the bastard first."

She looked shocked. "But Rick, you took an oath. You swore to do no harm!"

"That applies to humans. Butcher Ban is no human. He barely qualifies as an animal. The man is a narcopath."

Sassy looked surprised by his words. "Narcopath? What is that?"

"The simple answer is he is a messed up, crazy, nut ball. Shall I be more precise? A narcissist with no soul, who is also a sociopath. They are all about themselves. You are less than nothing. They have an inflated sense of self-importance, with a constant need for praise and admiration. They have an innate ability to fool others in order to get what they want, without remorse. But what sets these assholes apart is that the narcopath is unable to handle criticism or be viewed in a negative light, where a sociopath could care less what or how others perceive them."

I realized I have known a couple of narcopaths in my own lifetime. "What else?"

He flashed me a smile. "Narcopaths are boogiemen in disguise. They are wolves in sheep's clothing. Their abuse is sometimes so subtle you don't see it until your world is torn apart. Things move from zero to one hundred in seconds. You think you found your soul mate, but your gut says something ain't quite right, you need to slow down. Nothing is normal. They begin as a broken record of compliments, telling you things you always wanted to hear…"

"You sure you aren't describing your own personal opinion of your dad instead of Tarleton?" Sassy interrupted, her voice dripping sarcasm.

Rick stopped for a second, surprise all over his face. "Dammit, maybe I am." He thought a few minutes. "The narcopath's eyes are like windows to nothingness. They always lead the conversation back to themselves. Dad did not do that. His conversations most often led to the Revolutionary War. Narcopaths use big words with little substance. I'll give him credit. Dad was a wordsmith. He knew how to use words. Narcopaths are pros at passive aggressive punishment. Everything is all about them. You are less than dirt to them. You are just there for their use."

Sassy didn't say anything that time.

"Yeah, I know Dad was good at guilt tripping you. But he did love you. As much as he could. But, I do remember when he insisted what happened in

Boston was your fault."

Sassy hung her head as her cheeks reddened. "Maybe it was, Rick."

Rick snorted. "Yeah, sure. Gotcha. Maybe some of it was your fault, but not all. After all, Gramma Winslow raised him. She taught him well. I would say my Dad was a narcissist, to some degree, and I'm certain he wasn't the worst one we will ever meet. We had more good times than bad. In fact, overall, we had a pretty good life together, except for a few serious hiccups. And, I guess, everyone has some hiccups along the way."

Sassy nodded. "That's right."

"On the other hand, I believe my Gramma Winslow was a narcopath. I am convinced of it. My God, she was one mean old lady. She beat the snot out of you when you took Dad back and called off the divorce. This animal? Hell, maybe he's a plain old psychopath, I don't know, but there is something very wrong in Banastre Tarleton's head. He is one sick and sorry excuse for a man. But then again, you don't get a nickname like Butcher Ban for being a nice guy."

Sassy tried to smile. "I thought you were the big believer in 'presumed innocent until proven guilty.'"

Richard looked startled by her words. He pressed his lips together into a right slash but made no reply as he completed his examination of her. I averted my eyes as he checked her 'down there' and took a swab from inside her to check under his microscope. Finally, he answered her. "You're my mom. I believe you. Besides, the man has a God-awful, bad reputation. I'll check the swab now, but I'm going to culture it, too. As many women as he claims to have raped in the colonies, I'd be surprised if something doesn't grow. I have penicillin, and we are going to start you on a two-week round of it right now. And take this pill. It will keep you from conceiving a baby by him."

Sassy looked shocked but nodded and gulped down the morning after pill and the other pill he called penicillin.

I walked out of the room with him after he kissed her brow and tucked her into her bed. Richard stopped outside her door, shaking with apparent rage. "I will kill that sorry excuse for a man if I ever get the chance."

I shook my head. "Don't kill him. Neuter him."

Richard's head jerked around in shock. "What?"

"Castrate the sorry bastard. Cut his nuts off. Hell, cut his member off and shove it where the sun don't shine, like he did to your mama. Sassy says he never has children, but he lives past the War. Don't kill him. Castrate the sorry dog. He won't be raping anyone then."

I wish I had a picture of Rick's look of astonishment. "Damn, girl, you're tougher than you look."

I snorted. "You have no idea how tough I am, Richard Winslow."

And I hope you never will. I realized I was gritting my teeth.

In the days and weeks that followed, the light came back into Sassy's eyes as the smile reappeared on her face. Rick's kind and loving manner did wonders to help his mother begin to heal. I had not known a man could give so much, with such a loving, caring heart. The children's return a few days after Marc and Richard came back did a world of good to help both their mama and me get past those awful days when Tarleton and his men terrorized all of us at Belle Rose.

The children adored Richard. He taught Bella and Sassy's boys how to play with that silly little spinning toy he carries with him. I couldn't see much point to it, but the children seemed to love watching it spin. My heart swelled with unbidden emotions each evening as he danced around the parlor with Bella, who thought he was the greatest thing since her Papa and hot chocolate. Each time he waltzed around the parlor with my little girl, I must admit I dreamed it was me in his arms instead of Bella. I caught him looking at me a few times with hunger-filled eyes that told me as much as he loved dancing with Bella, he longed to hold me in his arms.

I wouldn't dare.

I didn't want Sassy to know that Tarleton's men abused a number of the slaves and free women of color, although they left me alone like I had the plague. Richard treated the women with the same care he gave his mother. Sassy awoke less often screaming in terror. We often talked about what she called coping mechanisms. I wasn't right sure what she meant other than it was supposed to help a person recover. She talked about healing, body, mind and spirit. I'll give her credit. She was damned determined to get beyond those horrible events and not let them mark her for the rest of her life.

In contrast, I was more of a hot mess as each day passed.

I prayed I could get beyond my past, too. But I kept remembering more and more. I wouldn't wake up screaming, but I would wake up gasping, crying in silence as memory after horrible, sordid memory of my childhood, long vanished to the dark recesses of my mind, fought their way forward to bombard me over and over again about events I had no desire to remember.

Sassy insisted I must remember before I can heal. But with each new memory, I felt angrier, more broken, more shattered. More soiled, worthless, used.

She reckoned it might be harder for me to recover from what she called my repressed memories of things long past than the horrible things that just happened to her. But, dammit, I wanted to forget and get on with my life. Instead, with each passing recovery of a suppressed memory, I felt more and more like I am losing my mind, more like I was shattering apart into a jillion, little bitty, jagged pieces.

And sure enough, like he promised, Calvin returned on July 15th. Marc and Richard talked to him in Will's library before they left, telling him what had happened. He appeared lost in thought as Marc and Richard rode away to rejoin Lafayette and his men. I sat, silent and tremulous, plucking at my hands, chewing my lip, as I waited for Calvin to speak.

"Did they hurt you?" he asked, his voice gruff with worry.

I shook my head as I looked up at him. "No, they avoided me like I had the plague. Tarleton commented I would be Duchess when this War ends. He seemed unwilling to sully the reputation of the Duchess of Ranscome."

I didn't mention Tarleton shoved his tongue into my mouth a couple of times.

Calvin looked up, both startled and perhaps a bit of guilt marring his handsome features. "He said what? But … but how would he know?"

I stared at him for a minute before answering. My heart began yammering in my chest as my hands became cold and clammy. "Oh, my God, Calvin, what have you done?"

He sniffed in disdain. "It was common knowledge Josiah Selk meant for you to be the Duchess. Lord knows I heard him call you his Wee Duchess many times. The estate is not entailed. It is in fee simple and goes back to the original barony. In fact, it was first given to a woman, Elizabeth Ranscome, who married Thomas Selk in 1565. Women have always been able to inherit fee simple titles in Ireland. I discussed marrying you with Jo years ago. I arranged to marry you upon your eighteenth birthday. Tom, the poor, misguided fool, died before then at Saratoga. I warned him not to go. I begged him to let us marry before he left. I would have married you the day Bella was born but it was all a bit too fast for you. I understood your reasons, but you must admit it would have been better for our daughter had we married before her birth instead of after. In any event, William never wanted the title. He understands if he owns Belle Rose after the end of this little Rebellion," he stressed the word with a scornful glance, "the King would indeed confiscate the properties and give them to his loyal soldiers. Tarleton might very well obtain Belle Rose, under those facts. T'was easy enough to convince Will to relinquish the Ranscome title to you, although it took over a year to get the King to agree. Your birth was a bit, ahem, unconventional."

I knew he was right. Tamsin was born on the wrong side of the blanket. So was I, even though I was adopted by Josiah and Belle Selk as a newborn babe. Still, it rankled for my own husband to refer to my ignoble birth as well as that of my daughter. My cheeks burned bright pink with anger and shame at my husband's words. I turned away from him lest he see my emotions written plain upon my face. In fact, it was the closest he had ever come to referencing my illegitimacy at birth. I understood Marc was a thorn under his skin, a constant reminder that I was not the true daughter of Belle and Jo, born of their marriage. Calvin and I never discussed it. It was a forbidden topic between us, the same as we never discussed those awful months during which Simon Le Grande abused me over and over again.

"I may have mentioned it to Charles that I managed to convince the King to transfer the fee simple title to you. I had no idea he would discuss it with his men. Charles will be most upset to learn of this. Most upset indeed."

My heart lurched with fear. "What will he do?"

"Rebuke the lout, in all likelihood. No matter how Sassy may or may not deserve some sort of punishment, she did not deserve this. His actions here were ungentlemanly and a poor reflection on the British officer. Charles will be most upset, especially in light of Tarleton's comments to you. He was way out of line."

"Well, he was right about one thing," I murmured.

He frowned. "Oh, indeed? About what, my darling?"

"I hope you realize that I will be a most reluctant duchess."

I shivered, despite the summer heat. All I could remember was Tom sneering at me, saying, "You'll never be a duchess, little girl."

"My silly darling. You will be a wonderful duchess." He chuckled and then changed the subject as he began to kiss me, demanding my attention, compelling my participation. I clung to my old man, trembling with unexpected passion, and he asked, "Want me to diddle you a bit before dinner?"

I nodded, but then pulled back. "Don't other people say that? Or is it our special word?"

Calvin laughed, his dark, chocolate-colored eyes twinkling with a flash of merriment. "I've heard other people use it," he answered with another deep kiss before he swung me up into his arms. I tucked my head to his shoulder as he carried me upstairs, still chuckling. "Ah, yes, I must be the luckiest man in the world. Married to a beautiful young woman, who is the epitome of a lady in every way, and yet who is my own little wildcat in the bedroom."

He told me once not long after we wed that I was his own little whore in the bedroom. His ill-thought comment triggered one of the biggest fights we ever had. Sobbing with anger, rage and humiliation, I punched him in the eye, and then slapped him over and over, until I collapsed, gasping for breath. I shouted at him not to ever call me a whore again. Hours later, after many tears, he managed to persuade me to calm down and carry on – but he damned sure knew not to call me his little whore ever again.

Since then, he called me his little wildcat. That still didn't thrill me, but it was better than the alternative. I sure hoped he hadn't told Cornwallis, that, too. I would die of mortification if I ever met him and knew Calvin told the General, I'm a wildcat in the bedroom!

He stayed a week, and then he told me he was leaving again. He did not say when he would return. I knew it depended how his visit with General Cornwallis went. I felt confident he would re-join Cornwallis and would advise him of Tarleton's actions at Belle Rose.

"I promise no other assaults on the residents of Belle Rose shall occur, my darling. I am quite sure Charles will not allow any further attack on the future residence of the Duchess of Ranscome. Take care and be sure to drink plenty of the renowned Belle Rose water. It seems to be agreeing with you. I am so very proud you decided to carry our child this time. I shall keep you in my thoughts and prayers. Take care of my heir, my darling. I shall return as soon as possible, but no later than mid-September." He frowned. "I still can't believe

Tarleton stole my stallion."

He bent from his saddle to kiss me, before he wheeled his mount around to canter down the path towards the road.

I shook my head as I chuckled. It somehow figured his last words were about his horse.

I hoped and prayed Calvin was right. We did not need another visit from Banastre Tarleton at Belle Rose. Once like that last visit was enough for a lifetime. I didn't need to explain Belle Rose was not entailed property. My lord, he already knew that, or else I could not have wound up with this blasted title! Plus, even if the title had been entailed, Daddy Jo bought Belle Rose with his own money when he came to Virginia Colony when he was a young man. Belle Rose would follow to Will and Will's children, no matter who held the title, unlike Ranscome Manor, Ranscome Downs, Ranscome Shipping, and the other Irish holdings. Of course, the title was not entailed, and as such, Daddy Jo could have given any part of the property to anyone he so desired.

Hmm. That was an interesting thought. Well butter my biscuits, I reckon I could, too.

.   .   .   .   .   .

"Well, butter my buns and call me a biscuit! Will's home!" I shouted as I spotted my brother ride up the drive to the house.

Will came home on September 8th, a full five months after he left to join Francis Marion in the Carolina swamps. Sassy threw herself into his arms, trembling with mixed joy that he was safe at home and terrified of telling him about Tarleton's vicious attack. She clung tight to him, struggling not to cry as he told us his story.

We were wrong. He was not with Marion all the time since he left. Will explained why he was unable to come home for their anniversary. "I got a request to join Washington the first of July. Of course, we all know I was expected to do as the General 'requested'."

Will confirmed the French and American Armies met at White Plains, New York on July 6th. "Sassy, I cannot say too much about how impressed I am with Rochambeau. Although Rochambeau has almost 40 years of warfare experience, he has made it crystal clear he came to serve Washington, not to command the combined forces. Heck fire, I was even more impressed Rochambeau never challenged Washington's authority. I swear, Rochambeau is the one soldier I think could challenge Washington with success. He could, but he has never tried to usurp power from Washington for his own glory. He insists he came to serve Washington, not to take over. Those two Generals discussed where to launch a joint attack. Washington favored hitting New York, because the French and Americans outnumbered the British there 3 to 1. Rochambeau argued the French fleet under Admiral de Grasse was sidling up to the US from the West Indies, and it would be easier to coordinate efforts at less populated places further down the Atlantic coast than at New York. Lafayette wrote they have Cornwallis's troops acting like a retreating army, burning all in their wake as they head for the coast. Lafayette stressed victory could be had in Virginia. Now, I already knew we are gonna end this War at Yorktown. Sassy told me that and my gal's never been wrong yet. I reminded Washington of your 'prophesy.' General Washington continued to probe a New York attack until August 14. That's when he received a letter from Admiral de Grasse stating he was headed for Virginia with 28 warships and 3000 soldiers, and de Grasse could remain until October 14th. De Grasse again urged Washington move south to Virginia to launch a joint operation."

Will grinned as he told how Washington called him in and asked Will's opinion. Without a word, Will pointed to the new missive from Madame X. "George, you already know what to do. We're gonna win at Yorktown. Hasn't she told you that all along?"

"She has indeed. And I must say, she has never once been wrong." Washington sighed, and then crossed to look out the window towards New York again. "Then, in accordance with missives from both Admiral de Grasse and Madame X, we prepare to go to Virginia, William." Washington then wrote an uncoded letter, sent by regular mail, as Sassy had recommended, that said the Americans would be attacking New York. Wiley old fox intended for the British to learn of the contents of that letter. I still can't believe they fell for it. But it seems the idea that Washington would leave New England and West Point unprotected in the face of a British assault was considered outlandish if not downright absurd. Now, we wait and see — and pray Sassy is correct and those British troops cannot get to Yorktown in time!"

They began the Celebrated March south on August 19th, with 4000 French and 3000 American soldiers. Along the way, they sent out fake dispatches that reached Clinton revealing the Franco-American army was going to launch an attack on New York. As a result, Clinton was even more convinced Cornwallis was safe in Virginia in the Yorktown area.

Will told us not everything was peaches and cream on the March south. "Well, you see, the combined French and American troops reached Philadelphia on September 2nd. The exhausted American troops flat refused to proceed unless they were paid one month's pay in real currency. They had been receiving Continental paper. Heck fire, we all know Continental paper don't hold shucks. It's worthless. Washington was most upset. I dare say he panicked. Rochambeau loaned Washington half the money from his supply of Spanish gold. Many of our brave soldiers had been serving over a year without one red cent of real pay."

"Did we loan him the rest?" Sassy asked.

Will blushed. "Well, maybe part of it."

"Good. I'm glad we were able to help. That's going to be the last payment they will get, too," Sassy commented. I noticed she didn't press Will about how much he donated to the Cause.

"Yes, but it will get them to Yorktown," Will said with a grin, as he reached over to squeeze her hand.

"And we helped," she said, her voice soft.

"We did indeed, darlin'." Will bent to kiss her cheek.

Will told us that on September 5th, the de Grasse fleet was spotted off the Virginia Capes. "De Grasse sent his French troops to join Lafayette and sent his empty transports to pick up the American troops. Washington then went home to Mount Vernon and let me come to Belle Rose." He smiled at Sassy and hugged her close to his side.

"But more happened on September 5th than that," Sassy demurred. "That is the date of the Battle of the Capes, between the British fleet, led by Rear Admiral Sir Thomas Graves, and the French fleet, led by Comte de Grasse. It was a very important battle, William. You see, it prevented the Royal Navy from making Yorktown with the 19 ships of the line sent from New York to assist Cornwallis. If they had arrived at Yorktown, Cornwallis would have had combined firepower of fourteen hundred guns, more than enough to provide adequate protection to Cornwallis and his seven thousand men. Without those ships, guns, and additional troops, Cornwallis knows all shall be lost if Clinton does not get more men to him right away. And of course, we know what is going to happen. Clinton's promised troops and supplies will not show up until after Cornwallis surrenders."

It was late when Will finished telling us all that had happened. I yawned, and as I arose, I told them I was heading to bed. Sassy looked terrified, like a deer caught in the headlights, as she puts it, whatever headlights are. She grabbed my hand to keep me from leaving.

"Please, Fancy, don't go," she begged. Her eyes shown like emeralds with unshed tears threatening to spill over.

I pulled her to me and hugged her. "It will be all right. Will loves you. This is private. You need to talk to him alone."

But, my best friend looked horrified. Sassy's eyes teared up, and her cheeks reddened as she struggled not to cry. I knew she wanted to tell him about her ordeal in private, but she looked more and more terrified by the moment. As her tears continued to well up, she whispered, "Please, Fancy. Don't go. Please."

I flashed a smile of encouragement to her, and murmured, "You are a brave, strong woman. You can do this."

She blinked over and over, as she struggled not to cry. She nodded as she tried to smile. Her lip trembled, and she snuggled tight into the bend of his arm, as close to his side as possible.

William sat stroking her back and bent to kiss her before he pulled her into his arms. "It's okay, Sassy, I know," he murmured, his voice filled with emotion as he tried to contain his own tears of anger and frustration. "It's okay, darlin'. I ran into Marc and Richard on my way here. Nothing that animal did could ever change the way I feel about my sweet Sassy girl."

I have to admit, tears welled up in my own eyes at Will's words. I was never so proud of my big brother as I was at that moment. It was exactly what Sassy needed to hear from the man she loved.

Sassy jerked her cap off and raked her fingers through her butchered hair. "He cut my hair off," she gasped as her eyes spilled over with a new wash of hot tears again.

"It's okay, Little Bit. Your hair will grow back. And you're still beautiful. You will always be beautiful."

And then, as she sobbed in his arms, telling him in halting, haunting words what happened when Tarleton returned, I slipped from the room. They needed privacy.

Chapter 6
Fancy, 1781

Calvin returned on September 19th, ebullient, filled with enthusiasm and high spirits. I will never understand why he stayed away so long, considering he was a mere 40 miles away at Monticello with Cornwallis for over a month.

"I am ecstatic we will be able to attend this battle, Fancy. Imagine, we will be present when Good King George defeats this rebellion. It will be a day of great celebration!"

"Great celebration for someone, that's for sure," I grumbled. I had heard too much from Sassy over the last few months to in any way believe the Americans were going to lose at Yorktown. I tried to convince my stubborn old mule of that more than once, but he refused to believe he was supporting the losing side. He could not accept the loss at the Battle of the Cape would somehow cause the British to lose all at Yorktown. I didn't even try to tell him Washington moved his army south. He would never believe it. Like they say, you can lead a mule to water, but you can't make the dad-blamed fool drink.

"Oh, you will see, my darling. I do wish you would relent and allow our little Bella to accompany us. She should be present the day that we trounce these rebels once and for all."

Of course. Every three-year-old child needs to experience war first hand. I'll be jiggered sideways before that's going to happen. I bit my tongue and continued to pack my things for the short trip to Yorktown.

I knew the battle would wage from September 28th until October 19th, when Sassy swore the British would surrender. In an abundance of caution, even though I felt it was overkill, I packed one trunk with enough things for three weeks. My husband insisted the Duchess of Ranscome must be in attendance and must look beautiful at all times.

"You must appear ravishing, my darling. You will be the highest-ranking person who will be in attendance. You are the personage closest to the King in title who will be there. It is imperative you look the part of Duchess at all times. It would besmirch the honor of the Crown for you too look anything less."

Well dad blast it, now I would besmirch the honor of the Crown if I looked less than perfect at all times. In the middle of a war. So, in addition to my pretty gowns, I added the packet of jewels I brought from Bermuda. Struggling not to laugh, Sassy even sent me with some of her jewels she inherited from Mama Belle. I laughed when Sassy pulled out a beautiful pink tourmaline, diamond, and aquamarine-covered tiara that Daddy Jo bought Mama Belle in Paris on their delayed honeymoon in 1722 when they attended the Court of young King Louis XV, at Versailles. The painting of Belle in the gallery at Belle Rose Plantation shows her dressed in her wedding dress, with her beautiful pink tourmaline and diamond ring, and wearing this tiara. I didn't take the dress, or her ring. Those were now Sassy's. I took several of Mama Belle's other court gowns I altered. I felt like a duchess for the first time clad in those beautiful silk mantuas, wearing Mama Belle's tiara and jewels. Replete with gowns, shoes, cloaks, and of course, the tiara and other jewels, we left on the afternoon of September 20th to journey to Yorktown.

It wasn't too hard to get there. We traveled by ship from the Potomac to the James River, and then overland to Williamsburg, where we spent the night. From Williamsburg, we traveled by coach on to Yorktown, a mere 11 additional miles, on the morning of September 21st. I did not understand why we didn't sail straight to Yorktown. We arrived in Yorktown before noon, waiting to be ensconced into one of the houses providing housing for the British.

That was when I saw the British ships in the Yorktown harbor, and the French vessels beyond. I realized there had been no reason to even attempt to sail straight to Yorktown. We would never have made it. In fact, we would have been blown right out of the water by the French ships guarding the harbor. With a sinking heart, I realized we were caught in a neat trap there by Washington's combined French and American forces. It was apparent, even to me, the English would be fighting a defensive battle. I knew that was not a desired plan of action at all.

Calvin was quick to find General Cornwallis, and the men were chatting when an unpleasant and familiar figure rode up before us, to quaff his hat to me. "Your Grace," drawled Tarleton, with a slow leer down my body.

Calvin's head snapped up at the word. His lips narrowed into an angry slash as he started towards the arrogant young man mounted on Calvin's stallion. Without a word, Calvin reached up and jerked Tarleton off Cole, and began to pummel him.

"You do not steal a man's mount, boy," Calvin hissed between blows to Tarleton.

The Colonel's eyes bulged in shock as he tried to fend off Calvin's blows. "Don't be a fool, you crazy, old goat. I had no idea the horse belonged to you. General, you aren't going to allow this kind of treatment to one of your officers, are you, sir?"

Cornwallis chortled, but the sound did not reach the look in his eyes. "I warned you. Never steal a man's ride, two legged or four. I warned you Hobbs is not young, but he is strong and has beaten far better men than you. Let it go. You overreached when you took the Earl's horse – and when you threatened to take his wife."

Wordless, Tarleton's sneer marred his handsome features. He wheeled around, glowering as he jerked an officer of lower rank off his horse before riding away without another word. Calvin may have regained his horse, but I was pretty dad-blamed sure he made a formidable enemy that day in Banastre Tarleton.

Calvin frowned when I refused to stay at the large house at the center of town. It was gorgeous, and a number of the high-ranking officers, including Cornwallis, were staying there. But, there was something unsavory about the house, a kind of pervasive excess that made me queasy. I couldn't put my finger on it, but even if I had not known about the bombing to come on October 10th, I could not have stayed there. Sassy had warned me the house would be destroyed during the battle. She urged me against staying there.

"No, Calvin, that house is far too noticeable. I bet the Rebels bomb it. They will think Cornwallis or I will be staying there. I cannot risk our child by staying in such an obvious target."

I did not add that something about Patrice Paddington's home made the hairs on the back of my neck stand straight up.

He pouted. I noticed my husband pouting more and more of late when he didn't get his way. "But, Fancy, darling, it is the nicest accommodation in town."

"I understand, Calvin. I refuse to stay there. I urge General Cornwallis not to stay there or let his men stay there either. It is too obvious a target. Find us something smaller, less pretentious, less an obvious target. Someplace safer, if there is any such place here. However, I suspect no place is safe in Yorktown right now." I sighed, frustrated he refused to allow me to stay in Williamsburg, but I had already lost that battle. Damn it.

We settled into the home of a very nice lady overlooking the harbor, near the edge of town. Mrs. Haggerty was sweet and welcoming. Bless her soul, I think she felt sorry for me. She understood Calvin dragged me smack into the middle of the war. A few days later, I told her how pleased I was to be at her home instead of Patrice Paddington's home, where most of the officers were ensconced.

She looked horrified. "Do you mean to say Sir Calvin intended to house you there?"

I nodded my head. "Oh, yes, ma'am. He was quite upset when I refused."

"Well, thank God you did. No self-respecting woman should enter a place like that… that house, and indeed, not a lady like you."

I felt like my skin was crawling. "What do you mean, Mrs. Haggerty?"

She shook her head. "Harrumph. No decent, self-respecting man should ask his wife to stay in a Gentleman's Club. I can't imagine whatever possessed Sir Calvin!"

Holy cheese on a cracker! My idiot old man tried to set me up in a bordello. "Maybe he didn't understand the true nature of her … establishment."

She sniffed. "Perhaps. But Sir Calvin never struck me as a stupid man."

I was flabbergasted by her words. Hours later, Calvin dragged in. Mrs. Haggerty served him the dinner she had kept warm for him, silent and distrusting. I tried to make conversation as he ate, sullen and ill-tempered. He glowered at me as he ate until he broke down and spoke. "Why are you wearing that? You look like a trollop."

I felt my face flush red with shame at his words, and I pulled the silk bed jacket he gave me close about my shoulders. "It's late, Calvin. I was in bed. We're in our own room…"

"I told you that you must comport yourself like a Duchess at all times here. That includes in this room."

I raised myself from the chair. "Oh, I beg your pardon. I suppose I thought you might not have meant I must dress like a lady in my boudoir since you tried to set me up in a Gentleman's Club."

He spat his tea out in shock at my words. "Wh…wh…what did you say?"

"Isn't that what they call Miss Paddington's establishment? A Gentleman's Club? In fact, isn't it called Miss Patrice Paddington's Elite Club for Gentlemen? My God, Calvin, whatever were you thinking? You mean to say you intended to set me up in a bordello filled with whores and soldiers?"

He stood up so fast he turned the table over, dumping the food and dishes onto the carpet. His face red, eyes glaring with anger, he spluttered as he managed to speak. "Madame, you are out of line. You owe me an apology."

My heart was clamoring like it does sometimes when I am scared or upset, pounding so hard that it hurts, but I was not finished. I was determined I would stand up for myself on this. I clinched my hands so he would not see them shaking. "I don't think so. No, Calvin, this time you owe me an apology. Would you have housed your pregnant wife in a whore house? After all your hard work to make me a duchess? And yet you claim to care about appearances? …I … I …" I raised my hand to cover my mouth as I stifled a sob.

His hand lashed out to slap me into silence. "Madame, you need to control yourself. Such discussion is unseemly in a wife."

My hand flew up to my cheek. I was stunned. Shocked. He had yelled at me, but he had never struck me before. I stood up straight, determined not to cave in over this. "And such behavior is unseemly in a husband. I have not rebuked you for spending every waking hour there. Just for trying to house me there. Of course, perhaps you meant to put me to work…"

His hand lashed out against my cheek again. "Madame, I warn you, enough."

My hand flew back to my cheek as I struggled not to cry. "I take it this means the honeymoon is over?"

"So, it would appear." He tossed down his napkin. "I'll be at Miss Paddington's. At least my motives are not questioned there and the girls are always most obliging."

My cheeks started to sting with embarrassment in addition to the slap marks. "That is uncalled for and you know it. I have never turned you down, Calvin. Not once in our marriage. Not even when the doctor warned us both against engaging in conjugal relations soon after both of my miscarriages. And you know as well as I do that this baby was conceived when I consoled you over Caroline's death."

"What? How dare you, Madame! Do not bring my dear, departed sister into this conversation. Perhaps you never turned me down, but who wants a woman big as a barn with a whelp inside her belly? You don't think any man there would want you, do you? You can't be that vain, can you, silly little twat?"

I stared at him in shock. Did he really call me a vain, silly little twat? I shook my head in stunned dismay. When I found my voice, I answered him. "Well, it's bound to be more fun in the bordello if your pregnant wife is not there. I will send your things over in the morning."

"Good. Do that."

"So why wouldn't you let me stay in Williamsburg, if not Belle Rose?" I asked as I struggled not to cry. Don't give him the satisfaction of seeing you crying. He wants you to cry. Just. Don't.

"You are my Countess, and the Duchess of Ranscome. I have explained all this to you before. Your reluctance to assume your duty to the crown boggles my mind. And after all the work it took on my part to secure this title for you. How many times need I explain all this, Madame? Why can you not comprehend that? I did not think you were mentally defective when I married you. Oh, dear heavens, is this what pregnancy does to a woman?"

I came really close to telling him yes, this is what pregnancy does to women. Somehow, I managed to hold my tongue. I didn't want to be slapped again. I hung my head, struggling not to cry as my husband stormed out of the house. And, all this ruckus over a perfectly lovely red silk dressing gown he gave me less than a year ago for Christmas. Now, don't that beat all?

The next day, General Cornwallis came to Mrs. Haggerty's house to see me. "General! What can I do for you? I did not expect to see you here."

He chuckled. "I was more than surprised to see you in Yorktown, my dear. I warned Calvin bringing you was not a wise idea."

I tried to laugh. "Well, he was quite determined."

"Hmm. Yes, I have to agree with you on that. In any event, I hear Calvin and you exchanged some cross words last evening, Lady Fancy."

I felt my cheeks begin to redden. I tried to laugh, but it came out more like a squeak from a little mouse. "Well, yes, sir... I reckon you could put it that way."

"I cannot leave the Duchess of Ranscome unprotected during this misbegotten battle, Your Grace. The King would never forgive me if something untoward happened to you."

"Well, hush my mouth," I began, my heart began beating faster, erratic with fear. My chest felt almost too tight to hold my wild beating heart. I coughed a few times, as I do sometimes when I am stressed and my heart races. "Oh, but General, I am not your first concern…"

"I agree, dear. But you are a duchess, and it is imperative that you must be protected. I agree that you should not stay at Patrice's establishment. It is a beautiful place, but quite unsuitable for a lady of your rank. I must admit I am quite concerned about the precariousness of our situation here, if Clinton's troops do not arrive soon. I pray they arrive before I am forced to surrender. I warned General Clinton if the replacements do not arrive soon, he needs to be prepared to hear the worst. In fact, the situation is grave enough that I must protect you. I brought along a contingent of young Irish officers. I would like you to interview them and select twelve to be Your Grace's Guard. If it please you, Your Grace."

My mouth fell open. I was not accustomed to being called Your Grace. Tarleton called me that the day we arrived, but no none else had yet. Cornwallis's obsequiousness was a bit overwhelming, to say the least. Obsequiousness. I think that is the word Sassy explained is a nice way of saying 'the fine art of ass kissing'. He sure was kissing up to my well-rounded posterior about then. I was plum dab astonished he admitted he was in an un-winnable situation, barring a miracle. But I was thrilled he realized I needed protection, and that he agreed I should not stay at Miss Paddington's. "General, that is so thoughtful. You have no idea how I appreciate it."

"Not at all, Your Grace. You must be protected against rape and mayhem."

Well, that took me aback. I expected mayhem but I had not considered rape before he mentioned it. I shuddered, horrified at the very notion.

The officers were introduced to me by rank, with the highest ranks first. He brought 35 for me to choose from. Of course, General Cornwallis had his 'little rebellion' to quell, and only stayed long enough to see I was comfortable questioning the men.

By 3 p.m. that afternoon, I was fatigued. By 5, I was plumb dab exhausted as the last young man was brought in to me. My heart was acting up, racing like it was a fine thoroughbred taking off at Ranscome Downs. "Your Grace, may I present Leftenant Winston Fitz Simmons."

My head snapped up in shock as I stared at a tall, slender, young man with curling, dark hair, startling blue eyes, and an uncanny resemblance to Marc except with the Selk coloring. "Leftenant Fitz Simmons. Are you a Cork man, sir?"

He smiled, his bright blue eyes twinkling. Selk blue eyes and black hair, I thought in dismay. "Yes, Lady Fancy. From Waterside."

I stood up so fast I knocked over the tea table. The young man rushed to help me. "Oh, Your Grace, I apologize. I did not mean to distress you."

"No, no, not at all. Does your family call you Winston?" I babbled as I began to nibble at the inside of my lip. I do that when I am stressed. Better to chew my lip than my fingernails, Charlotte always said.

He smiled and reached over to pat my hands. "My mother does. My father died when I was very young, before I was even three. He drowned at sea. Everyone else calls me Fitz." I must have been pale, because he reached out for my arm to steady me. "Are you all right? I am afraid I have upset you. Perhaps I should not have come."

I shook my head. "No, I'm not upset. I am a bit …"

"Rattled?" The word came out soft, little more than a whisper.

I nodded, still chewing my lip. "I would say I feel like I've been plum dab jiggered, but yes, I must admit I did not expect to meet you here."

He chuckled, his eyes sparkling with mischief and amusement. I would bet the poor lad never heard a duchess say 'jiggered' before. "Mother was afraid it might disconcert you to meet me like this."

"Mother?" I yelped. My heart began to beat irregularly, racing in my chest. I swallowed a couple of times, surprised at how dry my mouth was, and pressed my hand to my chest. "Is … is your mother with you?"

He shook his head. "Oh, no, Your Grace, she is home tending to Grandfather. She was sure you and I would meet once I arrived in Virginia Colony. She warned me it might come as a bit of a surprise to see me."

I was stunned speechless. I stared at him for a minute before I managed to gather my addled wits enough to respond. "Your mother is Tamsin Selk, right?"

He nodded.

"Might come as a bit of a surprise? Well, I reckon you could put it that way, to meet a brother, I didn't know existed until right now. I'd heard tell that she was pregnant when she went to Ireland, but I never knew what she had. Well, how clever of Tamsin to have comprehended the sudden appearance of my brother might somehow disconcert me," I snapped. "But, then again, why should I be surprised? She never bothered to write me about you. After all, she didn't bother to take me with her to Ireland when she ran off with your father seventeen years ago."

I arose and walked over to the window, to stare out over the York Harbor. I pressed my hand to my mouth as I struggled to compose myself and to not give into the tears I yearned to shed. She went off and left you, Fancy, she went off with nary a word and left you all those long years ago. Do. Not. Cry. Not for the likes of Tamsin Selk.

Leftenant Fitz Simmons looked shocked by my outburst. "But, she did," he blurted. "We both did. She had me writing you letters and drawing you pictures as soon as I could hold a pencil. And, she often cried because you were not with us in Ireland. I know she wrote many times to her father, Lord Josiah Selk, and later to her brother, Thomas Selk, asking that you be allowed to join her. They always refused. Grandfather Fitz Simmons always tells her not to give up her hope that she will see you again some day."

'Oh, she did?" I retorted, as I struggled to hold back all those years of tears. "So why didn't she take me when she left? Oh, let me guess. Perhaps her hands were too full of Michael, Marc and Lily's baby, and she had no room in her hands or her heart for her own little girl?"

My voice broke. I could not contain my anguish. I don't want her. I don't need her. She went off and left me. For that damned Irish rogue. I don't … want … her… But even as I chanted the old mantra, I felt the first unbidden tear snake down my cheek.

"What?" he whispered. He looked aghast. "But she told me she wanted to make sure it was safe to take you to Ireland."

I realized with a start what I was doing to this young man was wrong. It was clear across his face Winston Fitz Simmons had never heard anything about how Jay and Tamsin left me behind when they kidnapped Michael after Jay damned near killed Lily. Hell, this boy probably didn't even know they took Michael until I blurted it out. I would bet my bottom dollar he didn't know a dad-blamed thing about the attack on Lily. I took deep breaths, trying to calm myself before I said anything else, I would later regret I said to my new-found younger brother. I took another deep breath and started again. "I apologize. You're my brother. We have much to talk about. Come sit here by me and tell me all about Ireland. I have never been there, but I understand Waterside is quite gorgeous."

An enormous smile broke out across his face, and he scrambled over to sit down beside me. "Ireland is incredible, amazingly beautiful, and Waterside is the most beauteous place in all of Eire."

"Eire?" I pronounced it like he had, 'I yearn.' "Why do you call it that?"

He chuckled. "Aye, that is the way we Gaels pronounce Ireland. Tis the old way it has been said in the Gaelic since before recorded time."

We talked for hours. He can weave a tale as well as Will. He told me of their prayers each night that always included, 'and keep our Fancy safe from harm, healthy and well'. I struggled not to cry when he told me that, and I had to make another trip to the window to check on the ships in the harbor again to give me time to blink those dad-blamed tears back.

However, I could not hold my tears back as he told me how Tamsin, my grandfather and he all came to Virginia after Daddy Jo died to take me back to Ireland, to be rudely rebuffed by Tom when they arrived after their long journey. "He told Mother she would never see you again, that you didn't ever want to see her. And he made us leave without even a moment with you."

"I never knew," I sobbed as I twisted my handkerchief. "I never knew…"

I didn't tell him I was still recuperating from being deathly sick with the scarlet fever then and never knew they came.

And then he pulled out the most beautiful chatelaine. "Mother asked me to give this to you. She painted the miniature after we went to Virginia. She saw the painting of you in the parlor on the Duke's desk. She tried to make you look a bit older. I see it does look a lot like you. She carried it every day until she sent it with me for you."

I blinked, stunned by the beautiful chatelaine. I had forgotten Tamsin painted miniatures. She had painted me clad in my favorite green silk dress, with my hair trailing down curled over one shoulder. Small green beads and gold hearts hung from the little frame. The delicate ladies' watch extended down from the miniature. The painting was small but it was clearly me. I choked back tears as I clutched it to my heart. "Thank you, Fitz. I will treasure this."

At the end of the evening, Fitz was one of my guards. I liked my little brother and I felt confident I could trust him. If nothing else, I knew my father, Marcus McCarron, also known as Marcus Fitz Simmons, and my brothers, William Selk, Michael McCarron and Winston Fitz Simmons, would protect me come hell or high water from any storms that should ever come my way again.

And the chatelaine my mother sent hung at my waistband, where I could touch it frequently. I was still stunned she had painted the miniature of me and sent it to me.

I was surprised the next morning to see Lily and Marcus at the British medical tent when I went down to help Dr. Johnston. I rushed over to them and reached up to hug them both. "What are you doing here?"

Marcus frowned. "The better question is what the feckin' hell are ye doing here, lass?"

I clucked as I shook my head. "Daddy, watch your language. Calvin insists the next Duke of Ranscome be in attendance when Britain wins this 'little revolt'. Even if the child is still in my belly."

Lily chuckled. "Yeah. Sure. Like that is going to happen. So, where is Old Stubbornness this morning anyway?"

"My best guess would be with General Cornwallis. They're thicker than thieves these days. How on earth did you get here, Lily?" I asked as I again hugged her close. "Is Gentry well? Has she been delivered of her baby?"

She grinned. "I've learned a trick or two since I fell in love with Marc all those years ago. Gentry and the baby are fine. I would not have left otherwise. Where are you staying? I hear a lot of the soldiers are staying at Patrice Paddington's."

Marc glowered. "Ye'd best be telling me yer not staying there, Fancy."

I shook my head. "Oh, no, I'm at Mrs. Haggerty's. Calvin wanted me to stay at Paddington's..."

"Of course," Marc said through gritted teeth. "The sorry old fool. I swear, sometimes I think that man is in his dotage."

"Now, Marcus, be nice. He's not all that much older than you. I refused. Cornwallis appointed twelve young men from Ireland to serve as my guard.

They may be disappointed not to be at Paddington's, but they are good lads, all quite determined to keep me safe and well."

"I heard Cornwallis gave ye men for protection. I'll talk to them later and make sure they understand protection of the Duchess of Ranscome and her unborn child is their primary responsibility here."

"This is pretty," Lily commented as she bent to study the chatelaine. "Where did it come from? My land, the miniature looks like the painting of you at Belle Rose."

I tried to smile. "Yes, it does. I think they understand their priority is my protection, Lord Fitz Simmons," I replied, as several of my guards approached. "In fact, you might recognize a few. Leftenant O'Reilly and Leftenant Fitz Simmons are both from Cork. Gentlemen, allow me to introduce you to Lord Marcus Fitz Simmons."

Marc's head jerked around so fast it made me dizzy. "What? Indeed? M' god, Winston, I had no idea ye were here!"

Lily's eyes, large as saucers, blinked fast. "Oh, my merciful heavens."

I tried to laugh, but the sound was as dry as the crackling of autumn leaves. "Fitz, this is Lady Liliana Fitz Simmons, your Uncle Marc's wife. She is a well-known physician. We are lucky to have her with us. Lily, Fitz brought me the chatelaine. It was a gift from Tamsin."

Young Fitz grabbed Marc's hand. "Tis a pleasure to meet you, sir. My mother was most upset when I joined, but my Grandfather told her it was not just my right but my duty as his heir. I must thank you for convincing the King to name me to follow my Grandfather instead of you following as Earl. Mother was most surprised and delighted."

Marcus blushed. "Ah, lad, ye've lived in Ireland all yer life. I lived there 10 years. I lived almost 20 years in Virginia. I've lived more than 20 years in Indian Territory, where our son, Michael lives. We love our wild, beautiful country. 'Twas right you inherit. I have no intention to move back to Ireland. It was always my plan you should inherit. Your father should have had the title."

"I appreciate that, sir, but again, I thank you. But, if I may be so bold, Mother urged me to encourage you all to come to Ireland. Your father is getting quite old, sir, and is becoming more and more feeble. He talks about you often. I know he misses you with a vengeance. It would mean the world for him to see you again before his time to leave this world, even though he will be leaving us for a far better place."

I noticed Marc looked pensive at Fitz's words. "I'll give it serious thought, young man. I would love to see my Da and home again."

His words tugged at my heart. I never heard him call Ireland 'home' before, nor heard the raw anguish in his voice I heard then.

Well, other than the day he told me he was my sire. I will never forget the raw, visceral pain in his voice or mine that day, as first he told me he was my father and then as I lashed out at him in pain and anger. "What do you mean, you're my father? How dare you tell me this now, after all these years? How dare you?" I raged at him. "Where were you all those years I needed you? All those years I longed for a father to love and protect me? All those years I longed for you to be my father? Dammit, Marc, why tell me this now?"

I would never forget the unguarded look of anguish that flashed across his face as they left Belle Rose early the next morning. I remember staring out my bedroom window as they were leaving, and he turned to stare up towards me. He kissed his fingers and held them up to me as he had done every time he ever left, as long as I can remember. I did not send a kiss back that time as had long been our practice. Instead, I let the curtain fall with no other response. It just about killed me but I was still so dad-blamed mad I did not fling up the window and call for him to stay while I prepared to take Bella and go with Lily and him to Indian Territory. Oh, foolish pride! Might I never make such a rash, impetuous decision again. I cringe to think of the pain I could have avoided less than a month later if I had gone with them.

What is it Sassy says? Oh, yes. Don't make permanent decisions based on temporary feelings. Some days, I am just as rash as she swears Richard can be.

But I digress.

On the morning of September 28th, 1781, Washington led his troops out from Williamsburg to surround Yorktown. Like Sassy predicted, the French took positions on the left of the city while the Americans took positions on the right. The French fleet had arrived, blockading the city from the York River and the Atlantic. In all, the allied French and American forces equaled 17,000. Cornwallis had but 9000 men. Washington had Yorktown surrounded by land and by sea. Washington had Cornwallis by the short hairs.

Cornwallis hoped to protect his position until British troops arrived from New York with seven redoubts and batteries that linked the narrows of the

York River at the Gloucester Point. The General explained to me that a redoubt is a tall, earthen fort or fort system. The tall wooden fence around the redoubt is called the abatis. Together, the redoubt and abatis comprise an enclosed defensive emplacement outside a larger fort, or in this case, the city of Yorktown. A deep ditch was dug before each timber wall. Those ditches were lined with felled trees with branches still attached, to slow down any assault on the redoubt. A typical redoubt will hold up to 100 men and is armed with cannon. Redoubts are meant to protect soldiers outside the main defensive line. The word means 'a place of retreat.'

Cornwallis had two months to prepare and was proud of the defenses he put into place in anticipation of the battle. "I am quite confident, Your Grace, that a ground attack on Yorktown is not feasible."

I must admit the defensive measures he had taken were quite impressive. I was pretty sure Washington's review of the area showed him a ground attack on Yorktown in and of itself would not work. Strong defenses or not, it was clear even to my uneducated eye that defenses alone would not win the forthcoming battle. If Clinton's troops did not get here on time, General Cornwallis's efforts were doomed, as Sassy claimed they were.

I remained silent, but I still figured in this case, 'redoubt' should mean 'a place of second thoughts about what you are doing', you know, like you are having a 're-doubt'. It's pretty sad I could spot that, but the so-called geniuses in the British military were convinced they had the winning hand.

That same day, Washington reconnoitered the British defenses and decided they could be bombarded into submission. Lord a'mercy, you cannot imagine the incessant caterwauling of the bombs bursting in the air all day long! I understand the Americans and French slept out in the open overnight watching the light show created by the flair of the bombs. The British officers guzzled gin and frolicked with Paddy's girls. Lord help us, Jesus! Well, you wait and see. Come October 19th, these same men would have no idea how or why they lost this war.

The next day, Washington moved his army closer to Yorktown. British gunners opened fire on the American infantry and fired cannons on them several times. There were a few casualties that day. In basic terms, it was men on both sides flexing their muscles in anticipation of the battle to come.

Calvin voiced surprise when Cornwallis pulled back from all his outer defenses except for the Fusilier's redoubt on the west side of town and redoubts 9 and 10 on the east side of town. Instead, Cornwallis had his men focus on the earthworks surrounding Yorktown. He received a letter from Clinton promising a relief force of 5,000 men within a week. Yeah, sure. I'll expect those troops when I can see the whites of their eyes here in Yorktown. In the meantime, Cornwallis knew he had to tighten his lines to hopefully manage to hold Yorktown until Clinton's men could arrive.

I am quite sure Charles Cornwallis would have been shocked by the comments Calvin made about Cornwallis's poor judgment in pulling back. Calvin claimed if he were the General, he could have trounced Washington well before Clinton's projected arrival.

I shook my head in dismay as word came back the Americans and French had occupied the abandoned defenses and began to establish their own batteries in those places. With the British outer defenses in their hands, the allies began laying out works for artillery and deepened their trenches. It was obvious to both Calvin and to me that Cornwallis was underestimating his enemy. Night after night, Cornwallis and his men and my husband reveled at Miss Paddington's Elite Gentlemen's Club (in other words, brothel) until the wee hours of the morning while the Americans continued to dig in deeper. Or as Marc said, the Brits were digging into something else.

On September 30th, the French attacked the British Fusiliers Redoubt. The skirmish lasted but two hours, and the British were quite excited the French were repulsed.

However, by then, malaria was sweeping through Yorktown. The tidewaters region has long been well known for being malarial. The American and French troops had not been in the tidewater long enough to have sickened yet. The men from the tidewaters area had some immunity to the disease, as did Calvin and I.

At the same time, Americans were cutting down thousands of trees to provide wood for earthworks. As the Americans and French put their artillery into place, the British kept up a steady, increasing fire on October 2nd. The allies suffered moderate casualties. I knew the allies had a hospital tent established where I figured Dr. Crait and Richard Winslow were working.

I was amazed Washington continued to make visits to the front. His officers were concerned about that but he was always quite fearless.

Washington swore God was on the side of the United States. He believed God would not let him fail. Sassy told me later Washington was convinced he would not die in battle. Sure enough, he survived Yorktown despite his continual acts of daring-do.

Cornwallis was awed by Washington's courage and tenacity. Rather than following his lead, Cornwallis went back to drinking at Miss Paddington's. However, on the night of October 3rd, the British opened a storm of fire to cover movement of the British cavalry to escort infantrymen on a foraging party.

That night, Colonel Tarleton led the foraging party out across the York River, over at Gloucester Point. It was unfortunate he collided with Lauzon's Legion, and John Mercer's militia, led by the Marquis de Choisy. The British were quick to retreat across the York River to behind their defensive lines, but not before they lost fifty much-needed men.

I could taste my disappointment. Butcher Ban was not among the dead.

The next day, crazy Colonel Tarleton ordered the slaughter of a thousand horses rather than ever let them fall into American hands. I always wondered if he did that to pay back Calvin over the stallion since the beautiful animal was one of the horses Tarleton slaughtered. The soldiers left the carcasses on the beach below the town. What a foolish waste! God knows days later we could have eaten the meat had it not been thrown out to rot. As it was, a number of the women, myself included, crept down to the beach right after dark to butcher as much horse meat as possible. We pragmatic women salvaged large chunks of horse flesh, which we smoked or salted to help preserve it. Several women commented how surprised they were a Duchess would help them to do such a thing. I announced I would prefer not to starve to death at Yorktown. Despite our best efforts, thousands of pounds of meat were wasted, left to ruin as we began to starve in the coming days.

At times, I wondered if Cornwallis's brain was rotting from excessive alcohol quicker than the horse meat rotted on the shoreline. The nauseating stench hung over the town like a miasma of hate, anger, and death. Calvin began to question Cornwallis's decision making more and more as these scenes continued. In hindsight, I reckon Cornwallis was plain and simple overwhelmed. The more overwhelmed he felt, the less he seemed able to make competent military decisions. And let's face it. At some point, he had to realize all was lost. He was fighting a losing battle. It was enough to make many strong men turn to drink.

By October 5th, Washington was almost ready to open the first parallel. That night, the sappers and miners worked strips of line on the wet sand to mark the path of the trenches. The next night, allied troops moved out in silence in stormy weather to dig the first parallel, hidden from British eyes by an overcast sky. The trench ran some 2000 yards, from the head of Yorktown to the York River. On the northernmost end of the French portion of the line, a support trench was dug to bombard the British ships in the harbor. The French distracted the British with a false attack, but the British were warned of the tactic by a French deserter. As a result, British artillery fire was turned on the French from the Fusiliers Redoubt.

By October 7th, the British could at last see the new allied trench. I brought some of the men dinners and was present as Cornwallis realized the allied trench was out of musket range. "Damned cowards! The sorry bastards are out of range, Calvin."

Calvin patted his friend on the back. "Fear not, Charles. We shall yet prevail against these yokel upstarts. Farmer Washington shall not prevail."

Cornwallis did not say anything. He shook his head and stared across at the allied line.

Over the next two days, the allies completed the gun placements and dragged their artillery into line. The British began to waver and weaken when they saw the large number of guns the allies had.

"I warned Clinton we needed to disarm these ruffians," Cornwallis muttered. "But oh, no, he insisted they are farmers, ill equipped, with little more than a few old muskets and pitchforks. Looks like a far sight more than a few old muskets to me."

"Fear not, Charles," Calvin responded. "Clinton promised us troops. They are due any time now, no later than the 12th. Have faith, old man. The troops will get here in time." He looked about, his eyes nervous in his survey of the allied forces. "They must. He promised."

Good luck with that one. God knew we needed those troops, but I had grave doubts God was rooting for Britain in this battle. And, as the old saying goes, if wishes were pounds sterling, paupers could be kings.

I was surprised when Calvin came by Mrs. Haggerty's house that evening. "I do wish you would reconsider and come to Miss Paddington's to be with me. I quite miss you, my darling. I long to be with you again. Please come back."

I stared at him in stunned surprise. "You miss me? I thought you said who wants a woman as big as a barn with a whelp in her belly? I do not want to disgust or embarrass you with my repulsive condition," I snapped, my head erect, as I ran my hands over my growing baby belly. I was determined not to ever be a victim again, of my husband or anyone else.

His cheeks turned red even as his lips thinned into an angry slash across his face. He raised his hand as if he might strike me. I bit back my instinct to cringe back from him. I steeled my backbone as I stood up to him. "Go ahead. Do it. Hit me. It seems to make you feel like a big man."

His hand stilled midway to my face. "That's a lie. A damnable lie, Fancy. You know I have never struck you once in your entire life. Just like it's a damned lie that I ever said you repulse me."

I tilted my head. Was it possible he did not remember striking me the last time we met? "Oh, indeed? Perhaps your memory's not what it used to be, old man."

I was sure he would hit me then. Instead, he grabbed me, pulling me to him. He ground his mouth against mine, shoving his tongue into my mouth. I balled my hands and began to pummel his shoulders, but he continued to plunder my mouth, and to grope me, until my fists opened and I pulled him closer to me. Soon, I was meeting him kiss for kiss, gasping with the passion he roused.

"Still think I'm too old?" he asked, his voice hoarse with desire.

"You talk too much. Show me you want me," I gasped, clinging to him.

Later, our passion spent, I realized what he had done. Not only had he managed to distract me, he managed to entice me to engage in marital congress with him, when the old fool had been making merry with Patrice Paddington's high-priced girls for days. I rolled over, and slipped from the bed, eager to wash myself of his essence and his scent. Dear God in heaven! What if he brought some vile disease from those women? What if it hurt my baby? Sweet Jesus, what have I done?

"I am delighted you have decided you'll move to Miss Paddington's tomorrow."

My head jerked back up at his words. "What?"

He smiled and bent to kiss my cheek. "Of course, you'll be coming back now."

"Calvin, I told you my concerns. Even Charles agrees I should not be there…"

"Nonsense!" I cringed as he shouted. "You are my wife. You shall do as I say. You shall come to Patrice's house tomorrow. Either of your own volition or dragged there if need be."

My heart racing, all I could think was the next night, the allies would shell Yorktown hot and heavy, focusing on the large house in the middle of town. I slipped my arms up to stroke his face. "Calvin, darling, please…"

His eyes went cold as the eyes of a snake as it encircles its prey. "Oh, my dear, you shall come, one way or another. Of course, it is up to you whether it be if your own volition or propelled by Colonel Tarleton." Trembling, I tried to pull back as I paled at his words. "Oh, the idea does not appeal? Then I urge you to come on your own. After all, as you know, Ban can be a bit rough when administering … discipline. I should hate to see him forced to discipline my beautiful bride."

I could not control the trembling that racked my body. My mouth was dry with fear as I gasped, "You wouldn't dare."

The smile did not reach his eyes. "Do you want to find out, my darling? Be there by midnight. Or suffer the consequences."

"Calvin…"

"Until tomorrow night, my darling," he said, with another hard kiss ground onto my mouth, before he wheeled around to depart.

I rubbed my lips and as he left the room. I thought I was the love of his life when we first wed. But more and more it seems nothing I do is good enough. I give him everything I have, and believe me, he takes it all and then some. But, unless it is sex when he wants it, he gives me less and less in return. I suppose he thinks 'giving' me the title of Duchess is all I somehow need or deserve when it was the last thing I ever wanted. Now, I suspect the title was his goal all along. After all, he says Daddy Jo talked to him when I was a baby about making me his heir, and I know Calvin started talking to Daddy Jo when I was little bitty about a possible betrothal.

Now, I feel so empty. I had hoped no one would ever make me feel this way ever again. Sweet Jesus, what will I do?

Chapter 7
Fancy, 1781

I didn't sleep well that night. I warned Fitz things might get dicey later. I explained my husband demanded I move to Paddington's or else he might have to enlist the assistance of Colonel Tarleton to 'discipline' me.

Fitz's young eyes sprung open wide in shock. "That will not happen. We were appointed by the General to protect you. Protect you we shall, even against Colonel Tarleton, if need be. Rest assured we shall protect you against any scoundrel who attempts to force you to that scandal-filled house of ill repute."

I stared at the young man before me, so much like both Marc and Will. I wondered again how on earth two people like Tamsin and Jay ever produced such a fine young man. And then it hit me. Both our Grandfathers were in him as well, with all of their starch and strength of character. And, Jay did not have a hand in raising my brother. My Grandfather Fitz Simmons was the male role model who raised him with my mother.

By dawn, I was dressed and at the British hospital tent. Both Lily and Marc looked surprised to see me there so early. Marc grabbed me into a bear hug and a kiss to my cheek, as my Guard assumed their positions around the tent. "What's goin' on, to have ye up at the crack of dawn?"

I told him what Calvin threatened. "I can't go," I whispered, as I struggled not to cry.

"Nay, ye'll not go, and he'd best not send Bloody Ban after my girl, or there will be Hell to pay," Marc growled.

"Indeed not, m'lord," Fitz said with steel in his young voice. "He'd best not send that man or anyone else for that matter after my sister."

Marc clapped Fitz on the shoulder. "Thank God you're here, lad. 'Tis a blessing indeed you're at Yorktown. Now, we must plan how best to protect our sweet Fancy girl."

They slipped away with several other of my Guard to make ready their plans.

To say it was a hectic day would be a gross understatement. All the French and American guns were now in place. Word was out that among the American and French guns were three twenty-four pounders, three eighteen pounders, two eight-inch howitzers, and six mortars. At 3 that afternoon, the French commenced their barrage, driving the British frigate, the *HMS Guadeloupe*, across the York River. I was shocked to see the British scuttle the *Guadeloupe* although I understood they did it to prevent her from being captured by the French. The French and Americans then commenced to rip apart the British defenses. Even though I knew it was coming, and as exciting as it was to see the Americans winning, it was still heartbreaking to see the British trounced so thoroughly. After all, I'd been a British citizen all my life. I was a Countess by marriage and was now a Duchess in my own right as well. My emotions were complicated, to say the least.

The allied guns fired throughout the night. The barrage was so heavy that the British were unable to make repairs. Midnight came and went, with no one coming to drag me to Paddington's. Of course, British soldiers were dropping like flies and many others were deserting under the relentless onslaught from the French and Americans. Some of the British ships were damaged by the cannon balls flying across Yorktown into the harbor. My Guard and I stayed at the hospital tent all night and into the next morning as more and more wounded were brought for emergency care ranging from gun shots, to broken limbs and horrific burns. It was also considered to be the safest place in Yorktown, although that wasn't saying much.

And I thought the town stank from the rotting horseflesh? Ha! Add to that the smells of charred human flesh and rotting corpses. It grew worse by the minute, as did the hoard of flies feeding on the carrion.

I know first hand what Hell smells like. It smells like the Battle of Yorktown.

I thought I would about die the first time I saw Lily saw a man's leg off. I'll never forget that poor man's agonized screams as she removed his shattered limb. Somehow, I survived and managed to help her through that amputation as well as many more in the days to follow. If I live to be a hundred, I will never forget the screams of men and boys undergoing amputations in the hospital tent at Yorktown, with nothing more to ease their pain that a stick between their teeth as I held their hands.

By morning, I was so exhausted that it was all I could do to stand between helping Lily with men sick with malaria and men injured in the fighting. When I began to sway to and fro, Lily insisted I lay down on an empty cot. With Fitz standing guard beside me, I fell into a sleep so sound that even the incessant shelling of Yorktown did not disturb my much-needed slumber. While I slept, some of my Guard returned to Mrs. Haggerty's to fetch my belongings at the urging of Marc and Lily. Knowing my husband's nefarious plan to force me to heel, the men were quick to bring my belongings back to the hospital tent before Tarleton or anyone else came hunting for me.

I remained at the hospital tent much of the time for the duration of the siege, and I was never left alone by my Guard. I could not have asked for a more loyal or fearless group of young men to protect me.

And then, it happened exactly the way Sassy foretold. That evening, the Americans began shelling Miss Paddington's house, burning it to cinders in minutes. The cannon balls were heated until red and then fired into Yorktown. A heated ball from Washington's eighteen-pound cannon crashed into Patrice Paddington's establishment, where officers were eating dinner, among other things. Washington was correct in his assessment that Cornwallis was staying there, like I had warned my husband. Soon, our men were being brought in with injuries from the bombardment of the town and Paddy's Place as hundreds of cannon blasts bombed the town. Lily and I knelt in the tent, our hands clasped, praying we be allowed to survive the burning hell all around us. I understand some thirty-six thousand rounds a day were falling on Yorktown at that point. The noise and the danger from the missiles never ended. Believe me, I would have escaped if escape had been possible. Since it was not possible for me to escape, I prayed without stopping as I worked in the hospital tent with Lily.

And, then to make matters even worse, smallpox broke out. It was fortunate Lily inoculated me against the dreaded disease years before when I was a child. However, inoculations were still new, and many were afraid to have them. As a result, so many brave souls were struck down with the dreaded disease even as our food supplies dwindled to next to nothing.

Cornwallis then sank more than a dozen of his ships in the harbor. He said he was ensuring the French could not take the vessels, but I always wondered if he were intoxicated or if he had been eating opium when he ordered that. It was such a strange thing to do. I just shook my head in horror at the wanton destruction.

The French then began to fire on the British ships. The *HMS Charon* caught fire, and in turn, set other ships on fire. By afternoon, it was clear the British could not have escaped by ship if they tried. Their fleet was destroyed.

Sometime during the day, Cornwallis received word the British fleet would depart New York for Yorktown on the 12th. Cornwallis admitted he was unsure if we could hold out much longer. Our situation became more desperate by the hour.

On the night of October 11th, the Americans dug a second parallel 400 yards closer to the British lines. They could not extend the new parallel to the river because British Redoubts 9 and 10 were in the way. Throughout the night, the British fired over the new line, of which the British were unaware, since they were firing at the old parallel. In the process, they wasted much needed ammunition. By the morning of the 12th, Cornwallis was horrified to discover French and American allied troops were in position in the new parallel line.

By the 12th, our situation was dire. Our food stuffs were in short supply. Supplies were utterly cut off. Men began to complain that they could have eaten the horse flesh had the horses not been slaughtered and left to rot two weeks earlier. As the men grew hungrier, tempers grew shorter. The Americans had the British troops sniping at each other as much as against the French and Americans as we began to starve to death.

Lily told me a human can live without air for three minutes, without water for 3 days, and without food for 3 weeks. At that point, we were into the second week with little to no food.

Plus, by then, many of the British troops were sick with malaria in addition to smallpox. Those of us who grew up on the coast knew once you have malaria, you were not likely to catch it again for some time. If it didn't kill you. You might have occasional bouts of fevers and chills afterwards, but you would not catch the disease as bad again. I would have reckoned Cornwallis and his men from the Carolinas had suffered malaria in the past. However, many of the new recruits, including several of my Irish Guard, were new to the Tidelands. They were all stricken with the deadly disease. Soon, Lily fretted we were losing as many men to malaria as to fighting in the trenches. Malaria, smallpox, starvation, combined with the losing side in the war did not make for pleasant surroundings. Yorktown stank to high heaven of disease and death.

And Clinton's damned promised troops still had not arrived. I could tell Cornwallis was on the edge of despair.

On October 14th, we received word the parallel trenches were within 150 yards of Redoubts 9 and 10. The French and Americans began blasting the Redoubts without ceasing in order to weaken the Redoubts for an evening assault.

"Now what?" I asked Marc.

"The British cannot hold out much longer, *mo leannan*," he responded with a shake of his head. Like myself, he yearned for our brave new country to be free, while it still hurt to see Britain failing.

Did I say hurt? It damned near broke my heart.

Redoubt 10 was nearest the river. It held 70 men. Redoubt 9 was a quarter mile inland. It still held 120 British and German troops. Both had heavy fortifications with rows of abatis, obstructions formed from tree branches with the sharpened tops directed towards the Americans and French. General Washington, who in my humble opinion was grossly underestimated by the British, had the French launch a diversionary attack on the Fusiliers Redoubt on the other side of town. A half hour later, the French assaulted Redoubt 9 with 400 French regulars, under the command of Colonel Wilhelm von Zweibrucken. The Americans assaulted Redoubt 10 with 400 light Infantry under the command of Alexander Hamilton, Washington's aide de camp.

At 6:30 that evening, we heard gunfire as the French attacked the Fusiliers Redoubt. Movements were made as if the allies were preparing to attack Yorktown itself. This caused general pandemonium as the British panicked. I pinched Marc several times to stop him from laughing. "Stop it," I warned.

General Washington sent the 400 Americans who would take Redoubt 10 with his quiet encouragement, prayers, and best wishes. The Marquis de Lafayette and Lt. Col. Alexander Hamilton led the foray. Lafayette wanted a more experienced American in charge but Washington insisted this battle was

Hamilton's. He sent William along to be Hamilton's second in command, knowing Will had ample battlefield and leadership experience. The Americans then marched on Redoubt 10. Hamilton also sent troops to the rear of the Redoubt to prevent the British from escaping. The Americans reached the Redoubt and began chopping through the abatis with their axes. Gunfire was exchanged, and the Americans charged, their bayonets aimed at the Redoubt. They hacked through the abatis and climbed the parapet into the Redoubt through great shell holes from the bombardment.

About that time, I understand a tall, handsome Belle Rose officer, reported to have once been a Duke of the Realm, shouted, "Rush on, boys! The fort is ours!" How I wish I could have heard his call to arms!

The British threw hand grenades at the American troops with little effect. They still had not yet realized God was on the side of the Americans. As men in the trenches climbed on the shoulders of their comrades to climb into the Redoubt, the Americans took the Redoubt 10. Almost the entire garrison of 70 British soldiers was captured. The American's casualties numbered 9 dead and 25 wounded. I was relieved to hear Will came through it with nothing but a minor wound. I prayed it would not become septic like Tom's wound did at Saratoga.

The French assault on Redoubt 9 began at the same time. It was slower going because the abatis had not been damaged by artillery fire. As the French began hacking at the abatis, a Hessian sentry called out, inquiring who was there. When no response was forthcoming, the Hessians opened fire on the French as they poured over the walls of the Redoubt. The French fired back and managed to drive the Germans back. The Hessians then assumed a defensive stance behind some barrels. They soon threw down their arms as the French commenced a bayonet charge. I would have enjoyed seeing those pompous Hessians surrender to the French!

Washington then began shelling Yorktown itself from three directions. He moved some of his men into the Redoubts they had won that day. It was a long, frightening, noisome night with little sleep and frayed nerves.

Before sunrise on the 15th of October, a sober and very angry Cornwallis turned all his guns onto the nearest allied position. He sent a storming party of 350 men under Col. Abercrombie to attack both the French and Americans. They were given specific orders to spike the French and American cannons.

The French and American troops were caught sleeping, ill prepared for the pre-morning assault. However, Abercrombie's foolish, ill-timed cry to his men to "skin the bastards" awoke slumbering soldiers and enabled them to go to the defense. The British managed to spike six cannons. Cornwallis was disgusted later to realize all six cannons were repaired by the time the sun arose for another long day of battle.

Worse yet, Clinton's troops still had not arrived. French ships still blockaded the harbor. The British troops could not have landed to help if they had showed up and tried to land. The situation for the British was beyond dire.

Cornwallis talked with Calvin and his most trusted officers. Calvin informed me in hushed tones that Cornwallis was terrified he was about to lose all to the Americans. On the morning of the 16th, as the American fire intensified, Cornwallis ordered the evacuation of his remaining British troops across the York River to Gloucester Point. He hoped the British could get across to the Point. If they could, the troops might be able to break through the allied lines and escape to elsewhere in Virginia and perhaps they could get back to New York. One wave of boats made it across. But an autumn storm erupted with heavy squalls. Further evacuation proved impossible.

And that was when I received the summons from Cornwallis. My husband had sustained mortal injuries in the attempted evacuation to Gloucester Point. Of course, Calvin just went off and left his pregnant wife in the midst of the battle. Lily, Marc and I ran to the harbor, where we found my old man struggling to hang on. Lily tried to perform something she called triage, but Calvin told her to stop. "You and I both know you can't do anything to save me, Lily. Work on men you can save. Besides, I need to talk to Fancy."

When Lily nodded, I knew my worst fears were confirmed. Calvin was dying from blood loss after he took the shell that shattered his leg.

"It looks … like you … were right, my darling," he gasped as I held his hand to my cheek, slick with tears. "No, dearest, don't cry. I … I have to … tell you something…"

"No, Calvin, it will be all right. You'll see. Lily can patch you up," I demurred, even as Lily shook her head at me.

He tried to smile, but winced with pain. "Too much time with Sassy, my love. You lie almost as well as she does. No, listen to me. If the babe lives, don't name him Calvin. I hate my name."

That surprised me. I remembered how he huffed up when Richard commented on his name. "What would you have me name him?"

"Charles Thomas," he whispered. "But there is more. Bella… is my daughter. If … anything … happens to this babe…"

"Nothing is going to happen to our baby, Calvin. And I know you love her like she is your own. You always have…"

"Shush, my darling." He was gasping for air, as his words began to slur more and more. "Let me finish. I done … you wrong, girl. Tom and I both did. That last time I … came before he left. Damned fool wouldn't let us marry until you turned 18."

"Don't try to talk, darling." Tears were streaming down my face as I clung to my old man. He might not be perfect, I thought, but he's mine and he loves me. And now I'm going to lose him.

He shook his head, frowning with pain coupled with impatience. "Fancy, you must … listen. He let me give you a sleeping potion. He told me how. And when you were like a drunk, you became very…"

And then, I felt the old, familiar topsy-turvy sensation of my dreams. I gasped, horror in my voice, as I grabbed his hands. "No. Tell me you didn't. Please, Calvin, tell me you didn't."

Why, God? Why did he have to tell me this? Why? Tears streamed down my face, as my body shook, racked with sobs.

His lips now blue, he somehow managed to move his hand to my face. "Don't cry, my darling. I … I loved you for such a long time. I told you that night I loved you, that I would come back … for you. That we would wed."

"I know," I gasped, nodding, as I trembled at the memory of my topsy-turvy dreams.

"You will never know… how much … it meant when … you told … me you loved me, that night. Oh, my darling, I am … so cold. Why am I … so cold?" his voice cracked, the words not even a whisper.

I laid down beside him, hoping to give him some bit of comfort as he lay there dying. After all, I could not tell him I thought it was Tom that night, at last telling me he loved me. Or that it was Tom to whom I was telling my innermost feelings, sure at last my first love was pledging to somehow marry me upon his return.

"But how? I asked. How could we marry? And you said, I'll take you away and make you my bride, my darling. I promise."

"You do remember." He struggled to smile. "She's mine, Fancy. I … I love you so much. I knew … someday you … would remember. I had to tell you … before I go…"

And then, in a flash, the light was gone from his eyes. My old man was gone.

I cried and cried. For my lost childhood. For the man now dead beside me, who had just confessed a horrible crime 'in the name of love.' How can men justify rape in the name of love? I will never understand how they justify that evil deed in their minds. I cried because now I understood my topsy-turvy dreams. I cried because Tom never loved me. Because I trusted the wrong man with my love, not once, but twice. I cried because both men I loved were monsters. And I cried because I knew I was broken, shattered beyond repair. How could I ever trust myself to love again, after I gave my love to those two monsters?

How could I love anyone else? How could anyone love me?

When at last I arose, drenched in my husband's own life's blood, I reached into Lily's pack for one of her cards she used to find out what blood types people had. I wiped some of his blood onto one of the cards. His was B positive.

Like my Bella.

I still sobbed when Lily and Marc pulled me away from him and took me back to the medical tent. My Irish lads surrounded me, determined to keep me safe. Lily hummed an Irish lullaby Marc taught her years ago while she stroked my hair. I remember Mama Belle used to do that when I was little. No one else besides Mama Belle and Lily ever stroked my hair like that, all sweet and loving. My mother never did that, but then, I can't remember her ever kissing me either.

When I awoke the next morning, there was a message the General needed me. I managed to pull off my filthy gown, sponge away most of my husband's blood, and change into a clean, presentable gown. Lily, Marc and my Guard accompanied me to the General. He sat alone in a darkened tent that had replaced Paddy's establishment for his home away from home.

"Your Grace, I am so sorry…" he began, and then his voice cracked. "I have a letter Calvin left here with me to give you … just in case."

Numb, I reached out for the sealed envelope and slipped it into my pocket.

I would read it later when things were not so hectic and when I had some privacy. Maybe back at Belle Rose. "Thank you, General. He asked me to name the baby Charles, after you, if you don't mind."

He smiled. "Not at all, my dear. I would be honored to have a future Duke named after me." He looked bleak. "I have failed the Crown. I have failed you. Many a fine man has died here. Our situation is …hopeless."

"I understand, Charles. What can we do to help you?"

I sat down beside the British commander of Yorktown and helped him write his letter of surrender. When it was finished, Marc, Lily, Fitz and I all witnessed it.

"Can you take it to him, Lady Fancy? I know it's a lot to ask of you. But I don't think I can manage it."

It was then I realized he was ill. I noticed his face was pale and he was sweating something horrible. I reached over and was shocked at how hot he was. "Lily, you need to check the General. He's burning up with fever."

With a look of alarm, she was quick to assess General Cornwallis. "Malaria, General. You cannot take the letter yourself. We will make sure it gets to General Washington."

He nodded, and then slumped back in his camp chair. "Thank you," he croaked.

Two hours later, on the morning of October 17th, I walked through Yorktown, towards the lines. The town reeked of rotting bodies, not just of the dead horses, but of those brave and valiant British soldiers who died in this hideous battle. The bodies were left behind to rot where they fell. There was not time and not enough extra hands to inter their remains. Lily voiced concern that the hideous conditions made the town ripe for camp fever or epidemic typhus. Cases of camp fever were being reported. The sounds I remember beyond the never-ending blasts of war were the caws of crows as they pecked at the corpses of the dead. That scene and the overwhelming stench of death are etched in my memory forever. I lived through Hell at Yorktown. I would not wish to forget what Hell looks and smells like. God knows we all lived through Hell during those awful weeks there.

Right at 10 a.m., a twelve-year-old drummer boy marched in front of my brother, who carried a white flag. The young drummer tapped out the tune recognized to be a request for parlay. The white flag held by Fitz was the international sign to request a truce. I suspect the flag more than the drummer's tune was what caused the men on both sides of the line to hold their fire. I am not sure they could hear the rat-a-tat-tat of the drummer's tune over the sounds of shelling.

I followed a few feet behind, with Lily and Marc on each side of me. They had to help hold me up. I felt faint with exhaustion. I wore a dark blue, modest, silk gown stripped bare of engageants and fripperies, with a sheer linen fichu at my neckline. I held a perfumed handkerchief to my nose, hoping it would somehow help to allay the overwhelming stench of death all around me. I thought of tying it around my face, but I was pretty sure I would never get to Washington looking like a highwayman. The bombardment ceased as an American officer ran to us. We were blindfolded before we were taken behind the American lines to Washington. Once the blindfolds were removed, I spoke on behalf of Britain.

"Your Excellency," I began, my voice trembling with emotion, "As the Duchess of Ranscome, I am told I am the highest ranked British subject in Yorktown. Mind, it is not a rank I wanted, and it is a rank I was most reluctant to assume. However, now I have been appointed to tender to your hands General Cornwallis's written surrender this morning. You will notice he signed it in the presence of myself, as well as Lord and Lady Fitz Simmons, who are with me, and Leftenant Fitz Simmons, my brother, who is also here with me. Lady Liliana Fitz Simmons is an excellent healer and advises us General Cornwallis is quite ill with malaria. Congratulations, General Washington. You have won. I believe the war is effectively ended with the delivery of this document to your hands." I handed him the General's missive.

I knew Cornwallis's written surrender proposed a cessation of hostilities during which officers appointed from both sides would settle the actual terms of surrender of the posts of York and Gloucester to the Americans.

Washington's smile was tight, his features grave. "I agree, Lady Fancy, as long as it is understood, I and I alone shall dictate the terms of surrender. They shall be my terms and mine alone, or we shall continue to fight this battle to the bitter end."

Fitz blinked, surprised by the case-hardened steel in the voice of the American Commander-in-Chief. I don't know what the lad expected, but apparently, a voice hard as a honed Damascus blade had not been envisioned.

Fitz gave a short bow, clicking his heels together, and answered, "Of course, General Washington. We would expect nothing else, Your Excellency."

Washington gave a slight nod. I think he was pleased Fitz had the presence of foresight to address him as General and Your Excellency. Lily, Marc and I had stressed Fitz must be respectful of Washington and his rank. The British snubbed Washington far too long, refusing to address him as General. I often heard Cornwallis and Calvin refer to him as 'that presumptuous Farmer Washington.'

And then, it hit me. The British were surrendering four years to the day after Gentleman Johnny Burgoyne surrendered to the Americans at the Battle of Saratoga. Four years to the day since Tom died there, one of the last men wounded at that awful battle. My damned fool brother died of a paltry scratch Lily says went septic. Overwhelmed, I swayed, darkness welling up all around me as I slid to the earth in a dead faint.

Chapter 8
Fancy, 1781

Needless to say, I was not the one to negotiate the terms. There were experienced military strategists to negotiate the terms for both sides.

I regained consciousness in the American medical tent. Richard was frantic as he slapped my wrists and patted my face. "Francesca, wake up! Francesca!"

"Her name is Lady Hobbs, sir. She is the Duchess of Ranscome," I heard Fitz answer, his voice stiff with outrage at the presumed offense of the unknown American man touching me in such a familiar manner.

"Well, duh, I would never have guessed," Richard snapped.

"Oh, hush, you two," I fussed. "Enough of your caterwauling. Dr. Richard Winslow, this is my brother, Leftenant Winston Fitz Simmons. Fitz, this is Dr. Richard Winslow, my sister-in-law's adopted son, and my … my dear friend."

Both men looked askance but stopped their fussing.

I realized General Washington hovered beside my bed. "General, don't you have more important things to do right now than worry about me?"

"My dear, I have known you most of your life. My Patsy thinks of you as a daughter. She would most likely horsewhip me if I did not see to it that you are well."

About then, both Will and Sassy rushed in. I chuckled as Sassy began fussing in rapid fire, mile-a-minute Spanish. Will knelt down beside me. His concern was evident in the worry lines marring his handsome features. "Been through a tough time of it, baby girl?"

I tried to smile, but before I could control it, I started to cry. "He's dead, Will."

Sassy plopped down on the ground beside me. "Are you sure, Fancy?"

I nodded. "Yep, pretty much. He died in my arms. Took a shell to his leg that shattered the bone. Lily said he bled to death. I …I… I've seen men die since this war started, but I never saw anything like that before."

I laid my head over against Sassy as I sobbed.

I couldn't tell them. How could I? Lily found the Aldon Card with Calvin's blood. She understood what it revealed about the true parentage of Bella. I swore her to secrecy. I could not bear for anyone else to know what he told me that awful day as he lay dying.

The Articles of Capitulation were signed on October 19th by Washington, Rochambeau, the Comte de Barras on behalf of the French Navy, Cornwallis, and British Captain Thomas Symonds, the senior British naval officer at Yorktown. The British soldiers were declared prisoners of war. The enlisted men were assured they would receive good treatment in American prisoner of war camps. Officers were assured they would be allowed to return home after they were paroled, although all nine of my men who survived Yorktown were turned over to Will as were Lily, Marcus and I. We were never taken as prisoners of war, thanks be to God.

At 2 pm, the allied army entered the British positions, with the French again on the left and the Americans on the right. Washington requested I read the Articles of Capitulation to the troops since Cornwallis was still far too ill to attend the formal surrender. I remember my knees knocking and my hands trembling as I stood reading the Articles, but I do not remember much of what I read.

I wore a dark blue wool riding habit. I didn't have a black gown and it was the darkest gown I brought with me. I covered my hair with a linen cap and a demure, dark blue bonnet. In contrast, Sassy wore the red, white, and blue riding habit she wore in '80 to testify before Congress, with a delightful, outrageous bonnet with tall, red feathers. Yes, we planned our ensembles together before we came. The only thing I wore different than planned was Tamsin's chatelaine, which hung from my waist.

The British asked for traditional honors of war. That would have allowed them to march out with the Union Jack flying, their bayonets fixed, and the band playing an American or French tune as tribute to the victors. Washington, still smarting from years of the English refusing to acknowledge him as the

Commander-in-Chief of the American forces, refused to allow the traditional honors. He commented the British did not afford the Americans traditional honors when the British took Charleston the year before. Weapons would be shouldered and colors cased. Sassy whispered, "Payback is a real mother f—r, isn't it?"

The British and Hessian troops then marched past the stand with their flags furled and their muskets shouldered. They appeared dour, even peevish, with their faces taut with anger and humiliation. Since Washington said they could play an English or German tune, the band played a British tune. With a start, I realized they were surrendering to the tune called 'The World Turn'd Upside Down.'

Yes, the world did seem to be turned upside down that day. I could understand their choice.

British Brigadier General Charles O'Hara led the surrendering army onto the field. At first, he tried once more to snub Washington by offering his sword to Rochambeau. I could not believe his nerve! I swear, my hands itched to reach out and slap the snot out of the damned fool. Rochambeau frowned, shook his head, and pointed to Washington. Washington, in a pique, then refused the sword as well, and indicated O'Hara should tender the sword to Benjamin Lincoln. Stunned by the whole debacle, I stood there, mouth agape. I had pretty much decided the whole thing was going to hell in a hand basket until Lincoln, Washington's second-in-command, finally accepted the sword from O'Hara, who was Cornwallis's deputy.

"I thought the whole thing was going to fall apart," I whispered to Sassy.

She gave that sexy little shrug she does so well. "I knew Lincoln would accept it from O'Hara." I struggled not to laugh as she winked at me.

At that point, the British troops were to march out to lay down their weapons between the American and French forces. As each officer came past, I thanked the man for his service. Some were polite and surrendered their weapons with grace, like true Englishmen. Others acted in anger, throwing their weapons down so hard that their weapons shattered. One man commented the damned rebels would not be using his musket against his fellow Englishmen. I told him that was quite enough, and he needed to comport himself like a British officer, not like some fool hooligan. It was appalling. Their boorish manners were unbecoming of British soldiers when they comported themselves like this in anger. It embarrassed and upset me to see them act that way.

Sassy then advised the officers which Yorktown family would be feeding them dinner that evening and housing them until they would be transferred to New York. From New York, the officers would be paroled home. Most thanked her, although I noticed a few, still taut with rage, acted as if they did not hear her. Fine. Do without supper then if you are that stubborn. Some of Tarleton's men leered at her until I corrected them with a sharp word. They cut angry eyes at me, but each straightened up at the sharp correction from the Duchess of Ranscome.

We proceeded through all the men, until one jaunty, cocksure Colonel stood before us.

"Mr. Tarleton, you have not been invited to either dine or stay with a single family in Yorktown," Sassy began. "It appears your well-earned reputation precedes you."

It was the one time I ever recall Ban Tarleton look rattled.

"What did you say, Mrs. Selk?"

Sassy's smile was tight. She had bright red spots on her cheeks, and her eyes shone with unshed tears. I knew this had to be hard on her, but she was determined to do it. "Not. One. Family. No one will house you with their wives and daughters. It seems, Mr. Tarleton, that your reputation precedes you."

He whipped his head towards me. "Surely you can do something, your Grace…"

"No."

He looked shocked, paling at my word. "But, why, Duchess?"

I took a deep breath, and handed him a sheet of paper on which a number of charges were cited against Tarleton. His eyes began to scan down the sheet. He paled even more to a deathly grey as he saw the names of numerous women who made formal complaints that he raped them. It was rare for his hands to shake, but they shook as he realized the document was signed by General Washington, General Rochambeau and General Cornwallis. I knew this was one of Washington's terms to accept the surrender. Tarleton did not know that. Two American soldiers then came up from each side of Tarleton and clasped him into irons.

"Because, Mr. Tarleton, you are a horrible disgrace as a British officer and you are no gentleman. You are being taken into custody, to be transported to Philadelphia to stand trial for these war crimes of which you stand accused. Guards, please take this … this creature by the agreed orders from Generals Washington, Rochambeau, and Cornwallis." As his mouth curled into an ugly snarl, I said, "You didn't think you could get away with it, did you?"

"You little cu…"

"You didn't really think you would get away with raping Mrs. Selk, did you, Tarleton? In the presence of a Duchess of the Realm? Well, you remember, sir, you are … nothing. In fact, you are less than nothing. And by the way, you will *never* get your filthy hands on Belle Rose Plantation or any other Plantation in these United States of America. Or on me, you pathetic, sorry excuse for a human being. Take this worthless rubbish away, guards."

I realized I was shaking as he was dragged away, yelling curses and vile threats at me.

"Did he really say that?" Sassy whispered, her eyes large as saucers.

Grim faced, I nodded. "Yes, I believe he just threatened to rape me, skin me, and leave me for dead," I whispered, shaken to my core by his angry words.

She shivered despite the heat. "Jesus, I knew the man was crazy, but…"

"Sorry little bastard better stay away from my girl," Marc muttered, as he pulled me into his arms. "Or I'll kill him with my own two hands."

Later, it was confirmed the French casualties were 60 killed and 194 wounded. Among the Americans, 28 brave souls were killed, and 301 wounded. Among the dead would soon be added John Parke Custis, Washington's stepson who was known to all as Jacky. Lily said Jacky died of malaria, but Richard swears it was epidemic typhus. I tend to agree with him. A man raised in the Tidewaters would be unlikely to succumb to malaria at 26. After lengthy discussions, they agreed the final diagnosis would be noted as 'camp fever', which covers a number of illnesses.

I met Jacky Custis when I stayed at Mount Vernon when Bella was born. He was a handsome and charming young man who was a mere 26 years old at the time of his death. I know it must have about killed poor Patsy that her last living child died as a result of his participation in the last major battle of the war. It made her no difference if he died from malaria, epidemic typhus, camp fever, or anything else. Her son was dead. That was all that mattered.

I don't know if I could bear to go on if I outlived my child. And with the death of Jacky, poor Patsy had outlived all four of her children.

Will suffered a minor injury taking Redoubt 9, but he was healing well. He was fortunate Sassy knew to keep it clean. His scratch did not become septic, as his brother's injury did four years earlier.

The official British report listed casualties as 156 killed, 326 wounded, and 70 missing. We figured those 70 included some who came over to the American side, and others who slipped away into the night. Deserters. Sassy said some Hessians walked off, disgusted with the way Cornwallis mismanaged the troops. Lily says her father's ancestor was a Hessian who walked off in disgust from Yorktown. Cornwallis surrendered 7,087 officers and enlisted men and capitulated another 840 British sailors who were in the York River. Sassy said German accounts would cite the higher numbers of 309 killed and 595 wounded among the British.

It was ironic the fleet long promised by Clinton arrived on October 24th. Admiral Thomas Graves was advised by deserters Cornwallis had been forced to surrender days earlier. When he saw the French fleet, he left without attempting a landing. He could see he was outnumbered by nine French ships. He then sent the British fleet back to New York.

Sassy says when the British Prime Minister learned of Cornwallis's surrender, he exclaimed, "Dear Lord, it is all over!" He was reported to have hung his head and said, "My brave soldiers at Yorktown never had a chance when Clinton failed to get the fleet there before the arrival of the French fleet. Cornwallis had too few men and too few supplies. We gave him … Too little. Too late."

However, King George was another matter. Furious over the surrender by Cornwallis, it took almost two years for the king to capitulate to the desires of his people and accept the United States of America was a sovereign entity no longer owned nor ruled by Britain.

After Yorktown, Washington made a trip home to Mount Vernon to console dear Patsy over Jacky's death before he moved his army to New Windsor, New York. Dr. Franklin began negotiations in Paris. Franklin had been in Paris since 1776. He was in large part responsible for the assistance the French gave the States resulting in the win at Yorktown. Although fighting continued on the high seas, Yorktown ended the fighting in the American colonies. The formal Treaty of Paris ended the war almost two years later on

September 3, 1783.

We got back to Belle Rose at the end of October. As we rode along in comfort in the Belle Rose carriage, we passed a line of British soldiers, now prisoners of war, walking to their prison camp. It would be a long walk to Pennsylvania. Better them than me. And then, I sat up a little straighter as I realized we were passing Tarleton. Not so cocky without your fancy hat and high stepping horse, are you, sorry little worm?

I didn't say anything. Sassy lay curled up on the other bench, snoring as she slept. Lily sat beside me, reading something or other about the healing properties of various plants used by what she calls indigenous Americans. She smiled when I asked her what that meant and told me Richard brought her some books about Cherokee herbal cures. How she can bear to read such boring things I will never know. Give me a good romance any day!

I pulled out the letter Calvin wrote to me, in case he was killed at Yorktown, to read it on the way home. It was a long, detailed missive. Holy Sweet Jesus, I thought I would about die as I began to read it. Nothing could have prepared me for the horrifying details in which he spelled out how he had Tom 'train' me to be a good wife someday. Mortified, my mind reeling, my hands trembling, I slipped the letter to Lily. I felt like I used to feel when Tom abused me, like I was looking down on the scene, that it wasn't quite real. Lily calls that 'disassociation.' Well, I reckon it was an excellent time to disassociate. I could tell by the look of revulsion marring her face as she perused the letter that she was plum dab mortified, too.

"We can't ever tell Marc and Will, Lily. It would kill them both," I whispered.

She nodded. "Neither Marc nor Will shall learn from me of the way both Tom and Calvin abused you for all those horrible years. And both were complicit, even though Tom was responsible for the greater bulk of the abuse you endured. Calvin encouraged it and enabled it to happen. He also participated in at least some of the abuse. My poor darling, I promise I won't tell them."

She understood. More important, she wasn't telling me it was my fault. I have wished Lily was my real mother most of my life. She was more like a mother than Tamsin had ever been to me. I laid my head over on her shoulder and shed silent tears most of the way home. Lily sat there, again stroking my hair, silent, as I cried my poor, aching heart out. There were no words she could have offered that would have meant more to me than her gentle touch did.

Daddy Jo refused to betroth me to Calvin when I was a child. He felt I was far too young to be betrothed at age 4, or even at 10. He insisted we wait to see if we suited one another when I was older, closer to marriageable age. Maybe Calvin didn't pass what Sassy calls the 'smell test.' And maybe Daddy Jo thought the future Duchess of Ranscome could make a better match than an Earl, never before married, who was 35 years older than me. Maybe I will know someday what Daddy thought when we meet again in the Sweet Bye and Bye.

When we arrived at Belle Rose, Hattie Mae had a big dinner ready for us. I couldn't eat despite Sassy tempting me with foods she knew I love. Fried chicken, mashed potatoes, fresh peach pie, even fried pickles. Lordy, I do love fried pickles! I couldn't even eat one that night. Nothing looked appealing. I felt sick to my stomach. I don't think I ate more than a couple of bites of anything that night.

I began to tremble at the least little thing. I figured I was losing my mind. I cried enough to fill another river the size of the poor, polluted York. I didn't trust anyone to be alone with my precious Bella, not even Sassy or Lily. I even yelled at Uncle Tobias when he swung Bella up into his arms to give her a kiss. I was relieved they all thought it was combination of exhaustion coupled with Calvin's death. Lily and Richard both talked about something called 'PTSD', which Lily explained meant 'shell shock'. It was an easy excuse. God knows I was in a state of shock. Who wouldn't be in shock to learn your brother and your husband plotted and conspired to abuse you for years?

We interred Calvin in the family cemetery the day after we arrived. He always wanted Belle Rose. Well, now he had his own little bitty plot of Belle Rose soil, his for all eternity. Every once in a while, I walk across his grave and make sure to kick a little dirt at his face. I spit on it now and then, too. I don't reckon I will ever get over this anger.

Everyone seemed to expect my quiet and tears at first. But as the days passed, and still I wept, overwhelmed, disconsolate and angst-ridden, their looks became more and more worried. Finally, Sassy approached the subject one morning as we sipped hot chocolate and we ate croissants in the parlor. Let's face it. It would take a lot to kill my appetite for chocolate or croissants.

"Fancy, I know you are grieving. But we are worried about you. Is there anything we can do to help you?"

I stared out the window before answering, the croissant poised in my hand half-way to my mouth. I dropped the chocolate-filled pastry back to the plate uneaten. My hands were shaking too hard to even eat a fresh baked, chocolate croissant. There was no way I could tell her why I was so upset without everyone knowing. I love her like a sister, and she is my dearest friend. She has helped me through some real rough times. But she has a big mouth, and I had no doubt she would go straight to William in horror and blurt out anything I told her about Tom and Calvin if I confided in her. That could not happen. I never wanted Will to know those awful things. I shook my head even as the tears began to well in my eyes yet again. "No, Sassy. This is something I have to deal with on my own."

She reached over to take my hand. "But, honey, we're worried about you and the effect this may have on your baby…"

I arose so fast I knocked the pretty blue and white Dutch chocolate pot over. "You don't understand, Sassy. I can't talk about it."

I bent to pick up the chocolate pot and to begin to clean the spilt chocolate off the floor. Sassy bent beside me and gathered my shaking hands into hers. "Honey, it's okay. We know you loved him. It's natural you are grieving. We love you. We're worried about you."

I could not contain my tears. As she gathered me to her, I laid my head on her shoulder and gasped, "You don't understand, Sassy. He was not the man we all thought he was."

She knelt beside me there on the floor, smoothing my hair, as she murmured, "We know he was fatally injured when he tried to escape from Yorktown, Fancy. But…"

"No, believe me, you don't know all there is to know about the real Calvin Hobbs. You don't want to know. And believe me, God willing, neither William nor Marcus will ever know what kind of low life, sorry excuse for a man Calvin Hobbs turned out to be."

I jumped up and rushed from the room, sobbing. She came after me and gathered me into her arms, murmuring soft words of consolation. I turned into her shoulder and clung to my friend as I cried and cried. Damn the man. I was desperate to tell Sassy. I remember the feel of the soft wool gown she wore. I clung to her sleeve as if it were my life line, rubbing the fabric back and forth.

If she had pushed me right then, I would have told her. I would tell them all if it would not hurt them so damned bad. But what would it do to Marc or Will if I told them about the nefarious plot Tom and Calvin concocted and put into play over most of my life time? How could they live knowing what he did to me, what he encouraged Tom to do to me, when they left me with Tom all those awful, lonely years?

Tom agreed to do more than betroth me to Calvin. He also agreed to train me to be a biddable and responsive wife. For money. And thus, I reckon Tom became my pimp as he taught me how to be a whore in the bedroom and then sold me to his best friend. No wonder my husband said one time I was his own little whore in the bedroom. That's what Tom trained me to be. Calvin's whore.

I was Tom's baby sister. I realize it was through adoption, but he was still supposed to love me. Protect me. Take care of me when Daddy Jo died. He promised Daddy Jo he would do those things. Calvin swore with his dying breath he loved me. But those two men both hurt me in ways no child should ever endure. They robbed me of my childhood, as well as my innocence. It looked more and more to me like they robbed me of my sanity as well. If that is love, if that is the kind of love I could expect from a man, then I never want love again.

We were all surprised when Christmas Day came and the baby had not yet come. At least, I was no longer crying at the drop of a pin. I even managed a smile and a laugh now and then. As I felt the ice around my heart begin to melt, I began to realize how drawn to young Dr. Richard Winslow I was. But, could I dare trust myself to another man? And perhaps even more important, why should I?

We ate our roasted goose dinner and opened our gifts. Bella was thrilled with the new gowns I made for her, with matching gowns for her favorite doll. Marcus glowed with paternal pride as he opened the embroidered waistcoat I made for him. Sassy and Will sat in a corner whispering and kissing, while Lily poured over a new medical treatise Marc imported from the Continent for her. I sat by the fire, crocheting a little blanket for my soon-to-be-born baby. The children sat around singing some silly song Richard taught them called "Tom the Toad." He said he learned it when he was in something he called 'cubbies.' Later, he played that baseball game with the boys, telling them they were 'goo-goo-googly good.' Sassy laughed and told us Owen used to say that to Richard.

Then, as the children played with their new toys Richard carved for them that he calls fidget spinners, Richard handed me a small box.

I looked up at him, shocked. "Richard, I can't…"

"Oh, hogwash," he muttered. "It's a gift. For a friend. My dearest friend. Merry Christmas, Francesca. I know you can't wear them for a while because you're in mourning, but by damn, I'm giving this to you now."

My hands trembled as I opened the small jeweler's box to find aquamarine earrings. Set in gold, the earrings were exquisite, simple, classic, elegant, not to mention downright pretty.

My heart lurched. How did he know this was my birthstone? And where did he ever find such beautiful aquamarines? They were the prettiest I had ever seen, with oval center aquas surrounded by small, round, rose cut diamonds. I tucked the box into my reticule, and then flashed him a smile. "They are beautiful, Richard. Thank you. Wherever did you find such pretty aquamarines? But I didn't get you anything!"

"Your beautiful smile was gift enough. I found them on eBay, back home. Beyond."

I frowned. "Where is eBay?"

"It's a place to shop there. Hey, let's take the kids outside and let them run off some energy in the snow!" He laughed as he grabbed my hand and pulled me giggling from my seat.

It was still snowing outside, although the blizzard seemed to be over. All the children wanted to frolic in the fresh fallen snow. I bundled up Bella and myself, and we headed out with Sassy's three to make snow angels. I stood laughing as the children wriggled in the snow, to make angels, or threw snow balls back and forth at each other. Finally, a snow ball hit me square in the chest, knocking me off balance and I fell down. As I lay in the snow, Bella and Rick both rushed over to ensure that I was okay. When they saw I was laying there laughing, making a snow angel of my own, Bella flopped over and began making another snow angel next to mine. After the slightest hesitation, Rick flopped down on the other side of me, and began making a snow angel, too.

"It's good to see you laugh again, Duchess," he said with a grin, his amber colored eyes glowing.

I remembered Will told Sassy once that her hair was like firelight shining through a bottle of good corn whiskey. I wasn't sure it described her hair color to anyone except Will, but it sure described the color of Richard's eyes. Amber, like firelight shining through a bottle of good whiskey. Warm, and golden, comforting and inviting. Eyes I wanted to melt into.

I giggled like a school girl, snow sneaking down inside the collar of my cloak, and into my boots, as I reveled in the snow like I had not done in years. "It's good to be able to laugh, Richard."

He smiled, and I could see the longing clear in his eyes. I could see he was not laughing anymore. His piercing stare at me caused my mouth to go dry with unexpected yearning.

Impulsive, I reached over, and stroked his cheek, before I kissed it. "Thank you for the earrings, Richard. They are beautiful." I laughed at the look of startlement in his eyes – is startlement even a real word? Because that is sure enough how he looked. I rolled up to arise, as I grabbed a handful of snow to pack into a ball. He sprung up, and grabbed my wrist, pulling me close to him. As his head started to lower to my face, a sudden rush of fluid told me it was not the right time.

"Ooh, look, Gramma, Mommy broke water!" shouted Bella.

Laughing with embarrassment as my cheeks turned red, I corrected my daughter. "No, Bella, Mommy did not wet herself. But my water broke. That's different. It means our baby is coming."

Lily looked surprised yet pleased. "About high time this baby decided to come. See, Fancy, it just took a little romp in the snow to get things moving. Bella, let's get your Mommy back into the house. Looks like we're going to have a baby for Christmas after all!"

Lily and Sassy helped me change from my warm outdoor wear into a comfortable bed gown for child birth. Before nightfall, the new Lord Hobbs was born, kicking and squalling before he was even out of my body. Like his sister before him, it was an easy birth, especially considering all the problems I had trying to carry him at first. I laughed and cried at the sound of his first furious squall as he was born. The boy had a thatch of dark, curling hair, like his sire. His newborn baby eyes were bluer than blue. When he would yawn, I could see dimples much like Will's in his tiny baby cheeks. He would be a handsome lad, although time would tell if the color of his eyes would stay Selk blue or would change to the Hobbs brown of his father's eyes. But one thing was certain. The reluctant Duchess of Ranscome was safely delivered of the

Marquess of Ranscome, who would someday be the Fourth Duke of Ranscome, and was already the Fourth Earl of Spring Haven.

I was afraid I would hate this baby after all I learned about his father. Lily assured me I would love my baby. As she said, who can hate a sweet little baby? And thanks be to God, like with my Bella almost four years before, my heart melted when my baby boy was placed in my arms. I looked up at my family and smiled.

"His name is Charles Ranscome Hobbs," I announced.

Sassy looked surprised. "I thought Calvin wanted you to name him Charles Thomas."

I will not repeat the obscenity I said to myself when she suggested Thomas be part of my son's name. I felt my cheeks burning red with angry hot spots as I shook my head. "No. Your first-born son is named Thomas. Boy children born in this family almost always have the second name of Ranscome, especially if they may someday be the heir to the title. His daddy chose his first name, for his good friend, General Charles Cornwallis. Since I am the Duchess of Ranscome, I chose the second name. He will have the family name."

Sassy looked perplexed. "Well, if you want a different middle name, maybe a Christmas name, you could go with Charles Felix Hobbs. Felix means happy, as in *Feliz Navidad*, which means Happy Christmas. Or even Carlos Felix Hobbs."

I kinda gagged, as they all burst out laughing. I swear I tasted a little bit of vomit in my mouth. "No, Charles Ranscome Hobbs will do fine. I'll let you save Carlos Felix for your own Christmas baby you might have some day."

"Hmm. Carlos Felix. I like that. Maybe we will name the next one that." She laughed.

My glaring look made it clear I dared anyone to argue with my decision. I did not need to explain Thomas Selk would get no recognition from me for all he did 'for' me. And thus, Charles Ranscome Hobbs was baptized a few days later.

After Charlie's baptism, New Year's Eve was magical. Lily played Mama Belle's harp and we brought in the New Year singing Auld Lang Syne. I was touched anew by Richard's thoughtfulness as he danced around the room with little Bella. Bella beamed with joy, laughing with sparkling eyes, as Richard spun her around and dipped her as they danced. At the end of their dance,

Richard grabbed me up by the hand to dance me around the parlor, before he stopped beneath the sprig of mistletoe hanging in the doorway. And it was there as we ushered in the New Year, where he kissed me the first time. As he paused there under the mistletoe, it seemed like we must be the only people in the world. He dropped his head to mine, tentative at first. The kiss deepened when he realized I neither pushed him back nor pulled away. Instead, as my hands crept up to cling to him, to pull him closer to me, I had to acknowledge my feelings for him were growing each day. By leaps and bounds. All I could think was, please, dear God, let him be a good man. Please don't let him hurt me. And, please, dear Lord, don't let him hurt my Bella or baby Charlie. I sure would hate to have to kill this man, considering I think I may be falling in love with him.

As if he could read my mind, he bent again to brush a kiss across to my brow. "I will never hurt you on purpose. I may mess up sometime. All people do. We are all human. We may quarrel, we may hurt each other's feelings. But I will never hurt you or your babies on purpose. I promise."

His words touched me. More than he could ever imagine. But I had learned words come easy for some people. I knew despite his best intentions, the day might come when he hurt us. Could I trust him? Could I ever trust any man? I sighed, no longer laughing, but all seriousness. I raised my hand to trace along the side of his face as I tried to memorize his feature and this moment. "I know you will try, Richard, but…"

"Francesca, I would die to protect you and these children. So, help me God." And with that solemn promise, he kissed me again.

That night, after I retired to my room, I pulled Calvin's letter out again to read. God knows why I thought it would help me. I hoped I would perhaps find the way out of this emotional hell Calvin and Tom threw me into. I suspected the key to my sanity was hidden somewhere in the damned letter.

I long hoped and prayed Calvin did not know about the awful things Tom did to me. I realized the first time I read the letter Calvin was as much a sick, perverted bastard as my brother ever was. I could not get over the fact Calvin paid Tom a stipend each month commencing when I was just a little over four years old to train me to be the wife he wanted to someday marry. My skin crawled as I re-read his year-to-year instructions for my 'training'.

No wonder Tom thought I was little more than a whore. He sure tried his best to train me to be one.

I wadded the letter into a ball and raised my hand to throw it into the fire. But something stopped me. I could not do it. As much as I feared someone finding the damnable letter and thinking poorly of me, I knew the day might come when I wanted that letter. When I needed that letter. I smoothed it flat again and put it back into the secret compartment in my jewel case.

No, I would not throw it away. Not just yet.

• • • • •

The snow was deep in the prisoner of war camp in Pennsylvania outside Philadelphia. Banastre Tarleton shivered as he walked around the quadrangle again. Determined to keep his strength up, he forced himself to go out to face the wintry blast over and over again to walk the boring quarter mile quadrangle. At some point, he would manage to escape this frozen backwater hell, and when he did, he must be strong. After all, it was a long walk back to Belle Rose Plantation, and he had unfinished business there.

Chapter 9
Fancy and Rick, 1782

That winter was cold, snowy, and altogether different from winter in Bermuda. While I missed the pink sands, aqua waters, and temperate climate, Bella was enchanted with her cousins and the miracle called snow. She loved to bundle up to go outside to play with the twins, rough housing with snow balls and building snow man after jaunty snow man.

It was strange. Some days, I felt at peace. Happy, perhaps, although I wasn't sure I knew what this thing called 'happy' was. Contented. And other days, I cried over all Tom and Calvin stole from me. You know, the simple things in life most people take for granted. My childhood. My youth. My innocence. My hope, my trust. My very faith in my fellow man. Those things.

I knew people would most likely tell me to let go of all that, and to move on. But some things are too much to forget. I knew I would never again manage to forget all those two men put me through, no matter how hard I might try.

I wanted to feel normal, whatever that was. But how do you find normal when you aren't even sure what normal is? I was pretty danged sure my life had not in any way or shape ever been normal.

I was so pleased Marcus and Lily were still there. Spending all these months with them had been fantastic. I was thrilled every time I saw my father holding my baby. I realized he looked at Charles the same way he looked at Bella when she was a little baby back at McCarron's Corner. Maybe that was the same look he would have had for me, if he had been able to hold me and claim me as his own when I was a babe. I remembered how open and loving he always was when I was a little girl.

How I longed for a father like Marc when I was little. For Marc to have been my daddy, for Lily to have been my mama. It was the innermost desire of my childish heart. Dare I even say my life would have been ever so much better if I had been raised by them? I sighed. No sense fussing over spilt milk now or dwelling on the 'what if's.' My life was what it was, good or bad. I had to learn to deal with it, to make lemonade out of lemons, as Sassy says, instead of always trying to make lemons out of lemonade.

I commented I knew it must have been hard for Marc and Lily to give up their first Christmas with Miles, Gentry and Michael's baby. Lily retorted hogwash, this was the first Christmas for Charles, too. She was quick to point out she was able to deliver both of their grandsons last year.

One day when I was feeling pretty low, I asked Lily, "How am I supposed to move past all the things I learned about Tom and Calvin? I feel so lost. I forced so much of it out of my mind for so long. Now, it is pushing its way back into the open. Each new memory hurts like a knife in my gut. I smell something, and memories wash over me. I hear something, and I'm right back there again. I guess it sounds foolish, but I swear it makes my heart ache. What do I do? How do I manage to let it all surface, and then let it all go and move on?"

Bless her soul! Lily gathered me into her arms like she was my real mama and told me, "Those are triggers. You have to learn what trigger your memories so you can avoid them. In the meantime, take it one day at a time. This was a lot to take in. And God knows you have been to hell and back with all the shit those damned men put you through."

Wordless, I nodded. I reckoned she was right. I pondered her words before I spoke up again. "But Lily, I'm still in hell. I dream about it every night. I can't get it out of my mind. I'm afraid I am losing my mind. A smell or a word can, what did you call it? Trigger memories I didn't even know I had. Yesterday, I smelled the oil the men use to clean guns, and all of a sudden, I had this vivid recollection of Tom messing with me right there on his desk where he had been cleaning a gun. I reckon that's why the smell of gun oil always makes me so sick to my stomach." I did not describe the details of the dream or what else Tom made me do that day. "How do I get out of this hell they made for me?"

I felt her tremble again. "Take it day by day, honey. We all love you. We are all here for you…"

"But, I don't want the others to know!" I whispered, my eyes again filling with tears.

She bent and kissed my hair. "They don't have to know. But maybe they should. Why don't you go ahead and tell them?"

"No, not any of them! Before when we talked, you agreed they shouldn't know. Sassy would tell Will, and Will would tell Marc. You know that!" I pulled away from her and walked to the window to stare out over the frozen waters of the Potomac, my arms wrapped tight around my body.

She followed behind and placed a cautious hand on my shoulder. "Do you have any idea how much you remind me of your father at times when you do that?"

I frowned. "Do what?"

"When you go to the window and stare outside like you are searching for the answer."

I didn't answer. I guess I am more like Marcus than I ever suspected. I have noticed it is hard for him to talk sometimes, especially about things that are the most important to him, like it is for me. I swear, sometimes the words choke in my throat. I have seen him go over to a window more than once to peer outside, while he ponders upon something that bothers him. God knows I do that, too. Marcus claims it's not that he doesn't like people, it's just that he feels better when people are not around. Well, except for Lily. Yes, I know how that feels. He's lucky he has Lily. But then, so am I.

And some days, I think I am lucky to have Richard Winslow. But can I trust him? And just as important, can I risk not trusting him?

So, here I am wondering night after night, day after day, can I trust Richard enough to talk to him? Or will I make myself a victim to him if he knows those awful things about me? Could he accept me, despite all that happened?

I swatted at a tear that slid down my cheek. "Maybe there is someone I could talk to. Besides you. Maybe…well, maybe I could trust him…"

She grabbed my hands again. "Then do it, honey. He's a good man, Fancy. I'm not saying that because he's Sassy's son. Trust him. Talk to Rick. You know he cares about you. Trust him."

It startled me she knew who I meant without me saying his name. "How … how did you know? That I meant Richard?" I whispered.

She smiled, and tucked a curl under my cap. "Oh, honey, it is so obvious that young man is falling in love with you. Trust him."

I wasn't sure if I were shocked or thrilled, horrified or delighted she thought Richard was falling in love with me. Truth be told, I suspected it, too. I was afraid to say it. After all, what is love? I was not sure I ever wanted love again if what Calvin gave me was the best there was. I looked at Lily, thinking again how different her relationship with Marcus was from what Calvin and I had. I thought again how different Sassy and Will's love differed from what crumbs Calvin threw me, too. Oh, but he did make me a Duchess. Not that I wanted to be one, thank you.

Well, if nothing else, if I do tell Richard, it will tell me what kind of stuff Richard Owen Winslow is made of.

I sighed. Lily says, oh, what tangled webs we weave when we practice to deceive. I wasn't the one who wove those tangled webs. I'm just the little fly they trapped in those awful, sticky webs. I am the unfortunate fool dealing with the aftermath of all those snarls and tangles.

I swallowed hard again. How could I ever learn to trust again? Richard is so sweet, so kind, so solicitous. But is it real? Or is it like Calvin, all some weird act designed to get sex? Please, God. Help me. To be strong enough to trust Richard with all this.

And to be strong enough to accept it if he can't handle my past. All of it, because like Lily says, it's a hot mess.

But still my biggest fear remains. Will he change, too, like Calvin did, if I give him my love? Is he no better that Calvin? Or Tom? Is any man better? I long to trust him. But how?

Oh, my dear God in heaven above! Did I write that I love him?

And does Lily suspect that as well?

Sassy swears not all who wander are lost, but you must be lost to be found. Was this my chance for someone from Beyond to find me? To become Richard's twin flame, like Sassy said she is Will's?

And if he is, do I dare not to trust him?

* * *

Rick was fast becoming comfortable with his new role as doctor to the Belle Rose Plantation, big brother to Sassy's children, and a kind of uncle to sweet little Bella and baby Charles. Some days, he could tell Francesca was beginning to relax with him. To trust him. Others, not so much. On Christmas, they had the best time playing outside in the snow. He had never seen a smile like hers when she held her new born baby that night. And then, a week later, after that special moment on New Year's Eve, she was distant again, remote, distracted, and once more tearful. For every two steps forward they made, she seemed determined to take three steps back. But why?

How long would it take her to realize he loved her? And just as important, how long would it take her to realize she loved him? Rick sighed, wishing for the umpteenth time he knew how to get past the wall she built up around her heart every time it seemed like she was opening up a little bit. Why was she so guarded?

Good grief, how awful a husband was ol' Calvin Hobbs anyway?

Why, this evening, she cringed from him, slinging her arm up in front of her face with a shudder that had to mean fear. Rick worked as a volunteer at enough Women's Centers over the years that he knew that clear-cut sign for sure. Had her damned husband hit her? How could anyone have ever hit her, so she would respond like that?

Maybe it was a reaction to Simon Le Grande. Now, there was a pathetic excuse for a human being, as Will pronounced. And the sorry rat bastard had the audacity to horse whip her for refusing to go to his bed! Damn, if Le Grande wasn't already dead, Rick might have had to kill the sorry little son of a bitch. Some days, he resented his Mom was the one who killed Le Grande and that he had not had the chance to do it himself.

Lily kept urging him not to give up on Francesca. He had no intention of giving up on her, but he sure wished he could get past that wall she had built up. He suspected Lily knew things about her that Francesca was not telling even to his Mom. Maybe it was just conjecture. In any event, he was there for Francesca. He knew some people would think he was crazy to have traveled through time to find a woman he saw in a painting. But Rick knew beyond a shadow of a doubt his soul was inextricably bound to hers for all time.

He smiled. He had relationships before he came here, although no serious ones. More than friends with privileges, but no significant commitment on his part. Now, he was ready for commitment. Marriage. Family. The whole happy-ever-after gig.

And she wasn't. Again, the whole wall-around-her-heart thing.

In fact, that morning he talked about this very subject with Lily. He told her how frustrated he was about it. She patted him on the back and told him once again to be patient with Fancy. "She is carrying a lot on her plate right now, Rick. You have to give her time. You came here searching for her. In contrast, she had no idea you two might gave a future before you showed up unexpectedly, and she was married to another man then. This is all very complicated. And please, don't give up on her. She needs you as much as you need her."

"I know we need each other, Lily. And, I have come way too freaking far to give up on her. I refuse to let the memory of Calvin Hobbs ruin the relationship I am meant to have with the woman I love."

She tilted her head at Rick. "Love, hmm? You sure about that?"

"Never more so in all my life."

She smiled. "Give her time. And believe me: this grief she is experiencing is about far more than Calvin's death. She needs you, Rick. Every bit as much as you need her, if not even more. After all, not all who wander are lost, but you must be lost to be found. Right now, Fancy is very lost. It is your job to help her find herself."

"Not just for me to find her?"

She shook her head. "No. She has to learn what 'to thy own self, be true,' means. She is resisting finding herself. I went through this with Marc. It was harder for me to cope with Marc finding himself than to find myself in 1763. Of course, I thought then and I still think when I found myself in 1763, I had found my home."

Rick tilted his head at her. "Really?"

Lily nodded. "Really. They say home is where the heart is. My home must be here, in this era, with my Marc. This is where I found my heart. Anyway, I think Fancy is afraid of what she is going to find. Life has not always been kind to her. When she does figure all this out? Well, you want her to figure it out. But this is probably the most difficult thing she will ever go through. Believe me. She is good people. Be patient. No matter what. Even when she calls you Richard."

Rick laughed. He had always related being called 'Richard' to being in trouble before Francesca. She was the one person he could remember who had ever called him 'Richard' unless he was in trouble.

Lily smiled again as she told Rick about a time twenty years before when she had to be patient with a certain Irishman, she loved more than life itself, and she had to let him find himself so they could find themselves.

• • • • •

That night, I wept anew as I again read how Calvin had been overseeing my 'education'. I could not get over the fact that at times, he joined Tom in his molestation of me. At those times, I was well dosed with the juice of poppies, causing me to have my topsy-turvy dreams with little coherent or intelligible memories. I was always blindfolded and often Tom tied my hands to the bedstead when Calvin attended Tom's little 'soirees', as he referred to them in his letter. 'Soirée,' my eye teeth. The blindfold and restraints were to prevent my recognition of Sir Calvin. At those times, Calvin would slip into the bed beside me, sometimes fondling me while Tom watched. At other times, like the time right before Tom left for Saratoga, Calvin was alone with me, telling me he loved me and longed to marry me. I am not sure, but I want to think that was the one time he engaged in sexual intercourse with me before we married. I reckon he perceived it was his right, a kind of 'pre-marital congress.' That is a bit easier to accept than that he raped me. In any event, I choose to believe it was the only time. I don't want to know if I am wrong. Yes, while Tom always belittled me, now I remembered Calvin always told me how much he loved his 'darling little girl'. When I was older, he called me his darling. At least, he never belittled me until after we married. Strange, isn't it?

I was beginning to understand why the phrase 'little girl' made my skin crawl. But then, the whole sordid, disgusting story Calvin spelled out made my skin crawl, to say the very least. And then there was the whole last part to his letter that just about killed me every time I read it. "You must be wondering why I wrote you this. I want you to know these things because you will always be mine, my darling. No one will ever be able to take my place in your memories. You have been my one true love since you were my darling little girl. I was your first love. Think of me often. I will be there with you in your thoughts forever."

What kind of monster would tell you things like that?

I crumpled the damned letter again as I sobbed. And then, Richard was there, pulling me into his arms. He took the letter from me, and without ever looking at it, he laid the crumpled pages aside. "I think it's high time we talk."

I pulled a handkerchief out of my sleeve and wiped the tears from my face. I squared my shoulders, and with a ragged breath, I nodded.

"It's time you remember we all love you. We know you are having a real hard time. You don't have to say why, unless you want to discuss it. I figure what you saw and endured at Yorktown was enough to make even a strong woman like you have a hard time getting past it. But, Francesca, I'm here if you need to talk."

I nodded again. "I know. But I feel so broken, Richard. Like I am shards of broken pottery waiting to be thrown away. Rubbish." My voice cracked and I looked away from him, embarrassed to have revealed so much.

He came to me quick and turned me back to him. "Francesca, you are without a doubt the strongest, bravest woman I have ever known. Shards? Oh, no, my love. My real mother was shards. She let drugs destroy her life. The drugs broke her so she could never find her way back."

His words surprised me. I had never heard him mention his birth mother before. "I didn't know that. You never mentioned her before."

His cheeks reddened. "I'm ashamed to say I try not to think about Katherine Winslow much. She was a lot for a child to deal with."

"Why?"

He kinda laughed, but the sound came out hollow, empty, not like he was amused. "My mother was addicted to opium. At times, she dragged me around with her into some pretty sordid situations. I used to try to warn her she was killing herself each time she used that stuff. She would tell me to mind my own business and not to begrudge her what little bit of happiness she had. She was very different from you, Francesca. Mother was like a china doll that had been shattered. You? You are already far stronger than you realize. Don't you know? What doesn't kill you, makes you stronger. Mother never figured that out. She was too busy blaming Dad and Sassy for all her problems. I knew she was addicted to drugs way before Sassy ever came into our lives."

I dropped my eyes and looked away, embarrassed by his unexpected praise as well as by my need to tell him things I never told another living soul before. Things I hadn't even told Lily. Why, I hadn't even told Sassy, and she's my best and dearest friend. But of course, like I told Lily, Sassy would tell William, and I knew Will did not need to know these things about his brother and about all the horrible things Tom did to me for years. "Well, thank you, but I'm not so sure about that, Richard."

Richard nodded, solemn, and bent to kiss my scarred forearm. "I'm sure.

How did you do this?"

I trembled at the gentle touch of his lips, and with a shake of my head, I pulled my arm away from him. The old scars were faded and no one including Calvin had ever mentioned them before. "Richard, it isn't right that you kiss me …" I began, as I tugged against his hold on my arm.

He shook his head. "Oh, bull hockey. It's high time I did, Francesca," and he gathered me into his arms to kiss my mouth, soft at first, and then he pulled back a smidgen before he kissed me again. He wrapped his arms around me and pulled me close to kiss me with such urgency, such desperation, as his body curved close to mine.

I didn't want to respond. I struggled not to. But before I could stop myself, my arms were wrapped around him, my fingers once again entwined in his silken, tawny locks. How can blonde hair curl like that? I could feel his fingers tracing little circles on the strip of bare skin between my hair and my neck. I moaned into his mouth, yielding my body into his, before I pulled back, shocked by my own audacity, my own brazenness. More, I wanted to beg. More. Maybe Tom and Calvin were right. Maybe I was nothing more than a little mixed-blood whore. By damn, I would control my baser urges. I had to. I have children to consider. Like it or not, I was not merely the Countess of Spring Haven. I was also the Duchess of Ranscome, and now the mother of a future Duke. I had duties and obligations to uphold. Calvin was dead, so it would not have been adultery, but I was not about to do anything that would put my baby's paternity in question, no matter how much I wanted this man. And God knew I wanted Richard Winslow. Bad. So damned bad. I broke away from him and backed to the doorway. "No. You need to leave my room. This cannot happen. I refuse to be that kind of woman."

I was shaking like a leaf. Oh, dear God, I wanted this man! I do not believe I ever felt such unrequited desire before.

His eyes smoldered with the fire burning within his inner being. I think inner being means loins, but I'm not rightly sure. He rose and started to argue, and then his shoulders slumped. "I am not giving up, Francesca. We will be together."

I shook my head. "Perhaps in the future, Richard. But not yet. It is not possible. I am still in mourning. You may be from a different time, but you know the rules we live by in this day and age. Four months minimum for full mourning, preferably six. Another six months in half mourning. It has not even been four months, Richard. And I need time … to figure out if this little broken vessel can ever be mended. You say I'm beautiful. I have to decide I am not garbage. Please, Richard. Give me time."

I did not intend to wind up dying alone of an opium overdose like Katherine Winslow did. My children deserved so much more than that.

Richard and I both deserved more than that.

He looked like he had to struggle to get control of his emotions again. He shut his eyes, breathing hard, still leaning toward me as if it hurt to stop touching me. At last, he spoke. "A doctor told me years ago in Japan, if something, like a vase, is broken, they mend it with gold. They don't throw it away as damaged. They don't hide the damage. They fix it with something beautiful, making it more beautiful and stronger than before. If we push those awful memories into the dark recesses of our mind, we remain broken and always feel like we deserve to be discarded. We feel like trash. But if we face those awful memories, and work through them, we mend the broken vessel and make it more beautiful and stronger than before."

I stared at him. I ached with longing to believe him, to believe I could be mended. I shook my head. "But I am broken, Richard. How can I ever be fixed? How can anything ever fix that?" My voice trembled as I struggled to hold back the tears biting at my eyes.

"Francesca, what do you mean? We're all at least a little broken. But you survived whatever broke you. You are a strong woman. You are already mended. You are not worthless. You are not rubbish. You are a beautiful woman, and I don't just mean your outward appearance."

I walked over to the window, wishing I had drowned all those years ago in the cold, clear waters of the Potomac. "But that's my point. I am rubbish, Richard. Nothing more than broken shards…". My voice cracked as I felt my soul shatter. "My husband made that crystal clear to me."

"Then he was an even bigger fool than I ever suspected." He strode over to me and took my hand into his again and raised it to his lips. I trembled as he kissed the palm of my hand one last time. "I'll wait, my love. If you need time, I'll wait. Believe me, you are well worth the wait."

I didn't know whether to be terrified or excited. Right then, after all I had learned from Calvin, about what Tom and he conspired to do to me, I wasn't sure I would ever be ready for another man again. But I knew one thing. If I ever were ready for another man, it would be Richard Winslow. He was the one man I thought might ever understand me, who might somehow understand what I had endured. Who might actually be able to help me mend.

I realized the love of this man would be a far greater treasure than I deserved. But maybe, just maybe, with love like that, I could mend into something better and stronger, too, like the Japanese vase he talked about.

Hmm. What is a Japanese vase anyway?

A few nights later, I woke up in terror, still unable to verbalize the fears that choked me night after night. I arose from my bed, and paced back and forth, crying at the unbidden memory of scents and colors which made so little sense to me. Dear God, would this torment never end?

And then, before I could change my mind, I pulled on my bed robe and grabbed the letter from my jewel case. I swallowed hard, shoved it into my pocket, and left my room to go to Richard.

I paused for a second before I opened the door to his room. I could see he had a lamp lit there by the golden glow under the door. It was now or never. And I desperately needed to be able to confide in someone. Oh, let's be honest. I needed to be able to confide in Richard.

He was sitting at the desk reading when I came in, one hand fidgeting with that little spinning toy he carries around with him. He pushed his chair back, startled by my unexpected appearance. "Francesca? Are you all right?"

I realized then I was trembling. I pulled my bed robe tight around me and shook my head before I answered. "No. I had another bad dream."

He held his arms out to me, and before I even thought, I rushed to him. He pulled me onto his lap and into his arms, where he held me close as I trembled. "Wanna talk about it?"

I shook my head, and then stopped. I took a deep breath before I raised my eyes to his. "I don't want to talk. But I think maybe I have to…"

He nodded and picked up my hand to kiss it. Then, he frowned as he turned my hand over, so he could see the old, faded scars below the lace on my bed robe. He stood there, stroking those old scars, silent. Richard traced the faint, silvered lines that marred my forearm. "I noticed the scars before, but you weren't ready to talk then. How old were you the first time?"

I frowned. "I beg your pardon?"

Without a word, he traced his finger along the scars on my forearm again. I blushed and looked away as I tried to tug my arm free from his hold. I had learned so much in the past few weeks, but his focus on the scars was like a raw sore that wouldn't heal, almost like I had cut myself again after all this time. Richard noting the scars on my arm made me feel even more broken, more shattered. More worthless, kinda like Calvin's damned letter made me feel and when he told me he was Bella's real daddy. "I … I don't know what you mean."

He stared at me a minute, and then sighed before he rolled his sleeve up. I gasped at the ugly scar. I reached out a tentative hand to touch it.

"Why? When did you do that?"

He grimaced. "When I was fifteen, Mom fell down the stairs outside my Dad's office and broke her neck. I had a horrible fight with my Dad. I was convinced he pushed her."

"She swears she caught her heel and fell, but I'll tell you, we all think there is more to that story than she's telling."

Richard nodded, excited by my words. "The story never made sense. There has to be more than she tells. And, we all know Sassy can tell a real whopper. Anyway, I beat him up pretty bad…"

"Good," I muttered through gritted teeth.

He looked surprised. "Well, he called the police, and they put me in jail overnight. The next day, I was transferred to a mental hospital."

It took a minute to figure out what he meant. "You mean your own daddy had you put in a lunatic asylum? I've heard about those places. They are horrible! Oh, my God, Richard!"

He nodded. "Yeah. But that wasn't the worst of it. I was sexually assaulted while in the jail. In fact, the next morning, I stabbed myself with a fork at breakfast, and ripped my wrist open. I wanted to die. I felt so dirty, so used. I know my thinking wasn't very clear, but…" He kind of laughed, as if embarrassed. "I remember thinking, wow, that's a lot of blood. They said I almost bled to death. That's why they sent me to the mental hospital."

I stared, not quite comprehending what he was telling me. I was afraid to ask but I had to, even though I feared I already knew the answer. "What does sexually assaulted mean?"

He chuckled, but it didn't sound amused. It sounded hollow. "Francesca, I was raped."

I felt myself going numb like I used to do when Tom was messing with me. "You were…"

"Raped. I tried to kill myself afterwards."

"I didn't know a man could be raped…" I began.

He tried to smile. "Yeah, if a couple of big guys hold you down while another one shoves himself up your …"

"I get the idea," I snapped. "How did your mom react?"

"She was livid. Called Dad everything under the sun. She hired a lawyer, filed for divorce, and she got me out of the hospital. But I had already stabbed myself in my wrist to rip my vein open and damned near bled to death. Mom and I moved to Williamsburg. A few months later, Dad showed up on our doorstep. Cocky bastard figured if he showed up, she would be thrilled to take him back by then. Ha! No such luck. She cussed him up one side and down the other in Spanish before she slammed the door in his face. I remember a lot of 'sorry *pendejo*' and '*malditate*, Owen!' That means 'stupid eff-er' and 'damn you, Owen.' But they began talking, and then they started going to marriage counseling. Sassy took Dad back the next summer. They even renewed their marriage vows. Don't misunderstand me, I loved my Dad. But I never understood why she took him back." His voice faded to a whisper. "I never understood how she could take him back. I could never forgive him. I tried. I could never get past the fact I got gang banged because he had the cops arrest me after he knocked my mom down the stairs at his office at Harvard and broke her neck." He took a couple of deep breaths, and then said, "Hell, I thought, maybe Katherine was right and he was the reason she turned to drugs. And that's not fair to Dad or his memory. My mother did that to herself, all by herself, God rest her soul. So, how old were you the first time?"

I struggled with a myriad of my own memories and emotions. I decided not to ask what 'gang bang' meant. It was hard for me to believe he trusted me with so much personal, horrifying information as it was. It must be humiliating for a man like Richard to have to admit something so awful happened to him.

I struggled with my thoughts, my memories, my fears. Did I dare tell him? Would I always regret it if I told him?

As tears welled in my eyes, he spoke up again. "Look, I'm sorry. I've overstepped. Sometimes I have issues with boundaries…"

"Four," I stammered. I could tell my word startled him, shocked him. "I was four."

"You tried to kill yourself when you were four?" He looked stunned.

I guess I looked startled. "Oh, no. That was when it started. My mama ran off with Fitz's father and they all went off after them. My mama took Michael to Ireland, but not me. She up and went off with nary a thought about me. How do you do that? Just go off and leave your child? And, then while they were all gone to fetch Michael back, he started on me. Oh, he just touched me at first. But as it got worse, he swore he would kill me if I ever told. I was older when I tried to kill myself the first time."

"The first time? You did it more than once?"

I nodded. "Yeah. I guess I was about six or maybe seven the first time. Will and the girls were leaving to go back to Puerto Rico. I begged Daddy Jo to let me go with them. Mama Belle had died by then, and he wouldn't let me go. I was so scared. I jumped off the dock into the river. I remember how the water was so cold it felt like slivers of ice were piercing my skin. I was going to follow them or die trying. I almost drowned, too." I hesitated a moment. "Sometimes, I still wish I drowned that day."

He paled, surprised by my words. "You never told anyone?" Richard sounded anguished.

I shrugged. "I told Charlotte one time he hurt me down there. In my private area. She got mad and slapped me hard. She said I was a disgusting little liar. She told me not to ever say such a thing about him again, that it was very naughty. The same night, he hurt me worse than he ever had before. I remember I cried, begging him to stop. I could smell the oil he used to clean his musket there on the desk where he took me. My God, I hate the smell of gun oil. I think I bled the first time that night. He was rough with me. He wanted to make a point. Well, he sure enough did. He told me not to ever say 'no' to a white man again, but to spread my legs like he told me, to be a good little girl and to do what he said. He said … well, he said he would kill me if I ever told anyone again." I could tell Richard had not expected my answer when his eyes flared wide with shock. "I promised him I wouldn't. I even swore it on the Bible like he demanded I do. I remember he said if I told, he would swear I was lying and God would strike me dead right there on the spot. I was nothing but a little no-account, mixed breed girl and I was under his absolute control."

"Why do you call yourself that? A 'no-account, mixed breed girl'?" he asked.

I started to stammer. "Richard, I thought you knew. I'm a person of color. One-eighth black."

"Really? I always wondered if being mixed was part of my mom's self-loathing."

I looked at him, not understanding what he meant. "What on earth do you mean?"

He smiled. "My mom was half black. Didn't you know?"

My mouth fell open in shock. "Get out of here! You're making that up!"

He shook his head. "No, I'm serious. Ask Sassy. She'll tell you."

I stared at him for a couple of minutes. My mind could not quite grasp that he had more black blood than I did. I realized that must be where his curls came from. I reckoned he had some issues about that mixed blood, too. Huh. Go figure. I took another breath and started talking again. "Okay, now you really messed with my poor little old pee piddling brain, Richard."

He laughed again, but I could tell he was embarrassed when he spoke. "Why do you call me Richard instead of Rick?"

I shrugged. "Why do you call me Francesca instead of Fancy?"

He kinda laughed. I wondered if he would prefer I called him Rick, but I didn't ask. I had other things more pressing on my mind right then. I took another big breath and resumed my story. Now or never, Fancy girl. Spill your guts.

"Well, anyway, I got to where I was beyond scared, I was terrified. I couldn't sleep at night. They started giving me a glass of warm milk at bedtime with somethin' in it to make me sleep. Usually the juice of poppies. Sometimes paregoric. I remember the taste of both. Then, I would fall asleep at night and wake up with him … you know. Touching me. Making me beg for him to touch me." I turned my face from him as I struggled to contain my tears of shame. "Then, cry out, begging him for more. Making me touch him. Doing … all sorts of things grown men aren't supposed to do with little girls. It was a lot worse when I was little than when Simon abused me when I was seventeen, and that was pretty damned horrible. At least I knew what Simon was doing by then. Oh, the scars. You asked about the scars. Well, at some point, I figured out if I cut myself, I felt calmer. More in control of my life in which I had no control."

Richard cleared his throat. "Why are you telling me now?"

I raised my eyes to meet his. I could see pain all across his face. *Because I have to know if I could trust you. If you love me like you said you do, Lily says you can handle it.* I took another deep breath. "He's dead. He can't hurt me anymore. I reckon it's high time I tell somebody. And, well, the smell of the oil woke me up again. I hate it when I wake up smelling that gun oil. You men were cleaning guns downstairs today. The smell always makes me dream about … that. And this time, I decided it's time to talk."

And you won't judge me. At least, I hope you won't. Please don't judge me, Richard. Please don't disappoint me. Please. Don't betray my trust. This is so hard for me.

I think that was when he realized who I meant. "Oh, my God, Francesca. Tom. It was your brother, Tom. How did you ever survive all those years?"

I thought, how did I survive it? Why did you survive it? And then, my beautiful Bella toddled into Richard's room after me, and I knew why I survived. I shrugged and tried to smile as my little girl climbed into my lap and wrapped her arms around my neck. I tucked a dark curl back under her little night cap and kissed her unworried brow. God willing, this child would never have to endure even an iota of the hell I endured growing up. I took a deep breath. "You just do, Richard. I reckon I survived because the fire inside of me burned brighter and stronger than the fire around me that threatened to consume me. I could choose life or death. I chose life. But it wasn't always an easy decision, as you can tell looking at my scars. Of course, I wasn't trying to kill myself with all of those."

"You were self-mutilating by cutting," he mused, as his fingers traced gentle circles over the faded, old scars on my arm. "I used to do that, too."

"I didn't know there was a name for it. But, if I cut myself, I could make myself feel something. Calmer. And, it gave me a kind of feeling like I was in control of something, even if it was no more than how deep the cut was or how long I let it bleed. For a long time, especially after Charlotte died, I couldn't feel much of anything at all. The situation got a lot worse after she died. Before, he said he was training me, so I could be a good wife someday. A responsive wife, eager for her husband's touch. After she died, he insisted I had to take her place. I couldn't remember a lot of it for a long time. I still can't remember all of it. I reckon it was pretty bad if I can't remember it. I don't want to remember, but Sassy says I have to remember to be able to heal. Why is that, Richard?"

"Sometimes, we have to remember what we have repressed from our active memories to be able to mend ourselves."

I frowned. "What do you mean?"

"I'm not sure I can explain it. The best explanation I ever heard is the story I told you before about the Japanese vase."

I tilted my head at him. "I remember. Tell me how it helped you."

He smiled. "Remember I said a doctor told me the story? He was my doctor at the hospital after … my bad time… He was Japanese, and he said in Japan, if something, like a vase, is broken, they mend it with gold. They don't throw it away as damaged. They don't hide the damage. They fix it with something beautiful and make it more beautiful and stronger than before."

"I still don't understand how that applies to me, Richard."

"The same principle applies to people, Francesca. That's why I had the semi-colon tattoo put on my wrist. In the future, the semi-colon will be a symbol that says the author could have finished the sentence but decided to keep going. It's on my wrist because I decided I'm the author of my story. I could have ended my story right there with the scar, but I decided to go on. My story isn't over yet. I put it right next to the scar where I ripped my wrist out to remind me, I was broken but I was mended. I am a survivor. I refuse to live my life as a victim. If we push those awful memories into the dark recesses of our minds, we remain broken and always feel like we deserved to be hurt. We feel like trash. My real mother, Katherine, always felt worthless. I felt worthless for a long time. I thought I must have done something awful to deserve to be attacked like that. I tried to push those memories into the dark recesses of my mind and forget it ever happened. But if we face those awful memories, and work through them, we can mend the broken vessel and make it more beautiful and stronger than before. I didn't deserve to be raped. You didn't deserve it either. You are already a survivor. Now, you have to realize that."

I pulled his wrist over to me to look at the little tattoo at the end of the old scar. "Well, I'll be jiggered. And, this little mark helps you remember that your story isn't over yet?"

He nodded. I bent over and kissed his tattoo and scarred wrist.

"Why did your mother feel worthless?"

"Katherine was mixed. I guess in this day and age, they would say she was mulatto…"

"Your mama was really half black? You sure you didn't say that to make me feel better?"

He nodded. "Yes, she was. She never felt she belonged in either race. I think she always resented the fact my dad could fit in anywhere. She resented what she called his white privilege. I never understood why it impacted her like it did. Of course, I look white, too, like you do. And like I said, Katherine was a weak woman, besieged by her own demons. She chose to give in to the demon called heroin."

"What's that?"

He shrugged. "Heroin is a drug derived from opium. It is extremely addictive. My mother chose to hide in heroin rather than cope. Rather than survive. Rather than really dare to live. That's why I say she was weak. She wasn't a survivor, like you. In the long run, the drug that gave her temporary solace killed her."

I stared at him, shocked, before I continued. I ached with longing to believe him, to believe I could be mended. I shook my head. "Opium can make you feel frighteningly wonderful. You don't care about nothing when it's in your system. That's why Tom would give me milk with it in it. He liked the way I would be limp as a noodle, totally compliant, when he messed with me after he gave it to me. Hmm. Sassy says that I'm a survivor, too. But I am still broken, Richard. How can I ever be fixed? How can anything ever fix this?" My voice trembled as I struggled to hold back the tears biting at my eyes. "You don't know what all I went through. You don't understand."

"Francesca, what do you mean? God knows I was broken with the horror that happened to me. So was Sassy by what Tarleton did to her. But we all survived. You will survive it as well, my love. You are a strong woman. You are mending. Believe me, sweetheart, you are not worthless. You are not rubbish. You are a beautiful woman, inside and out. God made you, and God does not make trash. Just because that damned man tried to make you believe you are rubbish does not make it true."

I arose and walked over to the window, wishing again I had drowned all those years ago in the cold, clear waters of the Potomac. "But that's my point." My voice cracked as badly as I felt my soul was shattered. "My own mother went off and left me. And then, my own husband made it clear to me I am worthless when he left me that damned letter."

Richard's brow furrowed as he frowned, clearly not understanding. "What letter, sweetheart?"

Do it, Fancy, I thought. I pulled the crumpled letter out of my pocket, took a deep breath, and handed it to him. *It's now or never.* So, with my heart beating ninety to nothing and my hands shaking, I handed it to him. "This letter."

He hesitated a moment, and then took the letter. I sat there on his lap and turned my face to his chest so I could not see his face as he read. Bella sat in my lap with her arms tight around my neck, where she had fallen fast asleep again. Oh, to be able to sleep like that! To be able to trust like that!

And with a start, I realized I would not be there, clinging to him, if I did not trust him. I sighed and sank closer against him as he read page after damning page. At last, he spoke, his voice shaking with rage.

"Dammit, I knew I didn't like that sorry…"

I put my fingers up to his lips as I shushed him. "Shush. Don't talk like that. He was her father. She loved him."

He struggled to control his obvious anger. Once he regained some control, he replied, "I apologize for the profanity. It was inappropriate. You're a better person than I am, if you can do that. Yeah. You're right. It always hurt when Dad put Mother down as a drug addict. She was my mother, no matter … whatever else. Calvin was their father. I have to remember that. She doesn't ever need to know…"

"No, she doesn't. Nor does Charlie."

"But by damn, Francesca, I swear, if he were still alive, hell, if either one of them were still alive, they would have hell to pay." He wrapped his arms around Bella and me tighter and kissed my tear-stained cheek. "You aren't rubbish, sweetie. They were the rubbish. And no, I would never tell Bella and Charlie. But I will tell you the rest of your life. You are far better than those two so-called men ever dreamed of being. You… you are not just any old person. You sure as hell are not trash. You are the love of my life, Francesca. I may not have been your first love. I may not have been any of those other firsts it is usual for men to want to be. I want to be your last."

My heart swelled at his words. He couldn't know how much those words meant to me, could he? He didn't care he wasn't the first. He wanted to be the last. Take that, Calvin. Take that, shove it in your pipe, and smoke it. "You won't tell Sassy? It would kill Will and Marc if they learned…"

He shook his head. "No. That's your story to tell if and when you need to tell it. I promise, I won't tell. I love you."

My heart clinched as his voice broke, and I felt his tears fall on my face. But I knew then that I had my answer. I could trust him. Always. There would never be a time when I could not trust him.

As Richard says, I found my semi-colon, and with it, I grabbed my chance to write my own new ending.

Chapter 10
Fancy - 1782

The next weeks were the best I had ever experienced. Each night after I tucked Bella into her own bed, I slipped out of my room and into Richard's. We talked for hours. We kissed more and more each night. I didn't know there were so many kinds of kisses. Little lopsided funny kisses to the edge of my lip while we were laughing. Kisses to my nape. Kisses to the hollow of his throat right where you can see the pulse. Kisses to each other's eyelids. We held hands, snuggled up close on his narrow bed as we listened to the wintry winds howling outside.

And, yes, we finally made love. It had been four months since Calvin died. We didn't merely have sex. I know now I had nothing more than sex before that night. Richard showed me the difference. We made love, as sweet kisses became more and more passionate, and as our hands roamed each other's bodies with more and more daring.

Gasping, I pushed back as we inflamed. A look of disappointment washed across his handsome features. I sat up and lifted my night rail over my head and after a second, I dropped it. As the night rail fluttered to the ground, his eyes lit up. I lowered my face back to him, as I began to devour his kisses like a starved woman. I reached my arms around him and kissed him again and again. Soft and questioning at first. Is it okay if I do this? He moaned against my mouth, nodding, and his body melted against mine.

His hands began to roam my body again, first pressing down my spine and then pressing alongside my bare breasts. I gasped at the unexpected sensations and clung to him. I trembled as I moaned into his mouth, "More."

His irises flared at the unexpected word, and he gave me more. I hadn't realized there was so much more. He gave as much if not more than I gave. I became lost in a whirl of sensations I never experienced before as Richard taught me what physical love is all about. The sharing, the intimacy, the little laughs and touches. The moans and words begging for more from us both. And then, of course, the crashing crescendo at the end of that well-played symphony as we climaxed together.

No one ever tried to bring me pleasure before. That wasn't my purpose. Before, I realized I had been nothing more than a tool. Now, I was a partner. My partner wanted me to enjoy the experience as much as he did.

It was a revelation.

"I love you," he gasped as his fingers twined with mine.

"I love you, too." My voice was ragged and hoarse with longing and desire.

That night, as we made love, the twin flames of Richard and Fancy joined as one. We weren't talking about The Future, but I was sure we would be together. After all, if twin flames are separated, would they not snuff out and both flames die?

I knew I was no longer lost. I had found my center. I laughed with joyous sincerity as I found what Lily called my happy place. I could laugh until I cried with this man, who brought so much to my life. If home is where the heart is, like Sassy and Lily both say, then my home was meant to be with this man who made me whole. In fact, I realized I loved him when 'home' went from being a place where I lived, to being with Richard.

And then, one night, after I came back to my room, Richard followed to hand me my robe. "You forgot this," he laughed with a grin.

I jumped out of my bed and rushed to him, to pull him close to me for yet another kiss. And, then, we both jumped apart like guilty children at the sound of a man clearing his throat.

"I think it's high time we have a talk, young man," Will growled.

I began to tremble, but I grabbed Richard's arm as he started out of my room. "No," I insisted, "Stay here. You don't have to leave."

Will's face grew red. "Fancy, this is man talk, between Rick and me."

I shook my head. "Oh, no, it isn't, William Ranscome Selk. This involves me, and I intend to be involved in any discussion about Richard and me."

Richard held me tight and bent to kiss my brow. "If you want to know my intentions, Will, I can tell you I want to marry Francesca once her period of mourning is over. If she will have me. I would marry her right now if I could."

I blinked. "Of course, I'll have you, you dolt. What do you mean, 'if I'll have you'?"

He kissed me again. "I mean it is your decision, not Will's. I intended to talk to Will once the time was right."

"You're sleeping with my baby sister," Will growled. "Under my roof. Don't you think it's time?"

Rick cracked a hint of a smile. "Again, William, that's up to Francesca to say. Will you marry me, Francesca? I swear I love you more than life itself."

I kinda melted into him at that. "Yes," I exclaimed, as I wrapped my arms around him, tight. "Oh, yes, Richard."

"I haven't said I will give you permission yet," Will growled.

"I didn't ask for your permission," retorted Richard. "Any more than you asked mine before you started sleeping with my mother."

"As I recall, you were nowhere near us then."

I stood up to my full 5'5" and glowered at my big brother. "I am almost twenty-two years old. I am a widow with two children. And thanks to your meddling, I am a Duchess. He doesn't need your permission. He needs mine."

Richard's head whipped around to me. "And I have that, right?"

And then, when you think things could not become any more embarrassing, Marcus stepped into the hall, rubbing the sleep from his eyes with a broad yawn. "What's astir?"

Will and Richard both started talking at once. All I could make out were "sleepin' together", "claims he loves her," "I do love her," and "says he doesn't even need my permission to marry her."

"He doesn't need yer permission, Will. Mine, mayhap, but not yours. And he has mine, if he wants it. What do ye say, Fancy? Do ye want the man or no?" Marc asked.

I am sure my eyes were dancing with the joy bursting my heart. I threw my arms around Richard's neck as I answered. "Yes. I want him. Forever."

Will opened his mouth a time or two, before he turned to Marc. "And you're okay with this?"

He shrugged. "She's a woman grown, William. She's entitled to make her own decisions, like Sassy and you did. Like my Lee and I did nearly twenty years ago. She'll be twenty-two in a month. Tis her decision, not ours."

"But, what if she's with child?" Will looked anguished.

I laughed. "Then I would become a typical Selk bride on my wedding day. Pregnant, like Sassy was. But I'm not breeding, Will."

He jerked his head back to me. "How do you know?"

Richard sighed. "Oh, for the love of… we're using protection." When both men looked confused, he continued. "Birth control."

I snickered at Will's horrified look.

"What the blazes is that?" asked Will.

I noticed that in contrast, Marc looked thoughtful. "Birth control, hmm? Call me crazy, Will, but that seems like a wise decision. Gives them time to get to know each other well before they grow their family." He yawned again. "I'm goin' back to bed. You should, too, Will. Leave the young lovers alone. T'will be fine without our interference."

I pulled Richard into my room and stuck my tongue out at William before I slammed the door and pulled Richard to my bed.

Will was frowning the next morning as we came down for breakfast. Richard made a silly face at me as I bristled at my brother. "William, it's like Sassy says. You need to give it a nap."

"Give it a rest," he said without looking up from his papers. "Sassy says give it a rest. But that's not why I'm frowning."

I reckon I frowned at his comment. "So, what has you glowering like an angry bear today?"

He pushed the papers over to me with a sigh. "I reckon you need to read this. I honest-to-God don't know what to say. It makes my skin crawl to think about you doing this. Even for Washington."

He sighed and shook his head again.

Richard started to say something, but I put my hand on his arm and 'shh'd' him. I pulled the papers over and started to read them. When Richard started to interrupt me again, I said, "Hush. You need to read this, too. This is important."

Richard's lips narrowed as he leaned over my shoulder to begin to read. After a few lines, he looked over at Will, concern written all over his face. "When did you get this?"

Sassy came into the dining room and sat a plate of ham down on the table before taking her own seat. "It arrived this morning. I de-coded it, as you can see. We are both pretty much stunned he is asking it."

"He can't be serious, Mom. I mean, Washington can't be serious, can he? Is he asking Francesca …"?

"To spy on the British? Yes, I am afraid he is. In fact, I guess I kinda put the idea in his head."

I looked up, surprised by her words. "But why on earth would you have done that? I mean, I'm a Duchess…"

She shrugged. "That's why he thinks it would work. You would go to New York City as an emigre, intent on escaping back to Ireland. Lots of Loyalists are doing that. You would tell Clinton you wanted refuge until you could go. Let's face it. You're the darling of the Loyalists right now. The heroine of Yorktown, even if you are a Selk. I don't think Clinton would consider you could be a …"

"Spy? But that is what the General is asking her to do. Secure information pertaining to ongoing British action and report it. No. Absolutely not. It is far too dangerous. I cannot believe you would even suggest such a thing, Mom." Richard sounded furious, his lips thinned and white with rage.

I laid my hand on his arm. "Calm down, Richard."

He didn't even begin to slow down. "No. I will not calm down. You are asking her to put her life on the line. And if she did it? She could be caught. Imprisoned. Hung. Hell, Mom, you think I don't remember all that stuff Dad and you wrote? About the Culpers? About your obsession with Madame X? With Agent 355?"

"That's enough, Richard," Sassy snapped, as his fingers tapped nervously on her arm.

"Yes, quite enough. You do not understand what you are asking her to do. Hell, I remember. Was Agent 355 the same person as Madame X? Dad thought she was. You disagreed. You thought they were two women. We all know you're Madame X, even if your name won't be known in the future. But here's a news flash, Mom. Francesca is not going to play Agent 355 to your Madame X. You know the poor woman will die on a prison ship in New York Harbor. Hell, I thought Francesca was your friend, your best friend. If this is what you want for your best friend, I dread to think what you want for your enemies. No, absolutely not. She is too precious to us all. She is too precious to me! I cannot even believe you would ask her to do this."

My heart was beating hard and fast. I could feel the blood thrumming through my veins ninety to nothing. I felt lightheaded. They wanted me to be a spy. Me? I cleared my throat. "Did this Agent 355 get caught? Did she die on a prison ship?"

"We all have to make sacrifices…" Sassy began.

I jumped as Richard slammed both fists down on the table. "Dammit, no!"

Will huffed up at that. "Don't you talk to your mother like that, young man."

"Oh, for the love of… Will, Richard, calm down. I can't think with you two caterwauling like that. Did she, Sassy? Does Agent 355 die on a prison ship?" I was surprised. My voice sounded calm, in contrast to the terror I was feeling right then.

Sassy hesitated before she answered. "No one knows. She disappears. They say she was pregnant when they took her prisoner and she was held on a prison ship. Her pregnancy may have saved her from being hung right off the bat. It is unknown if she died there or survived."

"And her baby?"

"Her baby will be delivered and be raised by its father."

I raised my eyes to Richard.

"How do they catch her?" My voice was low, controlled, almost calm. Almost.

Richard wheeled around to face me. "You can't be considering this. For the love of God, Francesca, tell me you aren't considering this cockamamie plan! You heard Mom say even she doesn't know if this woman survives. Please, Francesca, after all you have been through already? We have a chance at our happy-ever-after. Please, sweetheart, don't throw our future away!"

"How did they catch her?" I asked again.

"Oh, for the love of God, you don't have to do this!" Richard shouted.

Impatient, I nodded. "I know that, Richard. How do they catch her, Sassy?"

"Clinton gives her bad information. He gives it to her, no one else. When Washington acts on it, Clinton knows he found his mole."

Richard threw his hands up in the air. "Oh, for the love of all that is holy! No, Francesca, you can't do this! You have little children to consider, if you aren't thinking about us. What happens to Charles if you are arrested for treason? To Bella? You can't do this. Marcus, thank God you're here. You have to talk some sense into your girl. This is insane!"

About then, Marcus and Lily came into the room. Marcus looked worried, his brows furrowed into a line across his forehead. Lily looked even more worried, gnawing on her lip, eyes filled with fear, as she stood there behind Marc, with her hand on his shoulder. Finally, Marc spoke. "What's going on William? Why is Richard so upset? Why does my girl look like she doesn't know whether to cry or run?"

"I'm all right, Daddy." My voice sounded calm, but I could still feel the blood pounding at the base of my throat, pit-a-pat, pit-a-pat, too fast, tripping along like a drunk racehorse.

"Tell him the damned truth, Francesca. Tell him what they want you to do." Richard's eyes begged me as strongly as his words did.

I cringed at the anger in his voice. "Richard, calm down. I haven't said yes."

Marcus frowned. "Said yes to what?"

Will looked up at Marc. "Washington wants her to go to New York and act as a spy."

Marc looked horrified. "My God, Fancy, tell me you aren't considering it."

Richard raked his hands through his hair. "Oh, yes, she's considering it. I can't believe it, but she is considering it. It will get her killed if she does. Please, sweetheart, for the love of all that is holy, you don't have to do this. After all this damned family has put you through? You can't give serious consideration to doing this!"

I paled at his words and started up from my seat. "Richard, you are out of control. You need to stop. Right now. Please, I beg you…"

Will's head whipped up at Richard's words. "What the hell do you mean, young man?"

Lily grew animated. I could see she was upset by the direction the conversation was heading. Her hands gripped the edge of the table so tight that her knuckles turned white. "Richard, everyone, please! We need to stay calm," she implored.

"What did ye mean, Rick? When ye said 'all this damned family has put you through'?" Marc's voice was low and controlled, but I could hear the steel in it.

I could tell the blood had all drained from my face. *Please Richard, don't do this*, I screamed internally. My heart was beating fast and furious. My hands were sweating and my stomach ached with unspoken fear. I felt light headed as I started up again. "Richard, please, no… you promised…"

"He raped you, Goddamnit! He…" Richard's words seemed to freeze in his throat as soon as he had uttered the words. "Oh, shit."

The room went silent. Sassy stared in horror. Marcus stood speechless as tears welled in his eyes. Will stared, uncomprehending what was being said. Lily began to cry.

"Sweetheart, I'm sorry…" Richard began.

I pushed back from the table, angrier than I knew I could be. My hands were shaking so hard I dropped my napkin. "You promised me. You promised you would never tell."

Richard looked like I had kicked his dog and he hung his head. He struggled to regain his composure.

Marcus managed to speak first. "Who raped her? Fancy? What is he talkin' about?"

I shook my head as the tears began to slide down my cheeks.

Lily pulled me close to her side. "It's okay, honey. You're safe here. We all love you."

"I didn't want them to ever know," I sobbed as I turned to cling to Lily. "Oh, Richard! How could you? You promised me you would never tell…"

Marcus slammed both hands down on the table so hard that the mahogany cracked. I jumped at the sound. "Goddamnit, somebody answer me. Who the feckin' hell raped my girl?"

Richard and Lily looked at each other like naughty children caught with their hands in the cookie jar. Sassy sat there, eyes big as saucers, horrified by the awful scene unfolding before her.

After a minute, I cleared my throat. I swallowed a couple of times as I clung to the edge of the table. At last, I answered, my hands shaking and my voice barely even a whisper as I revealed the secret I had meant never to tell. "Tom did."

All hell broke loose.

Chapter 11
Fancy and Rick - 1782

It was bad. God awful bad.

It seemed like we argued around and around and around. Nothing ever resolved, tempers higher with each passing hour.

Sassy was beyond hurt. She was devastated I had not told her. She refused to understand why I had not told her. *Oh, yeah, Sassy*, I thought, with significant bitterness. *You would make this all about you.* We yelled and screamed and cried at each other. It was bad. No, I take it back. It was far worse than bad. It was God awful horrible.

Of course, it no longer mattered. Richard broke his word when he told. My shame had been made public, and my wounds ripped raw anew, as if scoured with salt. I wanted to run away and hide.

That night, I locked Richard out of my room. He stood by my door in the hall, begging me to open it and let him in as I sat huddled on the other side by the door, crying.

"Francesca, let me in. Please, sweetheart! We need to talk."

I covered up my ears and refused to listen to him. I wept with anger, frustration, humiliation. All I could think was he promised he wouldn't tell and then he told. He broke his word to me. I wanted to die with shame.

But I did not expect to get up the next day and learn he had left. I grabbed the edge of the cracked table to steady myself. "He…"

"Damned son of a bitch left, Fancy. He's gone. Left in the middle of the night without a word to anyone." Will's voice was scornful. It was almost as if Will were saying, I told you so. You don't buy the cow when you get the milk for free.

Was it just two short days ago Richard and I were talking about marriage?

A week later, with still no word from Richard, I gave up. I agreed to Washington's request that I spy on behalf of the newly recognized United States of America against Britain.

Marc, Lily, my lads, the children and I left for New York. The lads did not know the hidden agenda in our trip to New York. They thought we were going home via New York City. Tobias and Hattie Mae accompanied us to serve as our 'staff'. Although Tobias is my great-uncle, and Hattie Mae is his wife, it would look like they were servants. They both refused to stay at Belle Rose without me again.

Of course, Will about had a fit of apoplexy when they both told him they were going with me. *Served him right,* I thought, my mood glum. *I wouldn't be going if his wife hadn't set this whole mess up.*

I felt empty. The love of my life had betrayed me, and then abandoned me. I was tired. Of the struggle. The pain. The unending heartache. Sassy promised me Agent 355's children would survive. I no longer cared if I survived or not. I went to New York to fulfill my destiny.

•　　•　　•　　•　　•

Richard rode long and hard. It was a long way to Washington's headquarters in New York. It was imperative he talk with the Commander-in-Chief and make him understand the horrible risk this plan put Francesca in if she agreed. Please, dear God, let me get there in time to convince him. Please.

God, what he would have given for a car right then. And decent roads. Better yet, a damned telephone. Or even a computer. He had to chuckle at the idea of tweeting Washington.

Sassy always warned him not to make permanent decisions based on temporary feelings. By God, he hoped he wasn't doing that now. But he couldn't let Francesca made a mistake like this. Please, dear God, don't let her make a permanent decision based on temporary emotions. She was so angry, she might agree to this cockamamie plan for no other reason than to spite him. Please, dear God, don't let that happen, he prayed again and again.

He galloped on as the ice and snow pelted his face towards his sole hope. Agent 355 would die as a spy. Richard was determined Francesca would not be the one sacrificed for some insignificant scrap of information. The war was good as finished. They didn't need her services now.

Her children needed her. Richard needed her. He came too far to find her. He did not intend to lose her now.

He couldn't.

He urged the horse on through the snow and sleet. Snow be damned. He would not fail the woman he loved again. Once was enough. He knew he would never forget the pain in her eyes he caused when his big mouth overloaded and he blurted out her innermost secret until the day he died. Dammit, every time he remembered the hurt in her eyes, he felt like he died a little.

Jesus, he thought again for the hundredth time. What if I did come back at the wrong damned time? Is my presence here now going to muck up everything I long for?

He rode on, pulling his cap down again even as the ice crystals froze to his face and eyelashes.

•   •   •   •   •

The same day we left, Sassy and Will left the same day to Philadelphia to testify against Tarleton. Three days later, they met with Alexander Hamilton, who had resigned his commission in the Continental Army after Yorktown.

"What the hell do you mean he's not here to be tried?" Will snapped the words out at Hamilton.

Hamilton flinched. "He escaped from the prisoner of war camp. We are searching for him, but so far, he has evaded us."

Sassy looked terrified. She began to shake at Hamilton's words. "He … he could be anywhere."

Hamilton nodded. "Yes, ma'am, Mrs. Selk. He sure could."

"I'll testify this morning but then we are out of here. I have to get back to my babies." She ran her trembling hands up and down her arms.

The young man nodded. "We understand."

Sassy and a half-dozen other women testified about the abuses they suffered at the hands of Tarleton. By 8 that night, the Ranscome's Revenge left the harbor in Philadelphia to head back to Belle Rose. Two days later, they made home. Will and Sassy loaded the children and headed for the safety of the sugar plantation located in Spanish-held Puerto Rico. Will dashed off a quick letter to Marc to warn he should be on the watch for Tarleton in New York.

•   •   •   •   •

The wind raged wild around the lone, determined man as he trudged with dogged determination through the snow with but one thought: Belle Rose. It was a long hike back to Virginia, but Tarleton knew he would manage it.

He trudged on, his anger and resolve growing with each step.

By late afternoon, he found a hatchet by a woodpile. He picked it up and tested its heft. His smile, as cold as the north wind howling down from Canada, did not touch his eyes. He walked into the cozy little cabin, where he killed the man with one blow to the back of his head as the unsuspecting man sat whittling in the rocking chair by the blazing fire. The woman shrieked with fear as she backed away from the man with the cold, dead eyes. He grabbed her arm, threw her on the bed, and had his way with her. The next morning, he left the cabin, clad in the dead man's furs and boots, carrying his Pennsylvania musket and a bag filled with food, while he gnawed on a turkey leg. He pitched a burning faggot on the thatched roof of the cabin and smiled as it burst into flames. He saddled the lone horse in the barn and rode out before the first light of morn. He should make Belle Rose within a week. They always say revenge is a dish best served cold. The bitches would never see it coming any more than these poor fools had.

•   •   •   •   •

I hated New York City from the minute we arrived. It was noisy, crowded, dirty. I had never seen so many people in one place before in my life. I hated the squalor and filth. I yearned to be back in Virginia. I realized I was not meant for the big city. I doubted I was any better cut out for espionage. I wondered again why on earth I ever agreed to this insane plot. And then I remembered. Richard left. Without a single word. I'm already dead. It killed me when he left. It doesn't matter anymore.

Nothing matters anymore.

I hadn't felt this empty in a long time.

It took us two weeks to get there. It was late when we arrived at the Georgian brownstone in Manhattan that had been a Selk property for over fifty years. The housekeeper expected us and had kept a warm dinner ready with a fire blazing in the large parlor downstairs. Numb, I slipped into a chair beside the fire, holding my sleeping child. Lily took charge of getting everyone assigned to rooms.

I had to admit it was a handsome property. It could use a woman's touch, but the rooms were large and comfortable, with lots of windows which should let in the light during the days. I knew Uncle William owned it before Daddy Jo inherited it. The townhouse was one of the properties now belonging to the Duchess of Ranscome. The furniture looked like it came from the 1740's and there were lots of heavy tapestries in hunt prints and dark colors. Lily pointed out several rugs were Aubusson. Yes, it needed a woman's touch, if we stayed here any significant amount of time at all. A lot could be improved with fresh paint, new bed linens, curtains, and slipcovers. The seamstress in me began thinking of fabrics and colors, as exhausted as I was that cold March night.

Marc told me the dinner was on the table and took Bella from my arms. I tucked her onto the couch to let her continue sleeping. "I think she has a fever, Lily."

Lily frowned as she bent to feel my child's brow. "A little. We'll keep a close watch, but I'm pretty sure it's just a cold."

We ate the lamb stew and fresh bread with a minimum of talk. I made sure to thank the housekeeper for the late supper. She appeared relieved at my words.

"I was afraid it was not enough," she began.

I shook my head. "Not at all, Agnes. It's fine. There is plenty of it. It's hot and filling. It was an excellent choice. We're all exhausted, the children most of all. Poor Bella doesn't feel well, and it has been a long trip. I'm glad we're here at last."

"I'll make a big pot of chicken soup tomorrow. It will help the little one fight her cold."

I nodded. "I'm a big believer in the healing qualities of chicken soup."

She smiled, curtseyed, and left to begin tidying up the kitchen. A few minutes later, I chuckled as Hattie Mae followed her. I knew it wouldn't be long before Hattie established she was the queen of this kitchen, the way she did at Belle Rose as a young woman, forty years before. Tobias helped the men move luggage to the various bedrooms. Within the hour, we were settled enough that I was able to tuck my children into their own bedrooms.

I managed to turn in for the night around 11. I remembered how I wished I could come to New York with Daddy Jo when I was little. I would never have guessed these rooms would someday be mine. I sighed as I sank into the plush feather bed that night. Tears welled in my eyes as I lay on that big bed, thinking of all I had two weeks ago that I lost in the blink of an eye. As the tears began to trickle from my eyes, I wondered again how we got so close to heaven to fall so fast and so hard back down to the hell I found myself in now. Hell? Well, I made it myself. I was the one who agreed to this insane charade. Richard tried his damnedest to talk me out of this folly.

I looked around the room again and I chuckled, the sound hollow, empty. If he hadn't left, I would not be here now.

I got up and stoked the fire in the fireplace. I pulled out the damning letter from Calvin and read it one last time. As I read each page, I ripped it into little pieces. I fed the pieces one by one into the fire, watching as each word curled into crisped ash and disappeared. Once I burned it all, I ripped apart my journal. I tore out each page, feeding them to the ravenous fire as well. As the last scrap curled into a wisp of nothing, I sighed. It was destroyed. I felt as empty as my hands. Nothing was left in writing to prove any of it ever happened. None of it could ever be used as evidence against the Duchess of Ranscome or her children.

It was March 18, 1782. I turned 22 that day. I had been surprised all day no one wished me a happy birthday, not even Marcus or Lily. I realized it had been a difficult couple of weeks. Believe me, I knew all too well how hard these weeks had been. I tried to tell myself my family were all exhausted and my birthday slipped their minds. It was nothing more than a birthday. It wasn't important.

But when a woman turned 22, she no longer needs anyone's permission to marry as she wished. Just weeks before, Richard and I talked about this hallmark birthday and its significance for me. For us. For our future life together. For the children he swore we would some day have. Now, he was gone.

My monthly began that morning. I had hoped and prayed for three weeks I might somehow have conceived a child while we were together, despite his insistence we use 'protection.' No such luck. If a pregnancy were to keep me from the hangman's noose in the months to come, it would not be the child of the man I loved. He up and left me without a word. I had no expectation he would return. Life had never been kind to me. I had learned to expect the worst, and life rarely surprised me. Why did it surprise me now that life was once again giving me lemons from lemonade?

I pledged my word to the General. I would do my duty to the country of my birth. My children would survive even if I did not go with them to Ireland. One day, God willing, Charles would be the Fourth Duke of Ranscome. If not? Gentry's children would come next, as spelled out in my will. I chuckled. Then they could move the tribe to Ireland to live on Ranscome lands. I have to admit, I would love to see that!

But why did I have to feel so cheated? For once, why couldn't things have gone the way I hoped? The way I prayed?

I rolled over onto my side, curled into a ball, and cried myself to sleep.

The next morning, I slept later than usual. When I managed to drag myself downstairs, Marcus extended me a letter. "It's from Will. He says Tarleton escaped."

I felt myself grow lightheaded as the blood drained from my head. I grabbed the edge of the doorway. "How? When?"

Marc extended the letter to me again. "Read it. Seems the bastard escaped during a winter storm. They learned he escaped when they reached Philadelphia. The women all testified and he was found guilty in absentia. Sassy is beside herself. They are going to Puerto Rico until the sorry rat bastard is re-captured, or it is confirmed he left the country."

My heart racing and my hands trembling, I took the papers from Marc. I read the missive before I looked back at him. "Once he realizes no one is at Belle Rose, he'll head to New York."

He nodded. "Aye, my exact thoughts. So, what do ye want to do? Stay? Or flee?"

I gulped, more scared than I had been since I agreed to this insane plan. "We need to talk to Cousin Rob, and to General Clinton, the British Commander-in-Chief."

"Aye, but it's in the paper that Clinton is soon to be replaced by Sir Guy Carleton. He is an Irishman from Tyrone County in the north of the island. He was Governor of Quebec before his assignment here. Cornwallis was already called home after the debacle, as they are calling Yorktown. Clinton will leave within the month. That's about all I know. Carlton didn't marry until he was nearing the age I am now. His wife is 30 years younger than him. They have a passel of children and he adores her. He should be sympathetic to the young widow of a war hero killed at Yorktown when he realizes Calvin was 35 years older than you."

I sniffed. "Well, that may keep me in widow's weeds longer but perhaps it will keep the sex-crazed young officers off my tail. And even though I'm not grieving over Calvin, I can sure enough cry at the drop of a hat."

We both lapsed into an awkward silence. The cause of my crying spells remained unnamed although we both knew who the cause was. I turned and walked over to the window that overlooked the busy street beyond. "Is it always like this?"

Marc laughed. "I've never been here before. It's quite amazing, isn't it? It makes me think of London. I remember a similar feeling of astonishment when I was a lad and we visited London on the way to Italy. I thought London was the most wonderful city in the world."

"You like it? I hate it," I muttered. "The noise never stops. It disturbed my sleep off and on all night. I don't know how to sleep with all that ruckus going on outside my window. There seem to be swarming crowds of people everywhere. And I never saw such filth before. I don't understand why anyone would want to live in a place like this."

"I can assure you New York City will get bigger, noisier, and dirtier in the years to come, and people will still clamor to move here. I rather like it. Always did," Lily said as she slathered blackberry jam on her toast. "Shall we send word to Robert Townsend today before we try to see General Clinton? Is Carlton here yet? I bet Robert knows Clinton and could advise us. He might have met Carlton, too."

I stared at the busy foot traffic for a few minutes before I answered. What could make people come to live in a city the size of New York? How could all these people find work? Heck fire, how could they find housing? Food? Water? If a body didn't have to be here, why stay in a city as dirty and crowded as this?

I hadn't even liked Yorktown and it was tiny compared to this behemoth. I turned to face Lily and Marc. "That's a good idea. Let's send Cousin Rob word we are here and ask him to come to dinner tonight. I can put off visiting the General for a day or two, but I want to talk to Robert first. After all, he knows General Clinton for sure. He might even introduce us."

"That would be good. And he might know if Tarleton is in town." Marc sounded stressed.

Lily's head whipped around in shock. "Tarleton? Here? But I thought he was supposed to be tried for war crimes in Philadelphia."

"The son of a bitch escaped." Marc's voice belied his anger and frustration that Tarleton was loose. I knew he did not intend for the little braggart to get his hands upon Lily or me, especially after the comments Tarleton made about coming back for me. I knew without a doubt Marc would kill Tarleton or die trying if Tarleton even tried to hurt either of us. I shivered and rubbed my arms. "Ooh, I feel like a possum walked across my grave. We can talk to the Ranscome shipping people and see when a ship might be able to take us to Ireland."

Marc nodded, his face grim with worry. "Aye, that wouldn't be a bad idea. I suspect Her Grace, the Duchess of Ranscome, might be able to get a Ranscome ship quicker than most people seeking to leave New York."

I nodded. I sure hoped so. The shipping line was one of the properties I now owned and would provide our means of escape to Ireland. If I could survive long enough.

I sighed. Dammit, I never wanted this title. I never even wanted to go to Ireland. Now, I prayed every night I would manage to get there with my skin still attached to my bones, and I would be able to grow old watching my children grow up. I might even be glad to meet Tamsin again, I thought, as my fingers caressed the chatelaine hanging at my waist. God knew she wrote Fitz often and he always read her letters to me.

Strange. For the first time in most of my life, Tamsin was becoming a real person to me. A person I might should meet, if I managed to live long enough. Who knows? A person I might even come to like. Yes, she ran off with Jay Fitz Simmons 18 years ago and left me behind. But maybe I understood a little bit better about people doing stupid things when they thought they were in love. And, maybe they were in love when they ran off to Ireland. I hoped she had some happiness in her life.

Children. A single, unbidden tear slid out of my eye even as I tried to blink it back. Now, if I could manage to keep my two precious children alive. After all, my hopes for a happy future and a big family walked out the door at the beginning of the month with nary a word.

Dad blast it, Richard. Why didn't you listen to me? Why didn't you trust me enough to give me a chance to refuse to participate in this ridiculous scheme? We could be halfway to Ireland by now, on our way to, what was it you called it? Oh, yes. To our happy-ever-after. Instead of this godforsaken hellhole.

I swiped at a tear and turned back to Marc and Lily. "Then it sounds like we have our plans for the day. A letter to Cousin Rob, asking him to dinner, a trip to the shipping lines, and a note to General Clinton asking to see him later this week to make our introductions. Find out if General Carlton is here yet, and if he is, arrange to meet with him, too. Anything else?"

Marc stared at me before he answered. His shoulders sagged as he raked his hands through his hair and sighed. My heart lurched as I noticed silver hairs amidst his strawberry blonde and tiny, fine creases at the corners of his eyes and mouth. I swear they weren't there last month. I realized with a start he must be at least fifty now. My daddy was getting old. "No. I guess that sounds like everything."

"Then, let's get started."

We hurried all day.

By late morning, I sent letters of introduction to my cousin, Rob Townsend, as well as to General Clinton, the current Commander-in-Chief. I asked Rob to join us for dinner that evening, if at all possible. We verified General Carlton was already in New York and sent a letter of introduction to him as well. I asked permission to see both Generals in the next few days, as their schedules might allow. I then sent word to Ranscome Shipping we would be coming by that afternoon as well.

We were walking out of the townhouse about 2, when a messenger came rushing up. I ripped open the letter and grinned at Marc and Lily. "Rob's coming tonight. He'll be here at 7."

"Excellent. We'll know soon enough what he recommends." Marc sounded relieved and pleased at my news.

"Hattie Mae is already cooking a nice pot roast for supper, so we will be able to feed him a good meal. Perhaps we can pick up a nice bottle or two of wine while we are out today," I suggested.

We hurried on to the elegant offices located across from the piers. After a brief wait, we were ushered into a beautiful conference room overlooking the harbor. I went to the plate glass window to stare out over the harbor as we waited for Captain Conrad Sorenson, who was in charge of the New York offices. I noted to my dismay and growing concern there were no Ranscome ships in the harbor. As I stared at the busy harbor, the door flew open and a handsome man who looked to be in his early 40's rushed in.

"Your Grace, I just heard you had arrived. I am honored you have come to Ranscome Shipping today. What may I do for you?"

I turned to smile at him. About 6' tall, light brown hair, with intelligent blue eyes filled with enthusiasm and eagerness. His face was scoured with the fine lines a sailing man gets from years exposed to the sun and elements. I held out my hand. "Captain Sorenson, I appreciate you seeing us on such short notice. This is Lord Marcus Fitz Simmons and his wife, Lady Lilliana Fitz Simmons. This handsome young man is Viscount Winston Fitz Simmons."

Sorensen was quick to kiss my hand before greeting Lily, Marc and Fitz. After some small talk, we all sat down around a big conference table set in front of the window overlooking the harbor.

"I notice there are no Ranscome ships in the harbor at present, Captain. I hoped we would be able to secure passage to Ireland."

Captain Sorensen looked horror stricken. "Your Grace, I thought you knew. The harbor is blockaded. Our ships cannot get here."

I blinked, stunned by his words. "We can't get out of New York?"

"Not by ship, unless you are on a British ship heading back to London. The Americans are allowing British ships to go home. We might be able to arrange for a Ranscome ship to reconnoiter with a British ship after it passes the blockade line."

"That would be wonderful! When do you think a British ship might sail?"

"Around April 10th, I understand."

Excited, I looked at Marc. "What do you think?"

He grimaced. "It depends."

I frowned. "On what?"

Before he could answer, Fitz answered. "Faith, it depends on whether or not Tarleton will be on the ship to Britain."

My mouth went dry as my hands went cold at his words. Butter my buns and call me a biscuit, I should have thought of that. I whipped my head first to Marc, then to Lily. Silent, both nodded. I wet my lips. "Yes, that would be a significant factor to consider. But, even so, if we could meet the Ranscome ship, what, thirty miles offshore? I think we could put up with him for that long. I would rather not, but…"

"You don't understand, Fancy. If the ships don't reconnoiter, then we could be on the same ship with him for the entire voyage." Marc's low, soft voice belied the emotional impact of his words.

My heart began beating erratically. "For…"

"The entire voyage, *m'inion*. A good forty, mayhap forty-five days. Stuck on the same ship as that sorry *mhac na galla*. I'm not sure I could manage it. God knows if he dared to touch ye…" his voice broke. "Well, I don't think I could control myself." I always love it when Marc calls me 'my daughter' in the Irish.

Fitz nodded. "Nor could I."

Captain Sorenson looked uncomfortable. "Well, you have a bit of time to decide."

"But not much," I snapped.

He shook his head. "No, Your Grace. Not much, if I am to arrange one of your ships to reconnoiter. However, we could arrange a ship to pick you up in Baltimore, if you don't mind back tracking a bit. Our ships can still get into Baltimore with no problems."

I was quiet most of the way home. I had a lot to think about. Would Tarleton get back before we left? If he did, and if he was sent home on the first ship, did I risk putting us on the same ship so we could reconnoiter with a Ranscome ship offshore? Or did I wait? Or should we go to Baltimore? I sighed. I guessed I would have to wait and see what happened. All I knew right then was my head was pounding, and I was bone tired.

I checked on Bella when we got home. She seemed better than she had for several days. Lily was sure she had what she called a 'little upper respiratory infection.' I told Lily I would have called it a cold. She laughed and said it was about the same thing. She'd started Bella on some of the medicine Richard had brought because she said Bella had an infection. I felt so relieved my child was getting the best medical care possible. Lily swore with the medicine, Bella would make a quick and complete recovery.

After I visited with Bella and Charlie for an hour or two, I retired to my boudoir, where I changed into fresh attire before dinner. My headache was worse, and I hoped a little toilet water splashed on my temples combined with a cup of willow bark tea would stop the blinding headache. I never had a problem like this consarned headache before. But, as Hattie Mae announced dinner was ready, my head still pounded as if besieged by demons. I tried my best to put on a happy face as I descended down the elegant stairway to the foyer, to welcome Cousin Rob to 'my' home.

My home. How odd. I still could not get over the riches the title brought with it. At the same time, I wondered if this property would remain mine once the settlement over the war was finished. I would have to write to Will and Sassy and see what she might know about such things.

I frowned as I remembered again the harsh words we both threw at each other two weeks before. Could we ever repair our relationship? Had I ruined my friendship with my best friend forever by not telling her about Tom and Calvin? Why couldn't she understand my view point? Well, that was typical of Sassy. She likes to be in control, always in charge, and the one who knows everything. I don't say that to in any manner belittle her. It's just a fact. It's part of what makes her the dynamic force she is. I thought again for the umpteenth time that Sassy was so much better qualified than I would ever be to serve as Duchess. Why couldn't William have kept the dad-blasted title?

"Cousin Rob, I am Fancy Hobbs. I am delighted to meet you at long last."

My heart fluttered as the handsome young man bowed over my extended hand and kissed it. I didn't recall anyone other than Calvin ever doing such a thing before. Oh, I forgot, Richard kissed my hand when he met me last summer. Shiny dark brown hair, cunning, brown eyes, a pleasant smile. Taller than most men in this day and age, at about 5'10", although shorter than most of the men in my family. I knew Rob was related somehow to Mama Belle, and he certainly had her coloring with his brown eyes and brown hair. Must be related to the Broussard's, I thought. I felt my tremulous smile falter at the unexpected touch of his lips to my hand. Suddenly feeling awkward, I pulled my hand back from his.

"It is a pleasure to meet you at last, Fancy. Will has written me so much about you. And of course, Uncle Jo often talked about you when he came to New York. I was sorry to hear of your husband's death."

My eyelashes brushed my cheeks as I tried to stop unbidden tears. "Thank you. Please, come in. I believe we have much to discuss this evening."

We ate supper with my Irish guard in attendance. After dinner, the men slipped away to allow us to visit in private. They had been told we had personal family business to discuss.

"I understand Tarleton may be headed to New York," Marc said once the men in my guard had left the room.

Rob nodded. "So, I understand. I never met the man before. How does that impact you?"

I gulped. "He made some serious threats against me the day he was arrested. I must admit I am more than a little bit nervous to think about him being here…"

"Given the project before us?" he said, his voice low, as he took my hand into his again.

I nodded. "Yes. Scares me plumb dab witless, truth be told. So, the question is, do we stay and tough it out? Or do we turn tail and head to Ireland?"

Rob got up and went to the door to the kitchen. He motioned for us to be quiet as he looked out the door. He relaxed when he saw no one was in the kitchen. He shut the door and went to the door to the foyer. He again checked for listeners, and then shut the door.

"We must be cautious about what we say. Walls are thin and loose lips sink ships, as the sailors say."

Lily nodded. "Yes, they do. Thank you for checking. What do you think?"

He sighed. "I warned our friend against this from the beginning. As you know, Felicity was arrested in October and accused of treason. She is the only woman who has ever been held on a prison ship. The British deny she was held on the ship, but I know different. I visited her there each week and took her food and other things she needed. They could not hang her right away because she was with child. They planned to hang her once the baby was born."

"No, I didn't know that. Did they hang her?" I asked.

He shook his head. "No. She died from complications in childbirth. Filthy conditions on that damned ship. The baby survived. I am raising him."

My eyebrows must have hit the ceiling. "He's yours?"

He nodded. "Oh, yes. He's my miracle baby. She was the love of my life. I still cannot believe she is gone. I would hate for such a fate to ever befall another woman."

I gulped and nodded as he looked me straight in the eye. "I agree. Nasty business, treason."

"Indeed, it is. It broke me. But I believe you wondered if I could introduce you to General Clinton. I took the liberty of stopping by his offices today and telling him you've arrived. He can see you tomorrow at 1, if that's convenient. I would be most happy to accompany you. I am sure he would have suggestions about getting you to Ireland soon as possible. I feel you should go soon, although I would love to have you stay here for a while."

"Have you met Carlton yet?" Lily asked.

He shook his head. "No, he does not begin his official duties for another week or so. They are planning a big ball April 5th, before Clinton leaves. I am sure we will meet him there, if we have not met him beforehand."

"But I am in mourning…"

"Yes, but mark my words, they will expect the Duchess of Ranscome to attend the ball of the year. Forewarned is forearmed, you know. Better be prepared. I have it on competent authority they expect you to attend, even though Sir Calvin just died in October. After all, you are a young widow and a Duchess. We don't have a Duchess ride into town very often. They want to show you off at the party."

"Wonderful," I said beneath my breath, not at all feeling wonderful about the prospect of being the prize heifer to dangle before the eligible bachelors at a big ball.

Marc's eyes narrowed. "She won't be able to get out of it since she is in mourning?"

Rob shook his head. "No, and she should go. Proper decorum and all that rot, you know." He lowered his voice. "And it might afford you the opportunity to learn some wee tidbit to send to our mutual friends about the party that might make it up to them for missing the event of the year."

I blinked. And gulped. Dammit, even if I managed to get on the next ship to Ireland, I was still caught in the middle of this insufferable intrigue. "Yes, Sassy always loves the gossip about town."

We were all agreed that any reference to 'our friends' would be about Will and Sassy. He might be considered a traitor to the Crown here, but he was my brother, and writing to him would be acceptable. Writing to Washington would not.

"I am sure your sister-in-law would be most eager to hear all about the party. Who was in attendance. How they were dressed. Hair styles. Dress styles. All that rot. And of course, you might even come across some delectable tidbit of gossip. I understand women love to get bits of gossip." He grinned, his brown eyes sparkling in the candlelight.

I nodded. Yes, Sassy would love all of that. Maybe it would even give me an opportunity to open up discussions with Sassy via correspondence towards a reconciliation. And maybe it would allow me the opportunity to ask about her wayward son. Something like, oh, by the way, have you heard from Richard? Does he ever intend to come back to me, or was it all smoke and mirrors? Or just so much fairy dust he blew to get up under my skirts?

We arranged to meet Rob outside the General's offices the next day a little before 1 o'clock. He would introduce us all to Gen. Clinton. We chatted some more about family matters before he left for the evening.

I stood in silence at the door as I watched him leave. Marc came up beside me and slipped his arm around my shoulders. "What do you think, *m'inion?*"

I smiled. I reached a hand up to pat his arm. "I don't know, Daddy, but we will figure it out. Lily, do you have anything for a headache? This headache is killing me. I don't think I ever had a headache this bad before in my entire life."

Lily came up besides us before she answered. "You were never asked to commit treason before, Fancy. It's no wonder your head hurts. The stress is so thick you could cut it with a knife. But we are here and we will not let anything bad happen to you. Now, why don't you go get out of your widow's weeds into something more comfortable? I'll bring you something better than willow bark tea for your headache."

Not fifteen minutes later, Lily brought me a pill for my headache. I gulped it down with the glass of water she extended to me, and then slipped into my bed. I hoped it would ease the unpleasant headache. It did ease it somewhat, although I awoke throughout the night with the recurring headache which seemed worse each time I awakened.

Chapter 12
Fancy - 1782

By morning, the blasted headache escalated to a whole new level of pain I never dreamed a headache could reach. "It would figure I would still have this dratted headache this morning," I complained.

Lily looked worried. "You still have it? I'm surprised. You're not prone to headaches."

I nodded. "I swear my vision is blurry and I feel downright sick to my stomach. And my neck is so sore I can barely turn my head. I don't understand this at all."

Her face lit up. "Oh, you have a migraine, honey! It's all this interminable stress. I think it will ease up after we get through today and come to some decisions. Remember, we're here with you. We love you and we are going to make sure your children and you are safe and sound."

I smiled at her. "Thank God I have you guys, too."

The morning passed quickly. Bella felt much better. She was laughing and joking, back to her happy-go-lucky self again. I read stories to her for an hour or so. We practiced her letters and she was writing her name before the morning ended. We were both very excited about her progress with her handwriting. She is young, not yet quite four, but she was very bright and wanted to learn. I was determined nothing would hold my little girl back. I sang Charlie a lullaby at nap time, and Bella and I ate a light luncheon before I went to dress for the appointment with the General. We left the house a little after noon and were outside Clinton's offices right on time to meet Cousin Rob. Rob ushered us right in to General Clinton.

"General, I would like to introduce my dear cousin, Lady Francesca Hobbs.

Lady Hobbs is the widow of Sir Calvin Hobbs…".

"Ah, yes, young lady. I was quite saddened to hear of your husband's demise at Yorktown. Sir Calvin was a fine man and loyal to the Crown. I understand you provided admirable assistance to our valiant men there. Please, come in, and sit down."

"Thank you, General. I appreciate your kind words. May I introduce my family, Lord and Lady Fitz Simmons, and Leftenant Winston Fitz Simmons? And these are the other gentlemen whom General Cornwallis appointed at Yorktown to guard me. Leftenant Martin O'Reilly, Leftenant Brian Callahan, Leftenant Corey O'Halloran, Leftenant Timothy O'Shaunnessy, and of course, Captain Damien McMichael. I could not ask for a better and more devoted group of soldiers to guard me. Each has proven himself invaluable to me."

He frowned. "I understood twelve were assigned to you?"

"Quite so. Unfortunately, three were killed protecting me at Yorktown. Another sickened with typhus after the battle ended. Another sickened with malaria and one with camp fever. Those three were shipped home from Virginia. These six young men remain of the original twelve. Each is a remarkable young man, brave, dedicated, and devoted. Each epitomizes the phrase 'officer and gentleman' to me. I am proud to have them guard me, and I consider each one to be a man I am proud to know."

I could tell my praise pleased him.

"General, you may be wondering why I am in New York. We are headed to Ireland. I never wanted to be the Duchess of Ranscome, but the King named me to follow in my brother's stead. It seems that since the estate was first established in Ireland in fee simple, my grandfather could bequest it to whoever he wished in his will. The will stipulated Thomas Selk first. Tom died at Saratoga. William second. Will plans to remain here and signed the lands and title over to me. I was the third listed to inherit. The King confirmed the descent and noted that it has twice before passed to a female relative since first established through Baroness Elizabeth Selk in 1563. I understand that it is a fee simple title, rather than an entailed title, so it could pass to me. I think the King felt better about it coming to me since I was married to Sir Calvin. In any event, I feel we need to get on to Ireland, rather than remain in the Colonies."

"You don't call it the United States of America?" he asked.

I felt my cheeks redden. "My brother does. Of course, he considers himself to be an American patriot. I … I consider him a traitor to the Crown."

An unbidden tear slipped down my cheek as I struggled to hold my hands still. Dammit, I am not going to start having Mama Belle's butterfly hands now. Not. Now.

"Ah, my dear young woman, you have no idea how pleased I am to hear you say that. Too many young people raised here in the Colonies have no idea what loyalty to King and Country is."

"Well, I do. My grandfather, Josiah Selk, the first Duke of Ranscome, was the third brother. He never expected to be the heir. Yet, he told me he followed his duty when both of his brothers died without issue. I am doing no less than my grandfather would expect me to do, or raised me to do. It is quite simple. This is not about my wants or desires. It is about duty. I shall do my duty. If it were about my own personal desires, I would take my children to Spring Haven in Bermuda. I love Bermuda, and have wonderful memories of our life there. I would raise Charles and Bella at Charles' home in Bermuda if I were not now the Duchess of Ranscome. But with this title came different responsibilities. It is important for both Charles and me to learn our way in Ireland."

We talked for the better part of an hour, about the war in the Southern Colonies, as he called Virginia, the Carolinas, and Georgia, how the Loyalists were flocking north to New York to seek transport to Britain, and about the new Commander-in-Chief due in New York any day. "In fact, there will be a ball held in honor of both of us on April 5th. I hope you will attend."

I glanced at Marc and Lily before I smiled. "I am still in mourning, but I shall do my duty, even though I may regret the timing. I admit I am not eager to start socializing…"

"Oh, nonsense. You are a beautiful young lady in a town desperate for a little beauty. Your husband died five months ago. He would want you to be out and about with young people."

I laughed, as I remembered Calvin's final words to me in his letter. "I doubt it. I will have to see if I have anything suitable to wear…"

"Excellent. Then it is settled. You will come and wear something less oppressive than your widow's weeds. We will see you on the 5th. Oh, and Mrs. Clinton is having a tea on the 1st. I know she would love for you to attend."

"Of course," I murmured.

Then, having agreed to his demands for me to appear and to be the key attraction at his parties, I finally broached my concerns.

"General, I am sure you are aware that the British and Americans both signed a warrant to arrest Col. Tarleton for war crimes," I began.

He made a dismissive motion with his hand. "Oh, yes, I understand Washington forced Cornwallis to sign the ridiculous document. In any event, the charges against Tarleton were dismissed. He is on his way back to New York as we speak. He should be back any time now."

My mouth went dry with terror. I poured myself a small glass of water and after a couple of sips, I continued. "Well, sir, I understand from my brother Col. Tarleton escaped his prison and did not attend the trial. William states …"

"Balderdash! I cannot believe the word of a traitor, madam. You yourself said your brother is a traitor to the Crown."

My heart pounding wildly, I paused for a moment before I proceeded. I pressed my hands together to stop the visible trembling. "General, my brother may be on the wrong side of this war, but he is no liar. I would believe him before I would ever believe Col. Tarleton."

His eyes narrowed as his lips pressed together into an angry line. "Why?"

I jumped a little at the harshness of his bark. I composed myself and sat up as straight as possible in the hard chair. "Because, sir, I was present at Belle Rose Plantation when Col. Tarleton came there last summer to 'punish' Mrs. Selk. I am quite aware she lied to him in January. She admitted that to me. However, she did nothing to merit being repeatedly violated by that man. I can perhaps justify the horsewhipping, although I thought 40 lashes were a bit excessive…"

"Violated? Do you mean to say… Rape? And what is this about a horsewhipping? Forty lashes? I … I don't know what you are talking about."

"Indeed, sir? Well, I have with me a copy of the affidavit I gave to General Cornwallis on 17 October 1781 at Yorktown. Perhaps you would like to read it. I also have copies of the statements of the 12 women who alleged he violated them, including Mrs. Selk. And a letter from my brother stating Tarleton escaped, that he did not appear at trial and he was found guilty in absentia."

Clinton blinked a couple of times, shocked by my staunch words. He snapped the papers from my hands and began to study the writings. After an uncomfortable pause during which he perused the documents at length, he looked up at me. "I … I had no idea. My God. Forty lashes to a woman. That of itself is a death sentence. I don't know how the woman survived it. Charles told me he was pressured into signing the agreement to try Tarleton as part of the surrender. Of course, backed by the sworn statements of a person such as yourself, Your Grace, well, I am shocked and horrified."

I nodded. "I understand, General. He is a handsome young man, with his flashing smile, sparkling eyes, and dapper style. He speaks well and usually comports himself well in polite society. He can be quite charming and well-mannered at times. At other times? Believe me, not so much. In fact, that last day at Yorktown, he made some threats against me…"

He made another dismissive motion in the air. "I am sure he meant nothing at all, Your Grace. I doubt he even recalls those words. Don't spend another minute worrying about it."

I paused again, not at all impressed with this man. He seemed far too eager to believe whatever lies Banastre Tarleton might tell him. "Well, General, that's the thing. I am very concerned about his threats. Among other things, he threatened to kill me."

"What he threatened to do to her was to rape her, skin her, salt her wounds, and leave her for dead," Marcus interjected, his low voice like honed steel. "I heard him. I took him very seriously."

General Clinton paled at Marc's words. "My lord, surely…"

"Surely, you're thinking, Tarleton was a young man embarrassed at being caught with his pants down, shall we say? Perhaps. But perhaps he is the scurrilous dog Fancy says he is. I believe Fancy. I have known her all her life, and I have never once known her to lie to me. Not once. She is certainly not lying about Tarleton's threats to her that last day at Yorktown. Let me speak plainly, General. You are the British Commander-in-Chief in North America. I expect you to protect the Duchess of Ranscome against the sorry excuse for a man if he returns to New York before we leave for Ireland. And if anything, untoward should happen to her, well, let's just make sure nothing ill happens to the Duchess, General."

General Clinton began to stammer as his face reddened with anger as well as embarrassment. "That goes without saying, Lord Fitz Simmons."

Marc glared at him before responding. "I should hope so, General. After all, she is a Duchess."

We stopped outside the building after we left the General's offices. "Well, that was interesting."

Rob nodded. "Yes, I have to admit, I did not expect him to defend Tarleton."

Marc tamped tobacco into his pipe. "It seems to me he wants to believe Tarleton. Who would like to guess the young upstart is already here and talked to Clinton before us?"

"That would be my guess," I said. "And that idea scares me witless."

•　　•　　•　　•　　•

Clinton walked to the window and watched as the Fitz Simmons party left the building before, he spoke.

"You heard all that, I presume?"

The handsome, dark haired, young man nodded. "I did indeed, sir."

"Cover your back. Watch what you say. Do not, I repeat, do not put yourself into any position of vulnerability with that girl. Stay away from her. Do you understand?"

The young man nodded. "Oh, yes, I do, sir."

"Very good then. Carry on."

•　　•　　•　　•　　•

My head raged with pain by the time we got back to the town house. I begged off and went upstairs to lay down. I hoped some willow bark tea and rest would ease my horrible, never-ending headache. A short while later, Lily came in to check on me. I gulped down the pain medicine she brought me. "Thanks."

"No problem." She leaned over to kiss my cheek, and then frowned. "Fancy, you're burning up!"

"Maybe that's why my head hurts so bad." I winced. "And my neck is so sore. I can barely move my head."

Lily paled at my words. "Oh, my God… I'll be right back, honey."

She hurried from the room.

I sighed and settled back against the pillows again. The bed was comfortable, the pillows plump, and the room dark. Maybe a little well-earned peace and quiet would help.

I had dozed off when Lily hustled back in. "Honey, I need to draw a little blood…"

I tried not to sigh or roll my eyes and held out my hand. She pulled my arm closer to her and drew a syringe-full of blood.

I frowned as I squinted at the blood sample. "What on earth are you going to do with all that blood?"

"Run some tests, kiddo. Try to go to sleep."

• • • • •

Lily quickly prepared the slide and fit it into the microscope. After an adjustment to the lenses, she frowned. "Damn. There's a shitload of white blood cells. I don't like the looks of that."

Marc looked up over his new eyeglasses from the book he was reading. "Whatever is the problem?"

Lily didn't respond. She grabbed one of the medical treatises Richard brought from Beyond and scanned through photographs of various bacteria. Finally, she stopped, paling as she realized what the bacteria was that had infected Fancy. "Oh, hell."

Marc strode over to his wife's side and peered over her shoulder at the open book. "So, what do ye think it is?"

"Meningococcal bacteria."

"Lily, *mo chroi*, I don't know what that signifies."

"It means she has meningitis." When Marc still looked confused, she sighed as she shook her head in frustration. "Brain fever. The girl has a brain fever."

Marc paled at her words. "*Ai, Dia*! Will she die?"

"Not if I can help it," Lily said as she grabbed together antibiotics and pain meds. "Jesus, I can't believe I missed the symptoms before. She told me she had a God-Awful headache and her neck was stiff. I should have been on top of this. She needs to be quarantined from the children and the young men. It's caused by a highly contagious bacterial infection. Not stress or emotional upset, like doctors would like you to believe."

"You know as well as I do doctors are loathe to admit bacteria exist," Marc said. "So now what?"

"The disease most typically hits young adults and young children. They all need hot baths, clean clothes and fresh bed linens right away. I will meet everyone in the parlor in an hour. I can start everyone on prophylactic antibiotics. I pray she will be the only one to come down with it."

•   •   •   •   •

I don't remember much of the week that followed. At times, I was convinced I had died and gone to Hell. My fever would rage out of control while Lily sat bathing me with alcohol and ice, struggling to keep my temperature low enough that the fever would not do permanent damage to my poor addled brain.

Later, she admitted she had worried I would not live.

I remember the searing heat would be followed by icy cold as she tried to reduce my fevers. Crying for her to let me die. Crying for her to get me out of the burning Hell in which I was trapped. Crying for God to forgive me of my sins.

Crying for Richard.

I dreamed he came to see me more than once. Each time, he wept, saying his foolish behavior brought me here to the place where I became so ill. He sat by me, holding my hand, begging me to get well. "Come back to me," he implored, over and over. "I love you. I need you. We all need you."

I struggled to form the words in my mind. "But where are you? I don't know where to come. And why did you leave?"

He didn't answer. It was as if he couldn't hear me. He put his head down beside me and begged again, "Come back to me, my love. I need you, Francesca. Your babies need you. Please, my love, we all need you. Please, come back."

And again, I struggled to answer him, to assure him I loved him, too. But no words came out.

And then I dreamed Calvin came. He told me I could join him for all eternity. "Please, my darling, come to me. I miss you so much."

I shook my head. "No, never. Not after what you did to me."

And then, Tom was there, too. I shrank back as he reached for me. "Aw, come on, little girl. We can party like we used to…"

I struck out at the person I could see in the room. "No, no, never! Get away from me! Don't touch me! Don't you ever touch me again!"

Even Simon Le Grande came. When he appeared, I couldn't understand what he said. I cringed away from his touch and screamed. "Go away! Don't touch me! You've done enough to me. Go away!"

Then Mama Belle and Daddy Jo came. I ran to them but couldn't quite reach them. They told me I could go with them, but it was not supposed to be my time. "You haven't driven the big bus across the bridge yet, Fancy," Mama Belle said. "And everyone should have the chance to drive that bus!"

I tilted my head at that. "What bus, Mama? What is a bus?"

She laughed as butterflies flitted around her in a myriad of color and movement. "Oh, you know, child! It's like a carriage, from Beyond. You drive your bus to the finish. No one else, just you. It's so exciting when the bus comes over the Bridge down to your parade. Don't let anyone steal your parade!"

I frowned. "Carriage? Bus? Bridge? Parade? What on earth do you mean, Mama Belle?"

Hmm. And how did she know about the Beyond?

Mama Belle laughed. "Ask Lily, darling. And tell her Mama Belle sends her love. Now, you get well. Your babies need you."

And then she was gone.

As I awakened, I could see the first lights of morn shining in through the curtains. I started to get up but I realized I was either too weak or else there must be a big pile of bricks on my chest. I couldn't see any bricks, so I figured I had been pretty dad-gummed sick. I looked around the room from my prone position and saw Lily sleeping with her head resting on her arm in the big chair pulled up next to my bed. I smiled and reached out toward her. "Lily."

Strange. The word came out like the croak of a big old bullfrog.

Her head snapped up at my voice. "Fancy? Oh, my God, Fancy! You…. You're awake! Marc, she's awake! Our girl is awake!"

And then she shocked me as she started to sob.

"Was I that sick?" I whispered.

She nodded. "I thought for sure I lost you a couple of times. Last night, I had a long talk with The Big Man Upstairs. I told Him I had done everything I knew to do and it was up to Him."

I smiled at Lily's irreverent referral to the Almighty in such a manner. "And did He answer you?"

"He told me 'It's up to Fancy, kiddo'. And then I had the strangest dream. You were driving a bus over a bridge. I had a similar dream about Belle once. I … I was sure it meant you were going to die. But, now you're awake!"

She reached down to stroke my hair, like my Mama Belle used to do.

"I didn't want to die." I shut my eyes and sighed as I pretended once again that Lily was my real Mama. "I love it when you do that."

She bent over and kissed my brow. "Good, because I don't want you to die. No fever. You love it, huh? I do it because I love you, Fancy."

Four days later, I was dressed and ready to go to the tea party at the Governor's house. I was weak as a kitten, and worried about the gaps in my memory. It seemed as though the fever had seared some memories smack dab out of my poor fried brain. Lily would mention something, and I would stare at her like she had grown another head. I was most frustrated I had to attend the dad-blasted party and aggravated over the dress Lily insisted I wear. Oh, yes, it was black, but it was black and white. Very stylish and chic. Not at all designed to keep men away from me. Dad-blast it!

"What did you call this style dress?" I asked for the umpteenth time as I peered into the mirror.

Lily laughed. "Sassy called it a zoned dress. They are popular in Italy now. She sent it for you. She felt it would be a good transition dress in mourning, and still be very elegant. Here, let me fix the bow."

I figured Sassy sent it as a way to apologize. I shook my head as Lily adjusted the red ribbon around my waist, with a cocky bow. "Oh, yes, just what every widow requires. A black and white overdress, with a white petticoat, and a red ribbon at my waist. Lovely."

I rolled my eyes.

Lily nodded, as if oblivious to my criticism. "You are the very picture of loveliness in this gown, sweetie. You look wonderful. White mitts. You should have a red ribbon around your throat, too, but I figured you would raise Billy Hell if I tried that."

"You figured right."

"At your age, you can get away with the pearl necklace and earrings even though you are a recent widow. You should leave the chatelaine here. It would be too much. Your hair looks lovely in that new hedgehog style. It's so flattering for curly hair. I understand it is the latest hairstyle from Paris, and I told you the gold-toned powder would tone down the red in your hair to strawberry blonde. Your makeup makes you look fresh as springtime, not like you are recovering from a horrible disease. My heavens, what a difference a bit of rouge on your lips and cheeks can make for a girl. Now you don't look like you are about to keel over and die. And of course, the exquisite zoned dress. I love the way it hugs your figure. I may have to get one made for me, as well."

"You can have this one." I sniffed with feigned disdain.

She laughed. "Yes, like that dress would fit me. I'm as skinny as a scarecrow. I must weigh a stone less than you, and I am a good five inches taller than you."

She sat an exquisite little black feathered frippery of a hat on top of my head and tied another jaunty bow. I shook my head and gave up my fight. I was still too tired, too weak to fight anyone over what I would wear today.

"Do we have to stay long?" I fretted.

She shook her head. "No, but the General made it clear he wants you to make an appearance."

"Fabulous," I snapped. "We mustn't disappoint General Clinton, no matter how sick I have been. After all, he's due to leave in what, ten days?"

Lily smiled. "Something like that."

General and Mrs. Clinton lived a few houses down the street from our house. We walked the three houses down, and announced we were there. The butler turned to the crowd to announce us as a handsome young man entered the door as well.

"Why, your Grace, I did not know you would be here." The young man bowed with a flourish and kissed my hand.

"What the hell are you doin' here? Didn't the General tell you to stay away from Her Grace?" Marc sounded livid.

The young man looked up at Marc with a shocked look. Mind you, at 6'5' tall, everyone has to look up to Marc. "I … I don't know what you mean, sir."

Marc snorted. "Tarleton, ye get away from Lady Hobbs right now…"

A look of surprise shot through the man's eyes at Marc's words. "Oh, but you are mistaken, sir. I am not Colonel Tarleton. I know there is a marked resemblance…"

"Poppycock!" Marc roared, his face growing redder by the second.

"No, sir, Banastre Tarleton is my cousin. Our mothers are identical twins.

The family say we are identical cousins. Allow me to introduce myself. My name is Captain Brice Darlington. My friends call me Brice." He extended his hand to Marc.

Lily looked astounded. "They're cousins. Identical cousins, and you'll find they laugh alike. They walk alike. At times they even talk alike. You can lose your mind when cousins are two of a kind. Oh! I'm sorry. Remembering the words to an old song."

Marc stood mouth agape, unsure what to do, especially in light of Lily's odd comment. After an awkward pause, I held out my hand. "It is a pleasure to meet you, Captain. Allow me to introduce Lord and Lady Fitz Simmons, and their nephew, Captain Fitz Simmons. And yes, I am Lady Hobbs, but my friends call me Fancy."

He swept low over my hand, to kiss it again. "I am delighted to make your acquaintance, Your Grace."

I pouted, you know, the way girls pout when they are flirting. "I said, my friends call me Fancy."

He flashed another dimpled smile at me. "Indeed, you did, Fancy. And may I take that to mean we are going to be … friends?"

I tossed my head as I giggled. "I certainly hope so."

He was charming. Sophisticated. Elegant. Urbane. His hair was the rich chestnut brown of Tarleton's (I finally remembered) except he had a silver streak beginning right in front. As I chatted with him, I understood for the first time how my mother was attracted to Jay Fitz Simmons all those years ago. What was that song that Sassy sang sometimes? Good boys go to heaven but bad boys bring heaven to you. Yes, he looked like that kind of man alright with those smoldering eyes and sultry voice. Oh, not enough to make a woman go off and leave her child, mind you, but, well, I could understand the attraction of the rogue. Darlington was all rogue with his daring smiles and crisp, English accent. I could even see for the first time the charm his cousin must have towards women, too. You know, if he were not busy violating and abusing women. Brice stayed glued to my side for the hour or so that afternoon at the tea. He then walked us down the street to our house, where he bent low over my hand again to kiss it once more.

I decided right then I could get used to this hand kissing thing.

"I look forward to seeing you again, Lady Fancy," he said.

I smiled. "I imagine we will see each other again at the ball."

After we walked on into the house, I realized Marc and Lily were silent. Fitz stood fuming. "Okay, so what are you all upset about?"

Neither Marc nor Lily responded. Fitz did. "What about Richard? I thought you told us you love him."

I shrugged. "Richard who? Oh, you mean the man who said he loved me and went off without a never-you-mind? That Richard? Yes, what about Richard? And where in the blazes is he anyway?"

Fitz lapsed into silence, also, as he shifted from foot to foot, looking nervously at Marc and Lily.

Marc turned towards the window and began muttering in Irish. I think I heard *mhac na galla*, but I was not sure if he was using the derogatory term towards Richard or Brice. I shrugged. "What? You guys know something about Dr. Winslow's disappearance that I don't know?"

I caught the quick glance from Lily to Marc, and the look of embarrassment that washed across both their faces.

"You mean to say you heard something from him and didn't bother to tell me?" I shook my head in disgust. "Well, don't that just take the cake."

"Now, Fancy, don't get yourself all riled up…" Lily began.

"I beg your pardon. Did you tell me not to get all riled up? Why shouldn't I get riled up? Why in heaven's name did he contact you and not me? When did he contact you?"

Lily looked at Marc again, guilt all across her face. Marc cleared his throat. "As I seem to recall, you were unconscious at the time. He was most distraught over your condition."

"I told you both he should have stayed," Lily murmured.

My mouth went dry with yearning and frustration. "So, the consarned man contacted you while I was sick? But he didn't have gumption to stay and talk to me when I improved? Well, wouldn't that figure."

I turned to head up the stairs, but halfway up, I stopped, and turned back to them. "His contacting you when I was sick does not in any way satisfy me as to why he failed to talk to me before he left Belle Rose. He's here? In New York? Well, young Dr. Winslow better high tail it over here to talk to me pretty danged fast if he wants to resolve our differences, because right now, Col. Banastre Tarleton would have about as good a chance of winning my hand as

Richard Winslow would."

"Fancy, you don't mean that…" Marc began.

"Oh, I don't? Oh, that's right. I forgot. I've been sick. I had a brain fever. It's left me plum dab addled. I couldn't possibly know what I'm talking about, could I? I am so dad-gummed tired of people thinking they know what I mean better than I do! I was sick. I am not mentally deficient. Do not treat me as if I lack the wits to know my own mind. Oh, you all make me so angry!"

All three of them looked shocked at my words as I turned and flounced up the stairs to my rooms. I slammed the door and ripped the ridiculous excuse for a hat off and tossed it across the room. I was standing there crying when Lily came in.

"I'm sorry…" Lily began.

"Oh, shut up. I don't want to hear it. I am tired of excuses. If he wants to see me, he needs to act like a man, come over here and apologize. I am sick and tired of this nonsense. Sassy always used to write to him not to make permanent decisions based on temporary feelings. I thought that was strange when she would write it. Now I understand the *boy* has a hot temper and acts before he thinks. Yes, I said boy, not man. Real men don't run away at the first sign of trouble. If he wants me, he better 'man up,' as you say, and put his big boy drawers on, as his mama says. I would never have come to New York if he had stayed at Belle Rose. I try to make logical decisions. He didn't trust me. He wouldn't wait for my decision. He got his knickers in a wad and went off in a snit. If I did something like that, everyone would be telling me how wrong I was, but you all are defending Richard."

"I know. You told me you would never have agreed to this cockamamie plan if he hadn't left."

"That's right. And where in the blazes has the dad-blasted fool been for the past month anyway?"

She started to say something and then seemed to bite back her words. "I think Rick needs to tell you that, honey. But I promise you, it is an interesting story, to say the least."

I snorted. "I figured it would be. After all, he is Sassy's son. No one can make up a story better than Sassy. But, yes, Richard needs to be the one to tell me these sweet little lies he's cooked up. Don't take the responsibility for them onto your shoulders, Lily."

Her eyes clouded with worry. "Honey, I don't think…"

"Well, with all due respect, Lily, it doesn't matter what you think. It matters what I think. And he better have one heck of a good story to sell if he thinks I'm goin' to buy it after he up and walked out of my life without so much as a how-do-you-do. He can come tomorrow, or any other day until the blasted ship sails on the 10th. I plan to be on that ship, with or without young Dr. Winslow. Hopefully, the Ranscome ship will reconnoiter with the British ship, but I am leaving then, with or without the good doctor or anyone else who doesn't want to step foot on the British ship. I want out of this horrid, dirty town. Now."

Lily huffed up at me. "Now, listen here, little lady…"

I wheeled back towards her and held my hand up. "Oh, I don't think so. This argument should be between Richard and me. Exceptin' now I am upset with all of you for keeping information from me. Why didn't you tell me he came? And where has he been the past four days? I have been ill, but I am not a child. I do not expect to be treated as if I am a child. Do you understand?"

Lily's jaw dropped. After an uncomfortable pause, she replied. "Yes, Your Grace. I understand."

Lily wheeled around and stormed out of my room.

"Oh, wonderful. Now I upset her, too." I sighed. For the life of me, I could not figure out why no one seemed concerned I was so upset.

Everyone was quiet the next morning. Fitz and the other boys in my guard looked nervous as they tried their best to avoid talking with me. Lily sat drinking her tea as she read some boring medical book. For the life of me, I will never understand how she can read those dull old books. Marc kept looking at me, worry lining his face. I ate my breakfast in silence, not willing to broach the subject of either Richard or Captain Darlington with any of them. Well, I could play that game, too. Probably better than any of them, if you got right down to it. After all, I learned from an expert how to give the Silent Treatment. When I finished, I left without a word to go up to the nursery to see my babies.

I was there in the nursery when he arrived.

I heard some noises downstairs but hadn't paid a bit of attention. I was busy reading a story to Bella. As I paused to turn a page, she jumped up and ran to the door. "Rick! Mommy, Uncle Rick is here!"

Well, butter my buns and call me a biscuit, maybe the man can be taught after all. He sure enough got himself over here after I threw my hissy fit last night.

I shut the book and pushed it aside, my heart clamoring ninety to nothing in my chest. Stay calm, Fancy girl. Stay calm. I took a big breath, held it to the count of ten, and then let it out. "Hello, Richard."

Not bad. I didn't start out screaming at him. I didn't rush to him to throw myself in his arms.

He almost smiled. Almost. "Hello, sweetheart."

He bent down to hug Bella. I sat silent as she showed him the new doll Marc bought her since we arrived in New York, and she told him all about her favorite park where Nanny Hobbs took her every day for exercise. He was patient and attentive as he listened to her for about five minutes.

"Bella Boo, Mommy and I need to talk. Do you mind if I steal her away for a little bit?"

"No, that's fine." She wrapped her arms around his neck and kissed him. "You be sure to tell her you love her."

He chuckled. "I will, I promise. Francesca, could we go to the library to talk in private?"

I nodded and arose. I don't know why, but it offended me he knew there was a library, but then, I knew he had been there when I was sick. Silent, I left the nursery to head downstairs to the library. Halfway to the stairs, he grabbed my arm.

"Please don't be angry with me."

I stopped, shocked more by his words than his touch. "That is up to you, Richard. Give me a reason not to be angry."

And dad-blast it, he looked at me with those pathetic puppy dog eyes. It was all I could do not to pull him to me. Somehow, I resisted the urge to become milk toast. I squared my shoulders, pulled my arm from his grasp and walked on down the stairs to the library as I blinked the tears from my eyes. I waited at the door until he entered before I shut the door securely. I went around the big desk to sit down before I spoke again. "So, why did you leave?"

He stared at me with those puppy dog eyes again. "At this point, what difference does it make? Does it matter?"

I bristled at his words. "What difference does it make? Does it matter? Are you serious? You sit there looking like I kicked you to the curb. Like I wronged you somehow. And *you* left *me*, Richard. In the middle of the night. Without a single word. No note, nothing. You just up and skedaddled. And you have the nerve to ask me what difference it makes?"

My hands gripped the edge of the desk so hard I broke a fingernail. I didn't want him to see my hands shaking, but this was ridiculous. I hate it when my hands flutter like little butterflies. I loved my Mama Belle, but I always thought it looked weird when she made those little twitchy movements with her hands. I folded my hands on the desk as I waited for his reply.

"You told me to go away. You said you never wanted to see me again after what I did."

I felt the blood drain from my face. "That is an outright lie and you know it, Richard Winslow. I would never…"

"It is not a lie, dammit. You told me that when you were sick. The first time, I thought you were out of your head with fever. But the second time you sat right up in your bed, pointed right at me, and shouted at me to go away and not to touch you ever again."

I was shocked. I could not believe I did these awful things! I was unconscious. With a brain fever. My heart began to beat hard and fast. "I…I don't believe you."

He just stared at me.

I tossed my head. "Well, I said you would come in here with some cockamamie story. All you had to do a month ago was wait until morning when I was going to refuse…"

"But you're here."

I stared at him before I answered. "You don't know me, do you? You don't understand me… or trust me…"

"I went to the General."

I blinked and rubbed my forehead. "Oh, Richard, for the love of God…"

"I asked him to let me do it. You have children. It's too dangerous for you."

That stumped me. "Oh, please tell me you didn't do that."

"Why? What difference does it make?"

I knew Sassy had told me some story about an incident in the future when a government official shrugged off something about a horrible murder by flippantly saying, 'what difference does it make?' I suspected Richard was echoing those words for some reason known Beyond. Maybe at some time in the past, I understood the significance. But right then, my mind was blank. The meaning was lost to my still foggy brain. I rubbed my temples as I struggled to remember what it meant. "I don't know what you want me to say. I don't even know what you mean."

He stood up and sighed, his shoulders sagging. "I was afraid you would say that. Good bye, Francesca."

I stared in shocked disbelief as he walked out of the library. I started after him. "Wait, Rich…"

He didn't stop. I hurried after him, but he was out the front door before I could catch him.

As I stood staring at the street before me, Lily came up. She frowned. "Where's Rick?"

"Gone."

"What happened?"

I tried to laugh but what came out sounded like a little sob. "He said … what difference does it make. I told him I didn't know what he meant."

She turned pale. "Oh, shit. Fancy…"

"Not now, Lily. Please. Not… right now."

I turned and trudged back up the stairs. At the top of the stairs, it hit me. What difference did it make? It made all the difference in the world.

I sank down to the floor, as my sobs overwhelmed me.

Bella ran to me. "What's wrong, Mommy?"

I gathered my little girl into my arms. "He left. And he never told me he loves me."

Bella held me as I cried. I cried harder as she began to stroke my hair like Lily does. "It's okay, Mommy. I love you."

I clung tight to my little girl as I cried even harder.

Chapter 13
Fancy

I swallowed my pride. I sent a message to Richard, begging him to come back. He did not reply.

On the 5th, we prepared to go to the ball. I wore a dark blue, English-styled gown with fitted waist. The gown was simple but elegant, with furbelows down the sides and around the hem. Matching bows of blue velvet decorated the stomacher. As I slipped fat pearl earrings into my ears, Lily came into the room.

"Why don't you wear the pretty aquamarines Richard gave you for Christmas?"

My hands stilled in mid-air. "Would it be appropriate? I mean, the pearls are already pretty daring…"

She smiled as she nodded. "It would be fine. I expect he will be at the party, and it will send a message to him that you want to talk."

I realized she was right. It was far more important to me, in the long run, that Richard and I mend our fences than people in New York think well of me. I would be leaving in a few days and I would never see most of these people again. I nodded and removed the pearls from my ears to slip the aquamarine earrings into my earlobes. As I did, Lily grinned, and then reached around my neck to fasten the most beautiful necklace I had ever seen.

"Happy Belated Birthday, Fancy," she said.

I gasped. "Oh, my heavens, Lily! Are you sure? Daddy gave these to you after Michael was born."

She nodded as she fastened the clasp. "Your father and I discussed it. I have worn them a few times, but not very often over the past 18 years. You're a duchess. It's right that you get the necklace. You will have lots of opportunities to wear it."

It was the prettiest necklace I had ever seen. I admit I had lusted after it for years. Three rows of fat pearls clasped together with a 20 carat, oval aquamarine, surrounded by rose cut diamonds. She pulled the choker around so the aquamarine was in front, kissed my forehead and smiled. "Now you look like you're the Duchess of Ranscome."

Of course, being me, I cried. She frowned and began to fuss. "Now, no crying! You are going to mess up your makeup and you look wonderful. Come on, let's go to the party. I intend to have a good time."

I sniffed a couple more times as I dabbed at my eyes. "It's the nicest thing anyone ever gave me. Thank you from the bottom of my heart, Lily."

She smiled. "I wanted you to have it or I would not have given it to you. We meant to give it to you for your birthday. Unfortunately, we were all so exhausted the day we arrived, it slipped our minds. Two days later, I realized I had not given it to you. I cried and cried, afraid you might ... well, you know. But thank heaven, you got well, and now it's yours. A combination birthday and get well present. Now, put on the tiara Sassy sent with you."

Daddy Joe bought the tiara for Miss Belle on their honeymoon long ago in Paris. I stifled back additional tears as I sat the tiara onto my head. Set in gold, it was adorned with aquamarines, pink tourmaline, and diamonds. I knew it was priceless. I smiled and squeezed Lily's hand. "I feel like a princess."

She laughed. "Well, at least like a duchess, which you are, Your Grace. What was it Jo used to call you? Oh, yes. He used to call you his Wee Duchess. I always thought that was so sweet. Now, let's go to the party!"

Lily was dressed in a beautiful teal silk gown we remade before we came. It was a perfect fit, enhancing curves usually unnoticed on her tall, slender frame. She wore her exquisite emerald and diamond wedding ring Marc gave her long ago. She doesn't wear it all the time. She always makes me laugh when she says it is far too nice to wear when she milks the goat at McCarron's Corner. She also wore emerald and diamond earrings which he gave her one year for Christmas. With her dark auburn hair, greens and emeralds always look spectacular on her. Marcus wore black evening attire, with his fair hair slicked back into a neat queue. They both looked regal and elegant. And while I expected Fitz to wear his dress uniform, he surprised me and wore black evening attire as well. My little brother looked every bit the Viscount he was. I knew we would be the most spectacular group at the ball.

"You're so much like our mam. You always want a blue dress," Fitz said.

I laughed. "I do love a pretty blue dress. But, I don't look anything like her. If anything, you do."

He smiled. "Nah. You're both pretty."

I smiled at him. "Thank you, Fitz."

Since we were in evening attire, the Ranscome carriage took us to the gala event. Fitz helped me down from the carriage after Marc helped Lily down. The butler announced us, and we entered the world of partying with English nobility and high society.

It was my first experience hobnobbing in such a setting other than the tea party a few days before. I had been to some elegant soirees at Belle Rose, but I was acting as housekeeper at those events, making sure everything was perfect. This was the first grand ball I had ever attended as a guest. I could not hide the fact I was impressed with the exquisite decorations. Thousands of candles lit the rooms with soft, romantic light as thousands of hot house roses scented the rooms with their delicate perfume. There was a long banquet table set up buffet style in the dining room. Musicians played in the ballroom, and people were already beginning to dance the minuet.

It was like a fairy tale come true.

As I stood there trying not to gape like a little country mouse as I took it all in, my eyes landed on a figure standing near the musicians. My mouth went dry as I realized the handsome man with the sun-blonded hair was Richard. "He's here," I whispered to Lily, my heart pounding wildly.

She smiled and waved to him. "I told you he would be here."

His eyes lit up as he saw us, and he started towards us. Then, he stopped as a funny look crossed his face and he dropped his eyes. I frowned and headed towards him.

"Go get him, girl," Lily said, with a little push of encouragement.

I glanced at Marc and Fitz. Both grinned and motioned me on. Head held high, I marched on to Richard.

"Nice party." I tried to sound cavalier.

He grinned and raised his eyes to mine. "Yeah, they have just about everything a girl could want."

"Yep. Just about. I know this girl saw something over here she sure enough liked."

He chuckled. "Francesca, I…"

I raised my finger to his lips. "No, let me. I knew there was some reason you asked me 'did it matter' the other day. After you left, it hit me. It made all the difference to those men at that Benghazi place in Africa when no one came to rescue them. The way it meant everything to me when you left. It broke me, Richard. I was sure I had lost my happy-ever-after…"

He looked stricken. "Oh, honey, I'm sorry…"

I raised my finger to him again as I shook my head. "No, please, let me finish. You see, then I made what could have been a permanent decision based on temporary feelings. I fussed at you for doing that. But, I did it, too. I was rash. Impetuous. I acted the same way."

He gulped. Worry was written all across his face. "So, what do we do now? What are you saying?"

I stared at him a minute before I answered. A minute to memorize his face. To keep this minute preserved in my memory for the rest of my life. "Why, that's simple, Richard Winslow. Now we claim our happy-ever-after."

His eyes lit up. "Are you sure?"

I nodded, wordless.

It was if his whole face alighted with joy. He grabbed my hands and pulled me close. "I love you."

I smiled as I reached up to stroke his cheek. "That's what I wanted to hear."

I expected him to kiss me. Right there at the ball, in front of God and everyone. I did not expect him to drop to one knee in front of me there. "Wh… what are you doing?"

He fumbled in his coat pocket and pulled out the most beautiful aquamarine ring I ever saw. About 3 carats, surrounded with diamonds, like the centerpiece of the choker I wore. As tears welled up in my eyes, he asked, "Francesca Marie Selk Hobbs, will you do me the honor of marrying me?"

I couldn't hold the tears back. "Of course, silly man. I thought you would never ask me."

He slipped the ring on my finger, arose to wrap me in his arms, and kissed me. As he finished, we heard the tinkling of a knife tapping fine crystal. "Ladies and gentlemen, I would like to announce the betrothal of Lady Fancy Hobbs and Dr. Richard Winslow. We are thrilled. It may be a bit early, but we are more than happy for Fancy and Rick. After all, our families have wanted this for years. Hip-hip-hoorah!" Marc said.

Everyone joined Marc in the cheer. There was much applause afterwards.

General Clinton came over and patted Richard on the back. "Congratulations, young man! I must admit, I had no idea this party would lead to a proposal, but I am not at all surprised Lady Fancy inspired it. Congratulations!"

"Thank you, General. Now, if you don't mind, I would like to dance with the prettiest lady at the ball."

Clinton laughed. "You two young love birds dance, but I believe Mrs. Clinton is the prettiest woman here. I will cede that Fancy is the prettiest younger woman."

I laughed. "Well spoken, General."

I curtseyed and the men each bowed towards each other before Richard and I made our way to the dance floor.

•   •   •   •   •

Rick was devastated when Fancy went off on him when she was sick, screaming at him to go away and never come back. Lily convinced him to come back one more time to talk. But things went God-Awful wrong when she spurned him again. When she didn't know what difference it made, it broke his heart. He hadn't felt that empty in years. Lost. Hopeless. Desolate. Like it was the end of his world.

She would never know how important it was to him that she came to him this evening. That they talked. Cleared the air.

That she said yes.

He didn't want her to ever know, but he thought about harming himself after she screamed at him to go away and never come back. Thank God Mom's old warning came back to him before it was too late when he saw the semi-colon tattooed on his wrist. The razor poised over his wrist, he hesitated when he saw the tattoo next to the old scar, and then he lowered the blade. For once, he resisted the urge to make a permanent decision based on his emotions.

Thank God Marc found him that evening and they were able to talk.

Marc's a good man. Always gives sage advice without sounding preachy. He helped Rick calm down and remember the story wasn't over yet. Thank God he listened to Marc and came tonight. And thanks be to God for answering his prayers.

He sliced open an old scar on his forearm after she yelled at him when she was sick. He learned long ago how to keep the number of scars down by recutting old scars. Damn, he hadn't cut himself in years. He wished again that Dr. Tanakawa, his old therapist, were here. He used to call him from time to time with problems. Doc helped him through that last year in med school after Mom disappeared. Now, he could damn sure use some counseling. But hopefully, he was back on track. On a level keel. Semi-colon, dude. Semi-colon. Remember the story is not finished. Give it time. Give us time. Semi-colon. Do it right this time. No. More. Cutting. Ever.

He dipped his head to kiss the woman he loved as they waltzed around the room.

•　　•　　•　　•　　•

"Well, that was unexpected. Now what?" Brice asked his cousin.

Tarleton shrugged. "Now we change our plans."

Brice frowned. "How?"

Tarleton smiled. "I am already planning it."

"But the ship leaves on the 10th..."

"Trust me, old man. I will have a plan by morning."

"You better. The ship leaves soon, Ban."

Tarleton did not reply as he stared after the radiant young woman laughing as she danced with her handsome young man. *Enjoy yourself, my beauty. You won't be laughing much longer.*

•　　•　　•

It was late when I noticed her. The demure servant stood behind her mistress, with her eyes averted, as she fanned the woman with a large fan. I winced as her arms trembled from the weight of the fan. She must have been doing this for quite a while.

190

In any event, I recognized her right away. How could I not? I'd known her most of her life. With skin the color of warm honey, light brown eyes, and dark, golden brown hair, I used to say they should have named her Honey or Amber. Maybe Sunny, because her disposition was always sweet and happy, no matter how much nonsense Tom dumped on her. It about killed me when he sent her away. At least, I thought he sent her away until when I saw her there. I realized my sorry, no-good brother sold her like she was nothing more than a cow or a goat. She wasn't livestock. She was a human being. My cousin. And she was my friend. My one friend back then.

I squared my shoulders and marched right over to the woman sitting beneath a palm tree. She was a pretty woman, in a bright pink dress and her hair styled high. She did not arise when I approached her, but she reached out a hand to me.

"Why, Your Grace, I did not expect you to approach me here. I am honored."

"Who are you?" My voice was rough as I demanded she identify herself.

She withdrew her hand as her smile faded from her heavily powdered and rouged face. "I am Patrice Paddington, ducky. Why?"

It startled me that the madam of a notorious bordello in Yorktown was at this party, but I was not dissuaded. Ignoring her question, I moved to my next one, as I motioned to the girl standing behind her. "When did you obtain this slave?"

She laughed and her eyes narrowed. "Who? Clairee? Why, I obtained her in March of 1780. You must know that."

My eyes narrowed. "And why would I know that, madam?"

"Calvin sold me half interest in the girl right before your wedding. He assured me you knew. He said you refused to live under the same roof with his Negro mistress."

I could feel the blood drain from my face. "No, I never told him that. He never mentioned he bought Clarissa from Tom or that you bought half-interest from him. Did my husband still hold half-ownership in her when he died?"

She laughed again. "Oh, yes, m' dear. In fact, that was why I brought her this evening. I hoped we could talk. I would like to buy you out. How much do you want?"

"Oh, no. I will not sell her. She was a free woman when Tom sold her to

Calvin. All children born in 1764 or later were free at Belle Rose. She was born in '64. I will, however, buy you out. Then General Clinton can authorize me to free her."

For the first time, Clarissa raised her eyes to mine. I could see she was shocked by my comments. I also thought I saw a glimmer of hope spark in her eyes.

Miss Paddington stifled her surprise at my words as she pouted. She appeared accustomed to those pouts getting her way with men. It did not work with me. I just stared at her, impassive to her coy looks. She eyed me speculatively. "How much would you give?"

I shook my head, impatient with her games. "What were you going to offer me to buy me out?"

She eyed me again, as she appraised my willingness to pay. I could tell she was going to lie. "£10,000."

"You are lying and we both know it. You can buy a slave girl every day of the week for less than £100."

She pouted again, and then perked up as Marc and Richard joined us. "My dear, that is for an average servant girl. Not a trained courtesan who is high in demand for her favors."

Marc nodded his head. "I hate to say it, but she's right, Fancy. A trained girl fetches a far better price than a housemaid. But £10,000 is a bit steep. I would say £2500 is more in line with her value."

Richard nodded agreement. I held back the smile, knowing he did not know the going price for whores in the Colonies. At least, he had better not know the price.

"Sounds fair to me. I will offer you £2500 for your half interest."

This time, she did not pout. She frowned. "Really? That is the best you can do? The girl is trained. She can make you a fortune. I will be losing a fortune when I sell her."

I tilted my head to study her. Patrice Paddington's hands were trembling ever so slightly, but I caught sight of that little tremor. A thin line of sweat had formed on her upper lip. I could see a faint pulse throbbing at her collarbone. She knew it was now or never. Behind her, I noticed Clarissa's eyes were bulging with shock and surprise.

"She's not goin' to bid against herself, Paddy," Marc said. "Be reasonable.

What do you want for the lass?"

Miss Paddington gave a sharp look at Marc. "What interest in this do you have, Marcus McCarron?"

He laughed, and his voice filled with all the charm of the Irish. "Ah, Paddy, m'love, she's kin. We always look out for kin. Ye know that, lass."

She pouted again, looking mighty aggravated. She waved her fan as if to dismiss the entire issue. "Fine. I'll take £5000, and not one penny less."

Marc started to say something, but before he could I said, "Sold. Bring her to the Ranscome Manor House in the morning at 9 and we will complete the sale."

She arched her eyebrows. "You don't want to complete it now?"

I frowned at the presumptuous baggage. "I do not run around town carrying that sum of cash. And I want her papers when you bring her. I will need proof she is transferred to me with the sale, all nice and legal."

She shrugged as if to dismiss me. "Fine. Take her now. I'll be by in the morning to conclude the sale."

Eyes shining bright, Clarissa walked away with me. As we approached the doorway, she touched my arm. "Sixty-two."

I frowned. "What do you mean? I don't understand."

"I was born in '62, not '64. She would have taken less."

"You were born in '62? I didn't realize that. Well, I don't care. You're my cousin. You're worth it. I would have paid more. Your grandparents are at the house."

She looked shocked. "Will sold you my Gramma?"

I nodded my head. "No. Will freed your Gramma in 1779. They both chose to go with me to Ireland. What about you? What do you want to do?"

"I have a choice?" Her voice sounded full of unexpected hope.

I nodded. "Of course, you do. I already said I intend to free you. This should never have happened. You can stay here, as a free woman of color. Or, you can come with us to Ireland. Or whatever else you choose to do. Why?"

She hesitated for a minute or two. I could tell she was pondering her options. "Could … could I go back to Spring Haven?"

I was shocked. My husband kept her as his mistress at Spring Haven before we married. My mouth tightened into a frown. "Why?"

"My child is there."

If I thought I was shocked before, I was aghast and agog with that comment. "Was it Calvin's child?"

She shook her head. "No. At least, I don't think so. I'm pretty sure he's Tom's child. He was born in the spring of '78. I was already biggin' when Calvin bought me. Of course, you know how they liked to…"

I put my hand to her mouth. "Shhh. Not here." I looked around, nervous she might have been overheard.

And then, I remembered a little boy at Spring Haven. Light skin. Bright, blue eyes. Brown, curly hair. "He was still there when we left last summer. He's a beautiful little boy. I thought he was the cook's child. I didn't know you had ever been there. He used to play with Bella. They were about the same age."

She smiled for the first time. "My Toby is still there?"

"He damned sure better be," I said as we met up with the others to leave. "And we'll get him freed as quick as possible, too." And then the name hit home. She named him after her Grampa, my Uncle Tobias.

Richard accompanied us back to the house when we returned from the ball. He saw me to the door and kissed me one more time. "Can I see you tomorrow?"

"I don't know. Can you?"

I laughed at his puzzled look and pulled him back to me. "Of course, you can see me, silly man. Send me a note when. And where."

He laughed. "Tease. Okay. Get some sleep. I'll send a message in the morning."

"Hold your horses. Aren't you coming back here tonight?"

He laughed and laid his head against mine. "You sure?"

I didn't say anything. I reached up and pulled his head down to mine so I could kiss him. As the kiss ended, I asked, "Do you have to ask?"

He laughed and pulled me back for another kiss. "No. Leave a light on. I'll see you later." The kiss was long and lingering, hinting of promised lovemaking to come. I giggled as I pushed him out the door.

Tobias and Hattie Mae were ecstatic to see Clarissa accompany us back to the house. Hattie Mae began to cry as I told her how I found her.

"My poor little lamb. Thank you, Miss Fancy…"

I shook my head. "Oh, don't you dare start that 'Miss this' and 'Miss that' business with me. My God, you're my Auntie. Here, give me a hug. I'm going to bed."

Richard slipped back in an hour later. I slept well that night after Richard left, sated from our lovemaking and my dreams filled with the promises of our happy-ever-after.

The next morning, I slept later than usual. Bella woke me up, tickling me. We snuggled together in my big bed for hugs and kisses. Finally, I said, "Richard asked me to marry him. How would you feel about that?"

Her whole face lit up at that. "Oh, Mommy, it would be wonderful! Will he be our new Daddy?"

"He'll be your step-daddy, honey. But he loves you."

She tilted her head at me. "Can I call him Daddy?"

I hugged her again, thrilled she was so accepting of the man I loved. "If you want, you may call him Daddy. It's up to you."

My heart bursting with happiness, we dressed and went downstairs for our breakfast. As we finished, Tobias announced that a lady was at the door asking to see me.

"It must be Miss Paddington," I commented. "Show her in."

I gave her the money. She gave me Clarissa's papers. Clarissa and her grandparents waited anxiously at the kitchen door as Paddy and I concluded our business. As Miss Paddington left, I heard them talking, their voices excited.

I entered the kitchen with a grin on my face that must have been as wide as my derrière is when I wear panniers. "It's done. Now, I will go to the General and find out how to free you. And on the 10th, when we get on the Ranscome ship, I will tell the captain to head to Bermuda first."

Clarissa's eyes were brimmed with tears as she danced with excitement. "Oh, thank you, Fancy."

Not much later, Clarissa brought a note in on a silver platter. I smiled and thanked her as I tore the note open.

"Sweetheart,

Meet me at the wharf across from the General's headquarters at 12. Counting the minutes until I am with you again.

I love you forever. R."

I clutched it to my chest and then realized it was already a little past 10. I bent to kiss Bella. "Mama has to hurry, sweet pea. I'm going to see the General and then have lunch with Richard."

"You mean my new Daddy." Her voice was solemn.

I laughed. "Yes, Richard, your new step-daddy. Who you may call Daddy."

She grinned and kissed me again before she skipped upstairs to the nursery.

It was a beautiful spring day. Trees were budding out and flowers were pushing up through the soil. Children were playing in the park at the corner as I passed. I waved to their mothers as I strolled the three blocks to the quay where we were supposed to meet. Although sunny, there was a cool breeze blowing in off the harbor. I was pleased I wore my new grey riding habit made of the light weight wool over the pale pink, silk blouse. With a small pink hat sitting at a jaunty angle, I felt fresh and pretty.

I went first to the General's offices, where he was pleased to help me complete the papers to free Clarissa. "I am very proud of you, Your Grace. Not many people of your status feel as strongly as you do about slavery."

I resisted the urge to tell him why. Instead, I smiled. "You're welcome, General. Of course, it was my grandfather's intention that all the slaves at Belle Rose be freed by 1800 at the latest. Children born in 1764 and later were all supposed to be free. Clarissa was born in '62, so she was not freed then. In any event, she is now. We are going to take her with us when we leave. She is excited about her new life in Ireland."

I did not mention the child at Spring Haven.

He stood up to shake my hand. "Jolly good, Your Grace. I hope to see you sometime in London."

I nodded. "I imagine we might well meet in London some time. And thank you again for assisting me with this problem."

I walked outside and stood looking out across the harbor as I waited. I smiled as I checked the time with the elegant little ladies' watch hanging from the chatelaine attached at the waist of my gown. At last, I felt a tap on my shoulder. I wheeled around with a big smile on my face that quickly dissolved to a look of horror. "Tarleton. What are you doing here? Haven't you been warned to stay away from me?"

He didn't answer but stepped closer. As I tried to back away from him, he grabbed my wrist as unfamiliar hands grabbed me by the shoulders and pushed me towards Tarleton.

"Hello, my beauty." He smiled, but it did not reach his eyes. They remained as cold and snake-like as I remembered.

I knew this was bad. Very bad. After all, this was the man who threatened to rape and kill me. Of course, he also threatened to convince the King to allow him to marry me. I struggled to get loose of the unknown hands behind me as Tarleton lowered a handkerchief to my face. I struggled even as the drug swept through me, immobilizing me. I quit struggling as I was overcome by the narcotic and darkness enveloped my world.

I awoke to the sounds and movements of a carriage moving. As I stirred, he bent towards me and smoothed my hair back from my face with a frightening gentleness.

"Ah, my beauty awakens." He bent to kiss me, and laughed when I turned my face away from him. "Do you think struggling against me will delay the inevitable?"

I struggled against him. "I can try, you animal. I won't make it easy for you."

He laughed. "Animal, hmm? I must endeavor to live up to your lofty expectations. But don't you know I love it when a woman struggles against me?" He lowered himself over me, pinning my arms above my head and began to ravage my mouth.

I was helpless. Totally at this madman's mercy. Silent tears coursed down my face as he unbuttoned my jacket and blouse to begin fondling my breasts. Don't fight him, Fancy. He wants you to fight.

"Your young man shouldn't have proposed last night, my beauty. I had to change my plans."

I didn't ask what plans he meant. Right then, I didn't want to know. I would learn soon enough. Don't think about it, Fancy. Think about Richard. Think about Bella. Think about Charles. Happy thoughts. Positive thoughts. Good thoughts. Not this. Anything but this.

I forced my mind to go away from what was happening, like I had done so many times before. This isn't important. This isn't me. This is nothing more than a horrible nightmare.

Concentrate on surviving.

Even so, I heard him laughing as he entered me. I couldn't stop the tears.

Chapter 14
Richard - 1782

Richard frowned as he looked at his pocket watch for what must have been the 100th time. It was 1:15 p.m. Francesca should have been there by now. He shook his head, worried. After the slightest hesitation, he crossed the street and entered the General's Headquarters. As he entered, the staff Sargent looked up and smiled.

"Ah, Dr. Winslow. I understand congratulations are in order."

Richard grinned. "Thanks, Sargent. I was wondering if Lady Hobbs were still in her meeting with the General. We were supposed to meet across the street to go to lunch at 1."

Sargent Allen frowned. "Why, no. She was here this morning. But she left around noon."

Richard frowned. Fancy was always very punctual. She never ran late. He strode right back outside but she was nowhere in sight. After a momentary pause, he glanced down. There lay her chatelaine. His frown deepened as he bent down to pick it up. She wore it all the time since Fitz gave it to her. He arose and started towards the townhouse. His internal alarms were sounding like a four-alarm fire. Something was not right or her chatelaine would not be here with Francesca nowhere around.

Tobias looked startled when he opened the door to Richard, alone. "Mr. Rick, we thought Miss Fancy was with you."

Richard's heart lurched. "I can't find her. Get the men. We need to organize a search. Now."

Eyes wide with shock, Tobias turned and began to shout, "Guards, to arms! The Duchess be missin'!"

The men rushed into the elegant foyer from all directions. And within minutes, the search for the Duchess of Ranscome commenced.

•   •   •   •

The following days were rough as the cousins took turns with me. Brice was a bit gentler than Ban, but let's face it. Rape is rape no matter what you call it. I learned fast to keep my mouth shut and not to struggle or fight. I somehow clung to my sanity telling myself this was a nightmare and it would soon end.

It didn't.

On the morning of the 10th, the carriage pulled into Wilmington, Delaware. I was given a choice. I could marry Tarleton, or else.

I chose the or else. Ban was livid. He beat me so bad Brice had to pull him off me. Brice was afraid Ban would kill me.

By then, I prayed he would.

I regained consciousness with a start, screaming with fear. I realized I was trussed up like a calf for the branding. I was pretty sure Tarleton had broken my nose and maybe my cheekbone. My lip was burst open and swollen. In fact, my whole face felt like it must be bruised and swollen. My ribs were painfully tender and I ached with bruises from head to toe.

I could tell I was in a small cabin in a ship by the movement as well as the look of the room imprisoning me. I was thirsty and I had a God-awful headache. And I needed to make waters in the worst way imaginable.

I called out for a while with no response. I grew hoarse as I called out over and over with no one coming to help me. Finally, in frustration, I began kicking the wall. After about ten minutes, a disgruntled sailor entered my cabin. He was a big man, about 6' tall and 250 pounds, all work-honed muscle. His head was bald and he needed a good bath and a shave.

"What do you want, woman?" His voice came out like a growl.

"I need to make waters." My own voice was hoarse, more like a croak than anything else.

He shrugged. "Do it right there." He turned to walk away.

"Fine. Tell the Captain I asked for assistance and you told me to urinate on the bed."

Sailor MacGrumpy wheeled back towards me. "What did you say?"

I swallowed hard as I tried to ignore his hammock sized fists. Could he hurt me any worse than Bloody Ban already had? "Please tell the Captain that Lady Francesca Selk Hobbs needs assistance to utilize the commode."

He blinked, surprised either by my calm demeanor or name. He nodded and hustled back out the door.

Great. I still needed to pee. Desperately. I tried to think about anything else, but it is hard not to think about water when you're at sea. My thirst grew and my urgency increased to the point of desperation when the door burst open and a muscular man peered inside.

"I'm Captain O'Malley. Creeps says you need something?"

My eyes flew open in surprise. He was a big man. Not just tall, but all muscle from head to toe. Shirtless and clad in his trews, stockings, and shoes, I reckoned he got those iron hard muscles working on ships for more than 20 years. His skin was golden brown from the sun, like Will's. His light brown hair hung long in dreadlocks, which he wore queued back. His brown hair had faded from the constant exposure to the sun and sea to a dirty blonde. His cool, intelligent, grey eyes looked appraisingly at me. He wore a beard, that hung into a point in the front, and gave him a sinister look. Then again, perhaps the sinister look came from the scar slashing across one eyebrow. This was what I would have thought a privateer would look like, not a Ranscome captain.

"Oh, my merciful heavens. You're Captain Kirk O'Malley? From Galway? Captain of the Ranscome Enterprise, out of Wilmington, Delaware? And isn't Anthony Francisco your first mate? Was that Creeps? Don't people call him Creeps?"

I never anticipated Sailor MacGrumpy was none other than Creeps Francisco, one of the finest first mates in our – my – line. He got the nickname because he can creep around without a sound despite his size. And I sure never guessed that carrying me away was the finest Captain on the fastest ship I owned. Huh. Go figure. Well, that just about defined irony.

O'Malley frowned and nodded. "Yes, but I don't see what could matter to you..."

"It matters plenty to me if you are Captain Kirk O'Malley of the Enterprise," I rasped, my throat burning from my screams.

His laugh came out like a bark. "Well, I'm impressed you know who I am and what line my ship is in. What do you want, woman?"

"I want to be untied. I want a drink of water. I want to use the chamber pot…"

"And why in the name of the Almighty do you think I would do those things for you?" he snapped.

I took a deep breath. "Because I am Francesca Selk Hobbs. I am the Duchess of Ranscome. I own this blasted ship. Now, cut me loose!"

He blinked a couple of times. "Well, now, I've had women try to bamboozle me before, and sell me a load of malarkey, but this one takes the cake. Why should I believe you?"

"Have you ever had a person know who you were when they had not walked under their own powers onto your ship?"

"Ha. You were passed out drunk."

I shook my head, impatient. "Yeah, someone sure enough bamboozled you, but it wasn't me. I was beaten and drugged before I was brought here. Surely you can tell looking at me that I have been beaten. And, why am I trussed up like a Christmas goose?"

He looked surprised at that. "The men who brought you aboard said you caused a brouhaha at Lady Paddington's and you needed to be relocated."

I narrowed my eyes at him. "Do you mean to say I look like a doxie to you?"

He began to squirm and bent over to untie my wrists. "Well, not so much now, ma'am, that you are sober. Although your blouse is ripped down to your woo-hoo. You look more like you stood up when you should have shut up."

I glanced down, and felt my face redden at the exposed flesh revealed by my ripped blouse. I sat up, rubbing my numb hands. I couldn't even try to cover my shift and stays until I could use my numb hands. "Thank you. I reckon I did just that. I refused to marry him. He said I would regret it. Could you please help me up? I can't feel my hands. And again, I swear I wasn't drunk. He drugged me."

"Sure, Duchess." His words dripped with sarcasm as he shook his head again in disbelief, but he helped me up. He motioned across the room. "The chamber pot is over there."

I arose slowly, my muscles complaining from forced disuse. I slipped behind the screen to relieve myself. After I finished, I tried to cover my stays, but you can't cover something when you don't have enough fabric to cover yourself. I sighed and asked, "How long was I unconscious?"

He shrugged. "I can't say. You've been on board for fifteen hours…"

I was shocked. "Fifteen hours? What day is it? Where are we now?"

"It's the 12th. We passed Charleston an hour ago. We should be at Savannah by morning."

I struggled to think and not panic. My God, those maniacs had me for at least 5 days, and I had been on this ship unconscious for the better part of the sixth day. "Isn't Captain Matthews in charge of Ranscome Shipping at Savannah?"

Captain O'Malley looked stunned. "Yes, he is. How do you know that?"

I sighed. "I told you. I am Francesca Marie Selk Hobbs. My family call me Fancy. I am the Duchess of Ranscome. I own this line. I am expected to know the ships, the captains, the harbor masters, the business, from top to bottom. Didn't Will know all those things when he was running the business all those years?"

"Will? How do you know Will Selk?"

"Oh, for the love of … he's my big brother. He gave up the title because he intends to stay in the United States once this dratted war is done."

His eyes narrowed. "So … where is he now?"

"He took his family to the Bella Linda Plantation in Puerto Rico the first week of March when the maniac who sold me to you escaped prison after threatening to kill Sassy and me. Sassy is his wife."

O'Malley blinked a couple of times. "Damn. You might be Mister Jo's Wee Duchess. I remember him referring to the lass that way long ago when we sailed to Ireland back in '64. I took Will and his family to Bella Linda last month."

I could not contain my excitement. "Yes, it's all true!"

"Just one problem, my Wee Duchess."

My throat went dry again. Nervous, I wet my lips. "What is that?"

"I paid a lot of money for you, sweetheart. I don't intend to lose it. I won't lock you in, but I recommend you lock the door after me. Otherwise, you might have some unwanted visitors. And don't go on deck without me. After all, every man on this ship knows there is a high-priced woman on board. They need to see you belong to me and no one else." He turned to exit the cabin.

My mouth suddenly drier than dirt, I began to stutter, flabbergasted. "But…but… I'm not a whore."

"Like it or not, the truth isn't important to those sailors. The appearance of truth is what matters. You were carried on board unconscious and beaten. They believe what they were told: you were knocked senseless in a fight in a bordello. To these men, that story would be easier to believe that a real live duchess was assaulted, kidnapped and sold as a slave when she refused some *mhac na galla's* hand in marriage."

"Captain O'Malley, I personally guarantee that my family will return your money. Ranscome Shipping will return the money with interest. I swear…"

He laughed again. "Oh, no, my Wee Duchess. I have other plans for you."

I blinked a couple of times, not quite comprehending what he was saying. "But, Captain O'Malley…"

"I'll not tolerate arguing, Fancy. You just need to understand you belong to me now."

My heart froze as he smiled. And I thought Tarleton's smile was cold? I shivered.

'Flabbergasted' was not an adequate word to describe my shock. I could feel tears welling in my eyes. I blinked to bat the tears back. I didn't want to cry. Not in front of this man. Wordless, I nodded.

He frowned. "You understand."

I understood I am betrothed to a man I love with all my heart and soul. I understood I have been kidnapped, beaten, and raped senseless for days. But I said nothing. It would not help me at that point. I just nodded again before I managed to choke out my answer. "Yes, I understand."

"Good. You'll find some fresh clothes in the chest. Feel free."

Hands shaking, I washed myself the best I could at the little hand basin and then rifled through the trunk and found clean shifts, petticoats, and leather jumps in the chest. Plain but wearable. I have worn worse in my life. You can survive this, Fancy, I said over and over. You have been through worse. You will survive this. You have to.

But how much more could I survive?

We didn't stop at Savannah. Or at San Juan. I kept trying to convince Kirk to release me. He just laughed. He didn't care that I was in love with another man. He didn't care that my family would repay him the money he spent for me. He had his treasure. He intended to keep me.

With a sinking heart, I realized we were headed south. Kirk O'Malley's home was Barbados, and I was the prime piece of human cargo he transported home on this trip.

It appeared Kirk O'Malley had a little side job slaving. We were headed to the Hell on Earth called Barbados, also known as the Sugar Island. Oh, sweet Lord Jesus, save me. How would my family ever find me now?

•   •   •   •   •

They hunted everywhere but she had simply disappeared. Without a trace. There was not a shred of evidence to be found, not even an iota to point the finger at Tarleton. Rick knew in his heart Francesca had been kidnapped just as he knew beyond any shadow of doubt that Tarleton was behind her disappearance.

They scoured the city. And on the fifteenth day after Francesca's disappearance, Fitz stumbled across a little girl who remembered a pretty lady dressed in grey fainting down at the quay. She said the two men with the lady lifted her up and carried her away to a nearby carriage and then the carriage sped away.

"Slick as greased owl shit," Fitz said. "The damned bastards stole her away in the middle of town in broad daylight. Right across from the Commander-in-Chief's headquarters. In the blink of an eye. But how? And how could they have known when she would be there? Clarissa, who brought the note that morning?"

She looked nervous as she shook her head. "I swear, Lord Fitz Simmons, I don' know. Some lil' child brought it when I was sweeping the stoop. I gave him a penny, brought the note in the house and gave it to Miss Fancy straight away."

"Thank you, Clarissa. That will be all." Marc waited until she left the library and then shut the door before he turned back to the other men. "I don't trust her. This happened right after she came into this house. I know Tobias and Hattie Mae are her grandparents, and they are fine people, but I can't help it. I don't trust that lass."

Fitz nodded. "I know what you mean. Something about her sets my teeth on edge. That girl is not right in the head."

"I sent the letter saying to meet me at 1. When Clarissa brought it to Fancy, it was altered to say 12," Rick said.

Rob Townsend frowned. "You also think she was somehow involved? Why? What about her sets your teeth on edge, too?"

Rick stared across the hall to the parlor where Clarissa was dusting. "Simple. I don't believe in coincidence. My dad said there is no such thing."

Fitz stared out at the pretty girl, too. "I agree."

"I say the same thing," said Marc.

They all knew Rick was beside himself, near out of his mind with fears about Fancy.

"So, what do we do?" Fitz asked.

"Give her the afternoon off. Put a tail on her to see where she goes, who she meets," Rob said.

Fitz nodded. "Who should we use?"

"It needs to be someone she doesn't know." Rick looked thoughtful. "I reckon she could recognize all of us."

Marc's eyes narrowed. "Hmm. Mayhap. Mayhap not. I have an idea. I think I have the right group of people to handle this task."

It looked like time to use some old skills.

• • • • •

Hours later, a handsome and dapper officer was observed slipping in the front door of Patrice Paddington's New York Gentlemen's Club. He smiled at the group of laughing young men standing outside swapping stories about their adventures that evening in the high-priced bordello. Boys out having a bit of fun. He could well understand that. He tipped his hat at the group as he entered the exclusive establishment.

About the same time, Clarissa slipped out of the servants' entrance at the rear of the elegant Selk townhouse to start down the alley. She paid little notice to the drunk staggering down the alley after her. She meandered for blocks before slipping into the servants' entrance to Paddy's new establishment, located a few blocks from the military headquarters. The drunk staggered on towards the nearby quay.

Clarissa hated working at the Selk house. She would have done anything for Tom Selk at one time. She even entertained his friends when asked. Of course, she knew better than to refuse Tom's requests she party with his friends.

And when you think you are in love with the man pimping you out to other men, you will do anything he asks.

She got over her infatuation with Tom when he sold her to Calvin. She was shocked by Tom's ugly reaction to her pregnancy. Still, she knew better than to quarrel with Tom. She went with Calvin to Bermuda without a fuss, where she lived as his mistress until two years after Toby was born.

If she was shocked when Tom sold her to be Calvin's bedmate, she was hurt beyond belief when Cal sold her to Paddy. He told her Fancy and he were going to marry. Fancy did not want Calvin's mistress in the house when she arrived at Spring Haven.

The men trained her well for a house like Paddy's. Even so, her anger over her initial sale turned to rage when her childhood friend refused to live under the same roof with Clarissa and Fancy's soon-to-be husband.

Who did Fancy think she was anyway? Fancy wasn't any better than her, even if she could pass for white. Tom used to treat Fancy the same way. He used her the same way. Clarissa remembered times Tom fed them both drugs for his 'little soirees' with Calvin. Of course, truth be told, Tom never used Fancy at his soirées with anyone but Calvin. You would have thought Tom believed Fancy was special despite the way he treated her day after day.

It about killed her when Calvin told her Fancy refused to live at Spring Haven if she were there. Oh, she might deny she said it, but Clarissa would never forget the feeling of raw betrayal she experienced when Calvin told her he was selling her at Fancy's request. That was the day her childish love for her cousin turned to hate.

Clarissa could not imagine how Cal ever managed to wangle the title for Fancy. The uppity little bitch sure came up in the world since ol' Tom was in charge of Belle Rose. How dare she tell Clairee not to talk about those days? Thought herself too good to be used like that, hmm? Clarissa smirked. She figured Fancy was getting her comeuppance about now.

It would damned sure pay Fancy back for making Cal sell her to Paddy in the first place.

She threw open the door to her old room and rushed into the arms of the tall, handsome, dark-haired man waiting for her. After the long kiss, she said, "Tell me all about it. Every sordid little detail. Did you make her suffer? Oh, please tell me how you made her suffer."

"It went as planned." Tarleton's laugh was low and his eyes reflected the hunger he felt for the beautiful mulatto woman. "But let's talk later, my beauty. First things first."

A young soldier came staggering down the hall and stumbled into the room. "Oh, sorry, old man. Wrong. Room."

As he turned to leave, Tarleton spoke up. "No problem. Feel free to join us if you wish. Clairee enjoys a good party."

Clarissa giggled and snuggled closer to her lover.

The young soldier blushed as he backed out. "Oh, no, sir, Colonel. I wouldn't presume. Please, sir, carry on…"

He shut the door without a sound as Ban Tarleton turned back to the courtesan.

The men were all waiting in the library with Marc when Clarissa slipped back in the house a few hours later.

"Clarissa, we need to have a wee chat," Marc said, his controlled voice belying the myriad of emotions he was experiencing right then.

Her movements were slow, languid as if she were well satiated. "Of course, my lord. How may I please you?"

Her eyes opened wide with surprise as she realized the library was filled with the lads, as Fancy called her guard. Rob Townsend stepped behind her to shut the door.

"We have a few more questions for ye, lass. Perhaps we can tickle your memories, and ye might find a bit more information tucked away in her pretty little head that might help us find poor Fancy."

Poor Fancy indeed. She struggled not to laugh as she envisioned Fancy sold to whore in some damned hellhole like she had been sold. She curtseyed. "Of course, my lord."

"Oh, but let's not be rude. Did you have a nice afternoon?" Marc sounded solicitous, calm and smooth.

She could feel her cheeks redden as she recalled the hours of pleasure in her lover's arms. "Oh, yes, my lord. Very … pleasurable."

"Excellent. And how was the Colonel today?" Marc continued.

She blinked. "The Colonel? I … I don't know what you mean…"

About then, another officer turned around to face her. "Perhaps you didn't realize your lover is a Colonel? Even though I called him 'Colonel' when I intruded into your room?"

Clarissa paled. "I … I swear, I don't know what you mean."

Rob Townsend shook his head. "That is the best you can do? Come on, girl. You can come up with a better story than that. Brian walked right in on the two of you not two hours ago."

"No, sir, he must be mistaken. I didn't see no Colonel this afternoon. I … I had tea with an old friend. That's all."

Rick snorted. "Tea, hmm? Is that what they call it at Miss Paddington's? Well, let me ask this. You want to go back there? Because believe me, sweetheart, we can arrange it. Or perhaps you would prefer something a little grittier? Perhaps the Colonel can help you find a job that's got a bit more edge. Who knows? Perhaps a rougher crowd would be more to your liking."

She tilted her head at Rick. "I have no idea what you mean, Dr. Winslow."

Rick studied her for a minute. She was a cool one, all right. He could almost believe she didn't know anything about Francesca's disappearance. Almost. If Brian Callahan had not heard her asking Tarleton to tell her 'all the sordid details,' he might be willing to accept her at face value. Instead, it was all Rick could do not to throttle the two-faced, lying whore. Watch it, Winslow. She may be the best source you will have to finding Francesca. Do not let your emotions cause you to make the wrong decision here. No permanent decisions based on temporary feelings, dude. Fancy's life is at stake. He took a deep, calming breath and then smiled as he forced himself to relax. "Well, I guess we were mistaken."

Marc cut his eyes at Rick in surprise. "But…"

Rick held up a hand. "No, Marc, if Clarissa says she doesn't know, then I have to believe her. After all, why would she plot with a sorry assed, scum dog like Banastre Tarleton to kidnap the woman who freed her minutes earlier? It doesn't make any sense. I always said it didn't make any sense."

Marc blinked. Rick had always been the one surest Clarissa was involved. Rob cleared his throat.

Brian Callahan stared in obvious disbelief. "Yeah, sure. And I have some fine farm land I'll sell ye in Connaught at a most reasonable price."

Fitz shifted, uncomfortable with Richard's sudden change in demeanor. "Well, we're all a wee bit on edge tonight. Thank ye for your time, lass. That will be all."

Brian frowned. "But…"

Marc realized something was astir, too. "Aye, that will be all, Clairee. Thank ye."

She curtseyed and left the library. Rob watched at the door until she was gone. "She's headed to her room."

"What the bloody hell was that all about?" Brian demanded. "We all know the feckin' bitch is involved. Hell, I heard her myself."

Richard nodded in agreement. "I know. She is most definitely involved all the way up to her pretty brown eyes. But it was clear she wasn't going to give us anything tonight."

"Think we played our hand too soon?" Marc asked.

"Maybe. That's why I tried to act like I'm a dumb ass and I believed her. You have no idea how bad I want to choke the truth out of the lying little bitch." Rick sat clinching his fists over and over as he continued to try to control his emotions from spiraling out of control.

"We all did. So, now what?" Fitz said.

"Well, I'm glad to know ye haven't slipped your noodle," Brian said. "I thought I was goin' to have to knock some sense back into your addled brain."

They all laughed at that.

"No, now we wait for one of them to slip up. And watch the cousin. What was his name? Oh, yes, Darlington. Watch him. He might be the weak link," Rob said.

Rick nodded. "She won't slip up without a lot more pressure. Nor will Tarleton. But Brice Darlington might. Hmm."

The others could almost see the wheels moving in Rick's brain.

"And remember. Don't make permanent decisions based on temporary feelings," Rick intoned. "Everything we say and do can impact whether we find Francesca."

"If it's not already too late," fussed Callahan.

Brian's words put a pall over the room.

"It can't be." Rick said. "I refuse to accept that. She's still alive. I know it."

Just like he knew his mom was alive when everyone said she was dead. He knew in his heart beyond a shadow of doubt Fancy was alive.

She had to be alive. He came too damned far to find her to lose her now. She was his heart.

Chapter 15
Fancy - 1782

We arrived at Barbados at the end of April, as the hotter, wetter season was beginning. It was hot but no hotter than I expected for the tropics. The sky was vivid blue, and the sun looked bigger and brighter than I had ever seen before. The waters varied from darkest azure to palest sky blue, depending on their depths. I stood in awe of the way the light glittered across the blues of the water as if diamonds had been sprinkled across the surface. The mountains were beautiful with verdant foliage and abundant flowers. The sounds of slaves chanting, birds singing and monkeys chattering filled the air. Of course, I realized it would be hotter in the wet, hot summer months to come, and that bright burning sun could turn into a red-haired girl's worst enemy. After all, the Africans called the Europeans 'red legs' for a reason.

Captain O'Malley and I left the ship at Bridgetown. It was the largest city on the island, with some townhouses as elegant as any I ever saw in Williamsburg or New York City. The harbor was filled with 40 or 50 ships. The town was bustling with merchants selling everything from calabash to rum to human cargo. There was still a strong and profitable trade in slaves.

O'Malley explained I had two choices. I could be indentured to him for a term of two years, at the end of which I would be free to leave if I chose to do so. I understood if I accepted that, I would essentially be his sex slave during my indenture. Or, if I refused his indenture of two years, I would be sold on the block for indenture. I knew the standard term for indenture was seven years. I might get lucky and be sold to work as a maid or field worker instead of warming an owner's bed. Might. Chances were another buyer would use me the same way O'Malley intended to use me, although I might be sold into a brothel or a breeding facility.

I am not a stupid girl. Naïve sometimes, but not stupid. Two years of servitude sounded much better than seven. I understood full well O'Malley would have the exclusive use and service of my body during that time. The contract specified any child born during my indenture would remain in his service for life. Of course, Kirk was most forthcoming that he hoped I would marry him if I became pregnant. If I did marry him, my indenture papers specified my indenture would end, and my child would be born free. Of course, if I married him, Kirk O'Malley would hold control over the Ranscome fortunes in his money-grubbing paws.

It was a devilishly clever plan.

He admitted he got the idea from Tarleton, who mentioned he would come to Barbados in four or five months and 'might deign to save me from indenture then by marrying me.' He thought that an odd offer when Tarleton mentioned it. Once O'Malley realized who I was, he knew what a treasure he held. There was no way he would let Tarleton snap the prize from him.

I realized if I became pregnant, the likelihood was I would miscarry, due to my weird blood condition. I never mentioned it to O'Malley. Chances were I couldn't explain it correctly if I tried. In fact, even if he did manage to force me into marriage, chances were I would never manage to bear him a child.

Of course, he would never manage to force me into marriage unless I were pregnant.

"You know my family will be searching for me," I said in a low voice after I signed the legal document.

Kirk shrugged. "It doesn't matter. You're mine for two years now, Fancy Hobbs. There is nothing they can do about it."

"Will could kill you."

His laugh sounded like a sea lion's bark. "Mayhap. But why would he do that? You would be sold at public auction to someone else for the balance of the term of your indenture."

I didn't answer. We had been around and around that mulberry bush more times than I could count. He saw no wrong in virtually enslaving the owner of the shipping lines for which he worked with the hope of forcing me to marry him.

Can you say 'soulless'?

I realized indenture was better than outright slavery, even on Barbados. It wasn't the Barbados of the 1650's when Daddy Jo said well over 500,000 Irish were kidnapped and sold into bondage on the Sugar Island, never to return to Ireland. Periods of indenture varied from a few years to life. Barbados alone received thousands of Irish prisoners of war who were considered outright slaves. Daddy Jo said Cardinal Rinuccini of the Vatican estimated 50,000 a year were taken for close to 20 years. Daddy Jo claimed over 100,000 Irish children alone were kidnapped and sold to the New World. Back then, children as young as 8 were stolen and sold into bondage. That sounds like some mighty high numbers, but I do know that trade for Irish women and children flourished, and a passel of them, probably some 50,000 to 80,000, wound up on Barbados between 1652 and 1657 alone. Add to that a twenty per cent death rate at sea was acceptable and you begin to grasp the horrors of slavery, whether from Ireland or from Africa. As Daddy Jo said, they were all treated like sub-humans by the British.

Hortense, Will's first wife, descended from an Irishwoman who was kidnapped, forced into indenture and sent to Barbados. Once there, she was bred to an African man and their children were slaves for life.

Nor would it be for me the hellhole countless Africans had been thrown into after being ripped from their homes and sold as slaves for life, especially in the harsh, early days when the land had to be cleared by hand for the tobacco and sugar crops to come. I had heard the horror stories of slavery on Barbados all my life. After all, my great-grandmother Ebony was sold here in the 1720's, when Daddy Jo bought her. Uncle Tobias was small when they lived on Barbados, but he still has vivid memories of the abysmal conditions for slaves. He described how his mother and he were forced to build a little lean-to for protection from the elements from sticks and mud, and how they ate cornmeal and whatever they could grub from the land. He told me how children as young as four years old were trained to follow the workers to collect insects and grubs to feed to the stock. He also told me of beatings to children as well as adults so severe that the slaves were scarred, if not disabled or killed. Life was cheap then.

My family were lucky that Belle and Jo traveled through the Caribbean in '27 and bought my Great-Gramma Ebony and my Uncle Tobias and took them to Virginia. Tobias was about 5 when they arrived in Virginia. They were still slaves when they got to Virginia, but at least they had clean clothing, decent little cabins, and adequate food at Belle Rose. The food and clothing improved after Gramma Ebony became a cook in the house.

Even back then, Daddy Jo refused to work children under 8. Until then, they received a basic education and job skills in a variety of areas. Tobias was 10 and had been working in the fields when the incident occurred that changed their lives forever.

Uncle Tobias told me that Tom and he were fishing in the Potomac one Sunday afternoon. Baby Will was playing nearby when the older boys heard a splash. Tobias looked up with horror to see the toddler bobbing in the waters 20 feet below them. Tom jumped up and was about to go in after his baby brother when Tobias dove right in. The water was deep and cold, but Tobias managed to get Will to shore and to safety.

Tom ran for help. Jo and Belle got there as Tobias dragged Will on shore. As he thumped Will on the back to make the toddler start to breathe, Belle sobbed, sure her baby was dead. I remember Daddy Jo said, "And then the wee lad vomited up dirt and water and started bawlin'. I realized the lad would live, though Belle cried and cried."

With that heroic act, Tobias was moved from being a field hand to training to become a footman. In the blink of an eye, his bravery saved Will, got Tobias freed, and changed history.

Gramma Ebony was pregnant by a white overseer on Barbados when Jo bought them. She told them she was Igbo, the name of her tribe in Africa, from the area called Ebonyi. From the area, Ebonyi, came her name, Ebony. The girl, my Gramma Maisie, was a pretty, bright girl. By bright I mean she was mixed, although I always heard she was smart as a whip, too. Maisie trained to become a seamstress and later became Mama Belle's lady's maid. Mama Belle mentioned once that Maisie could sew anything she set her mind to making. She adored Miss Belle and would have done anything for her. She offered to warm Daddy Jo's bed when Belle had the fourth miscarriage after Jenny was born, and the doctor warned another pregnancy could kill Belle. Both Belle and Jo initially refused, but the second year, in '41, Jo gave in and took Maisie to bed. She was sixteen.

Jo freed her mother and Maisie before he made Maisie his concubine. He said he wasn't going to have anyone ever say he abused his slaves or forced an unwilling woman. I reckon he didn't know a woman could feel like she owed her master something even if she had been freed. Or that a woman might still be afraid to tell the owner or overseer of the plantation 'no' even if she were free. The Lord knows I learned mighty fast not to tell Simon LeGrand 'no' when he was overseer.

Anyway, that was how Tamsin was conceived in 1741. And, of course, I am her child.

My Grannie Maisie died two years later in childbirth, giving birth to a stillborn son. Maisie had jumped over the broom with Horace by then. Horace was a field hand slave. I never knew my Grannie.

Tamsin never said much of anything about her mama other than to tell if it weren't for her, Tamsin wouldn't have been one-fourth colored, or a quadroon. That's what they called mixed folks like her back then. I am one-eighth black or an octoroon. Sassy says we are persons of color, even if we are light like me.

I've been around lots of slaves in my life but I had never been one before I signed those papers. I damned sure knew to keep quiet about my black blood. I never passed for white on purpose before, but I knew my black blood would have kept me a slave in Barbados forever had I dared mention it. Colored folk were not allowed to be free on Barbados at that time.

Daddy Jo had the reputation of being a 'soft' planter. He never beat his slaves. He did not abuse the women. He had a different attitude about the treatment of slaves than did most of the folk around the tidewaters where I grew up. But he still owned humans. He would have wept to see the price his manipulations to get me to be the Duchess of Ranscome cost me.

Yes, it was just two years, but during it I would belong to Kirk O'Malley, body and soul. He could use me any time and any way he chose. If I displeased him, he could beat me. And if I angered him too bad, he could sell my indenture. God alone knew what would happen to me then.

I figured I could handle anything unless he got furious and sold me to Tarleton. I would kill myself before that animal would ever lay his hands on me again.

I hoped Kirk O'Malley would be better. I had my doubts.

I was quiet as we shopped in Bridgetown to pick up supplies. I was surprised when Kirk insisted on buying me fabric so I could make myself some clothes. He explained his house servants wear blue, so he purchased blue cotton yardage. He chose some basic blue but added a beautiful piece of blue and white print. "Make yourself a jacket with that to have something to wear for special events."

"That's pretty. Yes, sir, I sure will. I can have those made in no time." I understood I would need to make myself a couple of petticoats, shifts, and caracols.

"Oh, you like to sew then?" he asked with his lopsided smile.

I nodded. I figured I did not need to explain I worked as a seamstress in the past or that I could sew a neat, elegant line. He would figure that out soon enough.

"Good. Mayhap you'll mend some of my things as well."

I nodded again. If sewing and mending were all my job duties would entail, I would be a happy woman, but I was pretty danged sure sewing would not comprise the full extent of my responsibilities. I understood I would also serve a function in his bed.

We left that afternoon to trek to the sugar plantation. I was glad Daddy Jo insisted I learn to ride at a young age. Even so, it was a daunting journey. Four hours later, we arrived at Seaview. Built on the side of a mountain with fantastic views of the Caribbean beyond, I could see why O'Malley named it that. I could also see that as far inland as it was, and as far as it was from Bridgetown, it was hopeless to even consider escape. It was not a possibility for a woman alone.

We crossed Seaview lands the better part of an hour before we reached the main house. As we crossed his plantation, O'Malley told me he owned 500 acres. Two hundred were tied up in sugar. The rest was pasture, timber, tobacco, ginger, cotton, indigo, and general food provisions for the plantation. Hmm. With the cotton and indigo, I should be able to dye fabric like Sassy taught me. I could even try some of the prints we had done in the past. There was a decent sized two story, Georgian house that reminded me of the house at Spring Haven. There was a boiling house, filling houses, cisterns, a still house, houses for the slaves, and stables. I was relieved to see the slave houses. I have to admit I feared I would find myself in some mud and daub shack like my Great-Gramma Ebony and Tobias did years before. At least that was not my destiny at Seaview.

As we pulled up before the house, a tall, dark man and a mulatto woman came outside to greet us.

"Fancy, this is Odo, my butler. He is my most trusted servant, unless of course, it is Dolly, my housekeeper. Dolly will show you to your rooms. Fancy will be here with us for a while."

"Yessuh, Cap'n. Where would you like Miss Fancy to be situated?" Dolly sounded as if it were reasonable and expected for her master to bring home stray women 'for a while.'

"In the rooms next to mine. I imagine she would like a bath. It's been a long voyage."

Expressionless, she nodded and turned, motioning for me to follow.

"Miss Fancy, these will be your rooms," she said when we reached the suite of rooms O'Malley stipulated.

"Thank you, but I'm not Miss Fancy. I'm plain old Fancy."

She looked at me sharply and then smiled. "Plain Fancy, hmm? I s'pect you are more 'fancy' than 'plain', girl. Come on. Let's get you situated, Plain Fancy."

The room was large and comfortable. Like myself, it was Plain Fancy. It held a large tester bed with a serviceable set of crisp, white cotton sheets, which I figured were woven from Seaview cotton. There were lattice-like wood coverings over the windows, which could open to let in the air and sunshine. A dressing table and mirror sat next to a wardrobe. I was aware I had no luggage, and that I must look like a raggedy beggar. I sat down and picked up the brush from the dressing table to begin to work through my tangles in my wind snarled hair.

"There be fresh clothing in the wardrobe. I'll have some water sent up and you can freshen up in the hip bath. We'll get you a real bath tomorrow down in the kitchen."

I smiled. "Thank you, Dolly. I admit, a real bath sounds mighty good. I would dearly love to wash my dirty hair." I frowned. "What do the servants call Captain O'Malley?"

"Most of us call him Cap'n."

I nodded. Silent, she nodded back as she left.

I would not have suspected her animosity if I had not caught her reflection in the mirror over the dressing table. Her reflection revealed fury there for a flash, but in that instant, I knew whose rooms these had been previously and who had been dismissed when I was brought in looking like something the blasted ol' Tom cat dragged in.

Damn. I did not need an enemy. I sat the hairbrush down, laid my head on my arms, and cried.

He came to me that night. He had come to me every night on the ship but he had never taken me. He came to me the first time when I awoke in terror, screaming like a banshee. He wrapped me into his arms and crooned to me until I calmed. Afterwards, he came each night to sleep beside me. He would kiss me each time and fondle my breasts as I squirmed about a bit. He would laugh as I tried to wiggle away from his big hands, roughened from years of sailing. But he never pushed the issue. And then, he would wrap me tight into his arms, where I would somehow manage to sleep, sound and dreamless.

That first night on Barbados, he came for more.

I expected roughness. Overt force. Violence. And the damned man gave me candlelight, wine, and roses. I thought Darlington was a rogue? I thought that line from Sassy's song described Darlington? The line about good boys going to heaven and bad boys bringing heaven to you? Ha. I was wrong. The phrase was designed for Captain Kirk O'Malley. I swear I never dreamed the Devil himself could be so charming.

I would like to say Kirk O'Malley was thoughtless. Rough. Heavy handed. Impatient. But he was none of those things.

He was superb.

He came to me after supper clad in soft, cotton pants that pulled up just over his hips. No shirt. Just the vast expanse of lean, hard, tanned muscles rippling across his chest and belly. I had never seen muscles like that on a man before Kirk. His clean hair shone with luster. His eyes gave away the passion he would no longer control. His hands as well as his mouth were demanding yet gentle, determined yet kind. He might look like an angel, but I knew this man must be the Devil. The Devil alone could beguile like this. Oh, yes, he is nothing but a damned Irish rogue. A seducer of women. A damned fine seducer of women.

I realized why the local girls clamored for him to be their first. I was shocked when I heard a girl in the kitchen call him the Virgin Slayer. I thought maybe he killed young girls. After a night of seduction in his arms, I could understand why the girls wanted to be taken first by him.

I had changed into a night rail and had brushed my hair out after I washed it. I couldn't bear to wait until the next day, so I washed it in the basin, towel dried it the best I could and then combed the curls smooth. My hair was hanging down my back loose when he came in.

I didn't hear him enter the room from his. It startled me when he lifted my hair up to rub it across his face. I must have jerked at his touch, for he laid a hand across mine and shushed me. "'Twill be fine, *mo leannan*," he murmured as he lifted my hair from my nape to kiss me there.

Mo leannan is Irish for my love. I did not want to be his love.

I trembled. I didn't want to respond to this man. "Kirk, you know I love Richard…"

He shushed me and continued. As he continued to kiss me, I knew I was headed for trouble with a big old capital T.

He bent down for another kiss before he left. "I love you, lass."

My lips thinned into an angry line. I said nothing.

He had done that every night since he started his 'seduction' on the ship. Each night, he required me to tell him I loved him. Each night, I protested. He would laugh and tell me to say it anyway. "I love Richard. You know that."

He shook his head. "Nay, lass, say it back. Now. And don't speak to me of another man. You're mine now."

I already knew he would not leave until I muttered the words he wanted to hear. "Fine. I love you."

He smiled. "See, that wasn't so hard. It will get easier each time you utter those words. And soon, you'll mean it when you say it."

I trembled with rage at his words. He knew nothing about love. And damn him, when I began to cry, he gathered me into his arms, determined to console me. "God's tooth, Fancy, I do love you. You're an easy woman to love. You'll see. Soon you will love me as well."

And then he kissed me again, all sweet and tender, like I meant something more to him than an easy meal ticket. That made me cry more. How? How could I respond to one man when I loved another?

I woke up screaming that night. Kirk came rushing back into my room ready to fight whatever demon was hurting me. When he realized I was having another nightmare, he held me close, crooning softly to me in his odd mix of Irish and English. I finally came to my senses, and realized I was not still in the clutches of Tarleton. As I cried, Kirk patted my back. Once again, I fell asleep in his arms.

Hmm. Maybe he isn't soulless after all.

The next night, he took me to his big bed. I slept there every night after that. When I had another bad dream, he gathered me into his arms, soothing me until the nightmare passed, just as he had on the ship and that first night on Barbados.

Soon, we had a pattern established. I helped Dolly during the day. It wasn't required, but I would have gone mad without something to do. I sewed and mended for the Captain. At night, I served my primary purpose as leman to Kirk O'Malley. I think that's the fancy word for 'bedmate.' And of course, each night before we slept together in his bed, he told me he loved me, and expected me to say the same back to him. If I awoke to night terrors, as he called my nightmares, he held me and comforted me until they passed.

He confused me more by the day.

"We don't have to wait until you're with child to marry, you know," he said one night after we had intimate relations. "I'll marry you as soon as you say yes, as soon as the banns are read."

I bet you would, sly devil, I thought, but I didn't reply. I figured I was going to hell anyway. I would rather go for fornication than adultery. I figured it was adultery to marry one man when I was betrothed to another. I was not going to marry him unless I had no other choice. Richard might not want me any longer, but I would hold out until the bitter end waiting for him to come, unless it became apparent to me I would have a baby while indentured to Kirk.

I would not let a child of my body be a slave for life, ever. No matter who sired it.

But as his kindness over my nightmares continued, my resolve began to weaken. As each day passed, I found myself more confused. Who was this man called Kirk O'Malley? How could be so cold, so mercenary, so ruthless, and then so warm, so loving, so compassionate?

And how could I respond to him night after night with open arms when I still loved Richard? Was Tom right? Was I nothing more that a little mixed-race girl, fit for nothing except pleasuring men?

I realized with a start, one night as I laid in Kirk's arms, after we made love I no longer hated him. How could I, when I felt safe in his arms? And as I learned to trust him, my nightmares began to diminish. My confusion endured, but my nightmares all but stopped.

As the days passed, I felt less empty. Less dirty. Less foolish. Less hollow. And day by day, my desire to die lessened, as I began to hate my life less.

Of course, I never told him my history. I would never trust anyone again with knowledge of the evil Tom and Calvin imposed on me. I would not even tell him about Simon LeGrand. And I sure wasn't about to mention that little detail of being 1/8 black. He thought I was white, and I did not dissuade him of that notion. For the first time in my life, I purposefully passed as white.

I knew it was wrong. I was raised not to lie. But, I was afraid to tell him I was mixed.

I did, however, begin keeping a journal again.

In July, amidst some of the worst heat of the year and torrential rains, Kirk decided to go to Bridgetown. I was surprised by his decision to go. I was thrilled when he decided to take me with him. After all, he knew I did not love him, and I had only been there a little over two months.

It was a hard ride into Bridgetown. The road was waterlogged, and our travel was slowed to a snail's pace. We bogged down in the mud twice and had to get off our mounts to encourage the horses to continue through the muck. In the months since I arrived on Barbados, I had learned Kirk hated idle chatter and lollygagging and abhorred whining women. I remained silent most of the way there. I learned years ago how to keep quiet around men, and I figured I should say nothing if I had nothing good to say. I sure had nothing good to say until we reached Bridgetown.

Kirk led the way through the narrow streets to the inn where we would spend a few days. I knew he hoped a few days in 'civilization', with shopping and visiting would motivate me to give him that big 'yes' he was so desperate to receive.

I tried my hardest not to look the innkeeper in the eye. I knew I must be a sight, with mud staining the hem of my gown as well as my hands and face. I could feel my cheeks burning with shame. He says he wants to marry me, but here he is, flaunting me as his mistress to one and all here in the capitol. How could I ever face these people after he brings me here like this?

Kirk bent over and kissed me. "You can go as far as High Street to shop, if you want. I'll be back before supper time."

I shrugged. "I'll most likely stay here and sew."

He frowned and kissed me again. "You aren't my prisoner. You can go out if you want. Here, I'll leave you a bit of cash in case you see somethin' you want to buy. Remember not to go further than High Street if you change your mind. It can get a bit rough down by the quay. I would rather you not go down there without me."

Wordless, I nodded as I tucked the money into my pocket, and he left to wind his way down the narrow streets to the harbor.

The innkeeper showed me to our room. He had the girl bring me a couple of pitchers of hot water so I could clean up a bit. After I washed up and changed my gown, I put our things away and pulled a chair over by the window to sew. The room had a beautiful view of the harbor below, filled with ships from all across the Caribbean and beyond. I could see Kirk's ship, the Enterprise, moored there. I knew she was in port. That was one of the reasons we came to Bridgetown, so he could tend to business.

I had not expected to see the Enterprise moored next to the Fancy's Revenge, Will's ship. Heck fire, if you got right down to it, I reckoned both were my ships since the Duchess of Ranscome owns the line.

"Oh, sweet Jesus," I whispered, as I tried to calm my desperate mind enough to figure out what to do.

Ten minutes later, I strolled downstairs with my hair covered by a cap and my face covered by a broad-brimmed hat bergere. With a straw basket in my hands to help hide their shaking, I began to stroll down towards High Street, taking my time to glance in the stores along the way. I bought some paper, pen, and ink in shops as I strolled along before I stopped in a café where I ordered tea and a scone. I wrote my note, slipped it into the envelope, and sealed it. I scrawled Will's name across the front and then strolled on down towards the harbor.

I gulped. Kirk was right. The people here were a rougher sort than above High Street. I swallowed back my fear and walked on down to the docks, where I found a lad lolling about, staring at the impressive tall ships.

"Take this note to that ship," I said, pointing to the Revenge, "And give this note to the Captain. He's a tall, dark haired man. His name is Captain William Selk. Don't give it to anyone else. Only give it to Captain Selk. Here's a penny. I'll give you two more when you come back and tell me Captain Selk got the note."

I bit back my laughter as the boy jumped up to attention and saluted me as if I were one of the captains. "Aye, aye, ma'am!"

With my heart in my throat, I stood in the shadows of a building as I watched the boy go on board the Revenge and ask for Will. My excitement turned to horror as he handed the letter over to Kirk rather than Will, who was standing a few feet away. Kirk glanced at the letter, and then shoved it into his shirt with a frown. He then turned to scan the crowd along the quay. His lips narrowed as he spotted me.

I began shaking like a leaf and turned to start back up the winding streets towards the inn. I had not gone far when I felt a rough hand grab my arm.

"Couldn't resist, could you, wench?" Kirk snapped.

He walked fast, so fast I had to run to keep up with him. His hold on my arm was so tight I was crying by the time we got back to the inn. Without a word to the innkeeper, he dragged me upstairs to the room. Still holding my arm with one hand, he kicked the door shut as he pulled the letter to Will out of his shirt with the other hand. He waved it at me.

"Silly little twit, do you understand I could have you flogged for this? I could take you right down to the Governor and tell him you tried to escape."

Defiant, I shook my head. "But I wasn't trying to escape. I wanted…"

"You wanted him to know where you are. And you figured that would get me into a passel of trouble."

My eyes flashed with anger. "I warned you…"

I cringed when his hand lashed out to slap across my face. "You warned me? Oh, no, my Wee Duchess, I warned you against such shenanigans. I warned you to mind me well and not go past High Street. You chose to disobey me. Bend over. Grab your ankles."

My throat went dry with fear. I had seen him do this a time or two with recalcitrant slaves. I fought the urge to back away from him. I saw him go into a rage with one girl who did that the week before. He was a pretty good master with his slaves, as slave owners go, at least for Barbados, I reckoned, but he had a temper that could turn nasty in the blink of an eye over what he perceived to be disobedience. Better not fight him, Fancy girl. You will make it worse. I gulped. "Yes, sir," I whispered.

I was terrified of what he would do.

My trembling increased as I bent over and grabbed my ankles. He jerked his thick leather belt off, flipped my skirts up, and swung the strap across my bare hips. I flinched and bit my lip to keep from crying out as he lashed it down across my butt three more times. I stood there, bent over still holding my ankles as he had ordered, struggling not to cry.

"Will you obey me the next time?" His voice was gruff.

I nodded my head.

"I can't hear you," he said with another pop of the belt to my naked flesh. I flinched again as the belt hit the tender flesh one more time. "Answer me, Fancy. Now. I'm not playing."

I nodded again. "Yes, sir, Captain O'Malley. I'll obey. I promise. I'm sorry."

I struggled not to cry. As patient as he could be over my nightmares, he usually hated it when anyone cried. He considered it to be weak, cowardly. I could see he was struggling to control his breathing. I remained in the position holding my ankles, afraid to move. At last, his breathing slowed, and he said, "Then you can get up. Don't you dare do it again, Fancy. Don't even think about it. You'll be damned sorry if you do. Next time, I'll beat you within an inch of your life. I don't care who you are."

Silent, I nodded as I raised up, my hand rubbing my aching, bruised bottom.

He slammed back out the door. I sank to the floor after I heard the click of the lock and his footsteps faded down the hall and I began to cry in earnest. I was not surprised he locked me in, but it seemed to drive home the hopelessness of my situation. I cried not over the bruises, but over the lost opportunity to contact Will. Why did the foolish boy give the letter to Kirk instead of Will? I told him Will was tall and dark. Kirk was tall, although not quite as tall as Will, and not nearly as dark as Will, with his black hair.

I would be sorry if I did it again? I was already damned sorry. Not for trying. For failing.

One thing for sure. That whipping had me angry at him again. Maybe I was right in the first place about Captain Kirk O'Malley. Maybe he was no more than a soulless monster. Maybe I needed to cling to that picture of him and not succumb to his sweet night charms again.

We left for Seaview three days later. I reckon we didn't speak a dozen sentences between us over those three days or most of the way back to the plantation. I spent much of my time locked in the room at the inn. I remained quiet, docile, subservient. I knew I did not want him to lose his temper with me ever again. I don't cotton to being beaten.

A week after we returned to Seaview, he left for a voyage north. He said he was to be gone two months. I moved back to my room, where I was surprised to have less and less nightmares. Maybe the journal was helping. Or maybe I was finally getting better. I figured whatever caused my nightmares to lessen was a good thing.

By the time he returned, I knew beyond a shadow of a doubt I was with child.

·   ·   ·   ·   ·

Kirk shook his head in frustration. The lass was a constant frustration. One minute, soft and submissive. The next, she would bow up at him, full of piss and vinegar. He could never tell where he stood with her. Just when he thought she might be falling in love with him, forgetting the damned fool man who let her be kidnapped by those feckin' animals, and not an hour later she was stiff, angry, recalcitrant. Bowed up at him like a damned Duchess glowering at her minions.

This time, he lost his blasted Irish temper.

It wasn't so much that she tried to contact Will. He planned to tell Will, once she softened her heart to him. But he told Will he had not seen her, when she was with him not an hour before the lad brought the note on board. He would hate to lose Will's trust, not to mention his friendship. It would just about kill Kirk to lose that. They had been friends for longer than Fancy had been alive.

He reckoned he should have confessed to Will that he had her, but he couldn't bear to lose her. Not yet. The damned woman had stolen his heart. He never intended to fall in love with her, but by Jove, he had.

It scared him shitless when he saw her there on the dock. By God, at times he thought the girl lacked good sense. The crowd down along those docks could be damned rough. As he looked out from the Revenge over dockside, he saw at least two sailors he knew were rough with women, and another who killed a woman with his bare hands in Cuba not six months before. He wouldn't have any of those in his crew, but they were wharf side, hunting for work … or pretty prey. Fancy could have been their prey had he not realized she had come to the quay. 'Twas why he told her not to go there. It made him sick to think she might have undergone another attack. The last one was bad enough. He wasn't sure she could survive another.

He had seen nightmares and night terrors before, but none worse than hers. He could kill the damned men who did this to her. He knew many of her injuries were inflicted by Tarleton when she refused to marry the damned maniac. If that worthless piece of human garbage showed up again, Kirk might well kill him.

Hell, discretion be damned. Kirk knew he would kill the sorry *mhac na galla.*

She began having the night terrors on the ship. He didn't know if she even remembered those nights when she woke him, screaming like a fecking banshee. The first time, he ran to her cabin, his pistol drawn, ready to shoot the bloody bastard molesting her. She was sitting up in the bed, eyes wide with the terrors she alone could see. He gathered her into his arms crooning to her like his mam used to croon to his wee sister when the lass would awaken in the night like this. Mam called it night terrors. T'was clear Fancy was terrified of whatever she was experiencing in her slumber. After the third night, he began sleeping there beside her, to be ready to gather her close to him when the demons of the night assailed her night after night. A man would have to be a cold-hearted bastard indeed to fail to respond to the gut-wrenching cries of a lass like those that tore from her heart.

One thing for sure. He would kill the next damned man who dared touch her.

Chapter 16
Fancy - 1782

Kirk was gone just over two months.

In an effort to charm me, Kirk brought fabric for me when he returned. He asked before he left if I had a color preference. I told him I would love a bit of yellow. It looks pretty with my red hair and yet Calvin detested the color. Kirk nodded and said nothing more about it. I figured if I were lucky, he would bring me a nice bit of yellow linen to make a blouse or perhaps a jacket. I was stunned when he returned with fifteen yards of exquisite golden yellow silk brocade from France.

"Oh, Kirk, it's gorgeous! But where will I ever wear a gown made of such exquisite fabric?"

He laughed, his eyes crinkling with amusement. "You can wear it to the Governor's Ball. Or perhaps to a wedding, lass."

My mouth went dry. "A… a wedding?"

He nodded. "Aye, ours, once you decide you'll have me, you wee, stubborn wench. Now, come and give the man who brought you this beautiful fabric a proper greeting, my Wee Duchess."

I gave him a prim, dutiful kiss. I never understood why he called me small. At 5'5", I am pretty tall for a woman.

Kirk laughed, grabbed me by the waist, lifted me up to his eager mouth, and kissed me long and deep. "No, lass, not a sweet little kiss like you would give your father. Give me a real kiss. A kiss for your lover returned from the sea."

I felt my face redden, and I tucked my face into the crook of his neck. Laughing, he swept me up into his arms and took me to his big bed where he made love to me until morning.

"Tell me you love me."

"I love you."

He laughed. "See, I told you it would get easier to say it with time. Do you mean it yet?"

I felt my cheeks redden. I said nothing.

Did he know? Could he tell? I smoothed my hands over my rounding belly the next morning, wondering if he knew without me telling him that I carried this child.

I did not tell him he had succeeded, that I was pregnant. If he figured it out, he would increase his efforts to force me into marriage. I wondered if he knew, but he remained silent. I caught him staring at me sometimes, with a questioning look on his face. A thoughtful look. But he didn't ask.

I suspected he knew. Oh, let's be honest. I figured he knew. It was becoming obvious.

It was ironic. I wanted Calvin's babies, and my body rejected them twice. I managed to carry Charles to term with the medicine Richard brought from Beyond. I wondered if that same medicine was why I was carrying this child. Wouldn't that figure?

I knew Kirk hoped to present me at the Governor's ball as his future bride, to tell people I was his fiancee come to Barbados to see my future home. I still had not agreed, but we both knew I would give in. What choice did I have, now that I was carrying this child? It was as Richard once asked me: what difference did it make now? And the answer was the same as it had been then. It would make all the difference in the world, at least for my unborn child. First, a child born to an indentured woman was a slave for life. My child would not be born a slave. Also, a legitimate child could inherit. A bastard could not. I might want Charles to inherit, but I knew many children died before they even reached age five. That was why nobles tended to have large families. Kirk was banking on the high infant mortality rates to make this child my heir, the future Duke or Duchess of Ranscome.

The better question was, what choice did I have? I knew the alternative to marriage was not acceptable even for a Duchess in 1783. In Ireland, women with illegitimate children were sent to nunneries. Some were even locked up in lunatic asylums. I didn't intend to wind up in either.

I kept dragging my feet. I did not love Kirk. Oh, yes, he had proven often enough he could arouse me to passion. He told me every night he loved me and insisted I say the same to him. He still insisted if I said it often enough that it would eventually be true. I was convinced he had no idea what love was. I had given up trying to explain it to him. It angered him that I insisted that was not how people fell in love. He said if he didn't love me, he wouldn't comfort me when I would awaken screaming in the night, he wouldn't care.

Hmm. Maybe he has a point. But, does caring about me mean he loves me?

Anyway, I realize if this were to be my future, my destiny, then I needed to learn my place in Barbadian society, my position as the wife of Capt. Kirk O'Malley. No matter how I longed for another life I once almost had or for the embrace of another man I still loved and craved. It was time. I had to learn to accept my destiny.

Each day, Kirk continued to try to sway me to his thinking. For Kirk, it was simple. If I were pregnant, he was sure I would marry him. After all, he understood I would not want my child to be illegitimate, much less a slave. I might not show very much yet, but I would soon.

And I'll tell you. The devil is Irish. He had the gift of the blarney. His words were affecting me as time was working against my resolve. Each time he uttered those words to me, he sounded more and more sincere. Each time he made me say them back, they came a little easier.

And he does hold me close when I awaken screaming. He never fusses. Never scolds. Never questions. He holds me tight, murmuring sweet words of love until I calm and can go back to sleep nestled close to his chest. He never loses his temper with me at those times. And, he has already proven he has quite a temper when push comes to shove.

I missed his solace when he was gone. His strong arms wrapped around me makes me feel safe and secure. I admit I sighed with relief that first night he was home again.

Home. Huh. I sure never expected to call Barbados home. How odd.

By the time we left for Bridgetown, I would be almost six months with child. It was fortunate, as with Bella and Charles, I still was not showing. Discerning eyes could probably tell, but for the casual observer, I appeared pleasantly plump. What Sassy would call 'curvalicious.'

Kirk seemed eager to take me with him to the capital this time. I couldn't complain. Long months of isolation at Seaview was enough even for a country girl like me. I longed to see other people who would talk with me and would treat me like I were more than a servant or slave.

Kirk promised I could do some shopping this time in Bridgetown in addition to our attending the Governor's ball Saturday night at the Governor's mansion. I knew from the earlier trips that there was a thriving market near the quay in addition to the row of shops, including the fabric shops I longed to visit again. Lord knows I do love pretty fabric. As the trip grew closer, I began to feel excited about the prospect.

Most days, I could push those thoughts of life I planned to have in Ireland with Richard out of my head. But now and then, those happy, hopeful days Richard promised would creep back, unbidden, into my mind. To torment me, torture me with 'what if's' of the promised happy-ever-after that it now appeared would never be.

Dreams I must give up if I married Kirk O'Malley.

Could I do it? Could I force myself to submit to another loveless marriage with a man determined to control and manipulate me? Dear God, was my whole life supposed to be at the whim of selfish men who cared more about marrying the Duchess of Ranscome and fathering babies by me than about me, Fancy, and my hopes and desires? Was that all women of our century could expect? Was I doomed to an endless loop of unhappy relationships?

Or would our marriage be loveless? It scared me to think it, but was I falling in love or in lust with my wild, Irish rogue?

I decided love is complicated.

I was still surprised Kirk was taking me to Bridgetown after the last trip. He kept me isolated at the plantation for those long months after I tried to get the message to Will when we went to Bridgetown in June. He must know, I thought again as he gave me another questioning look that ended with one of his lopsided grins. Perhaps he plans to pressure me in Bridgetown. To force my hand at this party.

As we prepared to go to Bridgetown, I realized I had not yet told him I was with child. My shoulders dropped as I sighed in defeat. I reckoned it was time to tell the man he had won and that I would marry him in Bridgetown in the blasted yellow silk dress.

That night, after supper, he pulled me onto his lap, as he often did. As he lit up his cigar, he asked his nightly question. "So, have you decided yet when you will marry me, my Wee Duchess?" He had taken to calling me that even more after the disastrous June trip. "There's still enough time for the banns to be read for a wedding when we go to Bridgetown…"

I swallowed hard. "All right."

The words came out little more than a whisper, but it was there.

I thought he would choke on the sip of port he had just taken. He sat the snifter down. "Are you serious? Or are you mocking me?"

"I'm serious. I wouldn't tease about anything this important." My voice wasn't much above a whisper, but I knew he could hear me.

His free hand slid down to caress my belly. "I wondered when you would tell me." He sat down the cigar and turned me to him. "You've made me the happiest man in the world, Fancy. I promise you won't regret this decision. I'll arrange to have the banns read before we arrive. The Governor will be excited for us to marry at his ball."

Funny. I already regretted it. I felt like part of me died when I uttered those two words. I blinked back tears I refused to shed and forced myself to smile. "Good."

After all, I thought with resentment, we want the Governor's Blasted Ball to be a smashing success.

Kirk rode into Bridgetown early the next morning to arrange for the banns to be read and for the wedding ceremony to be held at the ball. When he returned late that night, he brought more silk in rich blues and corals.

"The banns are all arranged. And I brought you a bit more silk. I thought the Duchess of Ranscome might like to have a few more gowns for her arrival in Bridgetown."

Oh, wonderful. More work for me. In fact, those new gowns comprised a lot of work. With Dolly's help, and the help of two other slaves, we finished the three extra silk dresses in time for the trip in addition to the yellow silk and the cotton ones I had already made. Yet, with each stitch, I felt more like I were sewing myself into my shroud. There was no joy in my heart for these dresses or this trip.

Kirk surprised me with his elaborate plans for my arrival. He wanted it to appear that Francesca Selk arrived by ship for the wedding, so he arranged for the Enterprise to meet us offshore below the plantation. They would send a rowboat ashore for my luggage and me. Dolly would accompany me by ship. Kirk and Odo would then ride to town and would meet us in the harbor for my grand entrance. He hoped with elegant clothes and hair, no one would recognize the indentured girl, Fancy, was Francesca Selk, the Duchess of Ranscome. I was pretty sure the Governor would realize I was the same girl, but I hoped no one else would.

Finally, the day arrived for our trips to Bridgetown. Dolly helped me pack everything. The bags were downstairs to be loaded onto the wagon which would carry us to the beach to meet the ship.

"Hurry up, Fancy. It's time to leave," Kirk called out as I started down the stairs. He sounded boyish, excited and eager to go.

Wordless, I nodded and hurried out. Kirk already had our things loaded and helped me onto the wagon. He reached over to stroke my face. "Smile, darling. You don't smile enough."

I flashed him a quick smile. I was sure it did not reach my eyes. He squeezed my hand, and then we started on our journey. And the end of my dreams.

An hour later, Dolly and I were rowed out to the ship, which would then sail Dolly and me to Bridgetown.

As we sailed through the beautiful blue waters, I turned my thoughts to more pleasant things. I was delighted that for once in my life, I would wear a beautiful yellow gown. I have always loved the color but I didn't wear it often. Tom kept me in drab grays like the other Ranscome servants. Calvin preferred pastel blues and pinks that always made me feel like a young girl. But come Saturday night, I would be clad in elegant watered silk the color of morning sunshine. My hair would be styled like Sassy used to love to fix my hair, in long curls shaped to look like roses. I had taught Dolly how to style it into the elegant roses. It would then be dusted with golden powder.

I sighed. Unless a miracle occurred in the next four days, unless my beloved Richard should somehow manage to appear and magically manage to rescue me, I would marry Kirk O'Malley at the ball. The yellow dress would indeed serve as my wedding dress as Kirk prophesied.

It was late afternoon when we arrived in Bridgetown. Kirk met the ship with a huge bouquet of hibiscus and frangipani. I wore the coral silk gown he requested with a large hat covered in matching silk. I realized he planned the yellow and blue flowers to contrast with the coral gown. I took the flowers from him, and he leaned forward to give my cheek a chaste kiss. The crew cheered as he walked me off the ship as if they were thrilled their Captain was about to marry the Wee Duchess, as they all called me now. Well, it was a far sight better than being thought a whore, I thought with a grim smile.

We walked up to High Street to the elegant inn where Kirk had arranged for us to stay. I was relieved to see Kirk brought us to a different inn this trip. He further surprised me with separate, adjoining suites. It would appear to the world that Lady Francesca Selk Hobbs, as I was registered at the inn, would be appropriately accompanied by Dolly before my wedding with Captain Kirk O'Malley. In reality, Kirk and I would share one room. Odo and Dolly would share the other.

Dolly was helping me unpack when she broached the subject. "You look pretty in the coral. I like it better than the yellow."

I chuckled. "What's your point, Dolly?"

She frowned. "I give you credit. You never mince words. Have you told him yet?"

I nodded my head. "Yes. But you can't convince me he didn't already know."

She nodded. "Yes, he waited for you to tell him, but he was sure. And you really intend to marry him Saturday night?"

I knew she was married to Odo, but I was sure she still had feelings for Kirk. I stopped unpacking and looked her in the eye. "Do I have a choice?"

She looked startled by the question. She could not hide the little smirk that flitted across her handsome features. "Do women ever have a choice?"

My lips thinned as I shrugged. "I haven't so far in this life."

She nodded. "So, you knew the answer before you asked it. But I am glad you have come to that realization. He is a good man. A woman could do far worse."

I'd be happy to give the devil to you.

Her head whipped up. She looked rattled. "Wh… What did you say?"

I stopped re-folding a shift and looked up at her in surprise. "Did I say anything? I didn't realize I spoke."

Her eyes narrowed as she studied me. "Perhaps I imagined it."

And perhaps I need to be more careful not to voice my thoughts.

Dolly appeared pensive as we unpacked. "Remember, Little Duchess, it is often in the darkest skies that we see the brightest stars. I thought I would die when my daughter died three years ago. But even as Kirk's interest in the child waned, Odo was there to rescue me."

I tilted my head at her. "Rescue you? Why do you say that?"

She folded the petticoat and placed it into the chest. "I wanted to die. Kirk could not stand to see the child. He blamed her for her mother's death. He no longer wanted to live. He drank far too much rum, even for a sailor. My daughter was gone forever. My granddaughter was not allowed to live with me. It was my darkest hour. And my Odo rescued me from myself. He stopped me from doing injury to myself when I could not keep Betty with me. Kirk will do the same for you now. He is a different man since you came. He loved my Anya, but not the way he loves you. I have never seen him like this before. There is a lightness about him he lost after Anya died. Let him be the brightest star shining in your dark night now. Let him rescue you as my Odo rescued me. You already rescued the Cap'n."

I stared at her, shocked by her words. "Wait, who was Anya?"

"My daughter. Did you not know? She was the Captain's woman for two years until she died in childbirth."

I was shocked. I realized the resentment I had seen in her face before was because I was replacing her daughter, not her. "I thought you…"

She laughed. "Oh, no, Plain Fancy. He lived with my daughter. He could not marry her because she was mixed, but he loved her. You know white men can't marry mixed girls on Barbados. I like to believe he would have married her if she had been white, but it was not to be. And now, the Cap'n needs you every bit as much if not more than you need him. You bring a lightness to him I had not seen since before my Anya died. And he brings you calm amidst your storms."

"I don't love him. I don't know if I ever can."

I cringed at the pitying look she gave me. "You must try, Fancy. For your own sake, not just his. And for the sake of the baby you carry beneath your heart."

I nodded. I still had grave doubts that Kirk loved me or anyone except Kirk. But Dolly was right. I owed it to the baby growing beneath my heart to try to be the best wife I could be to Kirk. "I will try."

She smiled. "You will see. You will be a good mother."

I lifted my head with pride. "I am already a good mother. I shall continue to be a good mother. This marriage will enable me to get back my other babies as well. Kirk promised me we will go to Ireland and I shall have my other children with me once we marry. Otherwise, I don't know that I could have ever said yes."

"Then you are already beginning to see the bright stars in the night."

Dolly's words impacted me. It was high time I quit lollygagging about, grieving for what might have been. It was high time I determined to make the rest of my life the best of my life.

We ate a quiet dinner in our rooms that night. The next day, we strolled along High Street and even ventured down to the market beside the quay. It was dreadful hot, so I wore a pretty Pierrot jacket and petticoat I had made at Seaview. I looked crisp and fresh in pale pink cotton dimity, and the heat felt much less oppressive than it felt the day before when I was clad in silk. Kirk was playful and laughing as we browsed through the shops and vendors. I bought some pretty cotton chintz imported from India and some handmade cotton lace. I held the lace up to the sleeve of the pink dimity jacket to show Kirk how it would look made into engageants for my cotton gowns. "Look, Kirk. Won't it look pretty?"

He laughed. "Beautiful, darling. Buy anything your heart desires. I want you to be happy here, my lady."

I debated whether to smile or stick my tongue out at him. Propriety won out and I smiled as I picked up white linen. "Well, then, I want ten yards of this linen to make you some new shirts as well. I can't have my husband looking like a raggedy beggar when he goes to sea."

He laughed and hugged me close. "You're too good for me, you know."

I felt my cheeks warm with color. "I know, you sly devil, but it's rude of me to say it."

He roared with laughter. He grabbed my hand, and we strolled on through the shops, our hands swinging to and fro as we shopped.

We continued our shopping and he introduced me to people around High Street as his fiancee. "We'll be married Saturday night, unless Francesca decides she cannot abide the heat here."

I stood fanning myself in the shade of the shop we had just visited. "Oh, it's not too bad today now that I'm dressed in cotton. It was pretty horrible yesterday, clad in silk."

Kirk grinned. "But you looked smashing in the coral silk, darling."

I arched an eyebrow at him. "I take it you don't think I look pretty today in the pink?"

"Sly vixen, you know better than that. Begging me for compliments, are you? You would look beautiful clad in a tow sack. The pink is exquisite."

I could feel my cheeks redden at the unexpected compliment. "I think I'll pass on the tow sack, Captain. It sounds a bit rough. But I appreciate the compliment."

He roared with laughter and pulled me close for a hug. "See why I love her? Wittiest woman I ever met."

I raised an eyebrow at him. "You must have known some dreadfully dull women then, Kirk."

I smiled at him. A real, honest-to-goodness, from the heart smile. He pulled me close and kissed me. I was laughing when he finished.

"Ah, that's my girl. Laughing and smiling. I love to see you smile. I see your smiles far too little. You look happier now. Less like you're about to turn tail and run back to the Americas at any minute."

I tapped his arm with my fan. "As if you would let me run away."

He grew serious. "No, I would never let you run away. It would break my heart if you left me, my love."

I blinked. My heart lurched as I reached up to stroke his cheek. I could almost believe he loved me. But, did I want him to love me? Did I want to love him? I sighed. Like Sassy would say, it's complicated. But how could I possibly be in love with two men?

Chapter 17
Richard - 1782

Six months. It had been six long, interminable months since Francesca disappeared from New York City. Rick had never been so freaking frustrated in his life. He came so far to find her to have the woman he loved disappear like this. But God willing, they were on the right path now. And God willing, she would be back in their loving arms — his loving arms — very soon now.

They broke Darlington in London the last week in August, where they found him in a gaming house. No surprise there. The surprise was how easy he rolled over and confessed what Tarleton did with Francesca. He even handed over the earrings Francesca was wearing when they took her after a little friendly persuasion. He swore he didn't know what happened to her engagement ring. Of course, Pretty Boy Brice did not like it when they roughed him up and talked pretty damned fast rather than suffer more indignities.

"But I thought you were a doctor," he protested as Rick pressed the knife into the soft flesh of his throat.

Rick's cold smile made Darlington cringe. "For humans. Not for scum sucking, bottom feeders like you. Now, tell me where she is before this knife slips…"

Brice let out a high pitched, rat-like squeal as Richard began to press the knife into his throat. "Alright, alright! Ban sold her…"

"To who?" came Rick's harsh reply.

"Some ship captain in Baltimore. I… I think his name was Kirk… yes, Captain Kirk…"

"You have got to be freaking kidding me. He sold the Duchess of Ranscome to some dude you claim was named Captain Kirk? You can do better than that, asswipe." Richard pressed the edge of the knife into Darlington's flesh, causing a thin, red line of blood to appear.

"Son, he doesn't have any idea what you mean. No context here," Will warned. "It's just a name. It wouldn't mean anything to me either except Sassy told me about that other guy." Then, William frowned as he stopped Rick's hand. "Shit. Are you talking about Captain Kirk O'Malley of the Enterprise?"

Brice nodded, terrified that Rick was going to kill him. "Yes, that's him! His ship was in Baltimore when we got there. Ban told him she was one of Paddy's girls, that she caused trouble and Paddy said to get her out of town fast. That Kirk fellow paid 5000£ for her. Ban was amused to sell her to one of the Ranscome captains. He thought it was hilarious."

"Are you serious? For someone he thought was a troublemaking whore? Why on earth would he pay that much for her?" Will demanded.

Brice gulped. "You must admit she's a damned good-looking woman. Even in the condition she was in then…"

Will jerked Brice to his chest. "What the hell do you mean? What condition was she in then?"

"Come on, Will, let me kill the sorry little rat bastard," Rick coaxed.

Will shook his head. "Oh, no. Mr. Darlington still has some answers he needs to give us. And maybe I will let him live if he gives me the information. Now."

Brice's eyes lit up.

"And maybe I'll be the one to kill him, Rick, if I decide he's lying. My patience is wearing pretty damned thin. Now, start talking, you little worm."

Darlington spilled it all. The kidnapping was quickly planned after the engagement was announced. He confirmed Clarissa's involvement with Tarleton and her help to get Fancy there an hour early. The repeated sexual assaults and beatings when she refused to marry Tarleton. He complained that Tarleton wouldn't let Darlington have 'proper' sex with Fancy, but only allowed him to have her 'through her back door.' Will had to pull Rick off Darlington when he told them that little golden tidbit. And finally, Darlington told them Ban Tarleton sold her to Kirk O'Malley.

Will frowned. "Did either of you tell him who she was?"

Brice shook his head. "No. Ban wanted her to suffer. He encouraged Kirk to sell her to a brothel in Barbados. He said he might go to Barbados later and buy her back…"

Will looked sick. "O'Malley was going to take her to Barbados?"

Darlington nodded. "That was what I understood. He said he has a plantation there."

Rick had never seen Will so furious before. "Dammit, the fecking man looked me straight in the eyes and swore he hadn't seen or heard anything about her. 'No, William, I've seen no new pretty, red-haired lass in the islands, much less here on Barbados.' I swear I'll kill Captain Kirk O'Malley myself."

He released his hold on Darlington and shoved him away. "So, help me, if you are lying, I'll come back and skin you alive and pour salt in your wounds. You understand?"

Darlington nodded. "Yes, sir, Captain Selk. I understand."

Darlington turned, and staggered away, shaking too hard to run.

They sailed that night to Waterside for Marc and the others. Now, they had all been on the high seas for six weeks, but Will swore they should reach Barbados by nightfall. Rick knew they would go straight to the Governor to begin their search.

They had been in the waters of the Caribbean the past week. Rick knew at any other time, he would love this cruise. He used to beg Dad to take them on a Windjammer cruise. Dad always laughed and said, "Next year." They never took the Windjammer cruise, but Rick figured this was even better, except for the bathroom alternative. Outhouses were bad enough, but he would never get used to chamber pots, he thought with a shudder of disgust.

The islands they were passing were gorgeous and the waters incredible. He might even enjoy the trip back, once they got Francesca back safe and sound. In the meantime, he grew impatient as they sailed through the endless waters.

"We'll be there in a couple of hours now. I know it will be a bit late, but we are going straight to Governor Smythe."

"Thanks, Will. I don't think I could wait another day."

For the first time in six months, Rick began to think things might work out yet. Please, dear Lord, let her be safe. Let us find her. Please, dear Lord.

He was afraid to say 'and let us have our happy-ever-after'. But, maybe, just maybe, they could still find it. Despite all the horrors she had been through since that fateful day in April when Tarleton kidnapped her.

• • • • •

Saturday night, I was a nervous wreck.

I broke down into two crying jags that afternoon. First, Dolly and I had to adjust the hem on my gown. I never in my whole life cried over a crooked hem before. I couldn't believe I was then. Dolly was calm and unruffled. She quickly fixed the hem, like I would have done at any other time.

She gave me a cup of tea. "Drink it. It is chamomile. It will help calm your nerves."

I nodded and sipped the tea. I thought I would be fine until she began working on my hair. To form the roses from the hair is time-consuming. It left me too much idle time to fret over the wedding. Not to mention a whole slew of 'what ifs.' Oh, dear God, I thought, can I do this?

And then, I couldn't breathe. I remembered Lily called this 'hyperventilating,' but that did not help much other than to let me know I might faint, but I would not die. I started crying when I realized I wouldn't die. After all, that would have solved my dilemma.

Lily was right. I didn't die. Dolly murmured calm, soothing words to me and I regained my sanity. At least, she said I did. I wasn't at all sure there was anything sane about this wedding.

At last, I was ready. Dolly and I walked downstairs where we met Kirk and Odo. Kirk beamed with pride as he took my hand.

"My God, Fancy, you are exquisite."

I tried to smile, but I could feel my lips trembling. I blinked back the threatening tears. I decided right then I hated yellow and that I would never wear a yellow gown again. I took a deep breath and forced myself to give him a real smile. "Thank you, Kirk. You look pretty wonderful, too."

He was clad in formal black evening attire. He had shaved the beard earlier in the summer. His face was tanned, making his grey eyes look even more striking. The months at sea had turned his light brown dreadlocked hair, almost blonde. Without the whiskers, he looked sweeter. Less feral. Aw, heck, he looked more respectable, less like a privateer, even with the dreads.

He leaned towards me and kissed my cheek. I must have looked at him funny, because he blushed – rare for Captain Kirk O'Malley – and said, "I mustn't mess up your makeup or Dolly and you will skin me."

His words surprised me and I laughed. "Yes, sir, we would. So, are you ready to take me to the ball? It seems to me I recall we have a wedding to attend tonight. Oh, but you may muss the makeup later. I promise."

He beamed, his eyes twinkling as he laughed, and gave me another quick kiss before he turned me away from him long enough to fasten a necklace around my neck. I glanced into the mirror and gasped at the sight of the flaming twin heart pendant. Done in gold filigree, it hung from a gold chain. There was room inside each heart for a miniature to be added, with a place where the hearts intersected for a miniature of the baby to come. I was touched by the gift and struggled again not to cry.

"Oh, Kirk, it's beautiful. Thank you." My voice quivered as my hands trembled while I fingered the pendant.

He frowned as he wrapped my hands in his. "Why are you shaking like a leaf? You should be happy."

Oh, foolish man, don't you know anything about me at all? I forced a smile. "Just a touch of wedding jitters. Don't you know? All brides get them. Come on. Let's go."

He hesitated but a moment as his face went serious. The seriousness was there just a moment more, before he grinned at me, once again all charming Irish rogue. "Aye, we have a wedding to attend, my love."

Kirk placed a delicate, embroidered shawl about my shoulders, and we turned to head out to the Governor's Mansion.

Calling it the Governor's Mansion is a bit pretentious, but it was a nice home. It was larger than the house at Seaview, although not as large as the townhouse in New York City. The exterior was of red brick, with a slate roof. Inside was a dining room on one side of the entry and a parlor on the other. The Governor's offices were past the parlor, and the bedrooms upstairs. The furniture in the parlor had been pushed back for dancing, with musicians at one end. Music was already playing as we entered. I remember thinking Lily would love the stringed ensemble, with the beautiful pedal harp. I always loved hearing Lily play the harp. One of my earliest memories is of her playing duets with Mama Belle. I smiled. "Ooh, I love harps! Mama Belle and Aunt Lily played."

Kirk cocked his head at me. "Do you play?"

I could feel my cheeks redden. "Not very well. My lessons stopped when

Daddy Jo died. Tom thought the lessons were a waste of time and money."

I didn't explain Tom did everything he could to put me down. The names he called me because I was mixed. Kirk would never know all the abuse Tom and Calvin inflicted on me, or about Simon Le Grand. I told Lily and Richard everything, and look where it got me. I would never tell anyone else. Heck fire, he didn't even know I was mixed. Of course, if he did, he couldn't marry me in Barbados. As Dolly said, white men can't marry mixed girls on Barbados.

Hmm. Now, there's a thought.

We mingled with the cream of Barbadian society and danced for a couple of hours. One minute I would be relaxed and laughing, the next I would be terrified — horrified — about what I was about to do. I still was not sure I could say 'I do' when asked.

Close to 10, Governor Smythe tapped a silver knife against a crystal goblet. The crowd quieted as he cleared his throat to speak. "Ladies and Gentlemen, we have a special event this evening. Lady Francesca Selk Hobbs has agreed to marry our own Captain Kirk O'Malley. Lady Hobbs is the widow of Sir Calvin Hobbs, who was the third Earl of Spring Haven. She was with Sir Calvin when he died at Yorktown. We are honored to have the heroine of Yorktown with us. Lady Hobbs assisted in the medical tent during that ill-fated battle. She was an inspiration to all who were there."

The crowd murmured at his words. Kirk beamed. I gulped as I shook even harder. I can do this. My baby will not be born a slave. I… can … do… this.

I gulped and took a deep breath. I must do this.

The Anglican minister of the local church then stepped forward. "I have published the banns between Lady Hobbs and Captain O'Malley at the church these past two Sundays. This evening, I am now publishing the banns for the final time. If anyone here knows just cause why Captain Kirk O'Malley and Lady Francesca Selk Hobbs should not be joined together in Holy Matrimony, you are bidden to declare it. This is the third time of asking."

I was shaking so hard I feared I might faint. Please, God, I prayed. Help me do this. Please…

"I object."

My head whipped around at the sound of the voice I had prayed to hear for six months. "Richard," I gasped, my eyes wide with shock and an odd combination of shame, horror, and excitement.

The minister frowned. "Who is this man, Madame?"

I stood up straight. "This, Reverend, is Dr. Richard Winslow, my betrothed. Well, he was my betrothed. I thought…um… I thought I… I lost him last spring."

Rev. Tipton frowned. "Then I suggest we adjourn to the Governor's offices while we try to sort this problem out."

I realized I was not shaking any more. My prayers had been answered. Pandemonium broke loose in the Governor's Mansion as the people realized the wedding of the year would not be happening as planned.

Kirk stormed into the Governor's offices with the rest of us following right behind. His face red, his lips thinned into an angry slash, he snarled, "I don't know what this is all about, but I am legally entitled to marry this woman."

The minister blinked several times. "But, Captain O'Malley, if she was already betrothed to this gentleman…"

"It is irrelevant. That betrothal is void. It occurred before even six months elapsed after her husband's death. Didn't it, Fancy?"

My mouth was suddenly dry as day old grits again. I nodded. "Well, yes, but…"

"There's no 'but' to it. The prior betrothal is void. She cannot be held to it. Barbadian law is plain on this subject. A betrothal entered into less than one year prior to the anniversary of the death of a spouse shall be deemed void. There are no exceptions."

I think that is when I started shaking again. I looked at Will. "Say something."

"I object as well," Will said. "O'Malley conspired to trick the Duchess into this marriage with lies and deception."

The Governor began stammering. "But… But…"

The minister stammered until he managed to gasp, "How, sir? And who are you? Oh, pray do not tell me you are another betrothed." And then it hit him. "The… the Duchess? Did you say this lady is a Duchess? Oh, my word!" Rev. Tipton sounded fretful.

"He's my brother. And yes, I am the Duchess of Ranscome."

The Governor looked stunned. "Oh, dear God, you mean I authorized placing a Duchess into indentured servitude? Oh, my, this is highly irregular. It was bad enough to learn you are a Countess. Oh, my merciful heavens, I don't even know if it is legal to put a Duchess into indentured servitude."

I had to force back a chuckle at that. The poor man was red-faced and looked like he swallowed a hedgehog whole. I thought he might have a stroke.

"I also object to the marriage," intoned Marc as he cast daggers at Kirk.

"As do I," snapped Fitz.

I could not hold back the smile. "And that, sir, is my father, Sir Marcus Fitz Simmons, and my brother, Viscount Fitz Simmons."

"Harrumph. This is altogether irregular. I have never had objections to a marriage like this before. There will be no marriage until I can determine the validity of Dr. Winslow's claim."

Kirk glowered at the little minister. "I already told you. His claim is void…"

"And by your logic, sir, so is yours. Today is the 16th of October. If Lord Hobbs died on October 17th last year, then the banns were read before the one-year anniversary of Sir Calvin's death. That would indicate the Duchess agreed to marry you while she was still in her year of mourning. No. I am sorry. This sort of muddle is exactly why betrothals are not to occur until a year after the death of a spouse. Gives the surviving spouse time to figure out what they want. Not be swayed by untimely emotions. There will be no wedding here tonight. I shall meet you all at my church tomorrow after services and we shall attempt to sort this mess out then."

Kirk was livid. He wheeled around towards Richard. "I can resolve this right now. I challenge you to a duel, Winslow."

I gasped as his hand lashed across Richard's cheek. "No, Kirk! Please, don't do this!"

Kirk gave me a scornful look. "Don't whine to me, Fancy. Your pretty boy has done this to himself."

Richard gave Kirk a thin smile. "I'm down with that. Dueling works for me, asshole. And since it is your challenge, I believe I have the right to choose the weapons."

"No, no! Please! You can't do this!" I began to sob and then I grabbed my chest. "Oh, my God, Lily, it hurts so bad. Why does my chest hurt so bad?"

I crumpled to the floor. I must be hyperventilating again. But why did my chest hurt so bad? It never did that before. Everyone began to shout as I fell into the darkness of unconsciousness.

* * * * *

"Richard, she's in arrhythmia," Lily snapped, as she commenced CPR. "I need epinephrine. STAT."

Richard paled but jumped right into action. Now he knew why he dragged the med kit with him from the ship. Forewarned is forearmed, as his Dad used to say. He jerked open his medical kit and extracted a bottle of epinephrine, which he quickly drew into a syringe.

As he was about to plunge the needle into Francesca, Kirk spoke. "What's that? What in the blazes are you doing to her?"

Lily never missed a beat. "Saving her life. He's a doctor. She has a weak heart. This will help it stabilize. She is in cardiac failure right now."

Kirk paled. "But…"

"No time for 'but's' right now, dude. We have work to do," Rick snapped. "Get out of the way."

Lily and Rick worked like a well-oiled machine, if there were such a thing in 1782, thought Rick. If only they had a defibrillator. Oh, well, they both knew CPR. As Fancy's heart stabilized, Lily stopped the CPR.

"She's stable," Lily said with a sigh of relief. She wiped off her face as she sagged with relief.

"Yeah, for now." Rick wiped the sweat from his brow as Fancy's eyes fluttered open.

"What happened?" Francesca asked.

"Just a little heart flutter, sweetheart. Everything will be okay. Gosh, you're beautiful. Even feeling bad, you are gorgeous." Rick smiled at her as he smoothed her hair back from her face. He squeezed her hand, and then checked her pulse again. Her color was better although it still wasn't quite right. She was still way too pale, even for a lady in the 18th century. She didn't need to know how close a call this was.

* * * * *

Wordless, I stared at everyone for a minute. "I need to talk to Richard. Alone."

Kirk started to protest. "Oh, I don't think so…"

"Five minutes, Kirk. Give me five minutes. Please."

He stared at me before he sagged. "All right. Five minutes. But, Lady Fitz

Simmons stays."

I cut my eyes at Kirk but I did not quibble. I waited until he left the room before I began. Jesus, give me strength. God knew I did not want to have to do this. "Richard, you have to back off."

He huffed up. "I have to? Why? I love you, Francesca. This man is using you…"

"Richard, I am with child."

His mouth fell open in shock. "Are … are you sure?"

I nodded, wincing at the anguish in his words. "Quite sure. It's … it's not yours. And if this baby is born while I am indentured, it will be a slave for life."

"This is a load of bull, Francesca! You mean to tell me…"

"I mean to tell you my child will not be born a slave, Richard. That is the sole reason I agreed to marry him. If I marry him, my indenture ends now. It is a term spelled out in my indenture papers. Then, my child will be born free."

Richard grew quiet as he shifted from foot to foot. "I would marry you anyway, Francesca. You know I love you. I'll give the baby a name…"

"You aren't listening to me, Richard. If I marry Kirk, my indenture ends. Then, my baby will not be a slave. Otherwise, my child will be born during my indenture. A child born to an indentured parent will be a slave for life. And I am indentured to him until May 1784. I could have another baby by then. Or maybe two."

Richard looked horrified. "But…"

I shook my head. "There is no 'but'. If I marry him, my child will be free. If I don't marry him, my child will be a slave for life."

"She's telling the truth, Rick." Lily's voice was soft.

"Please, darling, don't duel him. It would kill me if he killed you…"

It was all I could do not to touch him. I ached with longing to wrap him in my arms and never let go. Hang in there, Fancy. You can do this. You have to do this.

"But you're going to marry the sleazy son of a bitch? For the love of God, Francesca, don't do this to me. Don't do this to us!"

I cringed at the raw pain in his voice. I wanted so desperately to throw myself into his arms, to comfort him. To beg him to take me away. But if I dared touch him right then, I would never be able to stick to my resolve. He would go ahead and duel Kirk, and that would get them both killed, unless I missed my guess. I took a deep breath. "Please, Richard. Refuse the challenge.

Give me one year…"

"It's already been a year. We should already be married by now!" His voice cracked. He looked down, clenching and unclenching his fists as his voice broke.

I cringed again. I hated causing him this pain. I wanted to rush into his arms so badly. To console him, to kiss him, to tell him how much I loved him. But I knew I couldn't. I had to stay strong. "Please, Richard. Let this baby be born a free person. And I promise I will give Kirk O'Malley more than ample reason to divorce me."

Lily's eyes grew large with shock. "Oh, Fancy, you need to think about that…"

I raised my hand. "I have done nothing but think about it for the past six months. Please, Richard. I beg you. Please. Help me get free. We can never have a future unless I can get free."

He stood there looking like someone either kicked his dog or maybe like he was the dog that just got kicked. "I'll think about it."

"But, Richard…" I began to protest, as the door swung open.

"Your five minutes are up, Winslow. Get out," Kirk snapped.

Richard gave me another longing look. I thought my heart would break at the yearning in his eyes, clouding his handsome, aristocratic face. He nodded, and strode out of the room.

"You make him understand?" Kirk asked.

"I sure hope so," I retorted. Damn, did I ever hope so.

I doubted Richard understood all I was trying to say. To be blunt, I would bet Kirk was a better swordsman. He might even be a better shot. But Richard had the right to choose the weapon. I knew he had some wicked guns he brought from Beyond. Kirk would be no match for Richard armed with that fancy AR whatchamacallit rifle. If they dueled, Kirk would die without marrying me. That would not free me. It would result in me being sold again, as part of Kirk's estate, and my child would still be born into a life of slavery. It would mean the permanent decision Richard would make to kill Kirk based on the temporary anger he was feeling would result in my child being a slave for life. I could not allow that to happen.

Fare thee well, my own true love. But I'll be back. Though I go ten thousand miles. I'd heard Lily sing that song dozens of times. The words never rang as true as it did right at that moment.

"Kirk, I need to talk to the minister, please."

He stared at me for a minute and then nodded. A few minutes later, he brought poor Rev. Tipton into the room.

"You have quite a kerfuffle, my dear."

I kinda laughed. "A kerfuffle, hmm? I don't reckon I ever heard that before. If that means this is royally messed up, I reckon you're right. Sir, I have an idea that might resolve this awful mess."

His eyes lit up. "Well, then, by all means, tell me what you are thinking, my dear young woman."

I told him my idea. Eyes grave with worry as I began, his demeanor relaxed as I talked. As I ended, he nodded. "By Jove, I think you've got it, my dear. This might work…"

Chapter 18
Fancy - 1782

Neither Kirk nor I had much to say about the whole mess that evening. I will say he did not muss my makeup that night. I had never seen him so cold, so angry other than that day in June when I tried to get the message to Will. All I could think was, this better work. The next morning, Kirk was quiet, almost morose, as we prepared for church.

I walked downstairs to meet him in the parlor. His eyes softened and he smiled as I entered in the pink silk gown I made from the fabric he brought me. "Ah, there's my beautiful bride-to-be."

I curtseyed for him. "Thank you, kind sir. Yes, I'm pretty pleased with this gown. The fabric drapes beautifully." I pinned the little pink hat into place with a long hat pin.

About then, I heard the patter of little feet. I looked towards the entry and let out a squeal of delight. "Bella! Oh, Marc, I didn't know you brought my babies!"

I bent down as she rushed into my arms. After a big hug and many kisses, she looked around and frowned. "Where's Rick?"

I began to stammer. Marc spoke up for me. "Rick is with Sassy and Will, young lady. We will see them at the church. Now, let your Mama hug baby Charles, and then we will be off to the church."

Bella pursed her lips as she shook her head. "But he's supposed to be here."

"Well, he's not here. We will see him at the church." I took Charles into my arms, thrilled to see my children again after all these months. Charles had grown so much over these past months! I sniffed his clean, fresh, baby scent, as he wrapped his little fist around a long lock of my hair. As I extricated my hair from Charles' grasp, I resumed answering Bella. "Rick isn't here, honey. But I want you to meet Captain O'Malley..."

She stepped back as she shook her head. "No. He has funny hair. It looks like snakes, crawling around an unmade bed. He's scary. I want my Daddy Rick."

Kirk looked stricken. He bent down and extended a hand to her. "I'm very sorry Dr. Winslow isn't here then. Gentlemen should never disappoint their lady admirers. But perhaps I could be your friend, too? My name is Kirk, and I think your Mommy is the most beautiful woman in the whole wide world ... unless that is you, Pretty Bella. And I promise to try very hard never to disappoint your Mommy or you."

She tried to look serious but giggled as she nodded and held out her hand to Kirk. I smiled and handed Charles over to Marc so I could pull on my gloves. "Then, I reckon we should go."

I noticed right away that Richard, Sassy, and Will were not in attendance as we entered the church. I hoped it meant Richard was withdrawing his objection. Time would tell.

Near the end of the service, the minister said, "I know a number of you were present at the Governor's Ball last night. You are all aware there was an objection made to the marriage of Captain O'Malley and Lady Hobbs. The Governor and I have researched the objection. The Governor has a few words to share."

Governor Smythe arose, went to the lectern, and cleared his throat. "Ahem. Well, yes, it was a most eventful night. Most eventful. You may recall that Dr. Winslow objected to the betrothal of Lady Hobbs to Captain O'Malley on the ground that Dr. Winslow was betrothed to her in April in New York. Captain O'Malley raised the point that Dr. Winslow's claim was void, because it was made too early after Lord Hobbs' death. The objection was then raised that Captain O'Malley's betrothal to the good Lady was also void as premature. I was asked to ascertain if either betrothal were valid. My ruling this morning is ... both are void. Neither was timely."

The congregation began to talk in excited tones. The minister frowned and dropped a gavel several times. "We will have proper decorum here. This is a house of worship."

I cleared my throat and arose. "Am I to understand, Reverend, that neither betrothal is valid because both were made less than one year from the date of Sir Calvin's death?"

He nodded. "Precisely, my dear. I would also add I received a missive from Dr. Winslow, in which he states, 'I have decided to withdraw my objection to Lady Hobbs marrying Captain O'Malley.' Therefore, effective today, you are now free to enter into a betrothal, if you chose to do so."

I forced myself to smile and turned to face Kirk. "Then I should like to take this opportunity in front of God, my family, and friends to ask Captain O'Malley to marry me."

Kirk's eyes lit up. He took my proffered hand and kissed it. "I would be honored, Lady Fancy."

The minister smiled. "Excellent. Then if anyone here knows just cause why they should not be joined together in Holy Matrimony, you are bidden to declare it. This is the first time of asking. I shall ask again next Sunday, and if there are no objections, the wedding shall follow."

No one made a sound, although I was aware of a small hand tugging on mine. I glanced down to see my daughter wide-eyed, as if in disbelief. "Mommy…"

"Later," I whispered.

"But, Mommy…" she began.

I shook my head. "Later, Bella."

When we got outside the church, numerous people came up to congratulate us. I noticed Bella looked more and more sullen and unhappy. As the crowd cleared, I took her aside and asked what was bothering her.

"You told me you were going to marry Rick and he would be my new Daddy."

My heart lurched. I had indeed told her that, the last time she saw me before I was kidnapped. I took a big breath. "Darling, sometimes things don't work out the way we want…"

"But I like Rick. He's sweet to Charles and me. He bought me a kitten while you were gone. And I know he loves you…"

"Bella, sometimes things don't work out the way you plan. Things change. I am sorry…"

"But it's not fair!" Tears welled up in her Selk blue eyes.

Believe me, I know. Better than anyone here. I struggled not to cry, also.

Kirk bent down beside Bella and wiped her eyes with his handkerchief. "Ah, lass, it will be fine. And perhaps you can grow up and marry Rick…"

He winked at me.

My stomach lurched. I struggled to smile. God willing, she would never marry a man old enough to be her father and who had once loved her mother. "Maybe so. Who knows? But now, you have to understand…"

She stepped back, pulling her hand free from Kirk. "No. I want my Daddy Rick."

I struggled with my emotions. Me, too, I longed to say, but God knows we don't always get what we want. At least, I sure don't. I took a deep breath. Oh, Lordy, help me to help my child. I started again. "I'm sorry, honey. Sometimes, things don't work out…"

She jerked away from me. "It's not fair."

"Well, I'm sorry. Life isn't always fair," I snapped and then I cringed. My words sounded tight and angry. I was angry, but I didn't mean to sound angry at my child. None of this was her fault.

She turned and ran to Marc. He picked her up without a word, but then whispered something to her I could not hear. She turned her face away from me and laid her head on his shoulder.

Later that afternoon, Will came to see me. He was pacing back and forth as I entered the parlor. "I thought you might leave without saying goodbye. I am so glad you didn't."

Will looked grave. "Well, don't get too excited. I cannot comprehend why you are doing this. Rick is devastated. He hasn't said a half-dozen words to us since we left last night, but I know he withdrew his objection. He sent this for me to give you. He got them back from Darlington when the son of a bitch told us where you were."

My eyes widened with surprise as I unwrapped the aquamarine earrings. I pressed the little package to my chest. "Thank you, Will."

"Well, don't bother. I'm madder'n hell about all of this. But since you seem set on this route, I want Kirk's papers."

I stared at him a minute before I realized what he meant. "You mean his Captain's papers?"

Wordless, Will nodded.

I frowned and stood up straight and proud as a duchess should. "I don't think so. What's that Sassy says? 'Let's keep the stupidity like this to a minimum here today.' I don't need this nonsense. The last I heard, the Duchess of Ranscome owns the shipping line. The Duchess is the one person authorized to recall the papers of her captains. You gave up that responsibility when you dumped this damned title on me."

Will's face reddened as he began to bluster. "Now, you hold on a cotton pickin' minute, little lady…"

I shook my head. "Don't you dare take that tone with me, William Ranscome Selk. No stupidity today, remember? I am not the scared little girl everyone used to coerce into doing whatever they wanted. I didn't ask to be Duchess. You dumped this title on me. You didn't even bother to ask if I agreed to be the Duchess. You just dumped this responsibility on me. With it, came the ownership of the shipping line and all decisions pertaining to upper management. Unless you obtained legal relief while I was missing, to authorize you to make decisions in my absence, you are not authorized to ask for his papers. In fact, since I have been found, you are not authorized to act at all."

Will was shaking with rage, lips thinned, with bright pink spots on both cheeks. "Fancy, I don't trust him with the Enterprise…"

I tilted my head. "Why? I thought you always swore he was the best Captain we had, including you."

"That was before this," he growled.

"Well, too bad. I own the line. He remains the captain of the Enterprise."

Right then, Kirk came over to us, the broad grin still emblazoned across his face. He slipped an arm around me and pulled me close. "Will, did you know Fancy asked me to marry her this morning?"

Will cut his eyes from me, to Kirk, and back to me. He shook his head in disgust. "That has to be the dumbest decision you ever made."

He wheeled around to walk away. About twenty feet away, he stopped. "What did you say in the note you tried to send me in July?"

I pulled the crumpled letter out if my reticule and handed it to him. "Here. Read it for yourself."

Will frowned. "It's still sealed."

Kirk stepped over to my side and put his arm around my shoulders. "It wasn't addressed to me. It wasn't mine to open."

"It wasn't yours to open? Sorry son of a bitch, you expect me to believe you wouldn't open that letter? You lied right to my face in July." Will's brow puckered as he opened the note. It said,

Will,

I'm fine. I'm at Seaview. Capt. O'Malley rescued me when Tarleton tried to sell me to a brothel. He has been very kind. Please tell Richard not to worry about me. Everything will be fine.

Like Sassy always says: Don't make permanent decisions based on temporary feelings.

Fancy

Will snorted in disbelief and waved the note at Kirk. "Do you expect me to believe this is the letter you refused to allow my baby sister to get to me in July? I don't believe it."

He wadded it up and threw it down. Sassy was quick to snatch it up. Her eyebrows lifted in surprise as she read it. As she lowered the letter, she smiled. "May I take it?"

"Of course." I stepped forward and hugged her tight. "Sassy, I am so sorry…"

She put a finger up to my lips. "Shush, Fancy. There's no reason for you to be sorry. I understand better now. Lily and I have had a lot of talks. I'm sorry I overreacted. I always knew something awful happened after Jo died, in those years you couldn't remember. I suspected Tom hurt you. I overreacted. Everything will be fine, you'll see."

I tried to smile. I hoped she would know what I was trying to say in the note. In any event, I knew she would decipher it. I clasped her hands closed. "I hope so, Sassy. Please. Make him understand. Tell him I love him. I don't want him to leave like this…" I whispered, as I struggled not to cry.

She hugged me again. "I'll talk to him. And we'll see you in a year."

I blinked, startled, as I realized she had passed a message from Rick. I nodded, eager and excited. "Yes, you must all come to Ranscome Manor. Perhaps for Christmas."

She smiled and patted my hands. "That would be wonderful. And it will give these men a chance to cool down before they see each other again."

Kirk and I were married a week later. I gave in and wore the yellow silk. I was stunned by the beautiful ring Kirk had chosen for me. As he slipped the ring with the diamond flaming heart onto my finger, he said, "Let love and friendship reign."

I leaned towards him and said, "Oh, Kirk, it's perfect."

How can he be such a charmer at times? Well, they do say Satan is a Beguiler. As I recall, he was the favorite of God's angels before his fall from heaven.

At the end of the ceremony, I pulled a piece of paper out of my pocket and handed it to my new husband. The paper was rolled up and tied with a bit of yellow ribbon that matched my dress. "I would like to give you this as a wedding gift. I hope you will accept it."

Kirk winked at me with a broad grin as he untied the bow and opened the paper. His eyes grew wide, and he grabbed my hands to kiss them. "Fancy, are you serious?"

I nodded. "Yes. You deserve it."

It deeded the Enterprise to him in fee simple.

He bent over to kiss my cheek. "Oh, darlin', I never expected…"

"Well, I did it anyway." I trembled, dreading the fuss I knew Will would make later.

We left for Ireland within the week. I was showing and Kirk was delighted with impending fatherhood. Bella was warming to him, and Charles often laughed and cooed for Kirk. He was especially intrigued with Kirk's hair, which Bella no longer insisted looked like 'an unmade bed full of snakes.'

Kirk estimates we will arrive in Cork by mid-December. I sure hope so. My back is aching and my feet are swelling. I now realize a pregnancy at sea is not the best plan. I want to be on solid ground when I give birth. On Irish soil.

And in the meantime, I keep singing that song Lily taught me. Fare thee well, my own true love. But I'll be back though I go ten thousand miles. Like the song says, the rocks might melt, and the seas might burn if I should not return to thee, my love.

Just wait for me, my love. I don't rightly know how far it is from Barbados to Ireland, and from Ireland to wherever I shall find you again. But I promise, my darling: I shall return to you, though I go ten thousand miles.

Rick was quiet and withdrawn after his tirade that first night. Sassy would never forget the anguish in her son's face as he voiced his fears.

"But what if I came too soon, Mom? What if I mucked up everything arriving here before I was supposed to arrive?"

"Oh, *m'hijo*, everything will work out. You two are meant to be together…"

"But we aren't together, Mom. She was married to another man when I came. She's going to marry another man now. Jesus, Mom, she's pregnant by that scoundrel. Why the hell am I here? I can't handle much more of this. I can't. I'm sure I came at the wrong time. And that's mucked up my chance for a future with the woman I love."

They all tried to console him, encourage him. But he was inconsolable. He knew Lily came at the wrong time when she was ten and had to go back Beyond until the time was right for her to return. He obsessed he arrived at the wrong time and his coming at the wrong time somehow ruined his future with Fancy.

Sassy feared he might be right.

Sassy would have sworn Rick aged 10 years after he relinquished his claim to Fancy. He was quiet and withdrawn on the trip back to Belle Rose. She couldn't help noticing his wrist was bandaged. Had he been cutting himself again? Oh, dear, she thought he quit that long ago. She would have to keep an eye on that.

Will ranted and raved all the way back to Virginia. Sassy let him fuss. She knew he would calm down once he used up all his steam. After they left the elegant ship, Fancy's Revenge, named after Sassy killed Simon Le Grand back in '80, Sassy hurried to Will's desk to decipher the note from Fancy. She knew there was a coded message there. She applied the secret formula Washington shared with her to make the hidden lettering appear below the words visible. After a few minutes of fanning the document over a candle, she smiled. "Want to see the real message, Will?"

Will looked up, puzzled. "What do you mean, Sassy? What real message?"

"I had to find the hidden lettering beneath and convert it. Oh, Will, it is a shame you didn't get this in July. Maybe he would have sold her to you back then. The poor darling girl never catches a break."

He strode over to the desk to peer over her shoulder where he could peruse the newly revealed message hidden below the words in the original message which said:

Will,

I'm fine. I'm at Seaview. Capt. O'Malley rescued me when Tarleton tried to sell me to a brothel. He has been very kind. Please tell Richard not to worry about me. Everything will be fine.

Like Sassy always says: Don't make permanent decisions based on temporary feelings.

Fancy

Will let out a low whistle as he read the translation:

Will,

I'm Fine. I'm at Seaview. Capt. O'Malley bought me from Tarleton, who told him I'm a high-priced whore. Kirk paid 5000£ for me. When I told him who I am, he would not free me, even though I promised to repay him. I am indentured for 2 years. I'm breeding. Kirk will free me if I marry him. Tell Richard I love him, but I can't let my child be born a slave for life. I'll be fine.

Don't let Richard make permanent decisions based on temporary feelings. I shall return though I go ten thousand miles. I shall love him forever.

Fancy

Will shook his head. "My God, Sassy, I would have missed it if you hadn't checked. But, dammit, this sure as hell doesn't make me feel any better about her marriage to Kirk."

Sassy looked at him, her eyes shining with excitement. "Will, you're missing the real meaning here. She wrote this July 10, three months after she was taken. She already knew she was pregnant. She married Kirk so Rick's baby won't be born a slave."

He blinked. "But she told him it isn't his baby."

She nodded. "Of course, she did. Rick would never have left her there if he knew she was carrying his child."

Sassy could almost see the wheels turning in Will's mind. "But that would mean she was what? At least six months along when we were there…"

"That's my point. That's why she wanted to get to Ireland as soon as possible, before the baby is born."

Will finally cracked a smile. "We need to tell Rick."

Sassy shook her head. "Oh, no, darling. We can't. Not yet. Fancy would have told Rick that last night if she wanted him to know right now. That would have resulted in the duel going forward and one of the men being killed and her still a slave. We have to wait until this baby is born 'premature', like Bella was. You know Lily will do blood typing. She blood types everyone. She's obsessive about it. Heck, I'd be surprised if she hasn't already blood typed Kirk unless I miss my guess. Oh, Will, Fancy promised she would give Kirk grounds for a divorce! I thought she meant she would let him catch her *in flagrante derelicto* with Rick. When this baby comes a month early, he will have to know it isn't his. I never dreamed she was so good at deception. We might have to start calling her 'Little Sassy'. Damn, I should have had Washington recruit her years ago."

"So, what do we do now, Mrs. Selk?" Will's eyes started shining with something besides anger for the first time in weeks.

Sassy leaned against him. "Let's make sure everything is okay here, rest a few days, and then let's all head out for Ireland. We might make it by Christmas. She wanted us to come for Christmas."

"Yeah, next year. Aren't you worried there may still be a duel when Kirk realizes this baby isn't his?"

Sassy grinned. "I suspect she will be able to convince him it is either Tarleton or Darlington's baby."

Will scowled. "But will Lily be able to figure out who the real dad is?"

"Oh, darling, Rick is Rhesus negative, like Fancy is. Remember? We explained to you about her blood type and why she miscarried those two babies. The Rhesus factor explains how Fancy could carry this baby. I told you before Tarleton never fathered a child. Darlington could not have impregnated her by sodomizing her. And, I doubt the other men besides Rick are Rhesus negative."

Will sank to the chair and started to laugh. As his laughs deepened, he pulled Sassy onto his lap, and she began laughing as well. By damn, he never guessed his baby sister was quite so duplicitous. He would have to remember not to play chess with the Duchess of Ranscome. One thing was sure: Kirk

O'Malley had no idea what he got himself into with this marriage.

Their Daddy was right, thought Will. She might be little, but the Wee Duchess of Ranscome was fierce. And heaven help any man who tried to best that woman. What was it Sassy called Fancy? Oh yes. A bad ass survivor. His baby sister was a survivor the likes of no woman any of them had ever known before or would ever know again. And when she made a promise, she kept it. She would return.

Rick was going to be one very happy man. Some day. After all, she was more than the Wee Duchess. She was

The McCarron's Daughter.

About the Author

Sharon K. Middleton is a fourth generation Texan. Her family immigrated from Ireland in 1740, and Mexico in the 1880's. She learned Spanish from her Grandfather, who learned it from his Mother. She practices Law in Texas, but plans to retire to North Georgia next year where she will continue to write about the Cohutta Wilderness and the early years of the United States.

Thank you so much for reading one of our **Time Travel Romance** novels.
If you enjoyed our book, please check out our recommended title for your
next great read!

The Scent of Time by Alan T. McKean

"Alan McKean's distinctive voice presents epic drama and spiritual discovery
through time." —Leslie P. García, author of *Wildflower Redemption*

View other Black Rose Writing titles at www.blackrosewriting.com/books

and use promo code **PRINT** to receive a **20% discount** when purchasing